PRAISE FOR

TWO GIRLS
~ of ~
# GETTYSBURG

"Klein's weaving of the young women's stories to a shared
conclusion gives a fresh perspective on the complexities
of the Civil War." —*SLJ*

"Terrific action and lively characterizations move the story
along well. . . . Klein succeeds in bringing home the horror of war
within a finely told story." —*Booklist*

"Compelling . . . a worthwhile addition to Civil War literature."
—*Kirkus Reviews*

"The characterization of the two cousins is well defined. . . .
Both endure the blood and horror of war realistically. Each of their
stories could stand alone, but the view of the Civil War from
both sides works most successfully." —*VOYA*

Books by Lisa Klein

Ophelia
Two Girls of Gettysburg
Lady Macbeth's Daughter

Two Girls of

Gettysburg

LISA KLEIN

BLOOMSBURY

NEW YORK BERLIN LONDON SYDNEY

Published by Bloomsbury Books for Young Readers
175 Fifth Avenue, New York, New York 10010

The Library of Congress has cataloged the hardcover edition as follows:
Klein, Lisa.
Two girls of Gettysburg / Lisa Klein.—1st U.S. ed.
p.   cm.
Summary: When the civil war breaks out, two cousins, Lizzie
and Rosanna, find themselves on opposite sides of the conflict
until the war reunites them in the town of Gettysburg.
ISBN-13: 978-1-59990-105-3 • ISBN-10: 1-59990-105-6 (hardcover)
1. Gettysburg, Battle of, Gettysburg, Pa., 1863—Juvenile Fiction. [1. Gettysburg,
Battle of, Gettysburg, Pa., 1863—Fiction. 2. United States—History—Civil War,
1861–1865—Fiction. 3. Friendship—Fiction. 4. Cousins—Fiction.] I. Title.
PZ7.K678342Tw 2008   [Fic]—dc22   2008010322

ISBN-13: 978-1-59990-383-5 • ISBN-10: 1-59990-383-0 (paperback)

Book design by Donna Mark
Typeset by Westchester Book Composition
Printed in the U.S.A. by Quad/Graphics Fairfield, Pennsylvania
2 4 6 8 10 9 7 5 3

All papers used by Bloomsbury U.S.A. are natural, recyclable products
made from wood grown in well-managed forests. The manufacturing processes
conform to the environmental regulations of the country of origin.

In memory of Jan Reed,
and in gratitude for her son

Part 1

Lizzie

Chapter 1
1861

For the first fifteen years of my life nothing remarkable happened to me, Lizzie Allbauer, a shy, plain girl growing up in the ordinary town of Gettysburg, Pennsylvania. But all that began to change in the fall of 1860 when my cousin Rosanna McGreevey came up from Virginia to live with her widowed sister, Margaret, and her two little children on Baltimore Street. Rosanna was barely sixteen, with masses of curly black hair, flashing blue eyes, and a drawl that could charm a wooden plank, not to mention every boy in town. I set my sights on becoming her best friend.

Then, in November Abraham Lincoln was elected president, and the United States began to pull apart like a too-tight jacket ripping at the seams. South Carolina broke away, followed by Mississippi, Georgia, Louisiana, and Florida. People were saying a war was inevitable between the Union and this new country, the sinister-sounding Confederacy. With a toss of her black curls, Rosanna announced she would go back to Richmond if Virginia seceded. I prayed that wouldn't happen. I waited anxiously for the rumbling of war to shake the ground and split our town of Gettysburg right in half, sending my pretty cousin southward again.

But that didn't come to pass, not even after rebels attacked Fort

Sumter in April 1861 and war was declared. My papa, the town's best butcher, still went to his shop every day, I attended the public school, and Mama kept house. At home I still bickered with my twin brother, Luke, and coddled Ben, who was eleven and still a little boy. In May, Virginia joined the Confederacy, but Rosanna did not go back to Richmond. She said she was too fond of me to even think about leaving. I was both relieved and delighted.

Life in Gettysburg continued on its usual course until a warm day in June 1861, the summer before I turned sixteen. I was lazing in a field near the brickyard with Rosanna, my head pillowed on my book, perfectly contented. Through half-closed eyes, I watched the clouds and sun battle in the sky. First the sun poured its warmth on us; then the wind blew the clouds across the sun, casting shade over us. Rosanna lay on her stomach, propped up on her elbows. In the sun's brightness, she reminded me of an exotic flower blooming among the cabbages and potatoes of a plain kitchen garden. We seemed to grow happily together side by side, though we were as different as two cousins could be. And even after months of friendship, there was still much about Rosanna that was a mystery to me.

"Rosanna, do you ever miss living in Richmond?"

"Sometimes," she admitted, tipping her head sideways. "But not when I'm with my favorite cousin."

I smiled. "If you were back home, what would you be doing on a day like today?"

"I wouldn't be sitting in view of the town brickyard, reading a book, that's for certain! I might be strolling in the park, along walkways lined with flowers." She sounded wistful.

"Then let's go for a walk," I suggested. "Evergreen Cemetery is as lovely as any park, with its paths and wrought-iron fencing."

Rosanna laughed. "It's a *cemetery*, Lizzie. It's where *dead people* go." She rolled over and laid her head on my outstretched arm, so that we looked up at the sky together. "You are too serious, my dear cousin. We must liven you up with an adventure."

"I don't see many opportunities for adventure here in Gettysburg."

I felt disloyal saying this, for I was proud of my town. We had ten churches, three newspapers, eight hotels, and two thousand residents. We had a new railroad depot, a new courthouse, and gas lamps on the main streets. Still, in Rosanna's presence I felt restless, for I had never traveled farther than the next county. Richmond, Virginia, seemed to me as exotic and distant as London, England.

"Well perhaps we can find you a fellow," said Rosanna with a sly smile. "That would bring some excitement to your life."

"No thank you!" I said. I could not imagine what I would even say to a boy. Rosanna, on the other hand, was a skillful flirt. The boys listened avidly to her Virginia accent and eyed her shapely bosom. My own blunt figure and straight, wheat-colored hair would never draw such attention.

"Some day you *will* thank me, Lizzie Allbauer." She sat up and began to pluck at a daisy.

I often wondered why Rosanna had come to Gettysburg. Did she miss her sister that much? Did her parents send her? Rosanna's father hadn't even written, for he and my mother had fallen out years ago. But when Margaret's husband, Joseph Roth, had died, Mama insisted on helping with little Jack and Clara, saying that we were all family.

"Don't you miss your parents sometimes? And your Richmond friends?"

Rosanna pulled the petals from her daisy, one after the other.

"The girls at my old school were insufferable snobs. That's why I like you, Lizzie. You're not at all pretentious. Plainspoken, I would say." She looked at me with her eyebrows lifted. I had asked enough questions, I decided.

"We'll be going to the same school this fall," I said to change the subject. "Papa has agreed to send me to the Ladies' Seminary so that I can study to become a teacher. You and I can walk to classes together!"

I looked expectantly at Rosanna. In the distance I heard the faint trill of a fife, high-pitched like the call of a bird. Rosanna held up a tiny fluttering petal.

"See?" she said in a triumphant voice.

"I see a piece of a mangled daisy. You're not listening to me!"

"It's proof that he cares for me."

"Who?" I asked, curious despite myself.

"Why Henry Phelps, of course! Come, Lizzie. Let's walk by the carriage shop. If he is working today, perhaps he will come out and speak to me." Her blue eyes pleaded with me.

I groaned. "Last time we waited there, it was only the seminary boys passing by who gave you their attention. I could have died in my shoes, such foolish things they said to you."

"If you'd only smiled, they would have noticed you too, Lizzie," she said, pulling me to my feet.

Now the sound of the fife was louder, accompanied by the sharp, fast beat of a drum.

"Let's find out why the band is playing," I said. "Then we can go in search of your Henry Phelps."

Rosanna agreed. We followed the sound toward the Diamond, the town square. People were coming out of their houses and shops as if called by the pied piper's tune. I pulled off a handbill tacked to a fence. *A Call to Arms!* its wide black letters cried. The wind riffled the edges, nearly tearing it from my hands. At the town square, where the

Baltimore Pike intersected the east-west road between Chambersburg and York, a military band played. The gazebo was hung with red, white, and blue bunting. The wind made our skirts billow and threw men's hats from their heads. A few heavy raindrops plopped into the dirt, even while the sun shone against the metallic gray blue sky.

"It's a war rally!" cried Rosanna, breathless. "Do you see Henry here?" She balanced on her toes and scanned the crowd. "He would be so handsome in a uniform."

I pretended to look for Henry Phelps, though I couldn't understand why she was so wild about the boy. He was just one of my brother Luke's rowdy friends. He worked, when he felt like it, to support his widowed mother and went to school only occasionally. I didn't see Henry, but I saw Luke in a tree beside Mr. Swan's shop, his legs in their too-short trousers dangling from the lower branches. He must have been shooting peas through a narrow reed, because I noticed a large woman rub her arm and look around her, frowning.

"If Papa saw that, he'd haul Luke out of that tree and whip him. He sure could use it," I muttered.

"Lizzie, you're always griping about your twin brother."

"I can't help it. Mama said we were fighting and kicking each other even before we were born."

"Maybe you'll get your wish, Lizzie. I see your father now."

"It can't be. He never leaves his shop during the day."

Papa worked hard every day of the week except Sunday, in order to keep up his reputation. But there he was, standing near the gazebo, wearing a vest over his stained apron as if he had come in a hurry. Seeing him, I felt a surge of pride. Beside him was Amos Whitman, his hired man, who had once been a slave. The muscles in Amos's arms were thick, his hair coal black. Papa, though he wasn't yet forty, had gray strands in his hair, which used to be sandy like mine.

"You don't see Mama, do you?" I asked Rosanna. "I hope she's at home resting. And Ben is supposed to be doing his chores." I looked around, but Mama and Ben were not in the crowd.

Mr. Kendlehart, the town council president, climbed the steps of the gazebo. He was followed by the recruits, who wore everything from tattered work clothes to their best suits. Some carried old muskets, swords, or pistols. While Mr. Kendlehart spoke, I watched the men, who didn't seem to know quite how to react to the cheering crowd. Some waved while others stood motionless. I shivered as the sun disappeared behind a thick bank of clouds.

"Our noble cause, the cause of freedom, will endure. The Union will not be shaken, nor human rights abridged, not by the false claims and the foul wrongs of the secessionists!" Mr. Kendlehart shouted. Then the captain of the company, wearing a brass-buttoned blue coat, began his appeal.

"Step up now! Our company is in need of still more men," he called. At the wave of his hand, the band played again. The bugler sounded off-key. The crowd moved like something thick stirred in a pot. Mr. Stover, the carpenter, stepped up, along with Samuel Pierpont. His mother owned the Ladies' Seminary where Rosanna went to school—where I would soon study too.

Then Rosanna gripped my arm and cried out, "There goes Henry. Hurrah!"

We watched as Henry Phelps leaped lightly onto the stage with the other volunteers.

"Isn't he brave?" Rosanna said, blowing kisses toward the gazebo.

"But he's only seventeen—," I began, when the band struck up "Rally Round the Flag" and everyone began singing.

"Do you think your brother Luke will enlist, now that Henry has?" My stomach felt like I'd eaten something sour.

"Of course not. Anyway, he can't. He isn't sixteen yet."

Rosanna was bouncing on her toes to the music.

"Lizzie, don't you think it would be exciting to live in a camp and march to the sound of the band? Oh, I would go in a minute if I were a man!"

"You must be crazy," I murmured, wondering why Rosanna, a girl from Virginia, was cheering at a Union rally. I folded the handbill I had been clutching all along and handed it to her. "Here. At least you can take this for a souvenir."

The speeches went on, interrupted by applause and cheers. I saw Rosanna wave to Annie Baumann, the grocer's daughter, whose hair always formed perfect brown ringlets. Even the wind that day couldn't budge them.

"You've been at the Ladies' Seminary only a few months and you've already won over Annie," I said, amazed. "I've known her for years, but she doesn't have the time of day for a public-school girl."

"She thinks it's romantic that I'm from the South," said Rosanna, rolling her eyes. "As if I lived on a plantation and was waited on by hundreds of Negroes! My father doesn't even own slaves."

"Is he against slavery then?" I asked, but the band had struck up a loud marching tune, and Rosanna seemed not to hear me. A few more men signed their names to the enlistment roll. Finally, people started to drift away.

It looked like the last volunteer of the day would be a fellow who worked on the Weigel farm. Mr. and Mrs. Weigel always spoke German to each other. One of their sons and their daughter's husband had already gone off to war. Martin was the only boy left at home. He also attended the public school, though he almost never said anything in class. He stood next to his mother, who gripped his arm tightly. For some reason I felt sorry for him.

Martin looked in my direction and I lifted my hand to wave, but his eyes passed over me, and my hand fluttered awkwardly back down to my side. Maybe he hadn't seen me.

Following my gaze, Rosanna saw the Weigels and said, "That boy's mother needn't worry he'll run off. They wouldn't take him if he did. Look how scrawny he is."

"I think he's about my age," I said, unable to say anything else in his defense. Like me, Martin showed little promise of turning out handsome.

I saw Luke drop out of the tree and look around, and for a heart-stopping moment I thought he was about to enlist. But he sauntered away, and I sighed with relief.

Papa still stood near the gazebo. His arms were folded and he looked deep in thought. Why hadn't he gone back to the shop yet? He held up his hand as Amos began to leave. Then he untied his butcher's apron and handed it to Amos, who reached for his arm as if to detain him, but Papa gently pressed Amos back. I felt fear rise in me. I couldn't believe what I was seeing. My father took the steps of the gazebo two at a time.

"No, Papa! No!" I cried out, but my thin voice was lost on the wind.

Lizzie

———◆———

Chapter 2

That night our family ate supper in silence. My mother sat stiffly and avoided looking at my father. She did not touch a single bite of bread or pork, though Luke ate with his usual greed. Ben, who knew nothing of the afternoon's events, tried to tell about a snake he had seen run over by a wagon, but I frowned at him until he fell quiet. He glared back at me like a small devil, his red hair sticking up in tufts.

Papa chewed his food in a deliberate way, his jaw working hard. Then he placed his fork and knife with a clang across his plate to announce that he was finished eating. My brothers and I stood up. Mama stayed in her chair, holding the edge of the heavy oak table firmly as if to keep it from drifting away. I began to clear the table, but Mama shook her head, so we left the kitchen and sat on the back porch stoop.

Luke began to whistle "Yankee Doodle."

"Stop that now. How dare you make light of all this?" I hissed at him. He ignored me and kept whistling.

"Why wouldn't Mama talk to me at supper?" asked Ben.

The door was closed, but the windows were wide open, enabling us to hear Papa's raised voice.

"I will serve my country in this war!"

Luke stopped whistling in midnote.

"How can you go and enlist with no thought of this family? Nothing good can ever come of fighting between brothers. I thought we agreed on that." Mama's voice was high with anger. Papa often said she had the McGreeveys' passionate temper.

"Like it or not, we are at war," Papa said, enunciating each word. "It is a man's duty at such a time to consider the needs of his country."

"What about your duty to us? I left my family in Richmond to marry you, Albert. I've never looked back. Now you are telling me your country is more important to you than this family?"

Then I heard Mama sobbing and Papa murmuring.

"But Albert, we've never been apart. How will we get by without you? You know I haven't been well."

I was embarrassed to hear my mother pleading, yet I was angry at my father for being so uncaring. Mama had almost died of a fever when Ben was a baby. She had stayed in her bed for months, and ever since, she often had headaches that lasted for days.

"Lizzie can take care of the house and garden. Ben is old enough to be useful as well. As for the shop, Luke will manage, with Amos's help. The boy must learn to be more responsible."

I shoved Luke. "Do you hear that? It's time for you to act your age."

"Why don't you start *looking* your age?" He pinched the fat at my waist and glanced at my still-flat chest. Scowling, I slid far away from him on the narrow step and pulled Ben next to me as a shield.

"Amos has agreed to work around the house for additional wages," I heard Papa say. "It will only be for a few months. The war cannot last longer than that."

"The rebels can go to the devil for all I care!" Mama burst out afresh.

I was proud of her for not giving up, even if Papa was sure to get his way.

"I do not relish this war, Mary—"

"Then let other men fight it. Younger men, without wives and children. Stay here, and we will do our part peaceably."

"Every respectable and able-bodied man of this town is called. Men my age and even older have already joined up. If I do not go now, I will be reproached by all our customers, by everyone I meet in the street, every day!"

I heard Mama weeping softly in defeat. I turned on Luke.

"Why did you tell her that Papa had enlisted? It was not your business."

"I thought she would be proud of him. *I* am," he said defensively.

"Proud that he might get killed? You don't understand anything!"

"I know that there's a war going on and it'll be done with before I'm old enough to fight it." Luke pounded his thighs in frustration.

"You only want to go marching and shooting and pretend you are a man. But you're just a stupid boy!" I shot back.

"I could pass for eighteen. And I'm smarter than you think," he said.

"No, you're not. You and Henry Phelps skip school so often you can't even do sums, and you write like a ten-year-old. All you care about is having fun."

Suddenly Papa appeared in the doorway and told us to come inside. Mama looked grief-stricken as he told us that he was leaving in the morning and that Luke would be head of the family until his return. I started to cry. Luke touched my shoulder, but I pulled away from him. I tried to look at Papa and store up his image in my mind, but his face kept dissolving in the blur of my tears.

Before dawn the next morning, I heard Papa's footsteps in the kitchen. I tiptoed halfway down the stairs and watched him drink his coffee. The only light came from the stub of a candle on the cold stove. Mama barely spoke as she packed a satchel with bread and a jar of apple butter, a sewing kit, a clean shirt, socks, and a small prayer book. Papa put on his jacket, shrugging his shoulders as usual, and kissed her. Neither of them noticed me sitting on the stairs.

As Papa left the house, I followed him like a shadow, barefoot and still wearing my nightdress. In the middle of York Street, he stopped and turned around. I held out my arms, and he dropped his satchel and lifted me from the ground. He smelled of bay rum cologne and tobacco. His mustache tickled my neck.

"I'll miss you, Papa. I love you." I choked out the words.

"I love you, too. Be good. Be strong," he said.

Then he was gone.

We sat in the dark kitchen, Mama and I, listening for the sharp whistle of the train that would take the new recruits to camp. The train came and went, its familiar rhythm fading into silence. In a neighbor's yard a rooster crowed. A creaky cart rolled by in the street. Mama began clattering around the kitchen.

"Go rouse up Luke," she said. "He has deliveries to make this morning."

I climbed the steps to the garret where my brothers slept and called out, "Wake up, lazy!"

There was only silence. I opened the door. Ben lay huddled on the trundle bed, fast asleep. Luke's empty bed was heaped with covers and clothes. So he had snuck out early for some mischief with his friends! Now who would do his work? Growing irritated, I lifted each piece of the rumpled pile, as if he might be lying underneath, flat as a flapjack, with a teasing grin on his face. Instead, I saw an envelope with *Mother* written on it. A feeling of dread settled like a heavy cat on my chest.

In the kitchen, Mama stood at the stove, poking last night's embers into a flame.

"Up with you, too, Benjamin! I need wood for the fire!" she called. "Luke, move a little faster."

"Luke is not here," I said in a small voice. "This was on his bed." I held out the envelope.

"That boy! I can't count on him. What is it now?" She frowned and tore open the letter, and as she read it, her body seemed to collapse in stages, like a house hollowed out by fire. She lay soundless on the floor, and for a moment I feared she was dying, until she drew in her breath again and began to sob. I took the note from her hand. Luke had scrawled his message on a torn piece of a recruiting handbill.

Dear Mother,

I have joined the regiment too. It is a mans duty. If I cant fight because of my age I will learn to play the bugle instead.

Dont worry I will take care of Father for you.

Love Luke

Lizzie

Chapter 3

When Mama had calmed down, I made the deliveries myself. My hands on the reins shook with anger. I understood why Papa had to enlist. But how could Luke do this to Mama?

The deliveries took me all morning. When I was done, I stopped to tell Rosanna the news. As I rushed through the door of her bedroom, she looked up from the settee, startled, and a large scrapbook slipped from her lap to the floor.

"Oh, I thought you were my sister," she said, sounding relieved.

"Rosanna, you won't believe this! Luke has run off to fight the war! Why, I'm mad enough to shoot him myself." I whipped off my bonnet and crumpled it in my hand.

"I believe it. But can you really blame him? Do you think he would let Henry show him up?"

"I don't think Henry Phelps had anything to do with it. He was just trying to get out of the work here." I stamped my foot. "He is so self-ish! You should have seen Mama. The news almost killed her."

"It is going to be hard on you and Aunt Mary," Rosanna agreed. "But every man wants his share of glory."

"Luke's hardly a man," I said with disdain. "He'll do some foolish thing and get himself hurt."

"Come. Sit down and I'll show you my scrapbook," said Rosanna in a tone that was both soothing and tempting. She picked up the leather book tied with red ribbons.

I sat down, resting my cheek on her shoulder.

"I've never shown this to anyone," she said in a whisper. Her hands held the edges firmly. "I especially don't want Margaret to see it, so I hide it under my mattress."

I held my breath, suppressing my anger at Luke, my fears for Papa. What secret would Rosanna share with me?

"My whole life is in this book. I started keeping it when I was six." Slowly she opened the book and turned the pages. I caught glimpses of childish handwriting, pressed flowers, cards, newspaper clippings, sketches, and a yellowed handkerchief.

"Wait, slow down," I murmured. But instead Rosanna skipped several pages.

"I was working on this when you came in," she said.

She had pasted in the handbill from the rally and written beneath it: *Friday, June 7, 1861, Gettysburg rally, Henry Phelps enlists*. On the facing page she had sketched the gazebo draped in bunting and Henry Phelps with his arms poised above a drum.

"That's a good likeness," I said. "I wish I could draw as well as you do."

Rosanna ignored my compliment. The little space between her eyebrows had developed a furrow, making her look troubled. Her finger slipped between two pages she had flipped past, and hesitated there.

"What are you hiding there? Show me."

She opened the book to a photograph of a young man in a knee-length frock coat. He stood with one hand resting on the back of a chair, the other holding a book. He had dark eyes and the hint of a smile.

"He's handsome. Who is he?" As I lifted the book to get a closer look, several letters slipped from the nearby pages. Rosanna hastily tapped them back into place.

"His name is John Wilcox," she said lightly. "I used to know him, back in Richmond."

"Why, you've never mentioned him before," I said, looking at my cousin in surprise. "Are those letters from him, too?"

Rosanna seemed about to reply when we heard footsteps. She slid the scrapbook under a large cushion and grabbed a blouse and a handful of buttons from the stool near her feet as her sister, Margaret, swept into the room. She wore a dark green skirt and a white blouse with wide sleeves. Her hair was pulled back into a net, giving her a sophisticated appearance. She had the same dark hair, blue eyes, and long limbs as Rosanna. Once I told Rosanna that she had only to look at Margaret to know what she herself would look like in ten years, and Rosanna had pretended to be horrified, even though Margaret, at twenty-six, was still beautiful.

"Have you extra pins in here?" she asked in her soft Virginia accent, another trait she and Rosanna shared. Then she saw me. "Why, Lizzie!" she exclaimed. "You and your mother must be so proud of the brave men in your family."

I didn't have the heart to tell her that my parents had quarreled and that I was furious with Luke. But Margaret's attention was soon diverted by the pile of clothes on the settee.

"Rosie, haven't you finished with these buttons yet? Can't you visit and sew at the same time?"

I held my breath, hoping a squabble wouldn't break out. Margaret could be short-tempered, for her life was not an easy one. At twenty-four she became a widow. She sold her husband's tailoring business to settle his debts, keeping three sewing machines, which took up most of her dining room. Now she struggled to make a living as a seamstress and support her children, Jack, who was six, and Clara, four.

"Margaret, dear, I promise I will work into the night until I am finished," Rosanna said humbly. "Sit for a moment, and let me tell you all about yesterday's rally."

Rosanna shifted, hiding the scrapbook with her skirt. Margaret perched on the arm of the settee, like a bird about to fly away again, while Rosanna chattered on about the band, the singing, and the speeches. I began sewing on buttons, for someone had to do it.

"Did I mention that Henry Phelps was there?" Rosanna asked with apparent innocence. "He volunteered! He once told me he wanted to play a drum. Imagine how fine he will look in a uniform with red bands on his trouser legs. Did you see how he waited for me at the church social last week? Perhaps I will write to him while he is away."

"Rosie," began Margaret, hesitating, "I think you should be less hasty in matters of love."

The furrow between Rosanna's brows returned. Her lips tightened.

"Mother and Father expect to hear that you are growing more serious," Margaret continued. "I must be able to tell them, truthfully, that you are helpful to me and that your studies at the Ladies' Seminary are progressing—"

"And if I do not satisfy all of you?" Rosanna interrupted. "Will they summon me home to Richmond?"

I sensed a battle coming on and sat very still, wishing I could disappear.

"Since the war began, they would like us *both* to return to Richmond," Margaret said with a sigh. "But I will not live on Confederate soil, not even in our father's house."

"Your ideals are lofty," Rosanna said with a sniff.

"A woman cannot be too principled," said Margaret sharply. Then she relaxed into a pleading tone. "Mind me, please, Rosanna, other-wise Father will scold me for not being a good influence, and he will make me send you home."

"I doubt they would take me back," Rosanna replied coldly. "You know as well as I do why they made me leave."

Rosanna and Margaret locked eyes, but neither of them spoke. I thought of the picture of John Wilcox and the letters in her scrap-book. Did they have something to do with this?

"I understand how you feel, truly I do," Margaret finally said, lift-ing Rosanna's hair and combing it with her fingers. "But you can be so impulsive. And marrying young is not a good idea."

"Who said anything about marriage?" Rosanna shot back. "Any-way, *you* married at seventeen."

"Yes, I know. But I should be a lesson to you." Her voice started to tremble. "No one can ever be sure that, once married, they will live long together."

"Surely you don't mean that I should never fall in love because it might end sadly," argued Rosanna. "If you had followed that advice, you would never have been blessed with Jack and Clara."

A furrow that matched her sister's now appeared between Mar-garet's eyebrows.

"You are right," she said with a sigh. "But I hope you will at least acquire a useful skill. Someday you might have to earn your own living."

"It would not be sewing, I am certain of that," said Rosanna, unhappily eyeing the pile of shirts.

Just then Margaret's children burst into the room. Jack climbed onto the bed and began to jump up and down, while Clara grabbed her mother's skirts and screamed with delight, as if she had won a game of hide-and-go-seek. I covered my ears. Margaret picked up Clara and kissed her face a half-dozen times. I was glad to see her worried look dissolve into smiles.

"Come to Auntie Rose. I want a kiss, too," begged Rosanna, and Clara happily complied. When the little girl had disengaged herself, Rosanna, flushed with emotion, exclaimed, "How I love you and your sweet children, Margaret! I will try my best to be good. I don't want to leave here."

Lizzie

Chapter 4

I was eager to ask Rosanna more about John Wilcox. But Mama and I were busy planning with Amos how to manage with Papa and Luke both away. Amos, of course, did all the butchering. He loaded the cart and I made deliveries, taking Ben with me to help unload, while Mama watched the shop. The rest of the day, while I waited on customers, my hands, arms, and back would ache from the strain of trying to control the mulish horse. I didn't see Rosanna for almost two weeks. Then one day she left word with Mama asking if she and I might go on a picnic after church. Mama agreed, for Sunday was, after all, a day of rest.

That first Sunday in July was as hot as an iron. Reverend Essig droned on and on while the ladies fanned themselves, and it seemed like forever until we stood up to sing the final hymn. As the last chord sounded, I dashed out of church, which was in sight of our house, and within minutes had changed into an old calico dress. I grabbed a berry pail, in which I put a chunk of bread and a jam pot wrapped in a clean apron. Dodging the ruts and puddles in the road, I soon arrived at Margaret's two-story clapboard house. Rosanna leaned over the gate and waved.

"Why are you running? It's too hot!"

"I guess I'm eager to get away," I admitted, wiping my sweaty forehead. "I have to make the very most of today, for tomorrow means more work. Let's hurry before someone picks all the berries."

"At least your shop is closed Sundays. My sister received a commission for uniforms and expects me to help sew trousers today."

"You mean you can't come on a picnic with me?" My shoulders slumped with disappointment.

"I didn't say that. I made a bargain with her: Jack and Clara will come with us, and then she will get more work done."

"Then fetch them along, and extra buckets, too," I said, trying to hide my irritation. I had hoped to have Rosanna to myself, for I wanted to hear more about John Wilcox.

Margaret came out with the children, and I went up to give her a kiss on the cheek. "You look so pretty today," I said. She smiled, brushing her hands against her blue checked skirt and touching the brooch at her neck. She had recently stopped wearing mourning.

"Don't run off, Clara, but stay with Rosie and Lizzie like a good girl. Jack, be careful climbing on the rocks. Here are your buckets."

I took Clara's hand and Rosanna held Jack's as we set out, following the pike. At the crest of the hill stood an arched brick gatehouse, the entrance to Evergreen Cemetery. Despite Rosanna's opinion, it still looked to me like a park or a peaceful village. To the east, Cemetery Hill fell away and then rose again to form Culp's Hill, our favorite destination for picnics. On its westward slopes, rocks and boulders thrust through the grass like small islands. Blackberries flourished in dense tangles of canes as thick as a man's finger, with thorns like claws. The bushes arched high overhead, loaded with ripe fruit the size of shooter marbles. My mouth began to water.

Jack and Clara plucked the low berries, while Rosanna and I rose on tiptoe, snaking our arms between branches to grasp the berries hiding among the leaves, then popping them into our mouths. I loved the feel of the warm clusters bursting on my tongue, the sweetness afterward. The purple juice left dark stains on everything it touched. Jack and Clara laughed at the sight of each other's blue lips and teeth. Then Jack overturned his bucket and began to wail. We bent over to help him and saw that Clara had rubbed berries into her blond hair. Rosanna's sharp rebuke made her cry, too. I sighed, wishing we could have left the children behind.

Rosanna decided it was time to give up berry picking. We took our buckets and the complaining children along the path that led through the woods to a sunny meadow where a spring flowed through a marshy swale. We scrubbed the children's berry stains, bathed our scratches, and cupped our hands to drink. In the shade of an overhanging rock, Rosanna laid out our lunch on a towel. The children ate bread and jam, then ran off to play in the clearing.

"Stay off the rocks, Jack, they are slippery," Rosanna called.

At last we were alone and I had a chance to ask Rosanna about John Wilcox.

"Two weeks ago you were going to tell me about that fellow in Richmond, weren't you?" I prompted. "Then Margaret came into the room."

"Was I? I don't remember," she replied casually.

"Of course you do," I said. "You showed me his picture. I saw the letters you were hiding. You must have wanted to tell me about him."

Rosanna took off her shoes and waded into the marshy spring. I followed her. The grasshoppers clicked and buzzed in the grassy meadow.

Finally she said, "I thought about John Wilcox every day when I first came here." She paused. "But now I have to look at his picture to remind myself of him—for him to seem real." That little furrow showed up again between her eyes.

"Did he write you all those letters?"

She nodded. "I memorized every one. But the more I read them, the more hollow his declarations sounded."

"What sort of declarations?" I prompted.

Rosanna blushed. "Of love."

My eyes widened. I wondered if Rosanna had loved him back. But all I said was, "It must be hard to write it in a fresh way every time."

"Then maybe it's not love," she said in a quavering voice. She paused and took a breath. "I stopped writing to him. I would write a letter, but I couldn't send it." She sighed. "But now it's over, and I'm already forgetting him."

I looked at her doubtfully. "How did you meet him?"

"We met at a party, the first time I was allowed to stay up for the dancing. I wore a new blue velvet ball gown, and he danced with me more than anyone else. He was so handsome! All the girls were jealous. He led me to a nook in the hallway and we kissed. I wished I had not laced my corset so tight, for I almost fainted!" Rosanna giggled at the memory.

"Wait," I said after a moment, calculating in my head. "You were only fourteen then!"

"I was almost fifteen. That's not too young to be kissed," Rosanna said, lifting her chin. "And he was nineteen."

With a chorus of shrill whistles, a flock of cedar waxwings flew up from a thicket. Twigs snapped behind us and we turned to see a deer stepping from the woods. Clara and Jack gave chase, and the deer fled, her white tail raised in alarm.

"Come back now. It's time for a nap!" called Rosanna, and the children returned willingly and lay down in the shade. Rosanna resumed her tale.

"Then he began to call on me at home. But my parents disapproved of him. Mother said that Mr. Wilcox was an 'upstart merchant' and that Mrs. Wilcox put on airs. Father said I was too young to have a beau. They forbade me from seeing him, and I said they couldn't stop me. So they sent me away."

"Why, that's so unreasonable of them!" I exclaimed. I could not imagine my own parents being so heartless, but then I had never done anything to displease them.

"Yes, but I'm happy living with Margaret," Rosanna insisted, wiping away tears.

I reached out and squeezed her hand.

"Did your parents approve of your sister marrying Joseph Roth?"

She gave a bitter laugh. "His family was Jewish! Why do you think Margaret moved as far away as Gettysburg? But when Joseph died, our parents made peace with her, because of Jack and Clara."

I remembered my mother telling me how she, too, had left Richmond to marry my father. Had the snobbish McGreevey family driven her away as well?

"Does John Wilcox still write to you?" I asked Rosanna.

"No. I haven't had a letter from him in four months. But now I have Henry Phelps to think about." She pulled a letter from her skirt pocket. "Look, he sent me a photograph taken in his new uniform."

Henry's picture was out of focus. I thought John Wilcox more handsome but didn't say so.

"Papa hasn't written yet. Does Henry write anything about the war?"

"He says the company is still at Camp Wayne, learning the drills, but soon they will leave for battle. When their three months' service is up, he'll come home. And best of all," she said, glancing up from the letter, "he wants to court me then! I believe I shall let him kiss me."

I counted the months. "That will be September, and I'll be at Mrs. Pierpont's school with you, so you can tell me all about it."

While Rosanna thought about kissing boys, I was excited by the idea of schoolbooks and classes full of girlfriends. I laid my head in Rosanna's lap, and she began to stroke my hair.

"Do you think you'll ever go back to Richmond?" I wondered aloud.

"I suppose so. I was born there, and it is my home."

"But now it's the capital city of the Confederacy," I reminded her.

"No, it is the capital of Virginia, where I was born. But if Virginia is part of the Confederacy, then so am I," she said.

I sat up abruptly. "Well, whose side are you on?"

Rosanna looked at me in surprise.

"I mean, you cheered at the rally in Gettysburg in support of the Union troops, and yet you say you are a Confederate?"

Rosanna laughed. "Lizzie, you take everthing so seriously. This war is only a gentlemen's disagreement. The rallies, bands, and armies— they're all for show. Each side is trying to get the other to back down from the duel. It's been three months, and has there been a battle worthy of the name of war anywhere?"

"No," I admitted.

"You see? The war will be over by fall, and all the bad feelings settled," she said. "And it won't matter that Henry was in the Union army and that I am from Virginia."

I wanted to believe her, yet it seemed to me that there must be more to the war than bad feelings between gentlemen. So many states had separated from the Union that the country was like a broken pot. I worried that it was too damaged to be easily mended. And there was the problem of slavery, which had caused the states to leave the Union in the first place. How could it be solved by fighting?

"Lizzie, dear, don't look so worried," Rosanna said, taking my hand. "Tell me, does the war make any difference between us?"

I looked into my cousin's earnest blue eyes and felt a surge of affection for her.

"Of course not! We will always be the best of friends," I promised.

Reassured of each other's love, Rosanna and I gathered up the berries and the picnic leftovers and woke up Jack and Clara. The four of us walked in weary silence back to town, while the late-afternoon sun cast its lengthening shadows along the slopes of Culp's Hill.

Lizzie

Chapter 5

Not long after my picnic with Rosanna, there occurred a battle worthy of the name of war near a little river in Virginia called Bull Run Creek. The news of a Confederate victory reached Gettysburg a few days later. We read that hundreds of people had taken picnic lunches and ridden out from Washington to watch the battle from nearby fields and hills. When the Union army retreated, the picnickers found themselves amid the chaos.

"What did they expect to see?" Mama said, shaking the newspaper in disbelief. "Gentlemen dueling? A log-rolling contest at a county fair?"

I tried to imagine eating a cold beef sandwich while watching men kill each other, or being trapped on a road jammed with artillery, crazed horses, and fleeing soldiers covered in blood and dirt.

"That couldn't happen here, could it?" I asked Mama.

"Of course not. We have more sense than most city folk," she said.

Our Pennsylvania volunteers had not been in the battle. But the newspaper reported that over eight hundred men had been killed. And yet the battle had settled nothing. The war was not over; it was just beginning.

I thought of Rosanna. What would she say about the war now that there had been a real battle?

That very week we received our first letter from Luke and Papa. Mama cried softly as she read it, then without a word handed it to me.

24 July, camp on Carrol Hill nr. Baltimore
Dear Mama,

I had to go to war, I hope someday you will understand. Papa was angry and said think of your poor mother. I do every day but still I am staying here. I'm sorry.

I am not the only boy in the company. There is Henry Phelps too, a good fellow. Wilson Nailor is 16 but they let him enlist. He put a paper with the number "18" in his shoe and when they asked "Are you over 18" he could say yes without lying. He gets to carry a rifle.

I'm learning the bugle. We drill daily. I'm learning reveille (wake up) and drill call, tattoo and taps, and retreat (which we will never need!). Capt. McPherson says buglers are needed in the cavalry because the drum cant be heard over the horses feet. But I dont want to leave this company. So Henry is teaching me to drum. He will march at one end and me at the other.

We were not at Bull Run but if we had been our side would have won it.

Your loyal son Luke
P.S. to Lizzie, I am sorry for leaving you the work but I know you can do it better than me.

Luke's apology made me regret our quarrel and wish I'd been able to tell him good-bye. Papa had written too, but his letter was shorter, not counting the instructions for the shop and the reminder for me to help Mama after school.

Dearest Mary,

I have little to say except how much I miss you. The daily drills are pulling this diverse company of volunteers into a real fighting unit. We have been mustered into the regular army for 3 years or the war's length. Thus far, however, war is more tedious than dangerous. The rebels were simply lucky at Bull Run, and I truly doubt that it will last more than a year, so have no fears for me.

Your loving husband, Albert

The loss at Bull Run and what it meant for the Union was the topic of conversation all over town. Would Lincoln choose a new commanding general? Would the Confederates strike at our capital, Washington? On Wednesday I went with Mama, Rosanna, and Margaret to Christ Lutheran Church to hear a woman from New York who came to help the town organize a Ladies Aid Society. She stirred up the church full of ladies like a preacher calling us to a great cause. While she spoke, my eyes roamed the church interior, following the tall pillars and the graceful arches that met overhead in a point. In the stained-glass windows and the plaques on the walls I read the names of people who had died years before. It was strange, I thought, to be in a church preparing for war, not worshipping God.

"An excellent project for the young ladies is the housewife," the New York woman intoned as she unrolled a rectangular strip of flannel with many small pockets. "For scissors, needles, thread, buttons, and such like. It can be fastened thus with ties. Every soldier needs one."

Then Mrs. Pierpont stood up to ask for volunteers. She was tall, with completely gray hair and a smooth, unlined face. She seemed stern, and I hoped she would not be too hard on me as a new pupil. Marveling at her broad bosom and narrow waist, I remarked to Rosanna, "Look how her corsets have squeezed all her flesh upward." We both giggled until Mama glared at us.

Mrs. Baumann, Annie's mother, agreed to collect knitted scarves and socks, and Margaret volunteered to oversee the making of three hundred shirts.

"I'll probably have to sew a hundred of those shirts myself," said Rosanna with a groan.

When the meeting was over, everyone stayed to share letters from husbands and sons. Conversations about the war swirled around me. By now we all knew that our men would not be coming home in September, and the ladies debated how long the war would last. Mrs. Pierpont's voice rose above the rest.

"Now, Sarah," she was saying to Mrs. Brodhead, whose lips were compressed with worry against her large, uneven teeth, "we have already blockaded the southern ports and rivers, and it is only a matter of time before the Confederacy is choked off. Those rebels are not about to reach Washington."

Rather than talk of the war, I drew Rosanna toward the refreshments. But Mrs. Pierpont caught sight of us.

"Why Miss McGreevey, this must be your cousin, Elizabeth Allbauer. Young lady, your father spoke to me last spring. I am delighted you will be attending my seminary."

I merely nodded, too intimidated to reply.

"Frieda Baumann!" Mrs. Pierpont exclaimed, turning from me. "You can count on my schoolgirls for a dozen socks each."

"But I don't know how to knit!" said Rosanna to me in dismay. "Can't we do something else, a flag perhaps?"

"Mrs. Pierpont must think I'm an imbecile," I murmured.

I watched as Mrs. Wade approached Margaret with her daughters,

Ginnie and Georgia. Ginnie's brown hair was fixed in braids wrapped around her head like a crown. She saw me and gave a little wave. I smiled back.

"You're in luck. I think the Wades are volunteering to help Margaret sew shirts," I whispered to Rosanna.

"Who are the Wades?" asked Rosanna, eyeing their faded dresses.

"Ginnie is a very sweet girl. She's eighteen, I think." I lowered my voice. "A long time ago her father committed a crime and was sent to the asylum. People say he will never come home. Ginnie and her mother and sister take in sewing and laundry. They may be poor, but they won't accept charity."

Rosanna's brow furrowed. "Does she have any friends?"

"They keep mostly to themselves. I've seen people treat them unkindly."

"Why, they can't help their misfortunes! Lizzie, we must make Ginnie our friend. You say she's a seamstress? Why, she can help with my project. Forget the socks—we'll make a flag, a big one."

I gazed in confusion at Rosanna. "Why?"

"To send to the soldiers of Company K. To keep up their spirits. Think of how proud it will make your father and Luke."

"While you think of impressing Henry Phelps!" I teased.

Rosanna wrinkled her nose at me. "I'll find Annie and see if she wants to help too."

"But you hate to sew. Why not send Henry one of your drawings instead?"

There was no reply from Rosanna, for she had already jumped up in search of Annie, and I was left shaking my head in wonder at my impetuous friend.

Lizzie

Chapter 6

After the meeting, Mama was in a somber mood, perhaps due to the letter from Papa and Luke and all the conversations about the war. She went to bed early, saying she felt poorly. I stayed up and wrote to Luke, telling how I'd put up twenty jars of beans yesterday, and how Amos and Ben had fixed the shed. Then I peered in Mama's room and found her still awake, sitting up in bed. Her brown hair was streaked with silver, but spread out over her shoulders, it made her look young and pretty.

"Come in, Lizzie," she said. I went in and sat next to her.

"The war won't last three years, I'm sure," I said.

"How can it go on for even *one* year, when the right and wrong of it are so clear?" Mama said, a note of distress in her voice.

"Do you mean slavery?" I asked. I knew Mama and Papa believed that one person couldn't own another person, no matter his skin color, and I tended to agree with them. But there were folks in Gettysburg, even in our own church, who thought it wasn't any of our business to meddle. And in the Bible, people owned slaves. It was complicated, I could see that.

Mama didn't reply but went on speaking her own thoughts. "I'm less worried about your father than I am about Luke. He is so young, I'm afraid he will do something rash in battle."

"But he's a musician, not a soldier," I reminded her.

"A drum won't satisfy him for long," Mama predicted.

I knew what she meant. The thought of Luke with his hands on a gun was scary. He would have a lark, shooting at anything that moved, just to see if he could hit it.

"You know, Mama," I said to change the subject, "I'm excited about attending the Ladies' Seminary this fall. I admit I'm a little afraid of Mrs. Pierpont, even though Rosanna says she is not as stern as she looks. I will help out at the shop before and after school and work on the accounts at night."

Mama was regarding her hands in her lap.

"What's wrong?" I asked.

"I believe you can read and cipher well enough," she said.

Her words alarmed me. "If I'm going to be a teacher, I have much more to learn."

"The tuition is costly, you know."

"That is because the best families of Gettysburg send their daughters there," I said. "We are as good as anybody in town."

"That sounds like something a McGreevy would say," Mama said sourly.

"Don't you want me to succeed? To get an education?"

"Of course I do. But I want your father's business to succeed too."

Her words were like cold water splashed in my face. I drew in my breath sharply.

"It's not . . . not that bad, is it?"

"You know our income is falling—"

"But it's only temporary, until the war ends!"

"Some merchants are thriving because of the war, Lizzie. I've heard that large meatpackers out west are getting rich on government contracts. For small businesses like ours, however, there is real hardship ahead if the war goes on."

"Amos knows what he is doing," I said. I tried to sound confident, even though I thought that no one could be as capable as Papa.

"Yes, I trust him. But he cannot do the work of two men and one girl. I need you at the shop."

"But it's Papa who wants me to go to school. He even mentioned it in his letter!" I cried, growing desperate.

"Your father is not here now. I make the decisions. Ben will go to school because he must master the basic subjects. You, however, will not go to the Ladies' Seminary this fall."

I jumped from the bed and confronted my mother, my fists clenched so hard they hurt. "What? But you and Papa promised! It's so unfair!" Tears spilled from my eyes.

"I'm sorry, Lizzie, I truly am. All of us must make sacrifices . . . for a time."

Mama's voice broke. Usually I was afraid to see her cry, but this time I didn't care if I hurt her. I turned away and slammed the door behind me. There went all my hopes for the coming fall: new notebooks, lessons in poetry and literature, and walking to school every day, arm in arm with Rosanna.

❦

For days I sulked over this disappointment, my face stiff and heavy with resentment. Rosanna urged me to keep begging, but I knew it would be vain. Mama's mind was made up. After a few days, Amos asked what was bothering me, and the kindness in his dark eyes made me reveal everything to him.

"Oh, Amos, Mama says I have to give up school because we can't afford it. It's unfair, and I'm so angry." I felt tears rising up and bit my lip hard to stop them. "I know I shouldn't blame her, but I can't help it."

"Looks like you goin' to have to get an education in hidin'," he said. "Like my folk always done."

"What do you mean?" I asked.

"Well, I wouldn't say anything to your ma, if you was to bring in a book an' read in it from time to time," he replied, winking.

I felt myself start to smile. I borrowed *The History of the Roman Empire* and *The Legends of King Arthur* from Margaret, who had four shelves of books in her drawing room. I kept them in a box below the counter and read when there were no customers in the shop. Every day Amos made me tell him one thing I had learned, and eventually he was familiar with Julius Caesar, Nero, and Sir Lancelot. I borrowed a volume of Shakespeare, and Amos was as surprised as I was to learn that he had written a play about a Negro, *Othello*.

Though I escaped from time to time into a book, I soon began to realize that Mama was right, the business was in trouble. When I couldn't get the accounts to balance, I turned the ledger over to Mama, and she sat at the kitchen table until late into the night, poring over the invoices and the orders and shaking her head. It was undeniable. We were losing money.

It was not Amos's fault, that was certain. He worked from sunup until dark. I would sometimes pause to watch him butcher a hog, hanging its carcass by the hocks while the blood drained, flaying its skin and then pulling it from the body like a jacket. He would cut through the thick white belly fat and remove the heart and the glistening reddish brown liver. The entrails would uncoil and spill onto the ground, smelling of rot and death, and he would not even flinch.

37

With sure blows of his cleaver, he would separate the rib cage from the spinal column, then cut off the loins that hung like saddlebags on each side.

Eventually I could look at a carcass and know how the cuts would fit into a barrel of brine and then figure in my head how much income the meat would bring. It was never enough. I learned each customer's preferences and set aside the best cuts of meat for them. But some people just couldn't pay, and out of pity Mama extended their credit. We always wrote to Papa that we were managing fine, to keep him from worrying.

Amos also tried to reassure Mama. "Why, ma'am, it's jus' goin' to take us a while to all ketch on to the way Mistuh Allbauer run his shop. He always been the best in this town, and we are doin' our best too."

"Yes, Amos, you are doing a fine job," said Mama. "Business should improve when the farmers bring in their cattle for slaughter."

One day Amos set out to deliver a keg of salt pork to old Mr. Schmidt, the tavern keeper. Sometimes I rode along and talked with the customers while Amos unloaded the cart. On this occasion, Mr. Schmidt stood with his hands in his pockets and made no move to help Amos carry the heavy keg. He thrust some bills at me and I counted them. There were only twelve dollars. He owed me twenty-five. I glanced uncertainly from him to Amos.

"That's all yer gettin' this time," Mr. Schmidt said. "Last barrel, the meat was all rancid. This'n better be fresh." He glared at Amos.

"Yes, sir. Packed jus' this week, sir," said Amos. "Mighty sorry about that last barrel."

Mr. Schmidt stomped away. Amos climbed up and took the reins. I was shaking with indignation when we pulled away.

"We never would have sold him bad meat! And he underpaid me. You should have stood up to him."

"It ain't my place to challenge a white man, even if he's wrong," said Amos, his brow set in an angry frown.

Nor could I say anything, I thought, being merely a girl.

"That's mighty unfair, it seems to me," I said, hitting my thighs with my fists. I wished for Papa to return. No one would dare cheat him.

I was still boiling mad about Mr. Schmidt when Rosanna came into the shop later that day, wearing a pretty flowered muslin dress. Amos was working at a butcher block in the back room.

"Doesn't the smell bother you?" Rosanna said, wrinkling her nose.

"Animals are raised to be eaten. That's a fact. Even in a fine city like Richmond," I said, for I was feeling irritable.

"Well, it just seems . . . brutal."

"No, killing a man is brutal," I said, and flipped the pages of the ledger to show that I was busy.

"Well, of course," admitted Rosanna.

"When I see a hog, I think ham and sausage, or candles and soap, which we make from the rendered fat, you know," I explained.

"Please! I have just eaten," said Rosanna. "I only mean, I couldn't do the work you are doing."

"Well, I would rather be a shopgirl or a maid than a butcher's assistant," I admitted. "Better yet, I would prefer not to have to work."

Rosanna looked embarrassed. Her father was a banker, and she would never have to give up school to take a job.

"Does Margaret need a roast for dinner?" I asked in a businesslike tone.

"Oh, Lizzie, I'm so sorry that you aren't in school with me!" Rosanna burst out. She grabbed both my hands. "I want to tell you everything that happens, but I'm afraid to hurt your feelings."

"It can't be helped," I said, pulling my hands away.

Rosanna bit her lip and stepped back. "Lizzie, the reason I came was to invite you to come and work on the flag tonight. All my school friends will be there. They think it's a wonderful idea. Annie Baumann's father paid for the material to show his patriotism, since he could not go to war because of his bad leg." Rosanna put her hand over her mouth to stop her prattling. "I really want you to come, Lizzie," she ended simply.

"I'm terribly busy here, you see."

"Please come. I've invited Ginnie Wade, too."

"Oh, because we're both poor working girls!" I said before I could stop myself.

"No, because you are my best friend and I miss seeing you," said Rosanna with cool dignity as she left the shop.

I went home feeling miserable. Things were no better there. Mama looked exasperated and Ben was complaining.

"Sweeping and scrubbing? Those are *girl jobs*!" my brother groused, throwing the broom on the floor.

Mama forced the broom back into his hand, scolding him. "One more outburst and you'll stir the pot and wear an apron all day tomorrow."

"There's no reason you can't help in the kitchen, Ben," I said crossly. He was starting to act rebellious and lazy, like Luke, and that made me mad. "House chores are nothing to be ashamed of. I work twice as hard as you do."

"Stop bickering, you irksome children!" said Mama, and left the house. It was her night to go door-to-door collecting donations and taking them to church to box up for the soldiers.

Alone in the house with my crabby brother, I thought about how lonely I would be if Rosanna were no longer my friend. With a sigh, I borrowed one of Mama's skirts, because mine were getting too short, grabbed a shawl, and set out for Margaret's house. The declining sun cast long golden rays across my path, and the crisp air raised my spirits. A few leaves were letting go from their branches, as if choosing to be the first out of the millions that must fall.

When I arrived, Margaret was sewing uniform trousers for soldiers.

"Those girls are more inclined to gossip than sew. But thankfully Mrs. Pierpont came by and gave them a volume of Lord Tennyson's poetry to read aloud while they work. Go on in," she said, nodding toward the drawing room. "And help yourself to another book if you'd like."

I counted nine girls sitting in a circle, all stitching white stars as big as a man's hand. Ginnie Wade was there, and several girls I knew from church. Annie Baumann sat leaning on a sewing machine heaped with yards of red cloth. Rosanna was reading aloud, her features expressing a strange passion.

Let the sweet heavens endure,
Not close and darken above me
Before I am quite sure
That there is one to love me!

She caught sight of me and clapped the book shut. "Lizzie, you've come!"

I felt everyone's eyes on me. My face flushed and the skin under my arms felt moist and prickly. Did my hands still smell of brine? I wished I'd remembered to use Mama's lavender water. I smiled all around the room and said hello. Annie nodded just enough to stir the perfect brown ringlets of her hair.

"Let me show you our flag," Rosanna said with pride, unfurling a section of cloth with alternating foot-wide bars of red and white. "It will be more than twenty feet long, perhaps the biggest flag ever made!"

My mouth fell open in amazement. Rosanna had been serious after all when she talked about a grand project.

"Would you like to work on a star or a stripe?" she asked.

"What are you going to do with it?" I blurted out, forgetting my shyness.

"You know, send it to our soldiers, to show them our support," replied Rosanna patiently.

"But what will they *do* with it?" It seemed obvious to me that the flag was far too big to display or carry.

It was suddenly very quiet in the room. Rosanna looked offended. Annie stood up next to her and took hold of a corner of the flag.

"What do you mean?" she asked coldly.

I was thinking that the flag was big enough to serve as an officer's tent. That, cut into pieces, it would make enough blankets to cover fifteen men.

"Nothing. I don't know. I mean—it's a beautiful flag, but is it p-practical?" I stammered. An awkward silence followed. "I mean, it's too big to even fit on a pole." Red-faced, I sat down on a cushion between Martha Stover and Ginnie Wade. The girls all bowed to their sewing. Annie helped Rosanna refold the flag, and they sat down together on the settee. Rosanna showed Annie a letter I guessed was from Henry Phelps.

"How lucky you are to have a beau in uniform!" sighed Annie. She leaned her head on Rosanna's shoulder and stroked her wrist.

I watched, consumed with jealousy. Rosanna was *my* best friend, and Annie was a little thief! I forced myself to look away and make small talk with Martha and Ginnie.

"He's just been promoted to corporal," Ginnie was saying about her own beau, Jack Skelly, who had been one of the first Gettysburg boys to enlist.

"Don't you have a fellow, Lizzie?" Martha asked. I flushed, thinking she was teasing me, but her question was serious.

"The very idea!" I replied, for that was how the girls spoke to each other. But I only sounded silly. Why had I even come?

When the Shriver sisters rose, saying they had to study, I ducked out without saying good-bye and hurried homeward, welcoming the cool air on my burning face.

Lizzie

Chapter 7

By October, the corn that had been only a few inches high when Papa and Luke left Gettysburg was brown and rattled in the fields. Neighbors of the farmers who were at war helped with the harvest, but here and there a field was left for the crows to pick. My sixteenth birthday was on October 19. With half my family away, I didn't feel much like celebrating. Mama took me to the photo studio to have my portrait taken. I thought I looked terribly plain in it, although I wore my prettiest dress. Ben carved a wooden comb for my hair. Two of the teeth broke off, but I wore it anyway. Papa and Luke sent letters.

Dearest Lizzie,

I am sending my fondest love for your birthday, my dear daughter, whom I miss more than words can say. You don't know how much I treasure the embrace you gave me the morning I left. I know you are being a help and comfort to your mother; you have always been a blessing to me . . .

Papa's words brought a lump to my throat. But then he had written half a page of instructions for the business, including a request for Mama to send him a financial report. I went on to read Luke's letter.

Happy Birthday to us, Lizzie.

Could you send me a piece of your cake? On the march we ate nothing but soup from dried vegetables and hardtack which is like old leather but if you soak it in coffee it is edible. Every day we are covered in dust and dirt, even the food is gritty. Henrys feet got so blistered he bled from his boots. We are best friends and share a tent which means joining our canvas together and holding it up with a pole at the ends. I swear he gets more letters from our cousin Rose than most men get from their wives. Sadly the girl I fancy has not written to me.

My duties are digging latrines and hauling wood to build winter barracks. Papas job is to help the quartermaster supply fresh beef. He makes me go with him to services at camp on Sundays and Wednesdays. The preacher thunders on about our everlasting souls. You would not believe the number of men who play dice and drink, but not Papa.

We are eager to whip the Johnnies and come home by spring. The nights are getting cold and I would give anything for another blanket. And some of Ma's sugar pickles would taste good.

Your affectionate brother
Luke

P.S. You can have my old pocket knife for a gift, I have a better one now.

Despite some of its unpleasant details, Luke's letter made me smile. I was writing back to him when I heard Mama answer the door, and I recognized Rosanna's melodious drawl.

"Happy birthday, Lizzie!" she said, coming in and kissing me as if the scene with the flag had never happened. "Here's your present." She held out a frame containing a bouquet of pressed violets and daisies.

I thanked her and gave her one of the photographs.

"Why, it looks just like you!" said Rosanna, seemingly delighted with the picture. "I'll paste this in my scrapbook. May I have a lock of your hair to put next to it?"

I handed her the kitchen scissors and felt her snip some hair from the back of my head.

"Rosanna, I'm sorry I wasn't more excited about your flag," I said, watching her fold the hair into a piece of paper. "I'm not like your school friends. I can't help saying what I think."

"Well, that's what I like about you, Lizzie. Most people are far too polite. But if you want to be more like the other girls, let me help you dress your hair in a more becoming way."

"So that's it. I'm not pretty enough?"

Sounding exasperated, Rosanna said, "You've been awfully touchy lately. What is bothering you?"

I hesitated. I knew but one way to say it, the most direct way.

"Rosanna, you have everything. You're beautiful, the boys flock to you, and you go to a school where all the girls want to be your friend." I looked at my hands, which were red and callused, and sighed. "I work in a butcher shop. Why do you even want me for a friend?"

Rosanna stood with her mouth open. But she didn't say anything for a long time.

I looked down into my lap.

"Lizzie, you were the first person in Gettysburg who was kind to me besides my own sister. And I can trust you. I told you about John Wilcox because I knew you would keep it secret."

"That's another thing, Rosanna," I said, feeling all my discontent bubble up at once. "Sometimes I don't understand you at all."

"So? I don't understand myself," she said with a forced laugh.

"I'm serious. Why did you cut off John Wilcox, who said he loved you? Why are you so keen on Henry Phelps now? What is it you want?"

I watched Rosanna put her thumb and forefinger to her mouth and frown.

"I'm confused, all right?" she said. "I thought I loved John Wilcox, but perhaps I was mistaken. And Henry was . . . *here*. He is not quite the man John is, but he is honest and good. His letters are entertaining, and I know he cares for me. Well, I think he does," she finished uncertainly.

I was beginning to think that Rosanna was like a chameleon, a creature who changed colors according to her surroundings. When she left Richmond, she simply put John Wilcox out of her mind.

"What will I do if you get tired of my friendship and decide that Annie Baumann is your new best friend?" I blurted out.

"Oh, Lizzie! That will never happen! You are my dearest cousin *and* my best friend, always."

For the moment, I was more pleased than if she had handed me an expensive birthday present.

"And that's why I know you'll do me this favor." She took my hand imploringly. "It's about the flag. My friends have given up. They say their fingers are too sore or they have too much studying. Even Annie Baumann has lost interest. I'm afraid it won't be finished in time for Christmas. Won't you please help me?"

At the mention of the flag, my irritation flared up again.

"But why, if you are so proud to be from Virginia, are you making a Union flag?"

"The Stars and Stripes is the only flag I know, and until a few months ago, it was my flag as well as yours," said Rosanna, lifting her chin.

"But where do you stand on the war?" I asked.

"Why? Does it matter to our friendship?" Rosanna's tone was challenging.

"No . . . but . . . I think it must be hard for you . . . being from the South . . . and living in Gettysburg," I said haltingly. But it did matter. I wanted Rosanna on my side in all things.

"Lizzie, I've been up here long enough that I feel loyal to our boys in uniform. I care about Henry and Luke and Uncle Albert. I don't know any Confederate soldiers." Rosanna shrugged.

I would have to be satisfied with that. Rosanna had her reasons, even if they didn't make much sense to me.

So three weeks before Christmas, Rosanna and I sewed up the final seams of her flag, with Ginnie's help. We pieced together stripes of red and white and a field of blue with thirty-four stars into a flag that represented a country that no longer existed. It was split into North and South and torn from east to west as well, for there was now fighting as far away as Kentucky and Oklahoma. We didn't talk about the war, but worked in silence, our fingers busy with the futile task of stitching together something that could possibly never be made whole again.

Lizzie

———◆———

Chapter 8

As the December days grew shorter and colder, we hoped that Papa and Luke would be furloughed and come home for Christmas. But Papa's letter dashed that hope. Smallpox was keeping the company quarantined, and only a few lucky officers would be allowed to go home. Mama tucked the letter in her apron and tried to hide her disappointment. But that night I was awakened by the sound of crying in the kitchen. I crept down the stairs, as I had the morning Papa left for war, to see Mama sitting at the table. A lamp flickered beside her and she clutched Papa's letter in her hand. Her shoulders shook with sobs and her back curved until her forehead rested on the table.

"Albert! Oh, Albert!" she cried over and over again. The anguish in her voice made my stomach clench. "I can't do it without you. Oh, I miss you so much!" she wailed, more softly.

I felt my own tears coming, thinking of how powerfully Mama must love Papa. A sudden fear seized me that she would get sick from worry and too much work. So I started taking piles of her relief work to the shop, and between customers I scraped lint off of old rags. In the butcher shop, my books gathered dust. I worked on the accounts until they balanced so Mama would not have to stay up so late. I knitted a muffler with a red fringe for Papa, hoping he wouldn't mind the uneven edges and dropped stitches. Then I began a scarf for Luke, while Mama knitted up four pairs of socks. We packed these with two wool blankets, a ham, some pickles, and my birthday photograph, hoping that the package would reach their camp in time for Christmas.

It promised to be a lonely holiday, despite the caroling and the cheerful greetings exchanged in the streets. Mama and Ben and I decorated a small evergreen tree with strands of dried berries, candles, pinecones, and foil stars and stood it on the parlor table, where it gave off a piney scent. On Christmas Eve, Rosanna and Margaret and the children came over for dinner, so the house wouldn't seem so empty without Papa and Luke. Ben raced around the house with Jack and Clara taking turns riding on his back and shrieking with excitement. The aromas of savory ham, mince pie, and peppermint filled the house. After dinner we lit the candles on the tree and watched it with great care, for one year a neighbor's house had burned to the ground when a Christmas candle ignited the decorations.

Another letter came from Papa and Luke, thanking us for the warm clothes and food. They were snug in their new winter barracks and expecting extra rations for the holiday. Included was a photograph of Papa sitting before a white tent, holding his hat in his lap, and Luke standing with his hand on Papa's shoulder, his cap askew. Papa's mustache had grown long and curved like a ram's horn, and his face looked gaunt. Luke's face was somewhat blurred. We put the picture in a frame, set it beside the tree, and sat around Christmas morning gazing at it until it was time for church.

While Papa's letter cheered us, the end bothered me like a splinter in a finger. He had written: *Your good news about the business heartens me. You can consult Matthias Schupp the York butcher this winter; he owes me a favor. Make a good deal with A. Trostle to keep his fat steers coming.*

If Schmidt opens a 2nd tavern persuade him to double his order. Next time include with your summary exact figures re: expenses & income.

"What are we going to do?" I finally said to Mama. "We can't hide from Papa any longer that we're losing money."

"Put aside your worries for one day at least," she said, taking a steaming pie from the oven.

The door slammed and Ben came in, along with a blast of cold air and the smell of stables. My brother had found a small job brushing horses and hauling hay for a New York regiment stationed at the public school.

"How much did you earn this week?" I asked.

"I got two dollars, on account of Christmas." He held out the coins to Mama, who took them, leaving him four nickels. Ben tried to give her two of those nickels, but she wouldn't take them, even though we needed every penny of that extra money. Mama had sold the silver candlesticks to cover household expenses until we figured out how to increase our income from the shop.

Still humming, she tucked away the coins and began to fix up a hamper with a fresh meat pie, homemade preserves, and hot bread. I hoped her good mood would last through Christmas dinner. Every time we sat down to eat, the two empty chairs at the kitchen table filled me with longing. Mama would gaze at them and squeeze our hands tightly while saying grace.

"Why are you packing a basket of food?" I asked.

"It's for Amos. He deserves a good Christmas meal. In fact, I want you both to take it to him now."

"But I just got in! It's freezing outside, and the food will be cold before we get there," protested Ben, but he put his coat back on anyway.

Mama wrapped everything in a blanket to keep the heat in. "Be home by dark. And bring back the blanket and basket."

I was ashamed that I hadn't thought of doing something special for Amos. I put on my cloak and Mama's cape for extra warmth. Mama wrapped Ben's muffler around his head until only his eyes were visible.

"That will stifle your complaining," she said, giving him a hug.

We didn't know exactly where Amos lived, though Mama guessed it was on the southwestern edge of town, where all the Negroes lived. So Ben and I set out, walking briskly to stay warm. It was late afternoon and the sky was growing dim. The windows of the houses glowed with lamplight. Passing Mrs. Pierpont's school on the corner of High and Washington Streets, we heard someone playing a piano. Along Washington Street, we kept close to the houses to avoid the biting wind. At Long Lane we stopped, gazing down a long row of tiny clapboard houses.

"How're we supposed to find Amos?" asked Ben, sounding worried.

"We ask someone," I said, though there was nobody in sight. We passed a garden, where frozen stems and stalks poked up through the snow-covered furrows. I chose one of the larger cottages, a likely place for a respectable butcher's assistant to live, and knocked on the door.

A woman with skin like milky coffee opened the door. The faces of three small children poked from behind her skirts. Unfamiliar cooking smells wafted in the air.

"Lawd, miss, come in from the cold. And you too, young mastuh," she said with a look of surprise.

I held up the basket. "I've brought this for Mr. Amos Whitman."

"Why, he don' live here, miss," she replied, shaking her head. "Go to the end o' the lane and turn left. An' you'uns have a Merry Christmas now," she added, and gently closed the door.

We stumbled over the frozen ruts until we reached the end of the lane. There stood a mere shack made of bits and pieces of old planks nailed together. Rags were stuffed into the window openings, and a dilapidated door hung on rusty hinges.

"Amos can't possibly live *here*," Ben whispered. "Let's just go home."

"Someone lives here," I said, pointing to the smoke that rose from a tin pipe that served as a chimney. Just then the door opened and we jumped back, startled at the sight of a figure thickly bundled in old coats, with rags wrapped around his head, hands, and feet.

"Why if it ain't Miz Lizzie an' Mastuh Ben!"

"It *is* you, Amos," Ben said, sighing with relief.

"We came to wish you a Merry Christmas," I said politely, hiding my dismay at the sight of his poor shack.

Holding the door open, Amos motioned for us to enter, like a butler welcoming guests to a mansion. Ben and I went in together. The shack was lit by a small fire on the hearth. I could make out an old chest, a rough table and a stool, some pans and plates, and a straw mattress piled high with blankets and rags. The floor was packed dirt, covered with old rugs. Amos set another log on the fire and prodded it with a stick until it started to crackle.

A feeling I didn't quite understand, something like shame, was growing in me.

"Let me—I'll put these on the hearth. To—to keep them warm," I stammered.

"That looks mighty good," Amos said, sounding hearty. He pulled the old chest up to the fire and motioned for us to sit. Ben's toes barely reached the ground.

Then the words came out, before I could stop them.

"Oh, Amos, why are you living in such a miserable place?"

"Ah," breathed Amos, looking down at his feet. They were wrapped in rags.

"Where are your shoes?" Ben asked, noticing Amos's feet as well.

"I'm keepin' them from gettin' worn out," he replied.

I knew Amos was paid a decent wage, eight dollars a week. Mother gave him an extra dollar for heavy chores and repairs. Surely he could afford to live in a regular house. He was not a drunkard. Where did his money go?

"Why, Amos?" This time, my voice was a gentle plea.

"Let me tell you'uns a story," he said by way of reply. Sitting on the stool, he rested his elbows on his knees and gazed into the fire.

"I was born on a plantation in South Carolina 'bout 1836. My folk were field hands. They worked from sunup to sundown. When I was half your size, Mastuh Ben, I carried food an' water to the fields an' picked up the cotton what fell outta the bags."

He reached for the meat pie on the hearth, took a spoon, and began to eat.

"God bless your mama, this here's a mighty tasty pie. I grew up eatin' mostly corn bread, mush, an' greens. We'd go huntin' for rabbit an' possum so's my mama could make stew. I could pick off a critter with jus' one stone. Like this." He cocked his arm and pitched an imaginary rock into the corner, moving so fast his arm was a blur.

"Will you teach me how to do that?" asked Ben, bouncing with eagerness. Amos smiled and nodded, then went on with his story.

"Our mastuh was a mean 'un. He whipped my pa for being too high an' mighty, he said, then sold him. I was 'bout your age, Lizzie. After that, my ma weren't ever the same. Then mastuh's fortunes declined, an' he sold all five of my brothuhs an' sistuhs. Each time she lost one of us, my mama got smaller an' sadder. One day she jus' died. I couldn't keep her alive no more."

I blinked back tears. Ben sat perfectly still next to me.

"All I had left was Grace." Amos bowed his head.

I hardly thought that losing your whole family was a blessing, but

I had said enough rude things for one day. Then I realized that Amos was not talking about religion.

"My Grace, a woman as beautiful as kind. We was married by a preacher, after he baptized us in the river. She was a house slave, had a fine hand with pastries, an' a gentle touch with childern."

I was stunned. Amos had a wife! Did my parents know this?

"Then one day she was gone. Mastuh sold her, too."

Amos sighed. The log on the fire flared up, glowing a bright orange.

"Soon, Mastuh died from an apoplexy, an' my mistress, fearin' the Lord, freed the rest of her forty slaves. I won't ever forget the day I got my papers sayin' I was a free man."

Amos finished the pie and wiped his mouth with his hand. I handed him some bread and he used it to sop up the last bits of meat and gravy.

"What happened to Grace?" I asked in a hesitant voice.

Amos bit off and chewed another chunk of bread. "The day I was freed I set out to find her. She was not twenty miles down the river, owned by crazy ol' Mastuh Johnston. He laughed like the devil an' said I could buy her for a thousan' dollars. I 'bout fell over dead to hear that sum but vowed to come back an' set her free."

"You shoulda punched him in the face and run off with her!" said Ben, clenching his fists.

"If I'd've done that, I'd be dead, young man," Amos replied, shaking his head.

Then he reached over and tapped the chest we were sitting on. "It's all in there," he said in a low voice. "Every cent your papa paid me since the day I came to work fo' him, 'cept what I took out to buy food an' work clothes an' scraps to build this place."

"We're sitting on a treasure!" cried Ben.

"Hush, Ben," I said, finally understanding.

"In a few more months I can meet Johnston's price an' buy a horse an' cart to bring my Grace home in style," he said, then looked around with a wry smile. "Such as it is."

My head was whirling, it was so much to take in.

"Papa doesn't know this, does he? Or Mama? Why didn't you tell us before?"

Amos shrugged and spread his hands. "Ain't nobody ever asked."

I looked at Amos's deep-set black eyes, his glossy skin and big hands, as if I were seeing him for the first time: a man who had once been a boy who suffered as a slave and even watched his mother die. And how could my father have employed him for almost two years without learning that he lived in a hut worse than a barn to save money to buy his wife out of slavery? I felt ashamed for thinking of Amos only as someone to help us run the butcher shop.

But all I said was, "We must go home now. Mother will be getting worried."

Ben stood up but he didn't take his eyes off that chest. I picked up the empty basket and the blanket. Then I laid the blanket back down where I had been sitting.

"Good-bye, Amos," I said, then hugged him. It was awkward because of his thick layers of clothing. But his arms were strong as he hugged me back. He smelled of wood smoke and dust.

"Please stay warm," I pleaded. "Pennsylvania is not South Carolina."

"No, it sho' ain't. Merry Christmas, now."

Amos shook Ben's hand and we left. The icy air hit my face, and I realized how warm Amos's little cabin had been.

As soon as we got home, I told Mama Amos's whole story and described his tiny, cold shack, while Ben kept interrupting to mention the trunk full of money. All the while, Mama shook her head slowly from side to side.

"If you don't believe me, I'll take you there."

"I believe you, Lizzie. But what would you have me do?" She spread her hands in a gesture of helplessness.

"Have him live with us. He can sleep in the garret, and Ben can move into my room. Also, he would be closer to the shop."

"I can't split wood all by myself, Ma," chimed in Ben. "I need Amos's help on the big logs. And he could teach me how to hunt with a slingshot."

"But Amos is a free man. We cannot tell him what to do," Mama objected.

"We're giving him a choice, Mama," I said patiently.

"But to live with us?" said Mama doubtfully. "People might misunderstand."

"Why? He would be our lodger, not a servant. Even our neighbors have lodgers," I said.

Mama was silent and pensive. I suspected her concern had more to do with Amos being a Negro. As much as she hated how Negroes were treated, she couldn't quite bring herself to let one live with us. I thought that was wrong of her, and I wouldn't give in.

"We should treat Amos like we would any friend or relative in need," I said, looking her square in the eye. I could see that she knew I was right.

"He is your father's assistant, and an honest, respectable man," she admitted. "But we must not offend his dignity. I will speak with him."

A few days later, I overheard Mama conferring with Amos at the shop. She said that because of Papa's longer-than-expected absence, she needed a regular hired man. If Amos would agree to patch the roof, rebuild the shed, and chop firewood, she would provide room and board. His wages and duties at the butcher shop would be the same. Amos said he would consider it. In my excitement I ran to tell

Rosanna, but she wasn't home, so I told Margaret all about Amos—and Grace, too. She even cried a bit, but her eyes grew wide when I said that Amos might come and live with us.

Within a week, Amos brought his trunk and moved into the attic room. Ben was as gleeful as if a long-lost uncle had come to stay.

"Mr. Amos, can I see your treasure? How much money do you have in there? Is it in gold?" he asked.

Finally I warned him, "If you don't shut up about that chest, someone will hear you and creep into this house at night and steal everything and cut our throats from ear to ear."

That quieted him for a while, until he began pestering Mama for a rifle.

"Someone has to stand guard and shoot thieves," he said. "And I'll protect us when the rebels come."

"Don't talk such nonsense," she told him.

In the end, Mama persuaded Amos to deposit his money in the Farmers and Merchants Savings Bank. She also decided to increase his salary by fifty cents a week. When I started to protest that we could hardly afford that, she cut me off.

"You know it's the right thing to do, Lizzie. We will manage to get by. Somehow."

Lizzie

———✦———

Chapter 9
1862

Winter was always the busiest time for a butcher. Meat stayed fresh longer and people ate a lot of it, believing that it kept up their strength against the cold. So there was slaughtering, packing, and preserving to be done, but without Papa, Amos couldn't do the work alone. Mama and I agreed that we had to hire someone, and though we could scarcely afford the wages, she started spreading the word around town. That's how I ended up face to face with Martin Weigel, the boy Rosanna had laughed at the day Papa enlisted.

When he first came into the shop, I regarded him doubtfully. All gangly limbed, he didn't look strong enough to heft a side of beef. His wrists stuck out beneath his jacket sleeves, but I noticed his hands were big.

"I'm here for the job," he said.

I assumed he had already talked to Mama and been hired.

"When can you start?" I asked.

"Today," he said, looking right at me. His eyes were gray blue, wide set, and honest looking.

So I introduced him to Amos, who put him to work. Mama was pleased to have Martin working for us, thinking the Weigels and their many kinfolk would be good customers. He worked for eighty cents a day. Three days a week he helped Amos strip hides and hew carcasses into hams and ribs and loins. When Rock Creek froze, they drove out in the cart and returned with huge blocks of ice that they covered with sawdust and hay. The ice would keep fresh meat from spoiling in warm weather. What meat we didn't sell fresh, I rubbed with salt and placed in barrels of brine and powdered nitrate, which gave the meat a healthy color. I negotiated prices on the hides and had Martin deliver them to the tanner. I tracked orders and deliveries, invoices and payments. But as hard as we worked, business never rose to the level of the year before, when Papa was in charge.

At home, Mama imposed strict measures to conserve butter, sugar, coffee, and candles. She talked about taking in laundry. I didn't know where we'd find the time to do other people's washing as well as our own. But fortunately it didn't come to that, for Ben kept finding odd jobs that brought in fifty cents here and there. One day I saw Amos give Ben a dollar, and I realized that he was turning over some of his own earnings to help buy food. I didn't say anything, because we badly needed the money. But I don't believe Mama ever found out.

Nor did she discover that I sometimes still read books at the shop, for Amos was as good as his word and never let on. I finished John Bunyan's *The Pilgrim's Progress,* which inspired me to bear my trials with more patience, and borrowed Charles Dickens's *Hard Times* from Margaret. Some evenings I sat with Rosanna while she studied, hoping to learn something. My cousin was by her own admission a lazy student, and I often ended up helping her. One night in February I found her in a sulky mood, staring at the blank page of a notebook.

"What shall I do, Lizzie? Mrs. Pierpont has assigned us to write another entry about the war. But I don't have any interest in battles and generals," she said wearily.

I picked up her notebook. It was titled *A History of the War*. In it was a paragraph on the fall of Fort Sumter, copied from the newspaper in Rosanna's flowing hand, a list of Confederate states and the dates of their secession, and a sketch of Rosanna and her friends sewing the flag. I realized that Papa and Luke had not mentioned receiving the flag.

"Why not write a description of camp life in the winter? You said Henry's letters were full of such anecdotes."

"Yes, but I doubt that will satisfy Mrs. Pierpont."

"Isn't she practically an abolitionist?" I said. The whole town knew of Mrs. Pierpont's strong opinions. "You could write about Amos and how he plans to free his wife from slavery," I suggested, looking sideways at Rosanna for her response.

Rosanna clasped her hands. "Oh, yes, she will love that. Margaret told me the story. It's so romantic, how he loves Grace even though they are so far apart."

"What's romantic about Grace being a slave and Amos working so hard just so he can *buy* her?" I said, frowning at Rosanna. "People shouldn't be bought and sold."

Rosanna's eyebrows shot up. "I declare, Lizzie, this whole business with your hired man is making *you* an abolitionist!"

"That's not true," I shot back. I knew that abolitionists gave wild speeches and sometimes broke into prisons to free captured runaways. I would never do such a thing. But I had to admit that Rosanna was half right. I did want slavery to end. Yes, even if it meant the war would last longer. I felt sad and suddenly older, realizing what others had known for a long time: the war had to go on.

"Rosanna, don't you believe that slavery is wrong?"

"My father does not own slaves," she said, avoiding my question.

"But what do *you* think?" I persisted.

"If all the slaves were freed, who would farm the cotton and tobacco?"

"Pay them to work. Like Papa pays Amos."

"Not everyone agrees with your father," murmured Rosanna.

"What do you mean?" I demanded, but Rosanna merely shook her head.

"Lizzie, I'm glad Amos is free and I hope he and Grace are reunited. I don't want to defend slavery, but without it, the entire South would collapse. Is that what everyone wants out of this war? To humiliate and destroy us? Well, we won't let it happen."

With that, she grabbed her notebook and swept from the room. I gazed into the sputtering fire as worry gnawed at me. When Rosanna had said "us" and "we," she sounded like a Southerner.

Margaret came into the parlor and set about straightening and dusting.

"I heard your quarrel," she said, giving me a sympathetic look. "Rosanna's been upset all week. We got a letter from Mother begging us to come back to Richmond. It had to be smuggled out because there is no post. She writes that there is no food because of the blockade, and the whole of Virginia is a battleground. I would never take the children there." She paused in her tidying up and sighed. "But I think Rosanna misses our parents."

I wondered if it was John Wilcox she was missing. But I merely nodded and picked up my cloak.

"She's even touchy with me. I'm so glad she has you for a friend!" said Margaret, kissing me as I took my leave.

Soon our quarrel seemed forgotten. Rosanna purchased a map of Virginia to assist with her writing assignments. Together we marked the movements of the Pennsylvania volunteers. As we stuck pins at Hunter's Mill, Alexandria, and Manassas Junction, it was clear that

General McClellan was driving the Union army toward Richmond. Soon, it seemed, Company K would face the rebels in battle. But the army was moving at the pace of a snail. It was April, and they had advanced no farther than Fredericksburg.

"That's barely thirty-five miles from where they broke camp in March," I mused to Rosanna. "Why, you and I could walk faster than that."

"Not with fifty pounds of gear on our backs," Rosanna replied. "That's how much Henry says they carry."

"Can you imagine us living in a tent and having to dig our own latrines? I don't know how Luke can stand it." I shuddered.

"No, I wouldn't survive a single day," said Rosanna. "Why, who would arrange my hair?" she added primly.

The thought made us both collapse with laughter.

"I do wonder what McClellan's strategy is," I said, wiping my eyes.

"He is afraid to attack Richmond," Rosanna said firmly. "Because he knows that it cannot be taken."

"How can you be so sure?" I replied, trying to hide my irritation. I wanted Richmond to fall, for then the war would end, and Papa and Luke could come home.

"All the Union generals put together aren't worth one General Lee," Rosanna declared. "And we will fight harder, because we are *defending* our country from the Yankees."

There it was again—"we"—and Rosanna didn't mean she and I. I didn't want to quarrel again. I stood up and put my shawl around me.

"I think I should leave now."

"I'm sorry, Lizzie. Don't go away angry," Rosanna said, taking my hand in a beseeching way.

"I'm not angry," I said. I could not put it into words, my helpless regret that Rosanna was slipping away from me.

I heard the steady *zzzt, zzzt, zzzt* of Margaret's shears. In the dining room, Ginnie Wade bent over the sewing machine that clicked and whirred like a tiny train while she guided a pair of blue worsted trousers under the needle.

I nodded to them over the noise as I passed through and almost collided with Jack and Clara. The children had come marching into the room, making *pum-pum-pa-dum* noises with their mouths. They wore blue uniforms with jacket buttons gleaming in double rows. Clara's had a wide skirt, while Jack wore tiny trousers. Margaret must have sewn them from scraps.

Waving a toy sword, Jack shouted, "I'm going to kill all the rebels. Then I'll free the slaves." With his lisp, "rebels" sounded like "webels."

"No, I will!" cried Clara, fighting her brother for the sword.

Ginnie laughed and clapped her hands. I glanced at Rosanna, who stood frowning at Margaret.

"When did they turn into little abolitionists?" Rosanna said.

"Do not criticize my children," said Margaret, her voice clipped.

Ginnie looked down, and I held my breath, embarrassed.

"Our parents still live in Richmond, in case you had forgotten." Rosanna's voice rose with emotion. "Don't you care that the city might be attacked?"

"I do care," replied Margaret. "But Mother and Father—and your John Wilcox—will have to take care of themselves. What do you expect me to do?"

"You can stop *this*!" burst out Rosanna, gesturing to the sea of blue cloth and the pile of finished pants. "It's—it's disloyal. You're making money off of the South's sufferings."

"I have little sympathy with the Southern *cause*," Margaret said, stressing the word in disdain. "Gettysburg is now my home, and sewing is my livelihood."

Rosanna broke into tears and ran from the room. She whirled around in the hallway.

"And I don't love John Wilcox anymore, I love Henry!" she cried, and stumbled up the stairs.

I slipped out of the unhappy house, sick at heart.

Lizzie

Chapter 10

Ten months after Papa left, I finally learned why business had been so poor. The realization was all the more painful because it involved Amos. He was the one who helped keep a secure roof over our heads. He was Ben's friend who took him hunting and shared his pride at the first rabbit he brought home for stew. He was almost as capable as Papa himself when it came to butchering a sow or a steer. But to some people in Gettysburg, Amos was just a Negro, and that was too much.

It was May and the fruit trees were in full bloom. I was feeling thankful that we had made it through the winter without Mama becoming ill, when she came home red faced from a Ladies Aid Society meeting. She threw off her bonnet and collapsed on the sofa. I rushed to her, afraid that she had a fever, but I saw that she was hopping mad.

"Do you know what Frieda Baumann had the gall to say to me?"

I couldn't guess. Mama didn't particularly like Mrs. Baumann, but she had never had words with her before.

"I shouldn't even repeat it, it was so uncharitable."

"You brought it up, so now you have to tell me," I said, knowing she was so heated she wouldn't be able to keep silent.

"Well, Frieda and I were side by side packing bandages, and she said, loud enough for the others to hear, 'I really think a mother ought to watch the sort of folk she allows around her family, especially if she has a daughter.' And I replied, 'Martin Weigel is a fine boy, and I trust him completely to work alongside my Lizzie.'"

"Did you have to say that?" I groaned. "Now people will think we fancy each other." I didn't fancy Martin, not at all.

Mama went on, imitating Mrs. Baumann's haughty tone, "'It's not the boy I'm referring to, but that colored man who works in your shop.'"

"Amos?" I burst out. "Why, he is completely honest! And who does she think she is, giving you advice? Let her worry about her own silly daughter. I can take care of myself."

"That's what I told her, in so many words," Mama said. "But a woman like that won't change her narrow mind because of something I say."

"What did the other women think?" I asked.

"Sarah Brodhead kept her head down, but Mrs. Stover had a definite opinion. 'You've taken this Negro into your house, Mary? Do you really think that is suitable?'" Mama picked up a small cushion and fanned herself with it. "As if I need to be told by the ladies of this town what is fitting!"

I realized that Mrs. Stover no longer came into the shop. Nor had the Baumanns contracted with us since before Papa left for the war. I recalled the day Mr. Schmidt berated Amos and refused to pay for what he said was rancid pork.

"Then Frieda had the gall to say, 'Some people in this town take this Negro-loving business too far.'"

I drew in my breath. "What did you say to that?"

"I told them that Amos was like a member of our family, and I would not suffer their vile insults any longer. Then I walked out. Liddy Pierpont was there and she looked like a tornado about to strike.

Heaven knows what she said after I left, but I hope it flattened Frieda like a hot iron."

"Mama, I'm so proud of you," I said. But I was wondering how many other customers had stopped doing business with us because of their prejudice against Amos.

Suddenly Mama began to cry. "If only Albert were here! Lizzie, whatever shall we do now?"

"We'll do what's right, Mama," I said, sounding braver than I felt.

A few days later, I asked Martin to come with me to Mr. Schmidt's tavern.

"What is our business with Mr. Schmidt today?" he asked when he brought the cart around. It pleased me the way he said "our business" as if he were proud to be working with us.

"He owes us money," I said. "I just need you to stand behind me while I do the talking."

"You don't want me to rough him up?" Martin said with a hint of a smile.

"Not unless he won't pay," I replied with a laugh. But I was nervous. I had no idea what I would say to Mr. Schmidt. When I came face-to-face with him, however, I found the words. I told him that we had, as always, the finest-quality meats in Gettysburg, expertly prepared by Mr. Amos Whitman, and that if he wished to continue receiving them, we expected a full settlement of his account. Then I handed him an invoice.

Mr. Schmidt looked surprised. He turned to Martin, saying, "Eh, son?"

Martin hooked his thumbs in his trouser pockets and nodded in my direction, indicating that Mr. Schmidt should address himself to me. Old Schmidt harrumphed and stomped away, coming back in a few minutes with a bank draft for twenty-two dollars.

With shaking fingers, I wrote out a receipt. I felt like I'd won a battle without even firing a gun.

"That was well done," Martin said when we had left the tavern behind. His few words were enough to seal my small victory.

❧

I soon discovered that the prejudices of Mr. Schmidt and Frieda Baumann were not lost on Amos. One spring night he asked Mama to let him make the trip to South Carolina to free Grace.

"You don't need my permission, Amos," she said.

"Yes, ma'am, but I wouldn't leave if I thought you couldn't manage. The livestock pens are all in good order, an' the smokehouse is full. Martin's a good worker; he'll help you while I'm away."

Mama nodded. "If we need any slaughtering done, we can ask Matthias Schupp. And when you return, Amos, your job will be here waiting for you."

There was a long silence, while the sound of spring peepers filled the night air.

"P'raps it would be best, given what folks in town is sayin', if I . . . if Grace an' I didn't come back. If we went somewheres else."

A cry of protest escaped me.

Mama said, in brief but certain words, "Amos, I am not one to heed the opinions of my ignorant neighbors."

Amos merely nodded and withdrew a map from his pocket and spread it on the table. With his finger he showed us the way he aimed to take.

"I don't think that's wise," said Mama. "I've heard that both armies are gathered here in northern Virginia. Richmond may soon be under attack." Using a pencil, she sketched a route that would take Amos westward, then south through the Shenandoah Valley to the gap in the mountains near Roanoke. "You must keep clear of the armies around Richmond," she cautioned.

Looking at the map, I saw that Amos would travel through Virginia and North Carolina and well into South Carolina before reaching the red *X* that marked the plantation where Grace was kept. It was more than five hundred miles, all in rebel territory.

"You're not going alone?" I had heard about free Negroes being seized by vigilantes and sold back into slavery.

"I have my papers sayin' I'm a free man, an' I bought me a good fast piece o' horseflesh," he replied with confidence.

"Amos, I just had a thought," said Mama intently. "I know of a Massachusetts man who is an experienced scout. He was injured at Ball's Bluff and has been recovering with an uncle here in town. He plans to reenlist, but I think he could be persuaded to a different kind of adventure. Shall I arrange for you to meet him?"

Amos said he would be obliged to her.

When Frederick Hartmann came to meet Amos a few days later, I thought I had never seen a man so dashing and handsome. He had light brown hair that fell to his shoulders in curls. His blue eyes twinkled as he twirled the ends of his mustache between his thumb and forefinger. When I served him coffee after dinner, I couldn't meet his eyes without blushing. Ben, however, wasn't at all shy.

"Can I see your scars, Mr. Hartmann?" he asked. "How did you get shot?"

"Don't be rude, Ben," I murmured.

Mr. Hartmann just laughed. He tugged his shirt aside so that we could see the purplish dent where a ball the size of a marble had torn through his shoulder. It made me a little queasy to look at it.

"It was my own darn fault," he said, leaning back and lighting his pipe. "You see, one night a party of nervous scouts, green as spring twigs, reported a Confederate camp near Ball's Bluff. So the next morning our raiding party crossed over the Potomac only to find out there wasn't any camp, just a row of trees, their drooping branches looking like tents in the fog. Well there we were, with nothing to raid. So we poked around closer to Leesburg and ran into some rebels there." He tapped his pipe, letting the burned tobacco flakes spill onto the step, then blew them away.

"And then you were shot?" prompted Ben.

"Not yet, son. They chased us back to the bluff, where we were trapped with our backs to the ravine and the Rebel army coming at us. We'd no idea there was so many of 'em nearby. Men leaped off the cliff just to get away and others surrendered. I jumped into the river just as a minié ball hit me, but I kept swimming till a buddy fished me out and put me in an ambulance. Lots of men weren't so lucky; they washed up downriver, near Washington, dead." He shook his head sadly.

"Why do you think it was your fault?" I asked, curiosity getting the better of my shyness.

"Because if I had gone out with the scouts, I could have told a tent from a fir tree, and we never would have set out to raid a copse of trees! About half our men fell that day, nearly eight hundred casualties."

"Eight hundred men died?" asked Ben, wide-eyed.

"No, son, casualties is killed, wounded, missing, or captured. They took five hundred prisoners alone." He fell silent for a minute, then slapped his hands on his thighs. "Well, Miss Lizzie, how about another slice of that apple pie? I tell you, it's the best I ever tasted."

In an hour, everything was settled. Mr. Hartmann would travel as a

Carolina landholder, with Amos as his valet. Once they had freed Grace, she and Amos would pretend to be Hartmann's slaves until they reached Pennsylvania again. Mr. Wills, a Gettysburg lawyer, had agreed to draw up the free papers for Grace and the false papers necessary for travel. The final matter was that of Mr. Hartmann's fees.

"I already own a good horse, but I'll require a dollar and fifty cents per day, plus food and such expenses. It could be a six-week journey," said Mr. Hartmann. "A fair deal, I believe, given the considerable risks."

Amos barely blinked, but I was stunned. That sum of money was more than Amos earned in three months. Mama offered him a loan against future wages, but Amos consulted his account book and said that wouldn't be necessary.

At the end of May, Amos and Frederick Hartmann set out. They were fitted for the trip with a tent, oilcloths, extra clothing, and saddlebags full of bacon, beans, and bread. Hartmann had taught Amos how to use a rifle and revolver, in anticipation of trouble. As they rode off, Mama and I stood in the middle of York Street, waving.

"There they go, two more soldiers heading off to war. These ones have no army to back them up," Mama said with a sigh.

"They can do it, Mama," I said. "They will be back."

But the well of emptiness that had opened in me when Papa and Luke left only deepened as the two figures grew smaller, then disappeared down Chambersburg Pike. I wondered if I would ever see Amos again.

Lizzie

———✦———

Chapter 11

Every June the fields that soaked up the spring rains turned bright green with new corn and the trees swelled with young fruit. June had always seemed the most carefree month of the year. But June was also the month that Papa and Luke had gone to war a year ago. Now a feeling of dread settled over me, despite the green and promising landscape, for our volunteers were camped near Richmond, and any day they would begin fighting the rebels for control of the Confederate capital.

The battle commenced on June 26 at Mechanicsburg. A few days later, the *Sentinel* described how General Crawford's division, which included the First Pennsylvania Reserves, Company K, had "rained an unceasing torrent of musket fire while the artillery discharged shells, canister and shrapnel, confounding and scattering the enemy, whose losses tripled those of our brave federals." The reporter made it sound as if the end of the world, or at least the end of the war, was at hand. But it was only the beginning of the fighting, which went on for seven days. With grim forbearance, we waited for the casualty lists to come in. Mama barely slept, and gray circles deepened under her eyes. Ben did his chores silently, without complaining.

The dark news trickled in. General McClellan's army had been forced back toward Washington, and our Company K had suffered more than its share of casualties. When neither Papa nor Luke appeared among the names, we were weak with relief and gratitude. Then terrible news arrived. Mrs. Pierpont heard it first, for she was at the telegraph office when the message came in, and she told Margaret, who informed Rosanna: Henry Phelps had been killed.

The next day the whole town knew of it, and Henry Phelps's name was on everyone's tongue. When his poor widowed mother received the news, she felt a sharp pain in her chest and took to her bed. The next morning, she didn't wake up. People said it was proof that grief could kill a person.

I went at once to see how Rosanna was taking the news and found her lying facedown on the settee in Margaret's parlor, a pile of damp handkerchiefs on the floor beside her. I was afraid to say anything, lest it be the wrong thing. I had no idea what it would feel like to lose your beau in the war. So I imagined how sad I would feel if Papa or Luke died, and that was bad enough. I blinked back my tears and patted Rosanna's back while she wept softly.

A week later I hurried to Rosanna's again, clutching a letter from Luke. Its contents were already seared into my memory.

Dear sister,

I have seen enough of war and am ready to come home.

When the battle started we played to keep up the fighting spirit but in all the confusion could not hear ourselves so gave up. Then a bullet struck Henrys drum from the side and smashed it to pieces right off his neck. Capt. Bailey ordered us behind the lines where we lay down flat and I could feel the earth rumble and shake from the cannons roar. I could not see Pa along the line for all the smoke that drifted back around us like a stinky fog.

Then Henry and me were given a stretcher to get the wounded men to the hospital tents. We saved Matt Siplinger who fell behind the breastworks with a hole in his chest. Then we picked up someone with a blasted leg and a man whose face was bloody but swore his hurt was a small one.

It came as Henry stood up with his end of the stretcher, a high screaming sound. Down! I shouted but it was too late, the shell hit behind him and burst and he bore the brunt of it while only dirt and small rocks rained on my back. I carried him over my shoulder to the hospital and he made not a single groan but died most bravely. After a nurse said he was gone I started to weep most unsoldierlike. Dont tell anyone.

We did not take Richmond but were pushed back in defeat. We retreated through the swamp to the James River, abandoning supplies to the enemy and a field hospital with over two thousand wounded. I was deaf for two days from the sounds of exploding shells. I will proba- bly have nightmares for a long time.

I know you and Rose are friends and perhaps it will give her comfort to know how Henry died, but if it will be too painful dont tell her everything. Henry always did say how pretty she is. He said he wanted to do better in school to deserve her.

I wrote to one A.B. and received a letter in return so I guess we have a liking for each other but I hate this war.

Your brother, Luke

P.S. Pa and I would love some pickles or strawberry jam from home. Please dont tell Mama all about Henry, she will fear it will happen to me too.

Just thinking about the letter made the tears spring up behind my eyelids. I wished I could tell Luke that I loved him. More than anything, I wanted to see him and Papa again.

A frightened-looking Jack answered the door at Margaret's house.

"Auntie Rose is very sad and she won't come out of her room," he said. "And now she and Mama are quarreling."

"It will be all right. Go find Clara and play," I said, nudging him out of the hall. I waited uncertainly at the bottom of the stairs.

"I want Mother!" I heard Rosanna wail. "You of all people should understand how I feel."

"But I don't. Why run to *her* arms? You think she will be sympathetic, hearing you were in love with a Yankee?"

"But I have to get away from here. I can't bear to be here when they all come home except for Henry! I *am* going to Richmond," cried Rosanna.

"You will do no such thing! It is too dangerous. I forbid you to leave this room!"

The door slammed and Margaret appeared on the landing. When she saw me, a look of relief spread over her face. She hurried down the stairs and grasped my arms.

"Thank God you're here. Perhaps you can comfort her. Why, you'd think she's lost a . . . a *husband*. This boy was not . . . not even a suitor." Margaret faltered and threw up her hands. "Please talk some sense into her. She is desperate."

The idea of Rosanna dying from a broken heart like Mrs. Phelps scared me. I ran up the stairs and opened the door to her room. The curtains were drawn. Drawers hung open from the highboy, and petticoats and skirts had been flung from their hooks. A small traveling trunk lay on its end, as if kicked aside. Rosanna was sprawled on her bed, weeping loudly. The evidence of so much passion startled me.

"Rosanna?" I whispered. "It's me."

She seemed not to hear me. After a moment, I climbed onto the bed and began to smooth her messy hair.

At my touch Rosanna sat up, clutching a slim book of poetry. Her face was blotchy and swollen.

"*O for the touch of a vanished hand and the sound of a voice that is still,*" she said, sobbing. "I can't believe Henry is just gone. Forever."

"I know," I said softly. "I'm sorry." And even though I hardly knew Henry Phelps, I cried too, because he would never walk through Gettysburg again, smiling and teasing the girls.

"Lizzie, do you think God is punishing me?"

"Punishing *you*? Why?"

"For being fickle in love. For everything bad I've done!" She began to blink rapidly, and her chin trembled.

"Don't be silly, Rosanna," I said, trying to sound lighthearted.

"But I'm a terrible person. Lizzie, you don't have any idea," she said, fresh tears spilling down her cheeks. "Oh, I have to go away, but Margaret won't let me!"

"No. Don't go," I pleaded. "Stay, and we will do things together that will cheer you up again."

"You don't understand either." Rosanna sprang from the bed. "Where's my valise?"

"Wait, listen to me." I wanted to stop her and remembered the letter in my pocket. "I've had a letter from Luke. He wrote about Henry."

Rosanna regarded me with red-rimmed eyes.

"What did he say?" she whispered.

Suddenly I doubted that I should tell her about the letter, given her state of mind. But she looked expectant, even hopeful.

"That Henry was bravely helping to save the wounded . . . when he died. Luke wrote that Henry talked about you a lot."

"He did?" said Rosanna with a faint smile.

"He told everyone how pretty you were."

"Was there more?" Rosanna's voice trembled. "Did he tell your brother he loved me? Did he call out for me?"

I stared at my cousin. She seemed a stranger to me. Did she only want to know how much Henry loved her? Couldn't she be sad just for his sake?

"I had no idea he meant so much to you," I said, hearing a sarcastic edge to my voice. Rosanna didn't catch it.

"Did he say he loved me?" she asked again. Her eyes pleaded with me.

I hesitated a moment.

"No, not in this letter," I admitted, thinking the truth would be less painful than a lie.

But she began to cry even harder. All I could do was try to explain, hoping that Rosanna would see reason.

"I know Henry *liked* you, and he wanted to work harder to deserve you, but maybe he didn't, well, *love* you like you loved him, enough to get married, that is—"

"Are you saying that he never loved me at all?" Rosanna interrupted in a stricken voice.

"I . . . I don't know," I said. I realized I was twisting the edges of Luke's letter between my fingers. "Did Henry ask you to marry him or write it in a letter?"

"No, not exactly," she admitted. "But I hoped . . ." She shook her head and sighed. "I guess I've been a fool," she said, sounding forlorn.

Perhaps I should have disagreed. But I was relieved that Rosanna's turmoil seemed to be settling. She went to the window, pulled aside the curtain, and rested her forehead against the glass.

"Tomorrow should be a fine day," she said dully. She turned to me, her face without expression, her hair wildly disheveled. "If anything happens to me, Lizzie, will you help my sister look after Jack and Clara?"

"Of course," I said, puzzled by her apparently random thoughts. "But you're not going to die."

"No, I'll live. Did you think I would do something desperate?"

She turned from the window with a wry smile that did not reach her eyes. She put her valise back in the closet and righted the trunk. I helped her hang up her clothes, then said I should be getting home. Rosanna put her arms around me and clung to me.

"Oh, Lizzie, at least I know that you love me!"

"You're my best friend. I'll always love you," I said, returning her embrace and believing those words would always be as true as they were at that moment.

Lizzie

———◆———

Chapter 12

As Rosanna had predicted, the next day was a fine one. I thought of my cousin, and of poor Henry Phelps, a few times, but it was hard to be too sad on a sunny summer day. That night, after it had cooled off, Mama and I were preserving beans when Margaret burst into the steamy kitchen. Seeing her distressed look, Mama dropped her tongs into the canning pot and her hand went to her throat in alarm.

"Is it one of the children?"

"No, thank God, Ginnie is with them. It's Rosanna!" Margaret tried to catch her breath. "She didn't come home today. I checked her room. She took her clothes and left a note. She has run off to Richmond!"

I was stock-still with disbelief.

Mama pursed her lips. "Honestly, I'm not surprised. She's a dear girl, but so impulsive!" With an irritated sigh she picked up a wooden spoon to retrieve her tongs from the boiling water.

Finally I found my voice. "She wouldn't run away," I said. "Maybe she is with Annie Baumann."

Margaret glared at me. "The station master saw her board the train. And you stand here and pretend to know nothing about it!"

My mouth fell open, but not a word came out.

"Margaret! Please explain what you mean," said Mama.

"Rosanna told me last night she and Lizzie had planned an all-day picnic for today, and I even packed a hamper full of food. It seemed a good idea, to cheer Rosanna, but it was all a ruse so that she could catch the morning train instead. How could you be so deceitful, Lizzie?"

"I don't know what you are talking about!" My face was growing hot and I could hardly control my temper. "Rosanna said nothing about a picnic. When I left yesterday, she was calm and had changed her mind about leaving. You must have quarreled with her later, Margaret!"

"Lizzie!" My mother spoke sharply. "Where were you all day?"

"Today? Why, I was at the shop all morning, and in the afternoon . . . I made . . . deliveries."

I looked away, unable to meet Mama's eyes. In fact, Martin had made the deliveries. I had stayed in the shop alone, with the shutters closed, reading a novel.

"See, Aunt Mary, she is lying," said Margaret. "But what shall I do about my sister?"

Now Mama was simmering like a pot on a low flame.

"Stop worrying," she said. "We will send word to your parents in the morning. Lizzie, go to your room now."

But I would not obey her. Instead I ran from the house, letting the door slam behind me. I stood in the street, wondering where to go. Then, with long, angry strides, I made my way to the butcher shop. I locked the door, threw myself down on a pile of burlap sacks behind the counter, and cried until I fell asleep. When I woke up, the first rays of sunlight were slanting into the shop and someone was rapping on the door. I stood up stiffly, opened the door a crack, and peered out. Ben was standing there, looking worried.

"Are you okay?" he asked.

"No, I'm not," I replied, still stinging from Rosanna's desertion and Margaret's accusations.

"I've been looking for you since I woke up. Mama's mad, you know."

"I know, and I don't give a pile of pig's livers!"

"She says you'd better come home."

"*You* go home. Tell her I'm working. And if she won't believe me, maybe I'll run away too." With that I slammed the door.

A short while later there was a shuffling outside the door and another knock. I took off my shoe and flung it at the door.

"I told you to go home. And don't come back again!"

"Lizzie?" came Martin's voice.

"Oh, drat," I moaned. I had forgotten Martin was due to work today. Martin opened the door and stuck his head in.

"What's the matter in here?"

"Nothing!" I said, turning my back to him, for I was a rumpled, tearstained mess.

"Are you sure?"

"No! I mean, yes. Oh, everything's wrong. Isn't it obvious?"

I heard him come into the shop and close the door behind him. I glanced over my shoulder to see him pick up my shoe. Then he just stood there. The only sound was that of flies buzzing and bumping against the windows. I could see into the back room, where the sawdust on the floor was soaked with blood and the knives and saws lay on the trestle tables, bits of dried meat still clinging to their blades. I could smell animal remains starting to rot.

"I hate this place—it's filthy and it stinks!" I said as a flood of anger rushed over me.

"Well, let's take care of that first," Martin said.

He handed me my shoe and left, coming back with a bucket of water, a cake of soap, and a brush. With vigorous strokes he scrubbed at the stained tables. After a moment I picked up a broom and began to sweep the blood-soaked sawdust out the back door, then cleaned the knives and saws. On our knees, we attacked the grimy floor until it was clean and our hands ached.

"The shop was never so dirty with Pa and Amos working here," I said. "It's because of Matthias Schupp."

With Amos gone, Mama had to rely on the York butcher coming by when there was a calf or sow to be slaughtered.

"Schupp doesn't care about this place," Martin agreed. "I don't like working with him."

"I don't either, and I've told Mama." I sighed. "If only Amos would hurry back."

I sat back on my heels. Martin turned to face me. My hair hung in damp strands and my skirt was soaked with dirty water, but if Martin noticed, he didn't show it.

"Now, what else is bothering you?" he said, as if he were merely asking what the next chore was.

My chin started to tremble as I fought back tears.

"I bet you wish your father and brother were here," he said.

I nodded. Missing Papa was like a pain behind my ribs, as if the emptiness there would break right out of my chest and fill the room.

"Hmmm," he murmured into the silence between us, which only grew longer. There was nothing for me to say.

Finally Martin said, "Do you wonder why I didn't join up with the other fellows last summer?"

His question surprised me. I hadn't given it a thought.

"I just figured it was because you're under eighteen," I said. "Or because your mother refused to let you go."

"You're right on both counts. But the real reason is that I don't want to be a soldier."

"Why not? I thought all boys wanted a chance to shoot at the rebels. Even Ben wants to join the cavalry."

"Well, look what happened to Henry Phelps. And he wasn't even fighting; he was carrying a stretcher." Martin drew his eyebrows together. "I don't believe in this war, Lizzie. Neither side can call themselves Christian. The South wants to keep men in slavery, and the North wants to crush them for it. And after a year of fighting, the slaves still aren't free. Why, Amos has to go and fetch his own wife and pay for her freedom. That ain't at all just."

Martin's speech took me aback. I had rarely heard him say more than a few sentences in an entire day of working, let alone speak out about the war.

I nodded eagerly. "Martin, I didn't know you felt that way. I agree with you."

Martin looked embarrassed. He rubbed his hands on his thighs. We were both sitting on the clean floor, with damp patches drying up around us.

"But not everybody does." I sighed. "That's why I'm afraid Amos might not return. He knows how people feel about him, and that it's hurting our business."

"My mother doesn't like Negroes," Martin said. "But she's never met Amos."

"My own cousin defends slavery," I said, feeling my chest tense up. "I can hardly bear to listen to her."

"I bet you're worried about her, going off down there."

I turned to Martin, frowning. "How did you know Rosanna left Gettysburg?"

"I saw your brother. He told me."

"Well, I'm not going to worry about her." I picked up the scrub brush and tossed it into the bucket. "She led me to believe she would stay here, then ran off to Richmond and made up a story blaming me. That's not how you treat a friend."

"I'd be mad, too, if I were you," Martin admitted. "But maybe she was just upset about Henry."

I thought of Rosanna crying because Henry Phelps might not have loved her.

"No, my cousin only cares about herself," I said bitterly. "So, she can take care of herself. I have my own troubles." I picked up the bucket and broom and shoved them in the corner.

Martin stood up, wiping his hands on his pants and looking uncertain.

"Thank you for helping me clean this place," I said, to show him I was not angry at him.

"Well, I'll be off to see about Mr. Beeman's steers now," he said, and with that he left.

Alone in the shop again, my thoughts ran in bitter tracks. I wondered why Rosanna had gone to Richmond, and how she could have lied to me, her best friend. I told myself I did not care if I ever saw her again.

Rosanna

Chapter 13

<del>*A History of the War*</del>
My History During the War

July 15, 1862 Richmond

I have stolen away from Gettysburg undetected, boarding a train to freedom. I could no longer be happy there, though my sister treated me lovingly and Lizzie patiently listened to my troubles. One day they may forgive me and understand that not even kindness can cure grief.

The car sways almost like a cradle and the wheels clack in a pleasing rhythm on the rails, but I am too excited to rest. I see the Blue Ridge Mountains marching by in a stately manner. Camps of white tents dot the fields like haystacks, and at every depot soldiers and supply wagons cluster. A handsome Johnnie in light brown pants tips his gray cap to me. I am going home!

I hope Father and Mother will not be angry with me. I will say that I came home because I missed them and was concerned for their welfare. They would not understand my sorrow for Henry any more than they understood my feelings for John Wilcox.

Alas, I have had to leave my scrapbook with all its contents at

Margaret's, taking pains to conceal it well. I did not wish to carry along the evidence of my weak and faithless nature. I shall endeavor to better honor Father and Mother and make amends for my past behavior.

I did find my school notebook among my hastily packed things. Perhaps I shall keep a journal, as I no longer have Lizzie to confide in. So I have given the book a new title, *My History During the War.*

July 16, 1862

I needn't have worried. Father and Mother were overjoyed to see me, having received an emergency telegraph from Aunt Mary and fearing bad news. Mother was dismayed that I did not bring Margaret and her children, and I felt a brief stab of guilt at deceiving my sister.

Papa has a new job in the treasury department, a commission from President Jefferson Davis himself. It gave me a start to see the new Confederate banknotes and to realize that we are now citizens of a different country! Prices have soared shockingly, and the government responds by printing more money. Hard times are upon us, Father says, due to the Union blockade of our ports.

Arriving in Richmond, the first thing I noticed was the presence of wounded and maimed soldiers, many hobbling on crutches. The sight makes me want to turn away. Every church is a hospital, and every other house shelters a recovering soldier. During the recent week-long battle, people rode out in carriages and carts to bring back the injured and dead. Even my parents took in a soldier, a young farm boy from Alabama. Fortunately his wound was as slight as my mother's nursing skills, and he departed in good health just days before I arrived. But he lay bleeding in my very bed!

Lizzie's final words will not leave my mind. Perhaps Henry did not love me. He was not even mine to lose. He was his mother's—his country's—loss. What have I lost? Not life nor limb. Not even my heart, really, for that will heal, leaving only the memory of a wound. I think of Margaret, who is still herself despite losing a husband. I did not love Henry that deeply.

July 18, 1862

Now that I am in Richmond, my thoughts return again and again to John Wilcox. I dare not ask Mother for news of him. No doubt she believes I have forgotten him after two years. He cannot know I am in town, for I have not gone out except to telegraph Margaret of my arrival. Neither have we had visitors, for Father has a stomach complaint and Mother must tend to him constantly. I will try to persuade her to go to the shops with me tomorrow and see if there is anything to be bought.

Perhaps I will hear some useful gossip as well.

July 19, 1862

Today's outing revealed more of the startling changes in my home city. At the chemist's, I gasped at the high prices for medicines, but we had to have the magnesia for Father and a supply of quinine pills. The apothecary gave us a list of medicinal plants to be found in the woods and fields. He warned that most drugs are likely to become even more scarce because of the blockade.

A simple calico dress now costs ten times what it did before the war. Bonnets cannot be had, nor hoops, so wide skirts have fallen out of fashion. Coffee might as well be a rare Indian spice; Mother and Father allow themselves only a small cup on Sundays, diluted with chicory. They fear a shortage of wood and coal in the winter, not to mention food, now that the farms and fields around Richmond have been ravaged by both armies.

In spite of these concerns, relief and hope prevail in the city because the Yankees have been driven back. Lincoln has called for more troops, proof that the South has gained the upper hand. Perhaps, Father says, the nations of Europe will now recognize the Confederacy as a nation and send weapons to hasten our victory. It is hard not to get caught up in the fervor and to feel my Virginia blood stirring with pride. Oh, the war is not about slavery, as Lizzie believes, but about our way of life and our right to pursue happiness!

Alas, did not hear any gossip at all relating to the Wilcoxes.

July 20, 1862

Riding home from church in Father's carriage, the scent of a fresh-baked peach pie from an open window reminded me of Aunt Mary's kitchen. Lizzie's honest face came to mind. Perhaps it was wrong of me to leave as I did. But it was necessary, for Lizzie would have done anything, even call out the constable, to keep me in Gettysburg.

Mother has written a harsh letter to Margaret. I am afraid I let her believe that my sister neglected her duty to me. When the letter arrives, Margaret is sure to be upset. But she would have more cause if she knew how Richmond is suffering. To see this beautiful city ill-treated by war, the surrounding fields torn up by battles, stirs up my Southern loyalties. The land of Pennsylvania is not trodden to mud by invaders, and the people do not fear their homes will be burned, as we do in Richmond.

These days I wonder if it was some other girl who cheered at the rally in Gettysburg last year, stitched the Stars and Stripes, and wrote passionate letters to a Union soldier. This morning I whispered to the image in my mirror, "I doubt you ever really loved Henry Phelps," and it did not contradict me.

July 22, 1862

"Everything happens for a purpose," Mother said at breakfast, looking pleased to see me, then expressed her hope that Margaret would come home as well. Is it not enough that I am home? Seeing that I was sore at her, Mother invited me to stroll in the park with her and Mrs. Sullivan. We go now, so I shall write more later—

❧

Oh my prophetic mother! Her words at breakfast are the theme of this day!

In the park I left Mother and Mrs. Sullivan discussing politics and wandered down to the pond. While I gazed over the calm water, feeling dull-spirited and wishing for some pleasant diversion, I heard whistling, and along came a dandy-looking gentleman. He wore a fawn-colored suit and brandished a walking cane, and when he came into the sunlight, I recognized him at once.

"Is it John Wilcox?" I cried without thinking.

He approached me, his head tilted to the side questioningly. I noticed that he was taller and, if possible, more handsome, with curly hair, a square jaw, and a bearing more manly than I remembered.

"My dear Rosanna McGreevey," he said with surprise and, I believe, some pleasure. He glanced around, as if to ascertain whether we were alone, before taking my hand and kissing it. My entire arm tingled, and I felt my heart begin to pound. I stepped back, suddenly shy.

We exchanged a few pleasantries about the weather, which was nothing remarkable. Silence fell between us; only the sparrows twittered. The honeysuckle bushes sent up a warm, sweet odor that made me dizzy.

"How long have you been in Richmond? Why did you not let me know?" he asked, a note of reproach in his voice.

A faint breeze stirred the curls of John's hair, making me long to touch them. I said that I was visiting my parents, but declined to reveal more.

"It is not the best time to take a journey, given the recent hostilities," he said, searching my face. "Ah, you must have come to see me as well."

I admitted I had been thinking about him. Oh, I am sure I blushed!

With his hand he tilted my chin upward, ever so gently, and asked, "Why did you stop writing to me?"

Feeling the tears collect in my eyes, I blinked to hold them back.

"I was confused, John. After what happened between us, I didn't believe you could love me or forgive me—"

John suddenly let go of my chin and took a step backward. Mother was upon us, like an insect with its feelers erect, Mrs. Sullivan trailing after her. When Mother recognized John, she looked back and forth between us, suspicion and disapproval written on her face. John seemed ready to bolt, but I was loath to end our meeting while so many questions remained unanswered.

"Mother," I said, "Mr. Wilcox happened by this spot just moments ago on his way to an appointment. He wishes to call upon us tomorrow."

I sensed John start. Indeed, my daring surprised me, too. Mother hesitated, knowing that to refuse in front of her companion would make her look rude. With forced calm, she named four o'clock as the time. John bowed and took his leave.

My triumph was short-lived, however, for once we were at home and Mrs. Sullivan had gone, Mother turned on me.

"I don't want you to see that Wilcox boy, and you know it."

"He is hardly a boy," I said, indignant. "He is twenty-two. And I will be eighteen."

"When he calls, I will say you are indisposed."

"Please do not, Mother!" I resorted to pleading. "We have not seen each other in two years. We merely wish to have a conversation."

Mother gave a harrumph.

"You still do not trust me," I said, summoning hurt and a little defiance to my voice. "Well, then, take the matter to Father, and perhaps you two can send me away to Gettysburg again."

My words were cruel, but they did silence her. She glared at me before turning her back to me.

In the wake of our argument, doubts surged again into my mind. I recalled how finely dressed John had been when I saw him. Was he on his way to meet a woman? Alas, who am I to be jealous? What if he does not come?

And where will I find something suitable to wear?

July 23, 1862

I put on my prettiest day dress, a sprigged calico, and fixed my hair without Mother's assistance so she would not see how my hands trembled. John arrived precisely on the hour, bearing a bouquet, which he presented to Mother. I thought well of his manners, but she was like a nut, hard to crack. Then, under her watchful eye, John and I sat at opposite ends of the parlor settee, unable to say anything of significance to one another, though we longed to. Instead we talked about blockade runners (their audacity) and the weather (its unpredictability). Mother tartly proclaimed her dislike of both. She asked John, rather sharply, "Are you furthering your education then?" She might as well have said, "Why are you not in uniform like all the other young men?" John admitted to being no scholar and sat tongue-tied after that. It was a most uncomfortable forty minutes.

When I ushered him to the door, he murmured in a low and hasty voice, "I have not been able to stop thinking about you. May I call again?"

My heart gave an excited lurch, and I whispered back, "Yes, but do not come here. I will meet you by the giant oak tree in the park tonight."

His eyebrows shot up. I realized how accustomed I have grown to the social freedoms of Gettysburg. In Richmond, a well-bred girl does not venture out on the streets unescorted—especially at night, and especially in these dangerous times. In neither place should young ladies make secret assignations! Nonetheless, I named an hour, and he nodded and was gone. Mother did not suspect a thing.

I went to my room early, pleading a headache, and slipped out using the back stairs. The park was only a few blocks away, surrounded by black iron palings. The trees rustled their leaves like ladies do their silken skirts, and in the distance a nightingale called. Even before I reached the corner, John appeared and fell into step with me. The odor of his sandalwood cologne filled my nostrils.

"I couldn't let you walk alone," he said, taking my arm with assurance.

It was already a warm night, and his closeness made me flush until I had to open my fan and cool myself. I sought for some harmless topic of conversation and settled on that of his family. I knew that his father was involved in shipping enterprises and his mother was a society lady.

"The blockade has cost my father dearly. Otherwise my parents are well, though some dastardly sickness has been plaguing our darkies lately." He shook his head. "Such a lot of responsibility, like having a passel of children to look after."

My eyes grew wide to hear John Wilcox speak of his family's slaves. They own a dozen Negroes, most of whom are house servants or work on the docks. John even has his own valet and is very fond of him. I thought of Lizzie, who is similarly fond of Amos. But she would probably dislike the Wilcoxes because they keep slaves.

"Are your slaves happy, or do they clamor for freedom?" I asked.

"What a strange question," he replied. "They are not mistreated and have no reason to be discontented. Now tell me, Rosanna," he said, changing the subject, "why did you come back to Richmond? You should not be gallivanting around during wartime."

I was afraid that he was scolding me, but I saw him smile. Since I had been in Gettysburg, he had grown a small, trim mustache, and his dark brown hair was longer, curling over his collar. Again I put off the desire to reach for it and decided to answer his question levelly.

"A boy I had been writing to was killed in battle last month. I wanted to go away for a while."

We took several more steps before he said, "But you haven't forgotten him?"

I listened for a hint of jealousy in his tone, but his voice stayed neutral.

"I didn't forget you, not even after two years," I replied, avoiding his question. I asked how he had been occupying himself, hoping to hear that he was no longer idle but engaged in some honorable activity.

"I've been at my usual pursuits," he replied lightly. "Riding and hunting. Some gaming in the evenings."

I tried to hide my disappointment at hearing that he still gambled.

But who is drawn to a person only for his virtues? Is it not worthier to love someone despite his imperfections?

As we strolled through the grounds, my hand on his arm, I told John about life in Gettysburg, my sister's family, and my adventures with Lizzie. Then John and I came to a wooded grove within the park. We sat upon the trunk of a fallen oak tree. He was so near that his thigh pressed into my leg. I thought I should move away but did not want to, so remained touching him.

"Did you love . . . this soldier who died?" asked John.

The darkness made it easier to be truthful.

"I don't think I did. Not like—" I took a breath and let it out in a rush. "Not like I loved you." I was surprised to hear the tone of accusation in my words.

John spoke with difficulty. "I cannot forget that night, Rosanna. I have always regretted . . . my mistake in putting you in such a position. I wish you could forgive me."

"I too was in the wrong. But I don't wish to dwell on that night."

"You have moved on, I see," he said.

"And you?" I ventured to ask. "Have you kept company with anyone while I was away?" I held my breath, waiting for his reply.

"Yes," he confessed. Jealousy twisted my insides. "But," he went on, "your return has changed that."

"Indeed. How?" I prompted, but he offered no explanation. His hand brushed my hair and lingered there.

"Rosanna, you are as beautiful as ever. May I kiss you?"

"Please, John," I said, closing my eyes as I felt his breath on my face. The touch of his lips, familiar even after two years' absence, made the tears spring to my eyes, and through my head ran the thought: *I am home, I am home, I am home.*

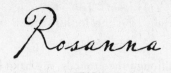

Rosanna

Chapter 14

July 25, 1862

Carried on a current of passion, my life rushes headlong like water over slippery rocks. I can no more resist than the stream that flows in its fated course!

Last night John and I met again at the park. The darkness made me bold and I ventured to kiss him deeply. He responded in kind before pulling back. He let out a low whistle.

"You do tempt a man, Rosanna," he said. "But we mustn't take any risks this time."

"We were younger then. Can't we trust each other now?" I said, wishing for him to draw me close again.

"Yes, but your parents will never trust me again," John said with a sigh.

I was silent. Father and Mother still did not know everything. I never could bring myself to tell them about the stolen money, the gambling debts. It was bad enough that they believed John had seduced their innocent daughter.

"What can I do to earn their regard?" he asked.

I feared the answer was "nothing." But that would not do. I fumbled for more hopeful words.

"They expect a man to have . . . some ambition in life. They are quite patriotic, you know, as I am—as are we all—and they tend to look unfavorably on someone who is . . . not in uniform or doing something for the Southern cause."

"I'm just too dashed lazy, I guess. A fellow even tried to talk me into helping the Confederacy by smuggling goods past the blockade, but it seemed like too much work. You see, it's not money I want, it's—" He broke off, rubbing his hands through his hair in seeming frustration.

"What is it you want?" I asked, my voice wavering between hope and fear.

But John shook his head. "It is late. I'll see you home before your father realizes you're gone and sets the law on me."

We walked in silence to the corner where we had met. He held my face gently in his hands, and the light from a gas lamp illuminated his face, where a struggle was being played out. It was I who plunged forward, letting the current of emotion carry me.

"John, I am going to tell Father and Mother that I love you. They cannot forbid me to see you."

"Not yet, Rosanna," he replied with sudden intensity. "Let me call upon you tomorrow afternoon, and we will see if your parents turn me away."

With that he kissed me hard, leaving my lips numb, then turned and left. Now I am apprehensive about tomorrow. If I do not sleep now I will look pallid and unwholesome when he comes.

July 26, 1862

Today at three o'clock John Wilcox came to our door, wearing a fine gray uniform, a saber at his side. Mother and Father were present as he announced that he had enlisted in the First Regiment of the

Virginia Infantry. We were all astonished. Even more so when John dropped to one knee and asked me to be his wife. Without a moment's hesitation, I consented! Mother fluttered her hands in a gesture of helpless defeat, and I heard Father murmur to her, "The same regiment George Washington once commanded. That ought to make a man out of him."

Resplendent is not too strong a word to describe John's appearance in his uniform. Truly there is something about it that grants him the status of a gentleman, though his family is not of the "old Richmond stock" that my parents value so highly. That he is a soldier is enough to persuade them of his good intentions and preclude mention of his past behavior.

July 27, 1862

I still cannot believe the words I say to myself: I am to marry John Wilcox!

There is no time to prepare for a grand wedding. I will wear my best baize dress (which I had the foresight to bring with me), resewn with some of Mother's lace, and the quaint bonnet that she wore when she wed Father. I do not think Margaret will regret missing the chance to create me a new gown. We shall be married in the drawing room, with only a few guests attending. It will be the 9th of August.

I must write to Lizzie. She must be happy for my good fortune, my newfound joy!

August 1, 1862

John's days are busy with military drills and routines, as his regiment is sure to be called to the front soon. Already we seldom see each other, and I am plagued with sudden doubts as I realize that I barely know this man who is to be my husband. What will he expect of a wife? Father has lectured me on obedience, and Mother speaks blushingly of vague "duties," leaving me none the wiser, only apprehensive.

August 5, 1862

Today we went to a military review and watched soldiers march by with admirable precision, the sun glinting on their polished rifles. I swelled with pride to see John among them! We also glimpsed the president on his gray horse. Mr. Davis has a wide and noble brow, wavy hair, and a beard on the underside of his chin. "Richmond can never be taken!" was the defiant boast on every tongue, "Dixie," the song on everyone's lips. I felt my individual fears dissolve in the common stream of patriotic feeling. We are not alone in the struggle but borne along and upheld by the strength of others.

August 10, 1862

Yesterday I wed John Wilcox. I carried a jasmine bouquet whose fragrance filled the room. John looked splendid in his new uniform. He stood firm as a rock while I felt myself trembling with emotion. A few tears escaped me, but thankfully did not stain my dress. Luckily I did not stumble over my vows, though my heart stuck briefly at the minister's words, "Wilt thou obey him and serve him?" But I said, "I will," believing that John would never demand of me anything that I am unwilling to do.

Then we clasped hands and faced forward together as husband and wife. We are making a new start and have promised to each other not to dwell on what is past, but to live blameless in the future.

Later we celebrated in private the sweeter ceremonies of marriage. I blush to recall my confusion and shyness, and his tenderness that overcame them. I could happily grow accustomed to such "duties."

August 11, 1862

John's parents have given us a charming cottage that needs only some furniture to render it cozy and homelike. They also gave me a sleek sorrel mare for riding, named Dolly. They even offered to send one of their Negroes to cook for us! Startled, I thanked them but said we had no need at present, and they had the grace not to seem offended. Then there is the matter of John's valet, Tom Banks. Without him, John can scarcely dress himself! I had thought that would become my duty, but John is quite particular about how his clothing is arranged. Only Tom's way will please him.

The truth is, I do not wish for us to keep slaves. Could this be Lizzie's influence? Or am I afraid to associate with Negroes? Whatever the reason, I cannot see myself ordering someone to do my bidding. This is a matter John and I will have to discuss in the future.

August 12, 1862

Alas, I knew it would happen, but so soon? John's regiment leaves in four days' time. I am too distraught to write more today.

August 13, 1862

John and I are careful with what we say to each other, that we may have only pleasant memories of these first days of our marriage. Yet there is so much I long to know before we are separated again! In particular, John's views about the war.

So this morning I asked him, couching the question in a caress, "Why did you enlist so suddenly?"

"How else could I have proved my worth and convinced your parents to let me marry you?" he replied with a smile.

"Don't tease me, dear. Did you join because you were about to be conscripted?" I asked sweetly.

"No, I did it for my love of you," he said steadily.

I did not want to hear that he had donned a uniform only for my sake. I hoped he was a man of deeper convictions.

"And I want you to know that I am proud to have a husband fighting for states' rights and defending Richmond," I said, fixing him with a gaze that I hoped conveyed my devotion.

"To be honest, Rosie," John said, looking embarrassed, "I didn't much consider the political aspects while enlisting. But I am trying to live a more honorable life, like a true gentleman would. Being a worthy husband to you is a matter of honor. And keeping the Yankees from meddling in our way of life is also a matter of honor."

He paused, regarding me carefully. "I don't mean to offend you, for I know you have Yankee friends up in Pennsylvania, where they harbor runaways."

My first impulse was to deny that my so-called Yankee friends had any influence on me. But I thought of Lizzie pressing me to denounce slavery, and Mrs. Pierpont making us read *Uncle Tom's Cabin*. Admittedly I had yearned for Eliza and her baby to reach safety in Ohio. To be free. Yet here I was, married to a man who owned slaves.

"I do pity the Negro slave who is abused," I conceded.

"My family has never abused any of our Negroes."

"Oh, I know they would not," I said in haste. "But surely many slaves are mistreated. My cousin Lizzie's hired man used to be a slave. He is in South Carolina right now, buying his wife's freedom with money he's earned."

"Did I marry an abolitionist?" John asked. Although he did not sound angry, he was frowning.

"No," I said, "but neither have you married a simpering Richmond belle with no ideas of her own." I tried to sound lighthearted, for there was nothing I wanted less than an argument, so soon before his departure.

"You know that's not what I expected in a wife," he said, gently kissing me. "But neither do I want one of those bluestockings who defies her husband and goes around speaking up for women's suffrage and against slavery and the churches."

"Why, I'm not that sort of woman at all!" I said with a laugh, and kissed him back. Of course I didn't want him to regret marrying me.

But the discovery that John holds such strong opinions unsettles me. Moreover, my own views about the war have grown so mixed and uncertain that it gives me some dismay. In the event of another argument on the subject, I would probably succumb.

August 16, 1862

John and I did not sleep at all last night, for we did not want to waste our final hours before his departure. We lay in each other's arms, exchanging affections, whispering our love, and in the intervening silences storing up every sweet sensation and word. I felt like Juliet, not knowing when she will see her banished Romeo again. "Parting is such sweet sorrow," she said to him, "that I shall say good night till it be morrow." But kissing my John again and again did not prevent his going, for he at last pulled himself free and was gone.

I wept loudly in my little house, for there was no one to hush me, and my crying echoed mournfully in the empty rooms.

Lizzie

———◆———

Chapter 15

It promised to be a long, dull summer after Rosanna left. The remainder of July was humid and stormy, mirroring the tumult in my own family. It took me a week to convince Mama that I had known nothing about Rosanna's plan to run away, that she had deceived both Margaret and me. Mama explained to Margaret, who eventually believed me as well. Although I was angry with Rosanna, I hoped she would come back, like a sorry puppy with her tail between her legs, eager to be friends again.

But Rosanna did not reappear, and it was not until August that I received a letter from her. She was sorry for the way she had left Gettysburg and asked me to forgive her. Then she went on to say that she was going to marry John Wilcox. I dropped the letter as if it were on fire. I could not believe what I was reading. I picked the letter up again, looked at the date, and realized that, in the time it had taken the letter to reach me, Rosanna had become Mrs. John Wilcox. I felt a stab of grief. My best friend was now lost to me, and it was my fault. By telling Rosanna that Henry Phelps did not love her, I had driven her into John Wilcox's arms. And now she was asking me to rejoice in her newfound happiness! I couldn't forgive her that much, not yet.

The news that Rosanna had run off to marry a Confederate soldier made for fertile gossip among the Gettysburg ladies, who all disapproved of her behavior. Annie Baumann was offended that she had not known about "this Richmond fellow" and blamed me for not stopping my cousin. Others said it was Margaret's fault for failing to control her sister. I could see that this gossip hurt Margaret, but she kept her head up and never discussed Rosanna in public. Privately, however, she complained to Mama that Rosanna was selfish and irresponsible, while Mama tried to soften her bitter mood by reminding Margaret of her own youthful romance. I wished Rosanna could see all the trouble and unhappiness her actions had caused us. She owed us all an apology.

One person who didn't agree, however, was Martin. He was unloading supplies from the cart and I was telling him how upset Mama and Margaret were at the news of Rosanna's marriage.

"I don't understand women," he said, lifting a bag of salt.

"Well, they think that Rosanna has insulted everything we stand for by marrying a rebel soldier, a man her own parents disapprove of," I explained, hefting a bag of salt and hurrying after him.

"It's nobody's life but hers. Everyone ought to leave her alone," Martin said.

"Well, that sounds simple enough, but don't you agree people should consider how their actions affect others?" I argued, not willing to let Rosanna off the hook so easily.

"Well, yes. For instance, you there struggling with that load makes me look lazy," Martin said. "Let me carry it."

"So you think I'm not strong enough?" I turned away, resisting him, then decided to tease him a bit. "It's nobody's bag but mine. Leave it alone!"

Martin laughed, and just then I lost my grip and the bag fell directly on Martin's foot. He yelped. Then we leaned over at the same moment and my head bumped his shoulder. He lost his balance and fell with his foot pinned under the bag, wrenching his ankle.

"I'm sorry! Oh, I'm so clumsy!" I freed his foot and he tried to stand up, but I saw him grimace with the effort.

"Give me your arm," he said.

I pulled him up and let him lean on me.

"You need to come to our house and have Mama fix you up."

"Fetch some ice first," he said through gritted teeth.

I ran to the icehouse, hammered off a few chunks, and wrapped them in a cloth. Martin climbed into the cart and nestled the ice around his ankle as I drove home.

Mama said she thought the ankle was only sprained, and she wrapped it up snugly. When she asked how it happened, Martin blamed himself.

"That's noble of you, Martin, but it was my fault. I dropped the load on his foot, Mama," I said.

"Well, then the least we can do is feed you," Mama said. "Lizzie, take your guest to the parlor while I finish up supper."

Martin did not object. Hobbling into the parlor, he sat in an armchair, resting his foot on a stool. I sat across the room, my hands in my lap. I couldn't think of anything to say. It was bad enough to have to look at Martin's swollen foot and be reminded of my clumsiness, harder still to make conversation with him.

"Pa was having me haul rocks from the field," he said. "I won't mind being off my feet for a few days."

Ben's footsteps sounded on the stairs. He peeked in the parlor, then disappeared, and in a moment I heard him say, loud and clear, "Ma, does Lizzie have a fellow now? It's about time."

I saw Martin try to suppress a smile. My face grew hot, but I didn't want to draw attention by fanning myself. From the kitchen came the clatter of dinnerware and the savory scents of bread and stew. Supper would be an awkward, painful meal. I was no longer even hungry.

"If you want to help your ma, I'm fine here by myself," Martin said.

"She would send me right back," I replied. "Does your foot hurt much?"

Martin shook his head.

A few more minutes ticked away on the parlor clock. I looked around the room as if I might discover some topic of conversation there.

"Here's a picture of Papa and Luke taken last Christmas," I said, reaching for the photograph on the mantel and taking it to him.

"It's a good likeness," he said, nodding.

I sat back down, holding the photograph. I thought of the photograph I had given Rosanna for her scrapbook. Was it pasted there, between pictures of John Wilcox and Henry Phelps?

"I had my photograph taken last year," I said. "You have to sit very still."

Martin's fingertips rested on the arms of his chair. Neither of us moved.

"We could be having our photographs taken right now," he said.

We laughed and I felt my shoulders loosen. But we didn't have anything more to say on the subject of photography. We listened to a conveyance creak along the street, growing louder as it approached. When it stopped in front of our house, I went to the window, eager for any diversion. A familiar figure was climbing down from a decrepit buggy.

"It's Frederick Hartmann!" I cried, and ran to the door, nearly colliding with Mama. "And Amos is with him!"

Then a woman stepped down from the buggy. She was a beauty, with skin and eyes black as jet and round, full lips. I couldn't take my eyes off of her. She gazed directly at me, too, without smiling. It was Grace, Amos's wife.

Supper was not the awkward meal I had expected after all. Mama got out the best linen and fixed extra ham and beans. There was plenty to eat, with fresh plums, cake, and cream for dessert. Everyone was talking, so I didn't have to make conversation with Martin. From time to time I stole a glance at Amos's wife, who sat next to him and spoke to no one. I wondered if she had ever eaten at a table with white folks before.

Of course we were all eager to hear about the trip, and finally Mr. Hartmann obliged us.

"It were quite an adventure, all right," he said, putting down his fork and wiping his mouth on one of Mama's linen napkins. "We spent two weeks running from a sheriff's posse that thought Amos was a runaway they'd been searching for. One night they chased us into a swamp where I thought the mosquitoes would kill us if the sheriff's men didn't do it first."

"We had to lie low for a while," added Amos. "Then another time, some deserters tried to rob us an' my horse was shot in the shoulder. I was 'fraid she was goin' to be lame, but she healed after a number of days. That slowed us some."

"Did you shoot anyone?" asked Ben. He had insisted on sitting next to Amos and giving him the largest piece of cake.

I saw Grace's eyes dart between Amos and Mr. Hartmann.

"Let's jus' say the villains got the worst of our encounters," said Amos. He took Grace's hand beneath the table.

Mr. Hartmann said the dangers had been greater than he imagined, but instead of expecting more money for his troubles, he made Amos and Grace the gift of a fine bed he had purchased on the way. Mama had them bring it inside, a clear sign that she expected Amos and his wife to live with us for the time being. Then she told Ben to drive Martin home in the cart, stay overnight, and come home in the morning.

My brother seemed pleased at being given the responsibility of driving all the way down Taneytown Road and back.

Martin had said nothing all evening, aside from thanking Mama for the food. I had almost forgotten about his injured foot, and watching him hobble to the door, I felt guilty.

"I'm sorry about your foot," I said. "Does it still hurt?"

"Not as bad as you'll be hurting if you apologize again," he said with a smile that made his grayish eyes twinkle. Why, his plain face looked almost handsome!

Lizzie

——◆◆——

Chapter 16

Summer ended early that year, the leaves on the trees turning yellow green and brittle even while gardens put forth corn and tomatoes and the cicadas persisted with their wild racket. Rosanna wrote a second letter, one filled with such sadness that I almost forgot my resentment. She also set me a task that brought some brief danger and excitement to my life: I had to find her scrapbook.

August 21, 1862

Dear Lizzie,

    I am so lonely. John has gone with his regiment, and I don't know when I shall see him again! Surely you understand, with your own father and brother away. Does the emptiness ever fill up?

    Lizzie, I hope this letter reaches you despite the blockade. I miss you and hope that you have forgiven me by now. I never meant for you to come to any trouble because of me. You of all people must know how weak and selfish I am, and that I cannot always help my passions. I have had a letter from Margaret, who remains unforgiving. Her accusations seem to me very unjust. Does she begrudge me my husband? Why can we not wish one another the same happiness? You, too, Lizzie, will find love soon enough.

I beg you to perform a favor for me as soon as you receive this letter. I trust only you to do this: find my scrapbook, which I hid beneath the bureau! As you know, it contains John's letters, pictures, and mementos, all of which now are inexpressibly valuable to me. You must find it before Margaret does—if she hasn't already found it and destroyed my treasures out of spite, and spilled all my secrets.

Please, keep it safe, and return it one day to your sad yet devoted cousin and friend,

Rosanna (Mrs. John) Wilcox

P.S. Whatever you read or assume to the contrary, know that my husband is a man of honor.

At this my curiosity overcame my hurt feelings. I could hardly keep from running to Margaret's house at once and turning Rosanna's room upside down. What secrets did the scrapbook contain? Somehow I had to search Rosanna's room without rousing her sister's suspicion, then remove the book without being seen. But what if Margaret had already found it?

The next morning, I went to Margaret's house on the pretext of recovering a blue shawl that I had loaned to Rosanna. In fact, I had brought it with me, hidden under my skirt.

"I have packed away all her clothes and I don't remember seeing that shawl," said Margaret with a dismissive wave of her hand. "But go upstairs and look."

That easily I gained entry to Rosanna's room. I peered beneath the bureau but saw only dust. Inside, it was empty except for some linens. A trunk stood against the wall. I opened it and saw Rosanna's clothes, a few books, and hair brushes. The scent of lavender mingled with that of old wood, making me miss my cousin. I searched to the bottom but there was no scrapbook. Had she hidden it elsewhere? I lifted the bedding and searched for an opening where she could have slipped it inside the mattress. Nothing. I went back to the bureau and rummaged through the linens again. Facedown on the floor, I stretched my arm underneath and felt around until my fingers caught on a satiny ribbon. The scrapbook was wedged between the struts on the base of the cabinet. By wiggling it back and forth, I finally freed it and sat back on my haunches with a groan, the book on my lap.

"What are you doing?"

I whirled around to see Clara in the doorway, regarding me with suspicion.

"You messed up the bed, Lizzie. Is that Rosie's book?"

"No, it's mine. I left it here. Go play now."

But she just stood there, frowning at me.

"Lizzie, did you find it?" called Margaret from the foot of the stairs, startling me. I tugged my shawl from under my skirts and laid it over the scrapbook.

"Yes, it was beneath the coverlet, of all places," I replied, then whispered to Clara, "Help me smooth out the bed." I winked at her, hoping she would enjoy keeping a secret. Then I hurried down the stairs and past Margaret, making sure she saw the blue shawl but not the scrapbook beneath it. I said I could not stay and visit, for Mama needed me at home.

For two days Rosanna's scrapbook lay underneath my mattress while I debated whether or not to read the letters. Finally I decided that Rosanna had granted me permission: *Whatever you read . . . know that my husband is a man of honor.* I waited until night, when I could read without being disturbed. I opened the scrapbook, and Rosanna's scent drifted up from the pages. Tears came to my eyes. On the page before me was my own picture, a lock of my hair, and, in Rosanna's slanted hand-writing, several quotations on friendship. I didn't pause to read them, but blinked until my eyes were clear and turned the page. There they were: the hidden letters from John Wilcox, mixed with copies of letters in Rosanna's hand. I turned up the flame on the lamp and began to read.

March 13, 1860
Dear Rosanna,

Forgive my impetuous behavior at the party. Never having met a girl of your lively beauty, I let myself be carried away by your charms. I do not think we were seen there in the garden. Will you let me kiss you again if I promise to stray no farther than the creamy skin of your wrists and neck? You know I have the greatest regard for your virtue.

Yours, John Wilcox

March 15, 1860
John: You cannot regard my virtue so highly as you claim. Indeed your flatteries strike me as excuses for your passion to run wild. Do you think

that "I love you" should act upon me like a key in a lock? And then to pry the latch against my protests! I regret the very little encouragement I gave you. It was too much.

Rosanna McGreevey

March 19, 1860

You are the one who holds the key

To my heart, which you turn against me.

I deserve your unbending cruelty, but I

Promise to reform if only you will love me.

Dash it, Rosanna, I am no poet, but if the lines are not suitable, perhaps the roses will persuade you to see me again.

Humbly, John

May 20, 1860

Dear Rosanna,

I don't blame you for calling me a cad and a bounder. I had meant to meet you but Hiram and the fellows wouldn't let me leave and before I knew it I had not a dollar in my pockets and couldn't find my way to the door, they had put so much whiskey down my throat. Won't you give me another chance? Sneak out into the churchyard while every one is singing the opening hymn. I will be there "praying" for your mercy.

John

June 5, 1860

Oh John, I fear I am losing my heart to you! I still can't believe that you prefer me over all the other

Richmond girls, some of whom are far prettier. I want nothing more than to be in your company, which makes me giddy with delight. Even your faults attract me. We are alike, for we relish taking chances. What fun to have a secret romance that Mother and Father don't suspect!

I treasure your photograph, which I kiss every night, that I may dream of you while I sleep. Here is a lock of my hair, tied with silk, to keep under your pillow.

—Oh dear, I blush to write this foolishness; I cannot possibly send it—

August 15, 1860
My dear Rose,

I am in narrow, not to say dire, straits, having incurred an inconveniently large debt. Cannot go to my father as we have had a row about my immoderate ways. I am willing to be temperate in all things except loving you, Rosanna! Could you persuade your father to give you money for some expensive trifle—say a new carriage or ball gown—then give it to me on the side? If so I vow to turn over a new leaf.

Yours most affectionately, John

August 23, 1860
Dear Rosanna,

Oh, everything be damned! It was wrong of me to make that request of you and now I shall live to regret it. Why did you take such a risk for one so unworthy? I am deeply ashamed. I will not gamble again. I never imagined it would break us apart. Such rotten luck, that your parents came in at that moment and mistook the scene so completely. No wonder they concluded that you were seduced and ruined. It was indeed a shameful exchange, but it was not lust. What choice did I have but to take the money you thrust upon me? I've settled my debt, but at the cost of our love!

I beg you to explain everything to your father so that we may be reunited. Tell me, why did you do it? Don't keep me in darkness.

Yours truly and sorrowfully,
John

September 10, 1860
Dear John,

It is too late. Mother and Father are sending me to live with my sister in Pennsylvania. I am forbidden even to speak of you. How would it help matters between us for me to confess to the theft? In my parents' eyes, my reputation is already ruined. I am certain they despise me and wish never to lay eyes on me again.

I don't know what came over me in Father's bank. It was the sight of the open till, Father's back turned, the pile of unguarded bills. Oh, it was the thought of your disgrace as a result of debt. I know you were tricked into that horrid betting game with no idea of the stakes. I wanted to help you. I thought this would show my love for you.

I gave no thought to the consequence of indulging such an impulse. Now I must live without my parents' respect and your love. All I have is the guilt of the crime itself.

I am unworthy of love. You must put me out of your thoughts.

Regretfully no longer yours,
Rosanna McGreevey

September 29, 1860
Dearest Rosanna,

Do not despair of our love. The greater part of the blame ought to be mine. I wrongly took advantage of your affection for me. Can you forgive me? Please come back and I vow to prove myself more worthy of your love.

Yours despite everything,
John Wilcox

With shaking fingers, I put the letter back in its envelope. There were more letters from John Wilcox, but I didn't want to read them. I wished I had never opened the scrapbook. Now I knew my cousin's secrets, and they burned inside me like bad cider. Two years ago, Rosanna had fallen for a gambler and had allowed him to take advantage of her. She had stolen money to pay his debts. Now, unbelievably, she was married to him.

I could not see John Wilcox as a man of honor, as Rosanna had pleaded. Indeed I believed him to be a preying fox. But he had not forced Rosanna to steal the money from her father's bank. How could she have committed such a deed and hidden it from everyone? She had been young, but that didn't excuse her either. Why had she told me none of her secrets? Rosanna had been my best friend, but I had hardly known her. She had hidden her truest self from me. All along she was bound by passion and wrongdoing to John Wilcox.

I turned back to the page that held my photograph and read the quotations Rosanna had copied there:

*"Friendship is the finest balm for the
pang of disappointed love."*
—*Jane Austen*

*"If I do vow a friendship,
I'll perform it to the last article."*
—*Shakespeare*

*"The only danger in friendship
is that it will end."*
—*Thoreau*

Fighting back tears, I removed my picture, closed the scrapbook, and tied the ribbons securely. Lighting my way with a lamp, I carried the book to the cellar. I wrapped the scrapbook in an old oilcloth to keep out the dampness, and stowed it beneath the shelves bearing the preserved bounty of summer, next to the dirt floor like the marker of a grave.

Rosanna

———◆———

Chapter 17

My History During the War

August 25, 1862 Richmond

Until John returns, the prospect of loneliness lies before me. When I expressed my sadness to Mother, she remarked tartly, "Perhaps you should not have been so hasty to get married, but waited until after the war." Why did I think she would be a comfort to me? It is clear she still disapproves of John.

I wrote to Lizzie asking her to recover my scrapbook. Soon she will have read the letters and will possess the full truth about her wayward cousin. But she has promised always to love me, and I trust in the goodness of her innocent heart, so unlike my own.

In my mind I relive that fateful scene in the drawing room. I have taken the money from my bodice, leaving the buttons carelessly undone.

"What have you done?" John says in horror, seeing the money in my hand.

"Take it. I did it for you. You begged me," I cry.

The locked door rattles and Father calls out in alarm, "Rosanna! Open the door."

We stare at the money between us, and in desperation John thrusts it into his pockets just as Father breaks the lock and bursts into the room with Mother behind him. My disheveled appearance and tearstained face, John's fumblings, and our guilty looks condemn us utterly.

"It is not what it seems," I plead.

"It is bad enough," Father growls, glaring at John, who is silent with mortification. "Leave!" he orders him.

John pauses at the door to say, "I love your daughter, but I do not deserve her," then disappears from my life for two years.

Now he is gone again, after pledging his love, and the tormenting memory revisits me. Have I made a mistake in marrying John? I lie awake fearing that he will die and leave me like this: full of doubts and regret at our past misdeeds, which still are unresolved.

August 26, 1862

In the light of day, last night's dire thoughts appear foolish and overwrought. Any day I expect a letter from John, full of loving reassurances. I have been sleeping with his dressing gown near my pillow. I will not wash it until he comes home, for the scent that lingers there comforts me.

August 27, 1862

Today I went shopping for household items but returned empty-handed. I could not even buy a new pot, for all the iron is being made into cannonballs.

I must find a way to occupy myself until John returns. Some women have taken up nursing in the Richmond hospitals, though not the better sort of ladies, as Mother fancies we are. And why should I feed and bandage some strange man when I have a husband whom I would gladly care for? But he is at war, and his valet, Tom, sews his torn clothing, launders his socks, and makes his porridge, while his wife sits idly at home, longing to perform such mundane tasks.

August 28, 1862

We live in a time of rare wonders indeed. My own mother, who has always maintained that no lady should ever seek paid employment, now has a position in the Confederate treasury department. On account of rising prices, the government prints thousands of bank-notes a day, and someone must cut and sign all those new notes. Mother's elegant handwriting and her friendship with Mrs. Davis helped her to the position. She says this is her contribution to "the cause."

Mrs. Sullivan invited Mother and me to tea and we went despite the stultifying heat. She served us real butter and sugar cakes, while relating how she had had to whip her slaves for taking food from the larder to feed themselves. She threatened to sell the poor Negro girl who served us if she did not remedy her manners. This only made matters worse, and the slave spilled some tea. Mrs. Sullivan's treatment of her infuriated me, but I dared not say anything. I blotted the spilled tea with a napkin and smiled consolingly at the poor girl. She did not smile back at me, but I think her dark eyes showed gratitude. Perhaps I will become an abolitionist and bestir myself from this lazy, pointless existence.

August 29, 1862

An accident has befallen my husband! Yet because of it, a course of action has been shown to me, and my dull spirits sparked with anticipation.

John's Negro valet arrived yesterday with the report that John had been injured—a blow to the head that left him unconscious for a full day. Unable to march on with the regiment, he remained behind at a hospital, from which he sent Tom Banks to beg me to come and care for him.

At once I began my preparations, and now Dolly stands laden with knapsacks full of provisions: a sewing kit; medicines and bandages; a plain, dark frock, apron, and light cloak; stockings and spare shoes; food and an old pot and fry pan; an oilcloth and blanket. I have fresh shirts, drawers, and socks for John—more than what is needed for this mission of mercy. But it would hardly do to go to war unprepared.

The valet is carrying a message to my parents, who would surely try to dissuade me if I were to inform them myself. We depart as soon as he returns. I am glad my husband wants me to come and nurse him, but I fear Tom may be underrating the seriousness of John's injury in order to spare me.

August 31, 1862 near Falmouth

We are traveling north, toward Maryland, behind Lee's army. The way is strewn with soldiers' gear, like the flotsam and jetsam of a great ship. I follow in its wake, accompanied by a slave. This is an adventure I never imagined!

Tom and I do not say much to each other. I estimate he is close to John's age, with the blackest skin I have ever seen. He prefers to sing to himself, both mournful tunes and foot-tapping ones, depending on his mood.

Yesterday I ventured to ask him why he had come to Richmond for me, when he could have escaped and headed north to freedom. He regarded me with some suspicion, finally replying, "Ma'am, I do what Master John bids me."

The subject seemed to make him uncomfortable. Did he think I meant to test his loyalty? I have no doubt that he is a faithful servant. Perhaps I will speak to John about the possibility of freeing him.

Dolly is a good mount, but I am sore from so much riding. The weather remains fair. Last night I lodged at a farmhouse with a woman whose chickens had all been confiscated by Lee's army, and two weeks later the federals came through and stripped the fruit from her trees. Yet she was glad to share what she had left, seeing that we were not soldiers.

September 2, 1862

Arriving at Warrenton Junction yesterday afternoon, we expected to find only a few convalescents remaining, as the army had moved on. Instead a scene of chaos greeted us. There were hundreds of new casualties from a battle at Manassas, the second one to be fought at that place. Some of the injured were being placed aboard trains to Richmond, while others were taken to makeshift hospitals nearby. I saw a dead soldier for the first time. The man's face had been shot entirely away and his body was unnaturally swollen. I turned away and vomited into the bushes. I was ashamed, but Tom said he'd seen grown men do much worse. After I drank some water, I dared to look at the body again and this time felt a great sadness that would have overwhelmed me had I paused to dwell on it.

It was John who saw me first and shouted my name. I ran to him, trying not to step on anyone in my haste. We kissed with restraint due to the presence of so many people, though no one paid us any heed. John's face bristled with a new beard that scratched my cheeks.

"Why aren't you lying down?" I asked him, noticing the bandage around his head. His hair stood upright, stiff with dirt.

"I am much better. My ribs are not broken after all," he said, causing me to catch my breath and demand to know all that had happened.

"In the middle of the night the alarm was raised. By the sound of horses it seemed to be a cavalry attack. I grabbed my rifle and rolled out of my tent when—so they tell me—I was struck in the chest by a horse's hoof and knocked down. Whether I was kicked again or hit my head on a rock, I don't know. Don't remember a thing." He shook his head ruefully. "Turns out it wasn't an attack at all, only some horses that had broken loose and stampeded through the camp."

I tried to get him to lie down and rest, fussing over him in a manner I deemed wifely. But he refused, saying he had to help sort the wounded.

Then he took my hands and said, full of tender concern, "Dearest Rose, I would not have asked you to come if I had suspected fighting would break out again."

"I could not have stayed away, knowing you were hurt," I murmured, touching his head. "At least you were not in the battle. You were almost fortunate to be kicked by that horse."

"No, it was our first test as a regiment, and even though we routed the federals, I failed by not being there," John said in a grim voice. I knew that his sense of honor had taken a blow.

Just then a man lying on the ground not ten feet away cried hoarsely, "Nurse, water!" I saw two women who appeared to be nurses in the distance, but none close by, and realized he was imploring me. I appealed to John, who looked about until his gaze came to rest on a man lying beneath a nearby tree, his face covered by a ragged cloth. John walked over and detached the canteen from the dead man's waist and shook it. Water sloshed within. He handed me the canteen and nodded. I bent down and held the canteen to the man's lips. I had to lift his head with my other hand. He smelled of sweat and blood. I had never been so close to a man who was a stranger to me, and I felt myself blush. But he gulped the water and murmured his gratitude as if there were nothing improper in what I had done.

Kneeling there, I breathed a prayer of thanks that it was not John who called helplessly for water or who lay in the stillness of death.

"What else can I do to help?" I heard myself say.

John took me to the assistant surgeon, Dr. Walker, who was so desperate for nurses he merely pointed to a box of bandages and handed me a pitcher, a basin, and a small flask of spirits.

"Save the whiskey for the worst cases," he ordered.

He turned away and I stood there stupidly. I had no idea how to determine a "worst case," let alone treat one. Seeing my confusion, John advised me just to clean the minor wounds. I thought he would stay beside me, but then he was called away. Finding myself alone, I commenced nursing those whose needs were within my small ability, wiping away dirt and blood and giving water and reassurances that I hoped were not in vain. The unaccustomed sights and smells bewildered me and nearly made me sick, and I doubt that I did much good. I thought to myself, I have come to nurse my husband, and here I am wiping the wounds of strangers!

Later I found John, cleaned his wound, and clumsily applied a fresh bandage. I asked him where I might find a bed to sleep in. He laughed and led me to a spot beneath a tree where he had devised a makeshift tent and placed my bedroll.

"Am I to sleep on the ground?" I asked in disbelief.

"A man in the army learns to sleep anywhere," he answered.

"But I am a woman!".

John looked embarrassed. He knelt down and unrolled the bedding.

"You are going to sleep beside me, at least? After all, I came here to be with you."

John smiled. "No, it would be unseemly. Darling, you shouldn't even be in camp, except that you are helping Dr. Walker. Tomorrow I'll settle you in a proper tent."

"A proper tent?" I repeated, finally understanding that I was to have no privacy with my husband and even less comfort. But I was too tired to argue further. I lay down and covered myself with a blanket. The ground was uneven and the noises of frogs and crickets, cries of pain from the injured, and shouting and laughter kept me awake for a long time. When the first rays of light woke me, I was so stiff and sore I could barely stand up.

September 3, 1862 Warrenton Junction

Tom has built me a narrow cot, and so last night I slept a little better. Forgoing the "proper tent," which was already crowded with two nurses and many supplies, I preferred my makeshift one. Reinforced with canvas on the ends, it shields me from view, and furnished with a tin chamber pot and small lamp, it is, I must admit, almost suitable. I wonder what Lizzie would think if she knew that I have been living out of a tent for three days now!

John's entire chest is discolored with bruises though his cuts are starting to heal. He is well enough to tease me by pretending to have lost his memory after striking his head.

"Who is this woman? I don't recall meeting her," he said to his companions.

"I am Mrs. John Wilcox, your wife," I replied, humoring him.

"No," he said, "I am General Robert E. Lee, and my wife is Mrs. General Lee."

The whole ward rocked with laughter, which is better than any tonic. As I write this, I am still shaking with mirth!

Besides John, I care for twenty or so convalescents, thankfully none of them with mortal injuries. I am very unskilled and the other nurses must be tired of my constant questions. But I have learned a few things. 1) If you keep a wound moist, the bandages do not stick.

2) Gentle pressure and elevation will stop bleeding in a wound that has opened up again. 3) A little whiskey is beneficial when poured in a wound, but does even more good if you spare a nip for the patient himself.

I even had a swallow last night and consequently slept well.

September 4, 1862

Thank goodness I am married, or my husband himself would ruin my reputation with his impulsive affections! I was going around the ward with my wash basin today when he drew me behind the hospital tent and into his embrace.

"What do you think you are you doing?" I whispered frantically as water spilled on my skirt.

"Why, kissing my wife." He drew back. "You are she, are you not?" His eyes twinkled merrily. Affection for my rakish, handsome soldier-husband welled up, and I returned ardent kisses.

"I had a dream about you last night," he murmured as his hands began to roam over my body. His touch was sweet and melting. I longed to be truly alone with him, in the dark, to permit his every caress! But duty called me back to the ward, and I returned to my work, a mite disheveled.

"What can I do for you, Baxter?" I asked my next patient.

"Why give me a kiss, like you bestowed on that lucky fellow," he replied, beckoning me closer. I felt my cheeks redden.

"Sir, that man is my husband. He is entitled to kiss me, while you are not," I said in a tone of rebuke. Then Baxter himself blushed, and I struggled not to laugh, for I saw the humor in the situation. So I said, in a softer tone, "But if you will behave, I will have you as right and healthy as he is now."

"I'd be much obliged," Baxter said meekly. Then, with some trouble, for his right arm was in a sling, he fumbled in his pocket and drew out a tintype.

"My gal. I'm going to marry her the minute I get home," he said longingly, showing me the picture of a young woman with fair hair falling to her shoulders.

"She's very pretty. I will gladly help you write her a letter."

So Baxter dictated, while I wrote. He had fine and true sentiments, and I easily forgave him for trying to kiss me.

At noontime I stirred the soup pots and managed to add extra beef and beans into the ration for my ward. All afternoon I laundered sheets and bandages and distributed supplies, including chloroform for the surgeons' use. After supper came another round of bathing wounds and writing letters. Dr. Walker came through the ward and soon left, saying, "I see I'm not needed here." I felt as if I had been paid a great compliment. In truth, I have never worked so hard, nor felt that I have done so much good in all my eighteen years as I have in these last three days.

When I told John this, as we sat beside a campfire kindled against the cool night air, he put his arm around me, and I know we were both thinking of our past wrongs. But we did not speak of them, though someday we must. Instead we talked about our childhood. I described how Margaret used to sew little dresses for our cats, which we played with as if they were dolls. John told me his two brothers died of small-pox when he was young and he barely remembers them.

I think that Tom is almost like a brother to John. It heartens me to see how he cares for John's welfare, and how John protects him in turn. Why should one of these men own the other, and there be such inequality between them? I kept this question to myself.

When nothing but embers remained of the fire, John and I parted with the assurance that we would see each other tomorrow, if only to exchange a look as we go about our duties and draw strength from the knowledge of our love.

September 5, 1862

This morning John and I had our first row, a terrible one. I am so shaken I can barely write.

I was washing out the breakfast pot when John came up to me, his hands deep in his pockets, and said that I should go back to Richmond now that he was better. I dropped the pot with a clatter. "Don't you want me here?" I asked in a stricken voice. He did not reply to that but said he was concerned for my safety. I said, "I'm worried about your safety, too, but I'm not telling you to go home." He reminded me that I was merely a civilian. Gesturing to the hospital tent, I said I was needed, couldn't he see that? Then he said he could not have his wife caring for strange men, like that Baxter fellow. "I have not done anything improper!" I said in outrage. "How can you doubt my virtue? Or is this something to do with your gentlemanly honor?" By now the hornet's nest was completely stirred up. I said he was jealous without any reason. He countered that he was my husband and I had pledged to obey him. Finally I said, "I won't go back to Richmond. You can't tell me what to do!" and stalked off. It was humiliating to be seen crying, so I hid in my tent.

It is after midnight and still I cannot sleep. Is it the common fate of wives to struggle against men's authority, then break, like wild horses made to take the bit? Perhaps Mother was right, and I should have waited to marry. But I thought marriage would make our love firm and enduring, like baking sets a cake. I should have learned by now that love can make one unstable. Is John now wishing he had not married me? Whatever will we say to each other in the morning?

Rosanna

Chapter 18

September 6, 1862

When I saw John after breakfast, he too looked as if he had not slept. I was afraid to meet his eyes. But he came up to me and said, "Rosanna, let us put yesterday's quarrel out of our minds."

"No, John," I said firmly, "I cannot simply forget what is unpleasant. It will come back to haunt us. We must talk." I took his hand in mine and drew him aside. "I must tell you, although I do not love the South's great cause—"

"Dash it, Rose, be more discreet!" he interrupted, putting his hand up to my lips.

I gently brushed it away. "Hear me out. I do love the South, though not the holding of slaves. Maybe it *is* because of my Yankee friends." I waved my hand. "That is not the issue now. Rather, in the last week I have come to embrace an even greater cause: relieving the suffering of those around me."

"Women do not belong in the field. You have no responsibility to these men," he protested.

"But I do feel responsible for them," I insisted. "And you cannot be more surprised than I am. I have always been the most selfish of creatures, I know. But now I am finding some reward in doing good."

His look was doubtful. He was not yet persuaded.

"I have another, more compelling reason, John," I said, speaking softly, though in great earnest. "Now that we are married, I cannot bear to be parted from you, not knowing when I may see you again. So please, let me stay and do some good."

John looked beyond me, his brows drawn together in an expression I could not read. My heart thudded, fearful of how he would reply.

"I want you to be happy. You are my wife." He sighed and looked down at his feet. "I will not oppose you."

And so we achieved peace. I had the good sense not to exult in my victory, but merely showed my gratitude with a kiss. John spoke with Dr. Walker, who agreed to let me to stay with the regiment, for he had need of another nurse.

I wrote to Mother and Father that I would not be returning to Richmond. I explained that a woman does not debase herself by contact with suffering, disease, and death. Rather, by nursing the wounded soldier she repays his sacrifice with her own lesser one. If they understand this, perhaps they will not think me so selfish and thoughtless.

September 7, 1862

Late last night I was startled by a movement outside my tent and, thinking it was some ill-intentioned soldier, nearly cried out for help, when I realized it was John creeping about! In a moment he was inside my tent. "I had to be with you tonight," he whispered, lying beside me. "Don't worry; no one saw me leave." Those were all the words he spoke, and even they were unnecessary. When I awoke he was gone. I was afraid to come out of my tent, for fear that everyone would see on my face what transpired in the night.

This morning, prisoners captured from a New York regiment were brought to camp. I expected to see them abused, but instead they were given food and their wounds tended to. Six or seven of them played cards with their guard, who had even laid aside his rifle. The guard gave them tobacco, and they all told jokes. Why, they could have been cousins or neighbors, not enemies at war!

September 8, 1862 leaving Warrenton Junction

Just as I was becoming accustomed to my rough lodgings and the routines of a field hospital, the army pulled up stakes to march northward. Tom brought Dolly to me, and I secured my belongings in saddlebags while he, in a flash, folded my tent, dismantled my cot, and loaded them on a wagon. I will ride Dolly and when it rains take cover in one of the ambulances, a four-wheeled wagon covered in canvas.

I am not the only woman traveling with the army. General Gordon's wife, whose name is Fanny, left her children in the care of a Negro mammy in order to be with her husband in the field. The officers dislike her, for she is considered quite demanding. She rides in her own carriage, while the nurses, Mrs. Throckmorton and Mary Ward, ride in an ambulance. Mrs. Throckmorton's husband and son are with the regiment, so there is no reason for her to stay at home. She is very devout, always reading from her Bible, and wears eyeglasses held firmly in place by folds of fat on her cheeks and brow. Mary Ward is the only one of us ladies with any training as a nurse. She is somewhat sharp featured and reticent, but capable. There is also a Creole woman who sells food and trinkets from a cart pulled by a donkey. Finally, some women I hesitate to call ladies follow the troops for entertainment of a baser sort.

An army on the move presents a magnificent sight, stretching for miles like a ponderous snake. The scouts and sappers clear the way for the ranks of infantry, or foot soldiers, who are followed in turn by the artillery. Teams of horses pull the cannons and wagons while the men march alongside. The caissons dig deep ruts in the road and sometimes roll into a ditch, and the whole line comes to a halt while they are heaved back into place. Mules laden with ammunition plod along, balking frequently. Then come the commissary wagons and ambulances, which sometimes stop to pick up a straggler. The rear guard follows, protecting us from being attacked from behind.

I was enveloped by clouds of dust kicked up by the artillery and supply wagons and had to tear a strip of muslin from my petticoat and tie it around my face in order to breathe. Mixed with sweat, the dust became muddy rivulets that collected about my collar. It was after midnight when we halted for the night, and I had no means of washing. Most of the men slept wherever their legs gave out beneath them. Mary Ward, Mrs. Throckmorton, and I slept in the ambulance.

September 9, 1862 somewhere in Maryland

This morning Tom brought me buckets of water for washing up. It makes me uncomfortable to be served by a slave, who must be unwilling in what he does.

I said, "You don't need to wait on me, Tom."

"Mastuh's instructions," he replied. I'm afraid I offended him by seeming ungrateful. I must try to do him some kindness in return.

I shared the water with Mrs. Throckmorton and Mary Ward, and at least our faces and hands got clean. How thoughtful of John. The ladies agree he is a gentleman.

As we marched through the town of Frederick, some citizens cheered us while others regarded us in silence, either from hostility or fear that their neighbors will take them for spies. The state of Maryland is bitterly divided between secessionists and those loyal to the Union.

John believes his regiment might be called into battle if reinforcements are needed at Harper's Ferry. Having enlisted without firm convictions, he is now, like the rest of them, eager to fight the Yankees.

September 11, 1862 South Mountain

At last, a real bed to sleep in and a washtub for bathing! While the regiment is bivouacked on the hillsides, Mrs. Throckmorton, Mary Ward, and I are billeted in a nearby farmhouse. (I am learning a new vocabulary.) The owner, Mrs. Alter, is a widow whose only son is fighting with the Confederate army in Kentucky. Mrs. Gordon lodges in a nearby house that serves as the general's headquarters, but she takes tea with us here. She talks incessantly of her children, making me miss little Clara and Jack.

The foothills of the South Mountains resemble paradise compared to the war-ravaged fields of Virginia. Acres of corn, their russet tassles swaying with the breezes, refresh the sight. Horses graze happily in fields of sweet timothy and clover. The trees are so heavily laden with apples and pears that their branches drag on the ground. The men stuff their haversacks with the fruit despite orders against stealing, but who can blame them?

The respite here is sorely needed, for the troops are in a weakened condition after the Manassas battle and the long march. Many can hardly walk, while others are dehydrated from heat or from dysentery, the bane of a soldier's life. Mrs. Throckmorton dispenses her own infallible remedy for loose bowels, an infusion of raspberry leaves and wild ginger. (Dr. Walker has resigned himself to the presence of women in his medical tents.) A dozen men lie ill with typhoid, and since quinine is already scarce, we gathered boneset leaves and scraped dogwood bark to make a tea that seems to remit the fever. Every day I learn more about the treatment of these common miseries.

To keep up my own health, I drink only the clearest water and always boil my tea. I make John do the same. The food unfortunately does nothing to strengthen the constitution. A cornmeal biscuit could break one's teeth, and last week the only meat was putrid beef. But today Mrs. Alter, the widow, baked sweet potato pies for us to take to our men: the general, Mrs. Throckmorton's husband and son, and my John. They devoured the pies in short order.

September 12, 1862

The news is that President Davis will sign an act accepting women nurses into the medical department. Soon I, Rosanna McGreevey Wilcox, will be an official army nurse! It is even said that we are to be paid for our service.

Wouldn't Lizzie be surprised to see me engaged in something practical! Even Margaret, who has a kind heart, could not object to my doing works of mercy.

Sunday, September 14, 1862

John and I went to hear the camp preacher, a small man with a mighty voice. He sermonized on the promise of salvation for those who died for their country and prayed for victory over "our evil oppressors." I was not so keen on the preaching but was moved by the singing, all the deep men's voices and but two high ones, mine and Mrs. Throckmorton's. Mary Ward has no religion, but Mrs. Throckmorton is attempting to convert her.

While the prospect of death makes some embrace religion, it disposes others to wilder entertainment. Every night the camp resounds with secular hymns played on fiddle and banjo, together with loud singing and dancing. There is even a troupe of actors. I wanted to see their play, but John said it was not fit for a lady and refused to let me accompany him.

Sensing that some aspect of his gentlemanly honor was at stake, I did not insist. But all day, resentment grew in me, along with a desire to see what was so unfitting for a lady, but not for a man. Then I began to wonder if there was another reason John did not want me along. Despite his promise never to gamble again, I feared he did so secretly, for his companion Hiram Watt was a notorious gambler. I had to know if John was being true to his word.

After fretting for hours, I hit upon a scheme. The cheeky Baxter, a conveniently slight man, happily loaned me a shirt, trousers, and a hat. At Mrs. Alter's, I changed into my disguise and on my way out came face-to-face with a startled Mary Ward. I said I only planned a little harmless mischief and hurried away.

The play had begun on the same stage from which the minister had preached in the morning. The role of a slovenly wife was acted by a soldier wearing an apron and rags stuffed into his shirt, while another, his face blackened with charcoal, played her Negro slave. They sang about tricking the woman's foolish husband, who then caught the pair together and whipped the Negro. The men hooted and roared with laughter at their lewd gestures. John stood near the stage slapping his thighs. My face grew red and I looked down, pulling my cap low on my forehead.

Then I noticed my shoes—delicate-looking shoes with heels— poking from beneath my trousers. I heard someone say, "Who is that lad?" and looked up to see Hiram Watt regarding me with suspicion. Reaching down to hitch my skirts, I grasped only my trouser legs, a gesture that further revealed my sex. I turned and ran without looking back, afraid that I, and not the actors, was the target of all the laughter I heard!

Returning to Mrs. Alter's I changed quickly and left a note on the kitchen table that I was laid up in my room with a headache. Truly I had given myself one, worrying that Hiram Watt would tell John that he had seen me. Then the men would mock him and John's anger at me would be fully justified, I thought ruefully. My mind gave in to wilder fears. What if they suspected me of being a Union spy and came to arrest me? It would be the punishment I deserved for mistrusting my innocent husband!

When hours passed and nothing occurred, my fears began to subside. Finally, my sense of duty drew me back to camp. Mrs. Throckmorton felt my forehead anxiously for signs of a fever. I believe I saw a slight smile of amusement cross Mary Ward's stern face. I borrowed Mrs. Throckmorton's Bible and read late into the night to my patients whose pains were keeping them awake.

September 15, 1862

I wish I had never sneaked into that silly play! This morning John told me that Hiram Watt said to him last night, "Saw a pretty young lad at the show who carried hisself in a way that reminded me o' your missus."

"Do I have a manly walk, then?" I asked with a coy innocence, while my deceitful heart pounded.

"No, you have a charming, womanly way in everything," he said with perhaps a bare hint of sarcasm. "But I wondered what he meant, so I said, 'Hiram, are you suggesting my good wife would spend the Sabbath, like you, in base entertainment?' He laughed and that was the end of it."

I meekly thanked John for defending me. But why did I not confess that I had been at the play and assert my reasons for going? Why did John tell me of his encounter with Hiram unless he suspected I had, in fact, deceived him? Are husbands and wives always destined to have secrets from each other?

I have so much to learn of marriage.

September 16, 1862

Yesterday Mrs. Throckmorton and I drove to Shepherdstown in Virginia, where we gathered several bushels of ripe vegetables donated by the good people there. We heard the muted sounds of battle somewhere behind us but were not afraid for ourselves.

Returning to camp near dusk, we learned that McClellan and Lee had clashed nearby. The First Virginia was called to the battle but arrived too late and ended up covering a disorderly retreat from South Mountain. The good news is that General Stonewall Jackson captured a garrison with federal stores and munitions at Harper's Ferry. The bad news is that General Lee was seen with his arm in a sling, either from being wounded or thrown by his horse.

Now the regiment will take up a new defensive position near Sharpsburg, expecting to engage the Yankees again. Once again we break camp, and I bid farewell to Mrs. Alter and her comfortable bed. I do not understand the strategy of war, but neither do the men fighting it. John says he does as he is ordered. I am amazed at how the men worship General Lee. They would follow him anywhere, even into the jaws of Death itself.

September 19, 1862 near Antietam Creek, Maryland

There are no words sufficient to describe the horrors of these past three days. I have crossed a threshold from which there is no return to a safer place. Hell has broken loose on earth in a battle with more casualties than there are stars in the skies. Among them my beloved John is numbered—to my grief and yet infinite thanksgiving, for although he was wounded, he is still among the living.

It began about dawn on the 17th. The field of battle lay between the little town of Sharpsburg and Antietam Creek. I was about a mile behind the lines with Mrs. Throckmorton, Mary Ward, and Mrs. Gordon. Dr. Walker railed against the presence of ladies so near the battlefield and forbade us to leave the hospital area. For what seemed like hours we listened to the steady thundering of cannons and the sharper volley of rifle fire, unable to see the progress of the battle. Though the hospital tents had been erected out of range of the artillery, from time to time a shell screamed overhead, followed by an explosion of dirt or the sound of a nearby tree splintering. I jumped like a skittish horse, and Mary, though more experienced, was almost as nervous. All the while, Mrs. Throckmorton moved her lips in prayer. I could barely focus on my desperate plea, "Lord God, preserve John from harm, and I will do anything you ask."

From time to time someone would dash through with a report that only worsened our fears: Lee was outnumbered three to one by McClellan. The fresh Union troops had gotten the better of our weary soldiers. Our flanks were weak and the enemy would shortly swarm upon us and we would all be taken prisoner.

Soon we had no leisure for worry or speculation. Following a brief lull in the fighting, the wounded began arriving in a steady stream. Ambulances disgorged their battered cargo. Men limped in using their rifles as crutches. Others staggered under the weight of wounded companions. I stood dazed with the shock of seeing the soldiers black with powder, mud, and dried blood, their torn flesh pink and bloodless white. Mary Ward thrust a basin and sponge at me. My hands shook, making me clumsy and almost useless. Soon, however, I fell into a rhythm of watering and bandaging. I lost all sense of time until someone touched my arm. It was one of the stretcher-bearers, telling me I was needed over yonder. I blew away the hair that had fallen over my face.

"I'm needed in many places, sir. Please hold this leg up for a moment while I bandage it."

"Ma'am, it's your husband, he says."

I froze with the linen and scissors in my hand.

"You'd best go, nurse. I can wait," said the man whose leg I tended, forgetting his own suffering out of concern for me.

Though I looked in the direction the orderly had indicated, my confused senses could not distinguish John among the dirty and bloodied men. Then I saw Tom kneeling and holding a man who was half sitting, half lying against a tree, his chest covered with blood. I ran to him and fell to my knees, covering his dirt-blackened face with kisses.

"Hello, darling," John said weakly.

I bit my lip to keep from crying. Tom and I lifted John and carried him to the hospital tent. It was already full, but even as we stood there, a dead man was carried out, so we placed John on his cot. Using my scissors I cut off his jacket and his shirt, exposing the wound in his upper chest. I felt dizzy and had to lower my head and close my eyes.

"I took a minié ball . . . near my collarbone, I think." He winced with pain.

I looked around in desperation. "Doctor! We need a doctor here now!" I shouted, but my plea was lost in the chaos.

"Rose. Don't panic," John said, plucking at my sleeve. "Tom, you can go. Help where you can."

"No, don't leave us, Tom. Tell me what to do," I said.

"You stay here. I'll find the doctor," Tom said, and I could see the look of fear in his eyes.

John lay perfectly still on the cot. His face was pale, his eyes closed, the only sign of pain his contracted brow. I could not believe how calm he was. Too calm. Mary Ward said that some men become serene when death is near. I started to sob, thinking I was about to lose him, and grasped his hand, squeezing it hard. His eyes opened. The pupils were wide and dark.

"I'm not going to die," he said. "I can breathe. It missed my lung."

Was he only asking me for reassurance? I felt for his pulse and there it was, beating against my fingertip.

"Yes, that's good," I said, encouraged. I seized a nearby basin and began to pour water on his chest and wipe the grime away with a sponge. Blood swirled when I rinsed my cloth, until the water in the basin was bright red, yet still more blood spilled from his shoulder. I began to panic again. His breathing was shallow.

"Oh, God, what now?" My voice was a ragged plea.

"Press on it. With your hand," John reminded me. I did, with both hands, and the blood seeped through my fingers, making them slick, until it finally slowed. My hands stopped shaking. I nudged the damaged tissue into place, then covered the whole area with lint and a clean, soft bandage. I folded his blanket beneath his head and whispered, "I love you" at his ear.

"No man . . . in the history of war . . . was ever better cared for—"

I shushed him, and he promptly fell asleep. Aware that I was shivering, I looked down to discover my sleeves and bodice soaked through with blood and water. My skirt was also stained. John's shirt lay in pieces on the ground, trodden into the dirt. I would clean up later. Only one thing mattered now: keeping John alive.

Tom returned with a strange doctor who, when he saw that there was nothing to cut off, said John was "in good shape" and left again. I went out behind the tent and gave way to great shoulder-shaking sobs that soon exhausted me. Then I returned to the man with the injured leg. I treated his wound as carefully as I had John's. He had been shot in the muscle and not the bone. I said I thought the leg would heal.

It was two hours or more before I had the opportunity to check on John. He was still sleeping. I also longed to sleep and decided to find Tom and ask him to stay with John while I rested. But these intentions fled the moment I stepped out of the hospital tent to see hundreds of men lying on the ground, illumined by the cooking fires, which flickered like torches of the devil. In the throes of their suffering, they bled and groaned and cried for mercy, for water, even for death itself. Mary Ward and Mrs. Gordon stepped between the bodies, carrying pitchers of water and broth. Forgetting my intent to sleep, I followed their example. I saw men with unimaginable injuries, wounds too horrible for words. I prayed they would be blessed with a quick death. My back as well as my feet began to ache from constant stooping. I nearly fell asleep on my feet and lost all track of time as diabolical images and the cries of the wounded mingled in my mind like a waking nightmare.

Vaguely I wondered why I didn't see Mrs. Throckmorton there. Later I learned that she had been with her son, holding his hand as he died of a wound to his stomach. Although I hardly knew him, I cried as if he had been my brother. I wondered if John would be the next to die.

In the morning, swaying from fatigue after a sleepless night, I stood by while Dr. Walker, using a long pincer, extracted the minié ball from John's shoulder. John bit hard upon a rag until the tendons in his neck stood out like ropes. The doctor said that a short time would tell if the wound would grow septic, and that I should watch for fever. After he left, I poured a liberal dose of whiskey into the wound before dressing it, gave John a great swig for the pain, and took the rest myself.

Still wearing my stained clothing from the day before, I laid down on an oilcloth spread on the grass and slept as if I had been knocked unconscious. If John called out for me, I was unaware of it.

Lizzie

Chapter 19

From June until September Papa and Luke's regiment was on the move, skirmishing with the rebels and falling back toward Washington. Papa wrote only a single short letter, sounding weary and discouraged. Hoping to cheer him up, I wrote back that Amos had returned safely. I didn't mention that Rosanna had run away and married a rebel.

Then we were all startled by reports of two battles fought not twenty miles from the Pennsylvania state line. Our reserves battled at South Mountain in Maryland, and three men in the regiment were killed. A few days later, they fought again. I read in the newspapers that it had been the bloodiest day in the history of the war that September 17, when almost five thousand men were killed and nearly twenty thousand wounded at Antietam Creek. Mama checked the casualty lists at the telegraph office at least twice a day. Mrs. Pierpont's son was among the wounded, but Luke and Papa's names never appeared. Despite my relief, I was afraid that their luck would soon run out. But at least the rebels had withdrawn from Maryland, for that meant they would not be bringing war into Pennsylvania, to be fought in *our* fields and towns.

Meanwhile Amos had returned to work at the shop, and Margaret hired Grace to look after Jack and Clara. Martin's sprained ankle healed quickly, but then Mama reduced his working hours to save money. The shop felt like an unsteady boat that a big wave might capsize, sending us all to the poorhouse. I couldn't let that happen. All summer, I had been thinking about what to do if Amos didn't come back—and what to do if he did. With winter and butchering season coming on, it was time to present my plan to Mama.

But unbeknownst to me, Mama had her own plan. In October, she sat Amos and me down and announced that we would form a partnership with the York butcher. It was a terrible idea, and I could barely contain myself.

"I'm afraid I don't agree, Mother," I said. "I don't like working with Mr. Schupp. He's too busy to consider our interests."

"Mr. Schupp supplies a good deal of salt beef and pork to the army. It would be to our advantage to share in those profits," Mama said, sounding determined. "Especially as the war is likely to continue through another winter."

"I still don't think that is the best course," I insisted. "Papa wrote how much the men hate salted beef, especially when they can easily get fresh meat. As for salt pork, Cincinnati ships it by the ton, and cheaply, too. We can't possibly sell it at a lower price."

Mother raised her eyebrows, but did not interrupt me. Amos regarded me thoughtfully. I continued laying out my plan, piece by piece.

"When Martin's neighbor, Mr. Trostle, came to the shop the other day, I heard him say that farmers are afraid that their cattle and hogs will be stolen in the night by Confederate raiders. Or else our government will take them to feed the soldiers. As long as the war continues, no one's livestock is secure."

"And what is your point, Lizzie?" Mama asked.

"People are worried about losing what they have and not being able to feed themselves. I predict that farmers will want their hogs and cattle butchered early and stocked safely in their larders rather than being left to an uncertain fate. So why not offer them custom meat-packing and preserving? We could do especially well curing hams and smoking beef, if we extend the cellar beneath the shop and build another smokehouse in the back."

"How can we possibly afford all that!" Mama exclaimed. It was not even a question.

"We would need a bank loan," I admitted. "But even with those expenses, I've figured out how we can make a profit sooner than you might think."

I handed Mama a sheet of figures and she examined it, lines of worry showing around her eyes.

"What do you think, Amos?" she asked.

"I 'gree," he said. "A ham in the cellar is safer than a hog in the pen. Miz Lizzie's plan sounds like a right smart one."

Eventually Mama was won over. She visited the banker, and soon Amos began digging a cellar with shelves for curing meat. We hired Martin full time and raised his salary from eighty cents to a dollar a day. Ben skipped some school to wait on customers in the shop, and I helped him with his missed lessons in the evening. I ordered the large quantities of salt, sugar, and powdered nitrate we would need for curing the meat. Mama looked worried as the invoices piled up.

"Sometimes you have to spend money to make money," I said as if I knew what I was talking about.

I took out advertisements in the *Sentinel* and *Compiler*. Finally, I decided we needed a new sign for the shop. Full of pride, I showed Mama my sketch:

ALLBAUER'S CLASSIC AND CUSTOM MEATS
Albert Allbauer, Owner. M. and E. Allbauer, Proprietors
Amos Whitman, Master Butcher

"The *M* and *E* stand for us, Mary and Elizabeth, of course," I explained.

Mama clapped her hands together. "Why, Lizzie, it's so . . . bold, but . . . yes! We will do it."

Soon the orders started coming in, and I was as pleased as I could be. Mama had convinced every woman in the Ladies Aid Society that a ham would make a lovely Christmas present to send to a soldier. I noticed her face had more color and the hollows under her eyes were not so dark.

"I'm glad you've been healthy, Mama," I said one night as we were peeling apples for pie.

She put down her knife and grew reflective.

"You know, Lizzie, before the war, I let all the cares of running the household and caring for you children overwhelm me to the point of illness. Life is even harder now, but it is also simpler. Nothing matters but that we are all alive and well."

"I've been so afraid that you would get sick again and I wouldn't be able to manage," I said in a rush.

"I'm not worried about that at all. You are quite capable, Lizzie." She looked at me and here eyes were misty. "You are also strong, here." She tapped my breastbone. "And that gives me courage, too."

I was stunned to think that my mother was inspired by some quality in me that I was not even aware of. Was it enough to make others admire me too? Were boys drawn to girls with inner strength? I wished I were beautiful and charming but decided that being strong would have to suffice.

So I was pleasantly startled one October afternoon when I was intent upon the accounts and heard a familiar voice say, "Good day, my dear Miss Allbauer. You are the picture of prettiness."

I looked up and straight into the clear blue eyes of Frederick Hartmann. I hadn't seen him since the day Amos came home with Grace. He swept his hat before him and bowed in an extravagant manner. I was suddenly aware of my old dress and ink-stained hands.

"What, not a word of welcome for your hero?"

I blushed all the way to the roots of my hair. Fortunately Amos came in, sparing me a reply. He was spattered with grayish mud, for he and Martin had been putting mortar on the chimney of the new smokehouse. Mr. Hartmann clapped Amos on the back.

"Congratulations, man! Master butcher Amos Whitman."

"That was Miz Lizzie's idea," said Amos, but I could see he was proud.

"Won't you . . . c-come by the house? To see Mama and Grace," I stammered. Although Mr. Hartmann had shaved off his beard and trimmed his long hair, he was still the handsomest man I'd ever spoken to.

Mr. Hartmann said he'd be honored, and his visit turned into a dinner party. Mama put on her Sunday best and allowed me to wear her lace shawl. I rubbed my skin with lemon verbena, hoping to overcome the smell of woodsmoke and brine that always clung to me. Margaret came, bringing Jack and Clara in their little uniforms. She wore a dark blue baize dress that matched her eyes and made her look as lovely as Rosanna. The thought of my cousin was like a sudden sharp pain.

"Have you any news of Rosanna?" Mama asked her.

"She does not write to me," said Margaret with a dismissive wave.

"I did hear from Mother and Father that her husband received some slight wound, whereupon she up and left Richmond to follow his regiment."

I put my hand to my mouth and gasped. Then I tried to picture Rosanna living in a tent with John Wilcox and marching with the soldiers, but I couldn't do it. My cousin seemed as remote and mysterious to me as the moon. I thought of Rosanna's scrapbook hidden beneath us, in the cellar. How much her secrets, if known, would add to everyone's distress!

"Let's not talk about my sister tonight. I intend to have a gay time!" said Margaret, flashing a charming smile as she held out her gloved hand to Mr. Hartmann.

Grace had insisted on cooking dinner for Mr. Hartmann. She wore a red scarf wrapped around her head as she chopped and stirred and baked, then dished up a pork loin, steaming cornbread, and plum pie. Mr. Hartmann had brought a bottle of wine for the grown-ups. He even poured me a glass. I sipped it slowly, and it stung my throat.

"I don't believe I've ever been waited on at my own table!" exclaimed Mama, slightly flushed from the wine. "I feel like a grand lady."

I was afraid that Grace would take offense, but she didn't seem to notice Mama's comment. I took an empty platter and set it next to mine, then slid down the bench, wordlessly inviting Grace to eat with us.

"Hey, watch your elbow!" Ben said as I bumped him.

Grace sat down at the empty place as if she had intended to do so all along.

Everyone was eager to discuss the news of President Lincoln's Emancipation Proclamation, which would soon free the slaves in the South.

In his usual blunt way, Ben said to Amos, "So you traveled all the way to South Carolina and paid that heap of money to free Grace, and if you had only waited a few months, President Lincoln would have freed her and you'd still have your money!"

"I'd do the very same thing again today. Money ain't everything, young man," he said.

A gentle look passed between him and Grace, who said, "Moses had a devil of a time freein' his people from the pharoah." Her voice reminded me of flowing cream.

"What do you mean?" I asked, curious but hesitant.

"I mean it ain't goin to be easy for President Lincoln. Where he goin' to get the power to free slaves in the states where he ain't even the president?"

"But he wouldn't make a promise he couldn't keep," I protested. "Doesn't he have some way to enforce the new law?"

"No doubt he hopes that it will make the slaves rise up," Mr. Hartmann said. "Southern masters have always feared rebellion."

Amos shook his head. "All Negroes know they be hanged or shot for takin' up arms 'gainst their mastuhs. So most be too 'fraid to rise up."

"But they could help the Union win the war," I offered.

"Miz Lizzie, you an' I know there's lots o' folk in the North, even here in this town, who don't want to fight jus' to free a passel o' slaves. They only wants to teach the rebels a lesson."

His point made me think. Would Northerners turn against Lincoln because of his proclamation? Then Mama asked where the Negroes would go, when they were all freed at once, and what I thought was simple good news had become a messy, complicated issue.

"I think President Lincoln is a great man and a brave one for taking a stand on freedom," said Margaret, always idealistic.

"Amen to that," replied Amos. "Freedom is God's blessin' but it don't always come easy."

Then Margaret asked Mr. Hartmann what had brought him back to Gettysburg.

"I'm on my way to join a cavalry regiment being recruited in Philadelphia. But the female company here is so charming, I just may change my mind and stay."

"Why did you shave off your grand mustache, sir?" Had that question really come out of my own mouth? It must have been the wine that made me so flirtatious.

"Well, more than once I've been mistaken for that rebel dandy, General George Pickett. Rather than let myself be captured or shot, I decided it best to alter my appearance," he said, winking at me. Under his gaze my neck started to prickle again.

When dinner was over and we left the table to gather in the parlor, Margaret took Mr. Hartmann's arm and steered him toward the settee so expertly that I was jealous.

"Won't you oblige us with the story of how you rescued our dear Grace?" she asked.

"Well, that's rightly Mr. Amos's story," replied Mr. Hartmann.

Everyone found a seat and Amos set down his pipe and began the story with their arrival at the plantation. He described a dark place overhung with moss-covered oak trees and an air of misery.

"Mistuh Johnston came to the door, lookin' like some wild-haired madman, his wife hidin' behind him. He denied knowin' me, though I could see he reco'nized me. I reminded him of our deal three years back. He said Grace were no longer alive, which about killed me to hear. But Mistuh Frederick demanded of Mrs. Johnston whether Grace were there. She nodded, her eyes round as marbles in her head. The old man cursed her, then started complainin' to us how hard times were. But I didn't fancy listenin' to his problems. I jus' held out my money, one thousand dollars like we agreed upon. Federal dollars, not·that worthless Confederate paper. But Johnston said, 'That gal ain't for sale no more. I got another one you kin buy instead.' I said, 'I'm only here fer Grace, and I ain't leavin' till she's mine.' "

Amos paused. I could see the emotion rising up in him. Mr. Hartmann took over the story.

"So I thought I'd put some fear into the old fleshmonger. I said to him, 'The war ain't going so well for your side, now, is it? Can't sell your cotton, can't come up with enough men or bullets. President Lincoln will free every blessed slave you own, and you won't get a dime for any of them. You'd best sell now while you can.' "

"What a clever gamble that was!" said Margaret.

"Well, the tough old devil replied that her price had gone up an extra five hundred dollars. Amos pulled out his purse again, but I grabbed it before Johnston could and growled, 'A deal's a deal. Bring out his wife now.' Then Johnston turned like he was about to run off, so I grabbed his collar with one hand and held up my pistol in the other and cocked it."

I heard Margaret draw in her breath. Mama was fanning herself rapidly. Mr. Hartmann smiled, enjoying the effect of his story.

"Well? What happened next, Amos?" I demanded.

"The mistress screamed and Johnston shouted for his manservant but no one came. Mistuh Frederick said, 'I'll shoot yer husband 'less you bring out the girl by the time I count to twenty.' She moved fast for an old lady, an' by the time he got to ten, Grace was in my arms, where she's stayin'.' "

Amos held out his arm and Grace came to him, resting her red-turbaned head on his chest while he finished the tale.

"Mistuh Frederick counted out the money we first 'greed upon an' made Johnston sign the papers. Then he said to Mrs. Johnston, most politely, 'I'm sorry to have to frighten you, ma'am. I know how much cotton costs these days. Buy yourself a new frock.' An' he took fifty dollars from his own pocket an' gave it to her, an' you could see her jaw drop to her chest, but she pulled it up again an' took the money with a smile like he jus' handed her a bouquet of roses."

Margaret and Mama laughed and clapped with delight. But a different feeling welled up in me, a deep appreciation for the sacrifices of Mr. Hartmann and Amos. Amos had spent every dollar he owned to redeem Grace from slavery, risking his own freedom to bring about hers. And Frederick Hartmann had put his own life and reputation on the line to aid them. I suddenly longed to do a brave and selfless act that would change someone's life. Mama said I had inner strength. But could I summon enough courage to undergo danger on another person's behalf? I wanted to thank Mr. Hartmann for his bravery, but as I started toward him, Margaret came between us, murmuring and dabbing at her eyes with a piece of lace. Mr. Hartmann fixed his eyes on her loveliness, and I, timid and plain, walked right past them, out of the drawing room and into the night.

But in the streets was an even greater commotion, as people ran around in a panic, calling for the militia and shouting that the rebels were coming to Gettysburg.

Rosanna

Chapter 20

October 15, 1862 Winchester, Virginia

We have been camped here for several weeks. Mary Ward and I share half of a run-down cabin, while Mrs. Throckmorton occupies the other room. Mrs. Gordon, enjoying the privileges of rank, lodges with her husband. General Lee is reorganizing his army, and new recruits arrive daily to build up the decimated ranks.

John's recovery is almost complete, the site of his wound a smooth indentation. His arm is still weak, but he has resumed drilling with his regiment. I showed Tom how to care for the shoulder by kneading it and applying a cold, damp cloth to ease the soreness and swelling. Sadly, we lost three men this week: Doone, from a blood infection following an amputation; Billings, who never regained consciousness after last month's battle; and Smith, from unchecked gangrene.

How constantly aware I am of the perilous nature of life! With the speed of an eye blinking, a bullet can shatter the body. In secret, infected blood can course through the veins, bringing unexpected death. It takes but a single step, a mere breath, to cross the threshold between life and death.

October 18, 1862

Frost glimmered on the grass this morning, vanishing within a few hours. I dread winter and doubt whether I am hardy enough to endure it under such rough conditions.

My wardrobe has been in need of some attention. The hems of my skirts were in ruins from tripping in the mud, so I cut them off and took out the fullness to make a more practical dress that falls just below the knee. I bought a sturdy pair of shoes from the sutler, whose tent is a veritable general store, and some cloth, which I made into a pair of long pantaloons to wear underneath my skirt for warmth and modesty. The first time I wore them, Dr. Walker criticized my "abominable dress," but I simply went about my work and he said nothing more.

October 19, 1862

Today Mrs. Throckmorton and I went in search of plants to substitute for the medicines that Dr. Walker can no longer obtain. We collected bark from the red oak, taking care not to damage the layer beneath. It is said to have disinfectant and astringent properties that promote the healing of wounds. Mrs. Throckmorton also makes a salve from slippery elm that relieves camp itch, a common discomfort. While we were in the woods, I remembered that it was Lizzie's birthday and grew melancholy with missing her. But it is no use writing to her, for the letters cannot be delivered across battle lines, and I have no wish to be accused of spying if I try to smuggle them.

A writer once said that friendship is the most sublime of affections, cementing souls across time. Such is the nature of my affection for Lizzie, though I have at times proved a poor friend. Still, I trust my scrapbook is in her hands, my secrets locked within the treasure chest of our friendship.

October 22, 1862

After so many weeks in camp, the men are restless for battle again. I said to Mrs. Throckmorton that I did not understand this yearning for danger. Have they already forgotten the horrors of Antietam?

"It is the same with mothers," she replied. "We suffer agonies in giving birth, yet still long to have more children. We always forget the pain and the possibility of dying."

I was struck by her calm wisdom and began to think about children. Later, while John and I strolled through a grove of trees with their glorious red and amber leaves, I asked him how many children he wished for. He paused for a moment as if imagining a peaceful future.

"I only require an equal number of boys and girls, for fairness' sake."

Startled, but remaining calm, I said that if I bore him three sons first (or daughters) I did not relish bearing so many more simply to even the number.

"And why not? Is that not your duty as a wife, if I require it?"

I stopped and stared at him. Were we about to have another quarrel?

"Are you still angry that I had my way before? So you will demand that I bear you twenty children just to even the score? I am not a brood mare."

At this John burst out laughing and took my hands in his.

"Rosanna, my dear, you are like a pile of dried tinder. At the merest spark, you blaze up. I am only teasing you! But I confess, I like to see you on fire."

He reached for me, but I slipped away, teasing him in turn.

"Rosanna, I will be happy with one child or twenty," he said, tenderly and still with a twinkle in his eye. "Now come here and kiss me."

I sidled over to him. "I do not intend to have twenty children, or even ten, though I might consent to three," I said, determined to have the last word.

But his was the last move as he eased me onto a bed of crisp, pungent leaves. After a while the chill of the earth began to seep into our bones, and we rose up again to return to camp.

October 24, 1862

Mary Ward surprises me. Today she showed me a pair of men's pants she intends to wear, saying she obtained them "from a soldier who won't be needing them again." She asked for my help in remaking her skirt to resemble mine, and I lent her my sewing supplies.

Then she suggested, "Why don't we wear our skirts *above* the knee to make them even less cumbersome? Indeed, why not dispense with them altogether?"

"Why, that would never pass muster!" Then I saw by her wry look that she was joking, and we dissolved in laughter together. I did not suspect she had a sense of humor!

October 27, 1862

All morning the men polished their arms, brushed off their uniforms and hats, and made themselves clean in preparation for a grand review of the entire corps by generals Lee, Pickett, and Longstreet. At two o'clock the scattered brigades came together on an open field, making a column at least a mile long. With their colorful standards raised high, the infantry marched to the brisk, rolling drumbeat, turned neatly as one body, and presented their gleaming rifles. I reflected that men, however mortal, when gathered into an army of thousands, appear to be invincible.

General Lee, erect in the saddle of his gray horse, conveyed a stern and quiet dignity. As he rode along the line, hurrahs sounded before him and traveled the length of the column like a wave. Passing near me, he smiled and raised his hat, then swept it before him and bowed. I was thrilled! John once said to me, "I would barter my life for General Lee's smile." Now I understand that sentiment.

Among the observers today were two English lords who could not have failed to be impressed by the spectacle. I overheard one officer remark to another that it would be a sad joke on us if they turned out to be Yankee spies! But judging by their accents and the fine manners they displayed when Mrs. Gordon and I served them tea, I am certain they were genuine nobility. Everyone has high hopes that England will come to the aid of the South, which would hasten the end of the war.

November 2, 1862

Early this morning the order went out to strike camp, and within hours all the tents were dismantled, the nurses' cabin abandoned, and the entire hospital loaded upon four wagons and a dozen mules. The sickest men we left in Winchester.

An icy rain has turned the ground into a quagmire with garbage trodden into it. Mrs. Throckmorton, Mary Ward, and I ride in a wagon. Rain drums loudly on the canvas. Whenever we hit a rut, the bottles and medicine tins clink in their crates and my pen skitters across the page. Drat! Poor mud-splattered Dolly plods alongside with her head down, deploring, as I do, this miserable weather.

Our destination remains unknown.

November 11, 1862

The routines of an army on the march quickly become habitual. When the line halts, for whatever reason, we dispense aid from the wagon, start a fire, and begin cooking. If it rains, a smoky battle ensues between the fire and the rain, sometimes ending dismally. Everyone then resorts to nibbling dried meat and moldy cornbread. At night, we nurses sleep in the wagons and Mrs. Gordon in her carriage. The soldiers huddle together on the ground with blankets and oilcloths heaped over them. The discomfort, together with the uncertainty of our movements, makes everyone tense and temperamental.

Occasionally, however, something out of the ordinary occurs. On the road yesterday a soldier climbed into the ambulance with Mary Ward, claiming stomach pains. As she later told us, the rascal promised her a share in his whiskey-distilling business if she would marry him. She kept a stiff-lipped silence, while dosing him with magnesia. But when he got over his pains enough to try and force a kiss from her, she braced herself on the inner struts of the wagon, put her feet against him, and with one great heave, rolled him out of the wagon and onto the ground. The cart in which Mrs. Throckmorton and I were riding nearly ran him down, and it would have been just what he deserved.

November 17, 1862 near Culpeper, Virginia

Two weeks of marching across the Blue Ridge and down the valley of the Shenandoah have revealed grotesque and depressing sights: hillsides and meadows plowed up by iron missiles, fences broken, fields trampled and burned. Hastily dug graves wash away, exposing decaying bodies. The skeletons of burned houses and barns stand black and forlorn.

I said to Mary Ward, unable to keep the anger from my voice, "We should retaliate against those who have done this to Virginia."

"No, for our soldiers would do the same, were they fighting in the North," she said. "That's the law of all war. It's never courteous."

"Then I would call the the generals together and advise them to grant a clean divorce between the warring countries and let each one live as it will."

"Ha! They would say to you, 'Who is that woman talking of marriage when we're fighting a war? Send her back to her cooking pot.'"

Mary's pompous tone made me laugh. She is an abolitionist, but she favors even more sweeping change, such as giving women the vote.

"We are more peaceable and compassionate than men and, if allowed to choose our country's leaders, would bring about a quick end to slavery and war," she argued.

"Perhaps, but Mrs. Throckmorton is the very image of compassion, yet she does not find slavery unjust," I countered. "I have heard her cite scriptures that uphold the ownership of slaves, and she often says that God intended for the strong to take care of the weak. She would never vote to overturn the natural order."

"Yet she is among the strong! Why, she would be a general if women could serve in the army."

"And you, Mary, would serve in Congress, if women were allowed to vote. But that will happen 'when pigs fly from their sty' as my cousin Lizzie would say."

For a while, we rolled along in the dusk of the gray November day.

"Rosanna, I'm afraid that what we do only prolongs the war," Mary said, breaking the silence. There was despair in her voice. "We patch up soldiers and cure their ills only to send them back into battle, where some of them will die."

"I can't bear to look at our work that way," I said, putting my arm around her shoulders. "I must believe that I am relieving the suffering around me."

I have not told John about my growing friendship with Mary Ward. He would not approve of her ideas, and if he should declare that she is an unsuitable companion for me, we would undoubtedly quarrel again.

November 22, 1862

Why is it that the thing we fear passes us by, while that which we ignored stops and strikes us instead?

On the evening of the 20th, I took John a bowl of stew and found him shivering though he lay close enough to the fire to become singed. He was in the throes of fever and speaking nonsense about his head being a cabbage. I took him into an ambulance and tended to him all night, keeping him warm by curling my body around his. We lay like two spoons nestled in a drawer. I hardly slept due to his twitching and murmuring. The next morning I told Dr. Walker he was not fit to march or to stand picket duty. I have made him ride the last two days, dosing him with Dover's powder for the fever, and ipecac and tea for his dry mouth and nausea.

November 23

No change in John's condition. He shakes and sweats, which makes him shudder again with cold. Twice today I changed his fever-soaked clothes & dried them. Dribbled tea between his parched lips. Dr. Walker says it is typhoid. I am so weary and afraid.

November 25

More men die from camp fevers and other illness than from battle wounds. I cannot bear to think that John, having survived being shot in the shoulder, might be carried off by typhoid fever. Oh God, help him!

November 26

Little change. He is alternately lucid & delirious mostly. I am almost sick myself with worry. Mary Ward made me rest while she tried to feed him. Several new cases of typhoid. An officer was carried off in two days.

November 29

At last! John's fever has subsided, but he lies flat with exhaustion and weakness. Mary declared him "almost out of the woods." Heedless in my joy, I kissed his forehead and hugged Mary. Said a prayer of thanksgiving and allowed myself to sleep.

December 8, 1862 camp near Fredericksburg

A damp and bitter cold has settled upon us. Overcoats and blankets are scarce, and those who threw them away in the summer to lighten their load now regret it. The lucky ones wear coats taken from dead Yankees. Pneumonia and typhoid are on the rise, and when they occur together, the outcome is usually fatal. John's strength increases daily, but he could relapse, for that is the habit with remittent fevers. Even Mary Ward has a touch of something but shrugs it off.

The Yankees are demanding the surrender of Fredericksburg, and if the city falls, they will press on toward Richmond again. There is likely to be a battle any day, and we are all wound as tight as watch springs.

December 10, 1862

Mary Ward has contracted the fever! I feel responsible, for what if she became ill by treating John? I wanted to nurse her myself, but Dr. Walker said she must be sent home. "We can't have womenfolk dying here," he said, as if camp were a place only for men to die. So we put her on a train for Richmond, where she will be treated, then transferred home. I made sure she was comfortably settled and gave precise instructions to the steward for her care. Then I said farewell, assuring her that she would come through this, strong as she was. Although she was dazed with fever and could not tell me her hometown, she murmured my name and gripped my hand. I could not hold back my tears. I shall miss her terribly.

December 12, 1862 Fredericksburg

The battle for Fredericksburg has ended in a victory for the South.

John's regiment was held in reserve and assigned to build a stone wall that served its purpose in stopping wave upon wave of advancing federals. Hiram Watt took a minié ball in his buttocks, by some accident or mistake of one of his fellows. Mrs. Throckmorton assisted Dr. Walker in that operation. The seriously injured have been sent to Richmond, and our hospital, an abandoned barn, shelters those beyond the hope of medicine. We do not have enough morphine to dull their pain, and their moans echo in the cavernous place.

One of my patients was a Yankee boy who had dragged himself by mistake behind our lines. He had a belly full of shrapnel, the kind of wound no surgeon can fix. He was afraid of dying, so I stayed with him, though many of our own men were also in dire need. The boy's name was Joshua Fuller, and I was surprised to discover that he was with Company K of the First Pennsylvania Reserves. Beyond that, I could learn nothing from him about the late battle or cousin Luke or Uncle Albert, for he rambled in his speech. But he did recount the story of his life, all eighteen years of it, from his birth on a farm in York, Pennsylvania, to this sad day.

When Joshua stopped breathing, I closed his eyelids. I cut off a lock of his hair and a button from his jacket to send to his mother. Writing the letter, I chose my words with the greatest care, knowing she will read them over and over, seeking comfort. Then I went to find John and poured out the boy's story, along with my tears for all the suffering and grief occasioned by this war. He simply took me in his arms, and I realized that it is his love alone that sustains and strengthens me.

Lizzie

Chapter 21

The rebels didn't come to Gettysburg after all, not on that night of the dinner party for Frederick Hartmann. It proved to be a false alarm that sent the town into a panic. The Confederate cavalry had rushed into Pennsylvania and captured the town of Chambersburg, twenty-five miles to the west. General Stuart's men had looted farms, stolen horses, and burned the railroad depot and the government warehouses, exploding the ammunition stored there. Then they had ridden toward Gettysburg but turned off the road at Latshaw's tavern, barely four miles from the edge of town.

We didn't sleep well for weeks after. Everyone expected the rebels to come galloping through our town without warning. Mama hid our silver and valuables in the woodpile. Many farmers decided not to risk losing their livestock to raiders, so Amos was busier slaughtering animals than he had been since the war started, and we processed a ton of cured beef in a single week.

In the middle of December came news of a battle at Fredericksburg, and, with surprising swiftness, a letter from Luke. I read it while walking home, then lied to Mama when she asked if there had been a letter at the post office. She worried that I looked pale, but I assured her that everything was all right, though it most decidedly was not.

December 14, Fredericksburg, Virginia

Dear sister,

This letter is for your eyes only. I know it is the fashion to write home what a lark it is to be a soldier but I cant lie anymore.

Yesterday I was on duty with the ambulance corps near Fredericksburg. Our men attacked Marys Hill but were forced back and the situation was growing desperate. On the last charge I picked up a rifle from a fallen soldier and no one made a move to stop me, every man being sorely needed. I ran forward in the dark with bullets whizzing by me until I came to a stone wall at the foot of the hill built by the rebels to stop us. It was doing the job and the ground was thick with the dead. I climbed over the bodies and aimed up the hill hoping to hit a reb and shot and reloaded I dont know how many times. Then the call came to retreat and I could not run fast enough. I was bawling with fear but thank God no one heard me through all the noise. Then I discovered that my rifle was rammed full of six or more loads, so in all the chaos I had not fired it. Or it had misfired and I had not known. Lord, it was enough to explode and kill me! We lost Fredericksburg badly in the end.

Our company is in a pitiful condition with 60 out of 94 men disabled by wounds and disease, besides those who died. Papa was not at Marys Hill because he was laid up with dysentery but now he is eating again.

I suppose I am considerd a man now and it will be my duty to bear a rifle in battle and to kill as many rebels as I can. The truth is I dread it. Do not tell Ma any of *this for she will be angry with me for fighting. Let her think I am safe. Only you know what a coward your brother is.*

                    Luke

How I ached for my brother! I longed to share my knowledge of his pain, but knew that I could not. It would only trouble Mama. I had to keep Luke's secret as well as Rosanna's. So I hid the letter at the bottom of my deepest bureau drawer. But I could not banish from my mind the image of my brother running in the dark and trying to fire his rifle while tears coursed down his muddy face. For the first time I knew in my heart—not just in my head—that war was frighteningly real and that Death itself pursued my brother.

The tidings from Luke enveloped me like a dark cloud all the way through December. Reverend Essig's familiar Christmas sermon about the Prince of Peace born in a stable struck me as hollow. Not even the little presents Mama, Ben, and I shared with each other cheered me up. But when the season's first snowstorm blew in just before the new year, it dispelled my gloom somewhat. I watched as giant wet flakes fell from a leaden sky. They hit the ground with a sound like fingertips lightly tapping on a coverlet. The snow fell so fast that soon it shrouded everything in white. Then it abruptly stopped and the sun shone again, blinding the eye. All along York Street, children ran outside to play, and their laughter and shouts filled the air. Ben and I shoveled a path to the well and the woodpile, then pelted each other with snowballs. Grace stepped outside into the snow for the first time in her life, a look of amazement on her face. Amos helped Ben fix the old sled and grease its runners with tallow.

Then Martin drove up in the cart and called out, "We have a delivery to make today. Let's go. It won't take long."

"I don't recall scheduling anything for today," I said, climbing reluctantly onto the seat beside him.

Martin hollered to Ben, "Toss that sled in the back and climb in yourself!"

The three of us set out, heading down Taneytown Road. A ridge of white hills marked with vertical black trees rose to our right. We stopped at the Hummelbaughs, and it took Martin, with Ben's help, all of five minutes to unload the cart and collect payment.

"This could have waited until tomorrow," I said.

"But now it's done and we can have some fun. Ben, want to try out a good sledding hill?"

"Of course. That's why I came!"

"Lizzie?" asked Martin.

I nodded, not wanting to spoil the fun.

Martin drove on until we came to a two-story stone farmhouse that sat at an angle to the road and near an even larger barn made of stone and wood. Behind the house and barn rose the ridge we had been following all the way from town. Two hills marked the endpoint of the ridge, sloping together in the middle like a snow-covered saddle.

"This is a nice farm. Who lives here?" I asked.

"I do," Martin said with pride. Seeing the direction of my gaze, he added, "We call those hills Little Round Top, behind the house, and Big Round Top, to the south. Good for hunting rabbits and deer."

"But not for sledding," said Ben, sounding disappointed as he looked at the thickly wooded hills.

"Just wait," said Martin. He jumped down from the cart and went into the house, returning with a jug of hot cider. We backtracked a short way, then tethered the horse to a tree, and Martin showed us a path that led through the woods and up the smaller hill. We skirted the hilltop, Ben dragging his sled through the brush, until we came around to the west side of the hill, which was lit by the afternoon sun. Above us, the hill was studded with huge boulders, but the lower slope had been cleared of trees, and icy paths snaked between the remaining stumps. Screaming, a boy whizzed past on a strip of oilcloth and two others slid downhill on a long plank slicked with tallow.

"My cousins," Martin said. They were delighted to see Ben and his sled, and soon the four boys were taking turns shooting down the hill and into the air after skimming the top of a flat rock.

"Come back up. It's our turn now!" called Martin. The way he said "it's our turn," as if we were together in this, made me suddenly shy.

"It's so steep. I know I'll get hurt," I said, shaking my head.

"Come on, you'll be fine. I'll steer," he said, taking my hand. Even through the layers of our gloves, I felt his touch. It was both compelling and reassuring. I nodded, and he sat down on the sled. Somewhat clumsily I sat behind him, crossed my legs, and laid my hands on his shoulders.

"You'd better hold tighter than that or I'll lose you for sure," he said. I barely had time to grab his waist before we were sliding, picking up speed, and I was screaming into the back of his coat. Martin leaned from side to side as we hurtled downhill, throwing up sprays of snow. At the bottom of the hill we took a tumble and rolled in the wet snow.

"That was so much fun. Let's go again!" I said, laughing. By the third time I was feeling reckless. "Over the flat rock this time!" I cried, and Martin guided the sled so that it skimmed the surface of the rock and hovered in the air for an instant before hitting the ground. Next I went alone and guided the sled down the icy course without crashing. It was a thrilling adventure.

Then one of Martin's cousins hit his head on a tree stump and we all realized our fingers and toes were numb. We drank up the rest of the cider, which had cooled, and went back to where the horse and cart were hitched to a tree. Martin and his cousins went back to his house, while Ben and I drove home in the cart, cold and tired. I ached all over and my wrist throbbed, though I didn't remember spraining it. But it seemed a small price to pay for such fun. I recalled how Martin and I had brushed snow from each other. How broad and strong his back was. How we had laughed together, our breath condensing in the air. His face was full of light and his whole person seemed changed when he smiled at me there on that snowy hillside.

I decided I was ready to have a beau, and Martin Weigel would do just fine.

Rosanna

Chapter 22
1863

January 1, 1863 Camp Petersburg, Virginia

We have turned the page to a new year. And here the conviction grows that in 1863, the tide of war will turn and a Southern victory be sealed. Winning Fredericksburg brought a store of hope and good spirits that lasted through Christmas, a festive occasion despite the cold and snow. The townspeople supplied brandy and cakes for the men, while Mrs. Throckmorton and I baked pies. I gave John a worsted shirt that I sewed by hand, a flawed but worthy effort. His present to me was a heart pendant fashioned out of melted lead, which I wear around my neck, close to my heart.

A storm last night buried the camp under two feet of snow. This morning the men engaged in a snowball fight of such intensity that it resulted in several minor cuts and sprains, which kept me busy most of the day.

January 6, 1863 Richmond

At our staff meeting, Dr. Walker noted my "growing competence in nursing" (his precise words!) and asked me to visit the hospitals in Richmond on his behalf. The city is only twenty-five miles from Camp Petersburg. Excited by the prospect of touring the newest hospitals in the country, I readily agreed. Besides, I feel a duty to visit my parents, and I do long for the comforts of home.

Arrived on the 4th to find Mother and Father quite disconsolate, for Margaret had decided it was too dangerous to travel at Christmas. Father said they would have slain the fatted calf for me, if there were any calves left in the city, which is more deprived than ever before. Poor Father hardly suspects how apt was his joke; indeed I am his prodigal daughter, unable to confess my wrongdoing.

January 7, 1863 Richmond

Mother fusses and frets over me until I want to scream. She says I should eat more, that my hair looks dull and my skin rough. Am I really losing all my looks? I know that cultivating beauty does not matter, and is hardly even possible, while living in a military camp. But nonetheless I have no wish to look like an old wife. Father took my side, saying I have never looked healthier, though I wonder about his judgment. He looks, if possible, more frail.

I have sent inquiries to several hospitals hoping for news of Mary Ward.

I miss John. We have been apart four days now.

January 8, 1863 Richmond

Wearing a fresh dress, Mother's good cloak, and fine shoes, I visited Chimborazo Hospital today. With Dr. Walker's letter of introduction in hand, I was given a personal tour by the matron, Mrs. Phoebe Pember. Compared to our field hospitals, Chimborazo is a modern wonder, with its heated cabins of whitewashed pine and the rows upon rows of medicine bottles on neat shelves. The wards have actual beds and the nurses wear starched white aprons. There is a central bakery from which fresh bread is distributed daily. Each division has its own laundry, kitchen, and bathhouse. The sick and wounded receive superior care; only one in five men dies, Mrs. Pember informed me. We discussed improvements I would like to institute in the field. Mrs. Pember observed that clean bandages and instruments seem to reduce the likelihood of infection, so washing them is desirable, but admittedly not always practical. I also learned that in certain cases, gangrene is less likely to spread once the skin is cut away. Why this should be interests me greatly.

In the evening I visited Mr. and Mrs. Wilcox, who have been consumed with worry for their son. Sparing them the more frightening details of John's injuries and illness, I assured them that he was well. Their household, including the Negroes, seems content and serene despite the upheavals of war. John's parents were generous to a fault, bestowing gifts and money (over my protests), and demonstrating affection. How happy they will be when we give them grandchildren, after the war!

January 10, 1863 Richmond

I received a reply to my inquiries about Mary Ward, a letter stating that she was treated at Bellevue Hospital and released on December 29. There was no address listed, so I cannot hope to reach her, but at least she is alive and well. Today I return to Camp Petersburg.

February 1, 1863 Richmond

My purpose in visiting Richmond this time is to collect medical supplies and items for the soldiers. Our neighbors have given several dozen books from their libraries and the congregations have also been generous. Now there will be no lack of books for the soldiers to read (even if half of them are Bibles). People have donated precious bottles of quinine and iodine, and the Wilcoxes' largesse and my own salary enabled me to purchase ipecac and sulfates.

All of Richmond is angry about Mr. Lincoln's proclamation concerning the slaves. President Davis said it proves that the North has always intended to abolish slavery and thereby ruin the South. In Richmond, Father informed me, almost half of those who work in the factories, ironworks, and mills are slaves, hired out by their owners. Even the hospitals, I have observed, depend on the labor of Negroes. If they went free, the Confederacy and its economy would collapse. I wondered aloud whether the Negro should be forced to support a system that denies him freedom. At this my father became so agitated I was afraid his heart would fail him.

By declaring the Negroes emancipated, President Lincoln has waved a red flag before a bull. The South cannot help but charge it. Any hope of a truce or compromise grows faint. I fear a terrible and decisive confrontation is inevitable, and I hope to be far from that field of death.

Mother gave me two petticoats she sewed from bedsheets after she saw how ripped and stained my old ones were. I have clean, fresh underwear for John, too. He will be so grateful.

February 4, 1863 Richmond

Today while I was departing for Camp Petersburg, Mother tried again to dissuade me, this time summoning the authority of Richmond society!

"Mrs. Sullivan and the ladies simply do not approve of what you are doing. It is difficult for me, too," she fretted. "Why not stay home and attend the sick in a decent hospital here in the city?"

"Tell Mrs. Sullivan," I said, choosing my words with care, "that our country desperately needs nurses in the field. Attending the sick, the wounded, and dying there is a duty and a calling of which my husband approves." There! I had cited the authority of my husband and my country.

"But how can you live in a cold tent with no privacy?" replied Mother, her mind on simpler matters. "And in the company of so many rude men?"

I explained that I shared a room in the camp headquarters with a stove and a good matronly woman and that I kept company with General Gordon's wife (a detail I thought would impress the Richmond ladies). Before Mother could summon any more objections, I said a firm farewell. But as I passed through the parlor with my valise in hand, I noticed a letter on the table and, recognizing Margaret's writing, touched it longingly.

Mother urged me to read it, making me suspect she had planted it there to waylay me. Dated Christmas Day, the letter described their holiday dinner, their gifts, the children's cleverness, and the weather. Margaret also wrote of her feelings for a cavalry officer, one Captain Hartmann. So my sister had a new beau! I wondered if he was handsome. Was he much older? Her letter didn't say, but its closing made tears spring into my eyes, and I seemed to hear her voice, exasperated but affectionate: "Though I know not where my sister is, nor if she be well, I pray for her safety and happiness daily."

On the table next to the letter was a framed picture of my sister with Jack and Clara, who had on their little matching uniforms.

"Margaret sent that to me at Christmas," Mother said, handing it to me. "But you may have it."

"I have nowhere to put it to keep it from breaking," I said, setting it down again. Oh, I wanted the photograph and would have treasured it. But their dear faces rebuked my selfishness. And Margaret had not meant it for me.

Once outside, having closed the door behind me, I gave way to sobbing.

February 10, 1863 Camp Petersburg

I believe John is keeping his word not to gamble, even though he is often in the company of Hiram Watt. I overhead a conversation between them in which Hiram was holding forth about the "natural inferiority" of the "rebellious Negro," while John did not contradict him. I can no longer postpone a discussion of this sensitive matter, namely John's views on slavery. If only I knew how to broach the subject without provoking a quarrel.

February 13, 1863

Today while we were taking a walk, the opportunity presented itself.

John mentioned something Tom had done for him, and I said, "Your valet is a man of virtue and intelligence. I am becoming fond of him."

"Yes, he is," agreed John, taking my arm to help me over a log in the path.

"I hope you do not hold the opinion that Negroes are our inferiors," I said mildly. "For I don't agree with those who say that they must be subjugated for their good and for our safety. Can you imagine Tom raising his hand against any person without just cause?"

"He would not, for he is a loyal family retainer. But he is exceptional among Negroes," John replied, not granting me any ground yet.

"Indeed, you treat him as kindly as if he were your brother, to your great credit."

"Yes, he is like one of the family," said John nodding, justly pleased with himself.

"Shouldn't your brother have the same freedom that you enjoy?"

John pursed his lips. "Tom does not desire his freedom."

I pulled my cloak tightly around me as the wind picked up. "How do you know? Have you asked him?"

"No. What would he do with it?" John was growing irritated at my questioning, but having brought the matter this far, I could not be silent until it was settled.

"Why, the same thing that you do. Make choices and act upon them."

"But he would simply choose what I wanted, for that is what he has always done."

"That is no reason he must continue to do so." I met each of his denials with gentleness, hoping to make him relent.

"Darn you, Rosanna," he said, running his hands through his hair until it stood wildly on end. "Didn't your mother teach you not to cross your husband so often? I will have things my way!"

"John, this is not about you and me—"

"Of course it is!"

"No, it is about Tom and his right to freedom."

"When I die, he will belong to you and you can do what you want with him!"

"Don't talk like that, please," I said, touching his lips. "I am sorry if I angered you," he said.

He took several deep breaths that condensed in the air between us. "I forgive you," he said.

"John, I do not want us to own slaves. When the war is over, will you grant Tom his freedom?"

John raised his head and looked up into the bare trees. A lone red cardinal perched there, repeating its song. In the distance, tin messware clanged, signaling mealtime.

"Rosanna, what did I do to deserve you?" I don't know what he meant by the question, but at least he managed to smile at me. "Upon my death, or at the end of the war, whichever comes first, Tom shall be free, as you wish."

"Not because I wish it, but because it is right," I whispered, feeling no triumph, only gratitude.

"It may be," he said, and turning around, he retraced the path to camp, seemingly deep in thought. I followed in silence.

February 27, 1863 Camp Petersburg

I am thoroughly sick of camp life and all its discomforts. Above all the lack of cleanliness disgusts me. One who has not been in a camp cannot imagine the smell of a barracks full of men who have not bathed in months. John is a little less revolting because I launder his clothes, and our patients are lucky in that they are kept as clean as can be, under the circumstances.

As for myself, I have not bathed since I was in Richmond over three weeks ago! I am wearing all my clothes in order to stay warm. My hair is flat and shiny with oil. I am ashamed for my own husband to see me. Surely none of my friends in Gettysburg would recognize me in such a state. Lizzie and I once joked that I could not survive a single day in camp; well, it has been nearly six months! And for the last five weeks we have had to melt snow to drink because the stream was fouled from the camp latrines.

But I have chosen this course and will persevere. Now I am able to treat wounds of all sorts and even set simple fractures. I know how to treat the ague and typhoid, and when to let nature run her course, for good or ill. Measles have broken out, and in some cases the infection progresses to the lungs or brain. I had the disease as a child, but John may not be immune, so I have instructed him to avoid anyone with signs of a fever or rash.

Good news! Mrs. Throckmorton has just interrupted my writing to announce that she has water boiling and a washtub at hand, and Mrs. Gordon has stoked up the fire, so we are going to wash our hair and take turns bathing. My spirits are already revived.

Lizzie

———✦———

Chapter 23

When the spring thaw came to Gettysburg, my wintertime worries also melted away. The shop had turned a good profit and we were able to pay the first loan installment on time. Mama had gotten through the bitter-cold months without any fevers, nothing worse than a one-week cough. I hadn't been sick at all, and Ben suffered a lengthy cold but still managed to grow two inches. I was concerned about Grace, however. She was often sick and didn't have much energy, but she refused to see a doctor. Then the reason she was ailing became clear: she was expecting a baby. She was so slim to begin with that her belly started to show in March with a baby that was due to be born in July. Amos treated her like she was glass, but I could see that she was made out of something more like iron. I thought most women became softer and somewhat dreamy when they were expecting their first babies, but Grace was not like anyone I'd ever known in that regard, or in any way at all.

Nor was anyone I knew quite like Rosanna, whose friendship was proving hard to replace. Martin and I were no closer to being friends than we were the day we went sledding on Little Round Top. To my disappointment, I seldom saw him, for he had to work on his father's farm nearly every day. I needed a companion and confidant, and Ginnie

Wade seemed the only good prospect. She always greeted me when I saw her in the shops or along Baltimore Street, where she lived with her mother. One day we fell into step together as I was going to Margaret's house.

"My sister is expecting her first child this summer," Ginnie announced. "I expect I'll be with her a lot." Georgia Wade had married her fellow, Louis McClellan—who was no relation to the general—when he came home on furlough. Now she lived just a few doors from Margaret.

"You are lucky. I always wished for an older sister," I said with a sigh.

"Oh, don't. It's no fun being the younger one. We always bicker."

"Grace is also expecting, you know. Since Amos is practically a member of our family now, their baby will be almost like a cousin to me."

"Goodness, really?" said Ginnie, raising her eyebrows. Was it disapproval I saw, or only surprise? She changed the subject. "I think Martin Weigel likes you."

"No! He does? How do you know?" I replied, all flustered.

"I saw him watching you in church one day. But maybe he was just distracted. It was a long sermon."

"Well, that's encouraging," I said with an edge of sarcasm in my tone. I couldn't tell if Ginnie was teasing me. With Rosanna I would have known at once. I could have told her that I was sweet on Martin, and she would have known what to do next. But Rosanna was no longer my friend.

"Annie Baumann told me she has been writing to your brother Luke and he has written back," said Ginnie, changing the subject.

Ever since the incident with Rosanna's flag, I had considered Annie mean and insipid. I wished Luke had chosen some other girl to write to. But if I told Ginnie this, she might tell Annie that I disliked her. It was wearying to have to watch every word I said.

"Annie thinks it's terribly romantic, your cousin being a field nurse, but her mother says it's shocking."

"Annie thinks so *because* her mother disapproves!" I blurted out. But I didn't want to gossip about Rosanna. It was like pressing on a bruise. "Will you and Jack marry when he comes home from the war?" Ginnie's beau, Jack Skelly, had joined the 87th Regiment, along with many other Gettysburg men.

Ginnie sighed. "I hope so. I'm almost twenty. It would be so exciting to be married, don't you think?"

I didn't think so at all. But I tried to be agreeable.

"It *is* rather dull here in Gettysburg," I said. "I mean, the war is going on out there, all the men are gone, and you and I are just sitting here." A new conscription law had been passed, and all men between the ages of twenty and forty-five were being drafted, unless they could produce a three-hundred-dollar bounty.

"I'm not bored," she said. "I'm too busy sewing and doing relief work. What else *could* we do?"

"We could fight, like the men do," I said idly, then told Ginnie about the girl from Philadelphia who had cut her hair short and joined a regiment. "I read about it in the newspaper. She wasn't discovered for a whole year. Then she was shot in the arm and the surgeon who removed the bullet noticed her . . . well, you can guess what. They drummed her out of the army, but at least she now has a story to tell her children someday."

Ginnie looked horrified. Rosanna, would have relished the story.

"Well, I think it was brave of her," I said. "And I understand why she did it. She wanted an adventure. I might do it, too, if I could keep from getting shot. Then again, if the rebels come back, you and I might have to learn to use a rifle, because there will be only boys and old men left to defend the town."

I said this just to shock poor Ginnie. I knew I could no more fight in a war than pigs could fly out of their pens. I didn't have the courage of a hero like Frederick Hartmann or even the blind bravery that made Luke pick up that rifle and dash headlong at the enemy, firing again and again. I would have turned and run the other way.

"Well," said Ginnie, "you're almost as wild as your cousin, I reckon. What's wrong with being a young woman with ordinary desires?"

"Nothing," I started to say, but Ginnie had turned in at the gate of her sister's house. I didn't even get the chance to ask her if she could find a way to let Martin know I liked him. I would just have to take matters into my own hands.

I saw my chance on a sunny May day that promised a glorious summer to come. Wildflowers bloomed in the fields and along the roads, raising my spirits. I felt as confident as spring itself. Nothing bad could happen on a day like this. I knew Martin would be coming to the shop to help Amos with a task. While on my way to the post office, I came up with a plan. I would start a conversation, then mention the church ice-cream social in June, and if he failed to pick up on that cue, I would lightly suggest that we attend it together. My stomach fluttered with nervous excitement as I waited in line at the post office. I wondered if I would seem too bold. The postmaster nodded at me. There was a letter for Mama. Now I would have to take it home before going to the shop. If I didn't hurry, I might miss Martin.

Mama was in the garden with Ben, planting corn and staking bean seedlings. She had gained some weight and I thought that, like the sun, she grew stronger as spring advanced.

"A letter from Luke," I announced brightly.

Mama said, "You read it to me, dear. My hands are muddy."

Though I was in a hurry, I couldn't refuse her, so I unfolded it and began to read.

May 6, 1863
Camp near Bull Run Creek, Va.
Dearest Mother and Lizzie and Ben,

I hope this letter finds you all well though I am sad & discouraged. We received word of our troops being whipped at Chancellorsville though we were greater in numbers by two to one. We do not seem to have a general who can stop the rebels from mowing us down like wheat. But they have lost General "Stonewall" Jackson who was shot by his own men in the confusion of battle.

Some of the men are afraid (or maybe hopeful) that this defeat will cause the northern newspapers to call for Lincoln to end the war on any terms. I for one cannot bear to lose the war, neither can I stand more fighting.

Now to my real reason for writing, I have bad news.

I paused. My heart had started to beat rapidly. I looked uncertainly at Mama. She motioned for me to go on reading. My hands were now shaking, so I sat down on the ground before continuing:

Last week Papa and a detail of men were sent to rustle up a herd of cattle in the Blue Ridge foothills. It was not expected to be too dangerous but only half their number returned (without the cattle), having been surprised by rebels and several taken prisoner, Papa among them. He was shot at but Devine Bernard who got away believes he was not hit or not seriously injured anyway.

When I heard, I was desperate to go out and rescue him but Devine told me not to be a fool and make my mother grieve over both of us. But I will not come home without him!

We are following the enemy north up the Potomac. Though we are weak from losses and in poor spirits, we are in the good hands of Col. Strong Vincent, his courage matches his name. I have heard that Lee wants to take the war into Pennsylvania. I dont mean to put fear into you, but to give you warning to be prepared.

Your dutiful son and brother,
Luke

Mama had dropped her hoe and was leaning against Ben, moaning. Ben held her up until they reached the porch, then eased her down onto a step. I put my arms around her, and we sat for a long time without speaking. I struggled to take in this new knowledge: that Papa was a prisoner of the Confederates. He might be injured as well. What would happen to him? What if he never—

"He's still alive," said Ben. It sounded almost like a question.

"Yes, of course he is!" I said quickly. I was worried about Mama. She was sitting motionless with her hands over her face.

"What are we going to do?" asked Ben in a small voice.

Mama lifted her head. Her eyes were dry.

"We will do our work, as usual," she said, pushing herself off the step and standing up. "Ben, go and finish planting that row."

I felt tears coming, and uncontrollable words poured out with them.

"Why did this happen to Papa? Is God punishing me for complaining? Being hateful to my brothers? Not praying enough?"

"It's not any of God's doing," Mama said grimly. "War is man's doing."

I swallowed hard. "What should I do?" I asked in a small voice.

"Please, go tell Margaret. I don't think I can do it."

On the way to Margaret's house, I saw Mrs. Baumann and Mrs. Pierpont near the courthouse and Ginnie Wade and her mother coming out of the dry goods store. I hurried by without stopping to greet any of them. I couldn't bear to say the words "my father has been taken prisoner" and see their pitying looks. I did not even consider going to the butcher shop to see Martin, for my own affections no longer seemed important.

Jack was sitting on the front steps of Margaret's house, his brown eyes wide with worry, and Clara leaned against him, sucking her thumb. Their sad looks confused me. How could they have already heard the news about Papa?

"What's the matter, honey?" I said, absently patting Clara's head.

"Our mama is crying. It's something to do with Aunt Rosie," said Jack.

"Now what has she done?" I said, feeling annoyed. It didn't occur to me that Rosanna might be sick or hurt. It was Papa I worried about.

In the kitchen, I found Grace trying to comfort Margaret, who was seated at the kitchen table, dabbing at her red eyes with a towel. Grace's belly stuck out, large and round, momentarily distracting me.

"Why, Miz Lizzie! How did you know to come just now?" she asked.

"My mother sent me. We just received a letter—"

"Then you also know." Margaret held up a telegram. "Father was able to get this through—oh, my sister, my poor dear Rosanna!" she lamented, wiping the corners of her eyes.

"For goodness' sake, what happened to her?" I cried. "She's not dead, is she?"

Margaret only sobbed harder, but Grace, with a mournful look, held out a telegram, and I took it and read the simple message that John Wilcox had contracted measles and dysentery and was dead.

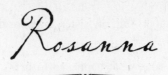

Rosanna

Chapter 24

May 6, 1863 somewhere (?) north of Suffolk

A few days ago I fell asleep, and when I awoke, my world had turned upside down. Oh, it pains me to put down the words no new wife ever thinks to utter:

My husband is dead.

When he showed signs of a rash, I thought it only a mild case and was not very concerned. Hadn't his strength already prevailed over two wounds and typhoid? Then I became sick, and while I was ill, he died. Alas, I blame myself, for if I could have held his hand, I might have pulled him from the jaws of death and nursed him to health again.

He died on the 3rd of May. I woke up on the 4th in a lurching wagon.

Mrs. Throckmorton said I had been delirious for two days. "Like a tree struck by lightning, you just toppled over. But you're strong; you'll heal." She cooed over me like a mother over an infant.

"Where is John? Is he well again?" I asked, still innocent.

Then she broke the sad news to me. At first I disbelieved her. But her sorrowful look confirmed the truth. She took me to her wide, soft breast while I choked out denials as if they would change the course of fate. I begged to go back, but even sitting up made me dizzy. Mrs.

Throckmorton said that Tom would arrange for John's body to be sent to Richmond.

"You should have left me behind too," I cried.

"I couldn't let you wake up to find yourself alone and a widow," she said tenderly.

"I mean, why not leave me to die as well?" I said, immune to all comfort.

"You mustn't ever say such a thing," she said firmly. "It is a sin against the Lord to wish for death. You were more ill from exhaustion than from measles. You were not about to die."

I turned away and lay facing the side of the wagon. Tears seeped from my eyes and the wagon rocked with the broken rhythm of my thoughts: My husband is gone! John lives no more. He is dead.

I passed the 5th and today sleeping, waking only to cry and sleep again. What will become of me? My face feels leaden, as if it will never lift in a smile again. The act of speaking is a great effort.

I asked Mrs. Throckmorton if someone was with him when he died, and did he call for me? She said Hiram Watt was with him. She made me sit up and eat, and said tomorrow I must try walking. Then she handed me my journal, saying, "It will do you good to write, empty out all your feelings, and make room inside for God's healing love."

But I am already empty and feel nothing.

May 7, 1863

I don't know where we are. Someone said we are marching to join the rest of Lee's army after its victory at Chancellorsville. I hardly care.

Today when we stopped to pitch camp, Hiram Watt and a few fellows came by to pay their respects. I managed to thank Hiram without breaking down in tears. He fiddled with his hat brim and, blinking, said, "John's last words to me were 'Tell Rosanna I love her.' So I'm tellin' you. Tom was there too, he heard it." At this I wept anew, but afterward felt a little comforted.

Then to please Mrs. Throckmorton, I walked around for twenty minutes and it tired me so much I had to lie down again.

May 8, 1863

This evening I took a longer walk down a little-used road. Mrs. Throckmorton means well with her prayers and ministration, but I wanted to be alone.

Robins and sparrows hopped along the path before me, chirping. May apples shaped like umbrellas spread over the shady floor of the woods, while bluebells nodded at its edge. Yet a curtain seemed to separate me from the freshness of nature. Can the flowers decide not to bloom or the birds decline to sing again because the winter was harsh?

No. But I don't know how they do it—how they keep growing.

May 9, 1863 near Petersburg

Today we forded a creek greatly swollen by the rain. I crossed on Dolly's back near the end, holding on to a rope secured to a tree on either side of the creek. The banks had been beaten into a muddy mire, and the water was turgid. Midstream, I felt the strong pull of the current and was tempted to let it bear me under and away. Through weakness, I believe, I lost hold of the rope, and as we began to drift, I panicked and screamed, clutching Dolly's mane. This startled her and she began to flounder, and water washed over her back, drenching me to the chest. I was terrified, certain that we would be drowned. There was a commotion on the bank, much frantic shouting and waving. I urged Dolly to the shore, and moments later her hooves found the muddy bottom. With a great effort she carried us out of the sucking stream.

It surprised me to discover that though the mind may yearn toward death, some force in the body surges up and demands to live.

May 10, 1863

Still clinging to my steady Dolly, still marching. It matters not where. I scan the ranks of infantry for the bright bandana John always wore around his hat for me. It's a habit. Then I remember he is gone and feel a dull aching deep in my chest.

Tom appeared late in the afternoon, riding a horse with bullet-scarred flanks. I was surprised to see him. I had not thought about his loss, I realized with a twinge of guilt. We were partners in grief, but did not speak of it.

"Did you know you're a free man, Tom?"

He nodded somberly. Sadness weighed down his features.

"Why are you still here, then?"

"I'm obliged to see Mastuh John's possessions rightfully bestowed," he said with formal dignity, handing me John's haversack and mess kit, his canteen, and his rifle. I hung them over the pommel of my saddle, except for the rifle.

"You keep this," I said, unwilling to take the heavy weapon. Tom shook his head firmly.

"That'd be askin' for a heap of trouble," he said.

"Of course. I wasn't thinking," I said.

"An' there's one more thing Mastuh John give me fo' you," said Tom, handing me a small leather pouch. I opened it up to find it stuffed with money.

"Not gambling money!" I said in dismay.

"No, ma'am. You know Mastuh John gave up gambling. This was all his pay he saved up. Said it was to settle a debt to your father."

I sobbed aloud, tears wetting my cheeks. I recalled my rash theft and our mutual shame. To think that John had been planning in secret to make restitution for my wrong! I felt a surge of love and belated longing for my honorable, dear husband.

"It's not really possible to put the past entirely behind us, is it?" I mused, more to myself than to Tom, as I caressed the pouch.

"I'm sorry, ma'am," said Tom, looking close to tears himself. "Well, I'd best be on my way."

"Where are you going now?"

"To Richmond, to accompany Mastuh John's body an' pay my respects to the elder Mastuh Wilcox and his missus. Then I'm goin' north."

"I will come with you to Richmond," I said, making my decision that very moment. All my belongings were with me. I bade farewell to Mrs. Throckmorton, asking her to explain to Dr. Walker that without John, I have no reason to remain with the regiment. She regarded me sadly but did not try to stop me from going, only called out a blessing as I veered away.

May 11, 1863

Though we were only fifteen miles from Richmond, it took us an entire day to cover the distance. Tom had repaired a battered ammunition wagon to carry John's coffin, and a wheel broke, delaying us. The road was crowded with soldiers who touched their caps out of respect as we passed. I wished for a veil to hide my naked sorrow from their eyes. To make better time, we detoured along the James River, passing factories and a prison camp for Yankees. Hundreds of tents were visible crowded together on an islet in the river.

A year ago I fled to Richmond, a foolish girl mourning a Northern boy who never loved her. Today I come home a Southern widow, fully entitled to grieve.

May 12, 1863 Richmond

All of Richmond grieves. It was the funeral of General Stonewall Jackson, hailed as the purest, bravest, and noblest of men. He died from wounds inflicted by the mistake of his own men at Chancellorsville, an ironic but nonetheless tragic end. I saw the procession pass, the general's warhorse with its empty saddle, followed by the black-draped carriage bearing his body. My grief for John flows on the general tide of mourning. Everyone who has lost a brother, husband, son, or father weeps not only for Jackson but for themselves, yet with that crying comes little comfort.

May 14, 1863

John's parents held a small funeral for him in their church. Prayers were spoken and hymns sung without my comprehending them. I have only one question for God: if he is the author of life, then who is responsible for death?

Tom was seated with the other servants behind the Wilcox family, but we did not speak. I wonder if he knows about my theft? He would lose all respect for me. It is time to bare the secret—to confess to my father and restore the money.

May 16, 1863

Alas, I could not bring myself to speak to Father, heaping old shame upon new grief. I tried to write to Margaret but gave up. Mother had already sent the news. Although I long to be in touch with my sister and Lizzie, what can I write that does not seem to beg for their pity?

Living in my family's house is like wearing a shoe that pinches my foot unbearably. Nor can I bear to live in the cottage where John and I spent a few happy weeks and where we planned to raise our own family.

Is there no place that I can call home? Richmond hardly resembles the city I remember. In April women took to the streets and rioted for bread, looting the stores until the militia drove them back. While people are starving, others grow rich running the blockade and parading in the streets like dandies. Everyone talks of slave uprisings, real and imagined. Yankee raiders captured President Davis's Mississippi plantation and most of his 137 slaves fled after robbing the house. Those who are recaptured will be tortured, maybe killed. This is the unseen consequence of Lincoln's freedom proclamation and the bitter fruit of secession and war: no one has a safe or proper home anymore.

May 20, 1863

I cannot shake off this lethargy. I sit in Mother's parlor writing, wearing borrowed black crepe, black cuffs, and a black collar. I am too young to be a widow—younger even than Margaret was when Joseph Roth died. Did she feel such guilt and anger as I do? One minute I blame John's death on the generals and presidents who stirred up this hornet's nest of war. The next minute I blame myself for being unable to save him. Then my other great character flaw rises up to rebuke me: lack of steadfastness. Once again I have abandoned my responsibilities and run away from the scene of my grief. I had hoped marriage would steady me, but lacking my husband, I bob and drift like a boat without an anchor.

May 25, 1863

In a volume of poems in Papa's library, I happened upon an elegy written by Tennyson on the death of his friend. It contains this memorable verse:

I hold it true, whate'er befall;
I feel it, when I sorrow most;
'Tis better to have loved and lost
Than never to have loved at all.

May this inspire me to put aside my vain regrets and rather dwell upon the brief happiness John and I enjoyed.

May 26, 1863

The business of settling John's affairs is almost complete, the signing of tax documents in the lawyer's office and the filing of pension requests. Sad indeed, that a man's life is reduced to a stack of papers.

Mother tells me that nurses are sorely needed at Chimborazo Hospital. Perhaps next week I will feel more like going there to inquire.

May 28, 1863

Today was a day of reckoning.

I returned the deed to the cottage to Mr. and Mrs. Wilcox. I sold most of its furnishings, taking a loss on everything we had purchased, but that is no matter. I told Mother and Father that I plan to lodge in a respectable rooming house and seek employment. To my surprise, they did not object.

Then, taking a deep breath, I produced the leather pouch with John's savings, combined with the money I had gotten from selling our furniture. I began my well-rehearsed explanation, taking care to emphasize my own guilt. I concluded, fighting back tears, "So it wasn't a matter of impropriety, as you thought. It was worse. I was dishonest and deceitful. I am sorry and I ask your forgiveness."

Mother hid her face and began weeping. Father looked at me, a struggle evident on his face. Then he took me in his arms and held me tightly. It has been years since he did so.

"Rosanna, my dear, that is all water under the bridge. Let it go, let it go. I forgive you," he kept murmuring, his voice breaking.

When we had all dried our eyes, Father insisted that I keep the money to establish myself in a new lodging. Mother kissed me and said she loved me. For the first time in years, I am at peace with them.

June 2, 1863

I was writing a note to the lawyer when a knock came at the kitchen door, and as the cook was away, I answered it. There stood Tom, dressed plainly but well. I led him into the drawing room, but he seemed uncomfortable there and remained standing. He did not immediately state his business, and I wondered why he had come.

"Do you need money?" I asked, ashamed of my selfishness. "You must have a portion of John's legacy, for you served him all his life, while I was his wife not even a year."

Tom shook his head, saying Mr. and Mrs. Wilcox had provided for him.

"At least let me thank you, for everything you ever did for my husband. It has been an honor to know you," I said, extending my hand. He obliged me by shaking it.

"You're welcome an' all, Miz Wilcox, but I ain't goin' nowhere just yet," he said with a firmness that startled me. "I done promised Mastuh John I would look after you if he was to die, an' be sure you would get on all right and keep goin' like you was. An' with due respect, ma'am, you don't look like you're doin' too well."

The tears pooled in my eyes at the compassion in his voice. I looked down at my ill-fitting black dress and clasped my hands to keep them from trembling.

"What do you mean, 'keep going like I was?'"

"John was right proud of you bein' part of the company and takin' such good care of all the men that was sick or hurt. For all the suffrin' he went through with bein' shot and gettin' the typhoid and all, I ain't never seen him so happy as he was since he married you. There, I've said my piece."

Tom's words were like a slim ray of light through a dark cloud. I had made John happy! And he had been proud of my work after all.

"Why, do you think I should return to my duties? That John would wish it?" I asked, more than surprised at the idea.

"That's not for me to say, Miz Wilcox." Tom looked away. "Perhaps I already said too much."

"No, Tom. You didn't."

He stood there while I tried to gather my thoughts, which were all in turmoil. Indeed, why should I stop my work on behalf of others because my own husband died? I was a capable nurse, and my services were still needed. Perhaps the work would even help to heal my grief.

"I will go back!" I said, grasping both his hands. "Tom, you have righted my ship and restored its course. Thank you."

To his credit he did not flinch, though I think I embarrassed him.

"It'd be best if I escorted you," he offered.

"My affairs here are almost settled. Give me two days," I said.

June 8, 1863 Essex County, along the Rappahannock River

It took me three days, not two, to finish settling John's estate and gather what meager provisions I could obtain in this starved city. Mother seemed newly hurt and bewildered, while Father, perceiving my determination, would not allow her to hinder me.

Tom hitched his horse to the wagon that had brought John's casket home, and I rode Dolly as before. Once we locate the 1st Virginia, he will continue northward. I wonder how we will find the regiment, but Tom plans to follow the river northwest until we overtake them as they march to meet the rest of Lee's army.

June 11, 1863 near Fredericksburg

Dr. Walker will be pleased. After a number of stops for supplies, I now have a substantial cache of sulfates, laudanum, candles, bandages, soap, and a portable medical kit for my use. I pray we are not robbed. Perhaps I should have brought John's Enfield rifle rather than leaving it with his father.

We took a few wrong turns before a farmer directed us to the road we sought. Unmistakably, an army has marched through here recently, strewing swords, mess kits, blankets, and garbage. A film of dirt covers this debris and the fences and fields, due to the clouds of dust stirred up by their passing. Where they pitched camp, the fields are trampled bare and scorched in patches from cooking fires.

June 13, 1863 south of Culpeper

Today we came within sight of the army's rear, and as we approached the hospital wagons, I felt my spirits lift with anticipation. When I embraced Mrs. Throckmorton, she gave me a knowing smile, as if she expected my return.

"I can't even count all the soldiers who asked about you and were disappointed that you had gone. As if these old hands of mine weren't capable enough," she said with pretended gruffness.

"I'm back now. I'm sorry for leaving. Only please don't treat me like a deserter and shoot me," I said, and we both smiled.

Dr. Walker seemed surprised to see me and was grateful for the supplies and medicines.

June 20, 1863 near Winchester

Last week, following the rendezvous of the armies in Culpeper, we began the march due north. Lee's army is in three corps under generals Ewell, Hill, and Longstreet, who is in command of the 1st Virginia. Tom changed his mind about going north. For now he remains with the regiment and is being paid to take care of the officers' horses. It seems that he also has developed unlikely loyalties and affections.

This morning we struck camp to march due north toward Martinsburg in West Virginia. Rumors about our destination have been flying for days. I hoped it was only the wishful talk of restless soldiers. But today the report is confirmed as true.

General Lee, with his full army now amassed together, will invade Pennsylvania and bring this laggard, drawn-out war to a head.

Part 2

———◆———

Lizzie

———❖———

Chapter 25

The war was two years old that June of 1863. Children who had been babies when the volunteers went off were now toddling around and starting to talk. Ben had grown about six inches. My mother had more gray hair, Margaret a few new lines around her mouth. I was still ordinary Lizzie Allbauer. I ran a butcher shop and had a liking for a boy who, for all I knew, took no interest in me. I thought about Papa and Luke every day and prayed for their safety. I wondered if Papa would detect anything different about me if he could see me now, at age seventeen and a half. Would he notice the inner strength Mama said I had?

I doubted I was very strong if I couldn't even summon the courage to tell Martin Weigel that I liked him. Even worse, he had said nothing to me. Our conversations at work were brief and businesslike. He knew as well as I did that the annual ice-cream social was approaching. I hoped he would ask me to go, but he never mentioned it. Did he have his eye on some other girl? I wondered who she could be and if she was pretty.

The second Sunday of June arrived. I went to the ice-cream social with Mama, determined to enjoy myself. The grounds of the Theological Seminary on top of Oak Ridge were dotted with white canopies, and trestle tables groaned under the weight of pies, cakes, meat, and fruit. Sure enough, courting couples were everywhere, walking hand in hand or sitting on blankets spread in the shade. Boys and girls lined up to turn the crank on one of the ice-cream freezers. I wanted to join them but felt too old for childish pastimes. So I merely observed the gaiety around me, thinking it strange that life went on as usual in Gettysburg. Despite the war, people were still capable of plain joys.

In the field Ben and the other boys ran a three-legged race and shouted as they tumbled over each other like a pack of half-grown dogs. Then the older boys took the field, Martin among them. I watched him join in the rituals of back slapping and fist pumping. When the race began, I clapped and cheered as his long legs became a mere blur, and his team finished in first place. I waited to offer my congratulations as he came off the field. Perhaps I would ask if he wanted to go for strawberries and cream. But Martin went off with the other boys, and they loaded up their plates with sausages and potatoes.

Disappointed, I wandered over to the dessert tents and filled a plate with fresh-picked strawberries. They had been slow to ripen, for spring had come late because winter had lingered until April. Now I savored each berry with its tiny crunchy seeds and soft red flesh and even licked my fingers, for no one was watching me. Ginnie and the other girls were sitting on a blanket, gossiping. Mama and the ladies stood in the shade of an oak tree, cooling themselves with palmetto fans. By the quick and agitated motions of their wrists, I knew they were discussing the war. I moved closer to hear their conversation.

"I know about the governor's warning, but I don't believe an attack on our state is imminent," Mrs. Pierpont was saying with her usual confidence. "We ought not to worry. Why would the Confederate army come to Gettysburg? Harrisburg or Philadelphia would be their aim."

"Well, I *am* afraid, living along Chambersburg Pike," said Mrs.

Brodhead, showing her irregular teeth. "I have hardly had a good night's sleep since those rebel cavalry came through last October."

"We've had so many false alarms," said Mrs. Wade. "But one of these days it will be the real thing."

"I am not so worried about a mere band of lawless Confederates," said my mother, looking into the distance. I knew she was thinking of Papa in captivity somewhere.

"Lizzie, come and join us!" It was Ginnie calling. I went and sat next to her, relieved to be included in a group. The girls were complaining about the lack of suitors, since all the young men had enlisted.

"And who wants to be seen with a mere boy? Why, I'm eighteen now," Annie was saying, as if her recent birthday were a great accomplishment.

"I saw Martin leave with those country boys," Ginnie said to me behind her hand. "That's too bad for you."

I shrugged, pretending not to care.

"Now, I could fancy that Weigel fellow," Annie said, apparently overhearing Ginnie. "The way his hair falls over his eyes makes him look dashing."

Was she taunting me? No one would describe Martin as "dashing."

"Well aren't you the fickle one, Annie!" I said, matching her light tone. "You'll break my brother's heart for sure." I smiled to show that I meant no offense, but she looked sore anyway.

"Come, Ginnie," she said, standing up and smoothing her skirt. "Let's walk by those two soldiers over there and find out if they are on furlough and for how long."

I was relieved to be excluded from Annie's invitation. I watched her waltz past the soldiers and pause, waiting to be noticed. Ginnie stood by demurely, while Annie preened like a bird. The soldiers nodded politely but moved away, and Annie's plumage wilted. I felt embarrassed on her behalf. Annie and Ginnie returned with their heads down. I sprang to my feet.

"I am going to climb up to the cupola in the seminary," I announced, hurrying off before anyone could join me.

Inside the building, the marble floors gave off a welcome coolness. My footsteps echoed in the hallways. I found the staircase leading to the cupola, and on the way up passed a girl and her fellow coming down the stairs, holding hands. From four stories above the ground I watched people moving between the tents and blankets and chairs below. In the distance I could see a patchwork of fields divided by fences, an occasional farmhouse, and rolling hills and woodlands extending for miles. To the east clustered the houses, stores, and steepled churches of Gettysburg. I decided it was good to live in an insignificant place where nothing momentous happened. I would wait for love to come to me, if it was meant to, not risk foolishness and hurt by seeking it out.

Soon the sedate and pleasant ice-cream social was a thing of the past. Around noon the very next day, carriages and wagons began to roll into town laden with chickens and pigs and household goods, and people cried, "The rebels are coming! Move out, move out!" Confused travelers headed every which way, for no one knew exactly where the rebels were. Someone said they were raiding Chambersburg again, while others said they were coming up from Maryland. I ran to the depot hoping to learn more. There I saw Annie Baumann's father and other shopkeepers loading their goods onto railroad cars. Even the bankers had emptied their vaults and were sending the money to Philadelphia for safekeeping.

Infected by the panic around me, I ran home to find our neighbors piling their furniture into a wagon.

"Shouldn't we leave too, Mama?" I realized I was wringing my hands.

"No, we are staying right here. Grace ought to be resting in bed until her time comes, not bouncing to Baltimore." If Mama was worried, she hid it well. My own mouth was dry with fear.

That night I started up from a restless sleep. It was after midnight. I went to the window just as an elderly gentleman ran crookedly by, huffing with each step and crying, "The rebels are on their way here, burning everything in their path!" Up and down the street, neighbors leaned out of their windows and ran outside in their nightclothes. Someone shouted that the sky to the south was orange with flames. All I could see was blackness over the housetops along York Street. I ran to Mama's room and found her already awake and dressed.

"So we *are* leaving?" I said, relieved. "I'll wake the others." But Mama seized my hand before I could leave the room.

"No! Not even the rebels would burn a town full of innocent people," she said firmly. "Stay here while I go out and see what the commotion is all about."

For what seemed like hours I waited, my mind racing with fearful possibilities. In the lamplight, the darkened window reflected my face, a picture of worry.

When I heard Mama at the door, I rushed to meet her.

"What did you find out? Why were you gone so long?"

"I had to wait for the news at the telegraph office. Twenty-seven houses were destroyed by fire in Emmitsburg. It was an accident, not a rebel attack. So I went to reassure Margaret. She was in a panic, watching the glowing sky from her bedroom window." Mama sat down heavily.

"Oh, those poor people! But at least it was only a fire."

"That's not all, Lizzie. The rebels did go through Chambersburg again, and this time they took prisoner all the Negroes they could find." Mama paused. "We must look out for Amos and Grace."

I didn't sleep the rest of the night. When the rising sun turned the sky pink, I got up and sat on the front steps, dazed with tiredness, as a cock crowed.

The rebels did not appear that day, nor the day after. I felt like a rabbit waiting for a hidden fox to pounce. The governor called for an emergency militia to defend the state. Even Mama decided it was time to take some action.

"If the Confederates come raiding, we won't make it easy for them," she said. She had Amos and Ben lock all the fresh meat in the small cellar beneath the shop with blocks of ice to keep it from spoiling. Then she visited Mrs. Pierpont, who agreed to let us use her large cellar for the rest of our stores. Amos fitted it with a thick door and a heavy lock, and he, Ben, and Martin cleared the smokehouse and moved the cured meat and barrels of pork there. I removed the signs from the butcher shop and hid all the knives and tools and account books so the shop appeared abandoned.

There remained the matter of the livestock penned behind the warehouse. Mama asked Amos to drive the stock to York for Mr. Schupp to keep until the danger was past. I saw the purpose behind Mama's request. So did Amos.

"I'll do it, Miz Allbauer, but I'm comin' right back to protect my wife an' this family, like I promised. I don't aim to hide out."

Mama asked Martin to go along and help Amos, but he said he was needed on the farm. I suspected his mother wouldn't let him go, and wished he would show some backbone. Ben pleaded that he was old enough to ride with Amos, and to my surprise, Mama agreed. Then I realized her cleverness. If the rebels came through Gettysburg in the next few days, Ben and Amos would both be out of harm's way. But what about the rest of us?

It rained the night of June 21 and the roads turned to muck, but by midafternoon of the next day the ground had hardened enough for travel. Amos would herd the dozen head of cattle, while Ben drove the wagon full of pigs. I felt a stab of worry as I watched my little brother climb into the driver's seat and take the reins. But with manly seriousness, he nodded to me and Mama, then flicked the reins. The pigs poked their snouts through the slats and squealed in protest as the wagon rolled away.

When Amos and Ben had disappeared, Mama looked in the opposite direction.

"Mr. Brodhead and a crew of men are riding out Chambersburg Pike today, Sarah told me. They aim to cut enough trees to block the road through the pass. That leaves"—she paused to count—"eight other roads leading into the town."

I knew what she was thinking. From which direction would the rebels come into town? Not knowing, how could anyone stop them?

It stormed again that night. Mama, Grace, and I sat in the parlor while the rain pelted the roof of the house and blew slantwise against the windows. Though Mama was nearby, with Amos, Papa, Luke, and Ben gone, I had never felt more alone.

Lizzie

———◆◆———

Chapter 26

On Wednesday, June 24, with still no sign of rebels, Grace set out to do some shopping, and Mama made me go with her. Though her belly was as big as a pumpkin, Grace stepped nimbly along. She clearly didn't need my help.

We stopped to watch the new Adams County cavalry drilling on the Diamond. Captain Bell looked like he had his hands full with his men, mostly Mexican War veterans older than Papa and some lads who looked as if they'd never held guns before. I doubted they could do much to protect the town from invading rebels.

"I wish Amos and Ben would hurry home. I'd feel a lot safer," I remarked to Grace.

"Just two more days," she said.

"More like three, I'd guess. They've got twenty-five miles to cover each way, and that road is bound to be crowded and full of ruts."

At South Street near the tannery we saw a family of Negroes laden with bundles. Even the littlest child dragged a burlap sack. Amos had said that many Negroes had taken to hiding from the rebels in the rocky gullies and thick woods of Culp's Hill.

"You'll be safer with Mama and me, especially if the baby comes," I said, hoping Grace was not thinking of joining them.

She nodded. "He's not due for another month yet," she said.

At the newspaper office, we heard that the train bringing the new volunteer militia back to Gettysburg had hit a cow and derailed, stranding the troops a good ways from town. They would be useless in case of a rebel attack in the night.

But the rebels didn't come that night or the next day. They were thought to be in the mountains to the west, probably raiding farms and driving horses and cattle back to their camp.

Then Friday morning wagons began to roll back into town from the east; people who had fled to York and Baltimore were coming home, believing the crisis to be over. They reminded me of dogs with their tails between their legs, ashamed for having panicked so easily. But there was no sign of Amos and Ben.

About noon the whistle of a train sounded, and the news quickly spread that the volunteer militia had finally arrived. I ran to the corner just as they marched by, resplendent in their new uniforms and bearing shiny rifles. Even if they were raw recruits, with less than a week of training, their sheer numbers—nearly seven hundred men—inspired confidence. Half of Gettysburg had turned out to welcome the volunteers with cheers and food. A photographer from Tyson Studios huddled under a black cloth, trying to capture the scene with his boxy camera. I found myself next to Annie Baumann, who was standing with her father in front of their store. She handed me a small flag to wave.

"The sight of these boys'll make the Johnnies run right back over the mountains!" Mr. Baumann predicted as the militia, with Captain Bell's cavalry in the lead, headed west along Chambersburg Pike. It was comforting to know that hundreds of soldiers were stationed between us and the rebels.

A light rain began to fall, and I hurried to the butcher shop, but only a few customers stopped in. It must have been about midafternoon when I was startled by the sound of hoofbeats, as if an entire cavalry were galloping through town. I couldn't see anything from the shop, so I locked up and ran home, thinking of my mother and Grace alone in the house. As I rounded the corner onto York Street, the crack of rifle fire made me halt in my tracks. The sound bounced off the stone and brick houses so that I could not tell where it had come from. Then another shot sounded, and a horse appeared around the corner, whinnying and foaming at the mouth. Its rider wore a faded gray uniform and waved a revolver. When he saw me, he let out a high-pitched holler and fired into the air. The sound stunned my ears.

The rebels were in Gettysburg!

The gray-clad soldier passed so near to me that I felt the heat of his horse's body and smelled acrid sweat. Stumbling through our gate I flung myself against the door, which opened suddenly, pitching me into Mama's arms.

"Thank God you're back! What took you so long? Grace is in the cellar; go and join her."

"No, I'm staying with you." Despite my terror, I wouldn't leave her.

"Don't disobey me, Lizzie!"

More shots splintered the air. We dropped to our knees so that we were below the level of the windowsill.

"You have to come with me," I said, grasping her arm.

So neither of us moved. Boots tramped in the street, wheels squealed, men shouted, and we waited for the next outburst of gunfire.

"I thought the militia would defend us," I said. "What happened?"

"I suspect those fresh recruits just lost their first battle," Mama said grimly.

A sudden knocking startled us. I peeked through the curtains to see four soldiers at the door. They were ragged and dirty, their trousers torn, their hair matted. One of the men raised his gun and rapped the butt against the door, more sharply this time. I felt my heart hammer against my ribs.

"They're rebel soldiers, Mama. We must hide! Quickly!"

"No! If they think no one is home, they will break in and search the house."

Before I could protest, she had opened the door and stood facing the soldiers. I decided she was out of her mind and would doom us all.

The rebels took off their battered hats and the one who had knocked on the door cleared his throat and said, "We're right hungry, ma'am, and we'd be ever so grateful if you was to spare us sumpin' to eat."

I could barely understand what the man was asking for. He said "raht" for "right," "may-um" for "ma'am," and "spay-er" for spare. But he looked Mama in the eye like an honest man.

Mama hesitated, then motioned for the soldiers to enter. They trailed her almost meekly to the kitchen, where they dropped their knapsacks and rifles on the floor like schoolboys. I noticed their shoes were nothing more than scraps of leather tied to their feet with rags. Mama laid bread and bacon on the table and the soldiers devoured the food like starving men. She told me to fetch a pitcher of fresh water and fill their canteens. My hands shook and I spilled a considerable amount of the water on the floor. One of the soldiers smiled at me, and I stiffened, full of distrust.

When they were finished, they wiped their mouths on their sleeves and stood up. They looked at each other and around the room. I held my breath, too afraid to move, as one of them laid a hand on the cellar door.

"The privy is out back," Mama said, opening the kitchen door. The rebels picked up their gear, nodded their thanks, and left.

My throat was dry, but I began to chatter like a hoarse jay.

"They looked pitiful, didn't they? Their hair must have been full of lice. And they smelled awful, but they were polite. I thought I would die with fear, but really, they weren't so terrible—"

I saw Mama sink into a chair, looking pale from the efforts of her hospitality, but after a few deep breaths, she pinked up a bit.

The cellar door opened and Grace stepped out, carrying an old ax that belonged in the shed.

"Nex' time we face the rebs together," she said, her black eyes flashing. "You ain't riskin' yore selves for me."

Mama said not to be foolish and made her go back to the cellar. The rest of the day she and I took turns peering out the windows for more rebels, but all was quiet. Just after dark, I stepped into the street where I could hear strains of a band playing "Dixie."

"They're still here," I called to Mama.

"Come inside, Lizzie!" Her voice sounded anxious.

But something had caught my eye, a glow in the sky to the northeast. Were the rebels burning the town? Before raising an alarm, I wanted to be sure. So I dashed toward the depot to get a better look. A small crowd had gathered, looking east along the railroad tracks as the bridge over Rock Creek burned furiously. The flames leaped higher, engulfing one car after another, until the entire bridge with seven burning cars collapsed into the creek bed.

"Damn rebels just destroyed the railroad!" growled one man.

"At least it's not our houses burning," said another.

"They cut the telegraph wires too. Now nothing can come in or go out of here—not troops, not news, not food."

"We're in trouble now."

I returned home to find Mama pacing the kitchen in agitation.

"Don't worry, it's only the railroad bridge they've burned."

She turned on me. "Elizabeth Ann Allbauer, I told you to come back, but you ran away instead! Must I put a leash on you to get you to obey me?"

"I only went to see if we were in danger from the fire!" I shot back, my own temper flaring.

"Do you think I want to lose all my children and my husband, too? I had no idea where you'd gone," Mama said, on the verge of tears.

"I wouldn't do anything foolish, Mama. You've got to trust me more," I said, putting my arms around her.

That night we slept on piles of blankets in the cellar, where it was as dark and quiet as a grave. In the morning the streets appeared deserted, and no sound came from the town square.

"Have they gone away?" Mama wondered aloud

"I'll find out," I offered, pulling on my shoes. "I promise to be careful."

First I checked the butcher shop and was relieved to find it undisturbed, though the windows of a nearby store had been broken. Knowing the telegraph was down, I headed to the courthouse as the likeliest place to hear news. About thirty people were listening to Mr. Kendlehart describe the prior day's events. He said our militia had met up with five thousand Confederates along Chambersburg Pike. Only one soldier was killed, but two hundred had been captured. Then the rebels had released all the prisoners and sent them home! This made me hope they would let Papa go, too.

After the battle, their General Early had come into town and demanded three tons of bacon, a thousand pairs of shoes, whiskey, and other supplies—or five thousand dollars in cash. Mr. Kendlehart told the general the truth: that all the town's goods and money had been shipped away. After searching the stores and finding them empty, there was nothing for the rebels to do but to move on.

"General Early was too late!" said one man, and his joke was greeted with laughter.

Everyone had a story about the soldiers demanding food or stealing chickens or horses. Not all the rebels were as polite as those who had visited us, but not a single person reported being harmed. We had been shaken up a little, that was all. Ginnie Wade ran up to me with the news that her sister had just given birth to a baby boy. I hugged her and even waved to Annie Baumann. I felt like dancing, I was so relieved. The war had come to Gettysburg and gone away again.

"Mr. Kendlehart," called out a voice in the crowd. "Where did the rebels go when they left here?"

"Why, they headed east, on to York. That was their intent all along," he replied.

At once my joy and relief gave way to cold fear. Amos and Ben were traveling on the York Road.

Lizzie

Chapter 27

It was Sunday, June 28, six days since Amos and Ben had left. Mama and I went to St. James, where every pew was full. Reverend Essig preached on the importance of being ready for Judgment Day in order to escape God's wrath. I would have preferred a more positive theme, in light of what we had just come through.

All afternoon Mama kept going to the door, where she would stand motionless, listening. Grace rocked in the parlor.

"Mama, do you think they ran into the rebel cavalry?" I asked.

She shook her head slowly back and forth. She didn't know any more than I did.

"Amos'll hunker down soon as he senses danger," said Grace. "I know they's all right," she whispered, rubbing her belly.

That night and all day Monday, rain fell from gray skies. I opened the shop and sat in a chair in the doorway, watching the raindrops plop into muddy puddles in the street. I missed the whistle and rumble of the train and thought of the ruined railroad bridge. With every wooden creak or clop of horse's feet, I looked up in hope that Amos and Ben had returned, only to be disappointed.

To my surprise, Martin Weigel came into the shop. He took off his hat and a puddle of rain water formed on the floor around him. I managed a half smile of greeting.

"There are no deliveries today, Martin."

"I know," he said, still dripping. "I think I'll just dry off a bit."

I wondered why he had come, but, being lonesome, I didn't want him to leave.

"I saw you at the ice-cream social," I said nervously, watching his face for a response.

"I saw you too. You had a pretty dress on."

My heart skipped, then beat a little faster.

"Why didn't you come and talk to me?"

"I wanted to, Lizzie, but the fellows would have teased me."

I didn't know whether to be pleased or hurt by his answer.

"Did you hear the news?" he asked, changing the subject. "York surrendered to General Early and gave up twenty-eight thousand dollars in cash and a ton of supplies."

My eyebrows shot up. "Goodness! I'll bet half of that was money and goods that our merchants sent there for safekeeping. But where did you get the news? The telegraph is down."

"I saw Mr. Rupp, the tanner, returning from York this morning."

"Did he run into any rebels?"

"No, but he said there was fighting in Hanover."

"Why, that's only a few miles off the York Road. Did he say if he had seen Amos and Ben along the way?"

Martin hesitated before replying. He must have seen how worried I looked.

"He asked if my butcher had come back from York yet, and when I shook my head, he said Amos might have a bad time of it if he doesn't stay clear of the Johnnies running everywhere."

I put my hand to my mouth and blinked back tears. Martin took a step forward.

"Maybe . . . I can help," he began. He looked up again, his forehead creased in an expression of seriousness. "I'll ride out and look for them. You can come along, if you want."

I gulped. Martin even seemed surprised by what he had said. But he met my gaze steadily with his grayish eyes.

"My mother would never allow me," I said. "I can't leave her and Grace."

"And my mother would tan my hide all the way to next Sunday," Martin said with a wry grin. "But she doesn't have to know. I'll sneak away."

"I can't let you do that for us," I protested. "Amos and Ben will be back tonight or tomorrow, I'm sure of it."

"Amos has been a good boss to me. I want to help you and your ma. If they are not back by tomorrow night, I'll go looking for them the next morning," Martin said firmly.

"Wait," I said, touching his sleeve. "You were afraid to speak to me at the social with the other fellows around, but you're not afraid to go out looking for Amos and Ben with rebels everywhere?"

Martin merely shrugged, put on his hat, and went back out into the rain. I stood in the doorway, baffled. I would wait until Wednesday morning, I decided, to see if Martin Weigel was as brave as his word.

That night, Mama and I went to a Ladies Aid meeting at the Lutheran church on Chambersburg Pike. We listened as Mrs. Pierpont read from a Baltimore newspaper that Lincoln had replaced his top commander with a new one, General George Meade. Mrs. Weigel sat next to me, rolling bandages with rapid fingers.

"The rebels must think we're getting desperate, changing generals like they were *Hosen—ach,* I mean trousers," she said, tapping her forehead.

"So far none of our generals has been any match for Lee. If he were on our side, the war would have been over long ago," said Mrs. Rupp, the tanner's wife. Her bold statement was met with a surprised silence. "Well, it's true," she insisted.

Mrs. Weigel leaned over and said to me, "*Bei Himmel,* this is one time I'm glad I don't live in town. I feel safer *auf das Land.* It makes me nervous to travel by Long Lane, where *die Negerin* live, you know." She tended to lapse into German when she became distressed.

"Why?" I asked. Then I remembered Martin telling me his mother did not like Negroes.

"*Sie konnt Mühe machen,* make trouble. If the rebels come back again. *Ja?*"

I could not agree with her, so I just held my tongue.

"I don't think we've seen the last of those rebels," said Mrs. Brodhead in her worried way. "Every night I see their campfires burning on the mountainside near Cashtown."

Mrs. Pierpont, with her usual authority, attempted to settle the question.

"The Confederate army has come through once already and found nothing worth taking. They will not return. There is no strategic or economic reason to do battle over our humble town."

"I hope you're right," said Mrs. Brodhead, but she didn't sound convinced.

"Lizzie, *meine Liebe,*" said Mrs. Weigel, laying her hand on mine, "if those rebels come back to town, you and your *Mutti* come to *mein Haus*. It is like a fort. They will not get in."

I smiled politely, thinking that Martin's poor mother had no idea what he had promised to do for me. I felt a bit guilty for keeping it from her.

When the meeting ended, Mama and I climbed the church's bell tower in order to see the rebel campfires Mrs. Brodhead was so worried about. They appeared as tiny red dots scattered along the base of the mountains between Gettysburg and Chambersburg. Even as I watched the distant flickering, I felt certain that God would never allow Gettysburg to be destroyed in battle. It would be a punishment none of us deserved. I was certainly no saint, but I did attend church almost every week and prayed every day. I would even pray for the entire Confederate army, to show my good intentions. Standing there in the church tower, even with the enemy in sight, I felt reassured. I reached for Mama's hand and squeezed it.

The next morning, that fragile peace was shaken. It was Tuesday, the last day of June. Despite the bright, sunny skies, there came a rumble like that of a gathering storm. I heard shouting in the streets and yelled for Grace to hide. The shouts changed to whistling and cheers. Soldiers were coming all right, but this time they were Union cavalrymen riding up from the south, stirring up huge clouds of dust. So instead of hiding, we joined our neighbors in handing out pies and cakes and sandwiches to the passing soldiers, expecting that they would ride on through town and head north.

But General Buford and his cavalry apparently intended to stop in Gettysburg. Word flew around that they were building defenses to the west, beyond the Lutheran Seminary, and that pickets were guarding every road that led into town. Soldiers descended on the shops, purchasing shirts, tobacco, and trinkets. They dusted off their blue uniforms and posed for photographs at Mr. Tyson's studio. Then they formed long lines in front of the taverns, until the general halted the sale of liquor in town.

Seeing the opportunity for some business, I brought several hams and smoked sausages out of storage. Mama didn't want me to be at the store alone, so Grace came with me and we sold all the meat as well as several jars of preserves. I didn't know whether to be flattered or angry when one of the soldiers called me a "pretty little country girl" and winked at me. Pretending not to hear him, I asked his companion if he knew whether the road to York was clear of rebels. He said he didn't even know where York was, and they left the shop laughing. Grace mumbled good riddance to them, and we went home in worried silence. It had now been eight days with no sign of Amos and Ben.

As I was drifting off to sleep that night, I heard the sound of gravel hitting my window. I opened the sash and peered out into the darkness. After a moment I made out the figure of Martin in the street below.

"I didn't want to wake your ma. Ben and Amos back yet?" he asked in a loud whisper.

"No. Wait there. I'm coming down." I started for the stairs, then realized I was in my nightgown. I grabbed my frock but decided it would take too long to get dressed. I saw in the mirror that my hair was a mess, too. Smoothing it down, I grabbed a long shawl and wrapped it around me for modesty, then dashed barefoot down the stairs.

Martin took a step back when he saw me. I wished I had taken the time to put on my dress.

"Sorry," I said, "I was almost asleep."

"Wow, you look . . . different. With your hair all around your shoulders like that."

"Martin, you shouldn't go," I said quickly. "Let's ask ask one of the cavalry officers for help finding them."

"I expect they have other concerns, Lizzie. Don't you trust me?"

"I do. I just don't want . . . anything to happen to you. Your mother would be upset."

"That's thoughtful of you," he said with a smile. I could barely see his face in the moonlight.

"Martin, I know I should feel safer with our soldiers all over town, but I don't. Do you think they're planning to fight a battle here?"

"I don't know," he said. He reached out and tugged up the edge of my shawl. It had slipped down, exposing my shoulder, and I hadn't even noticed. I hoped he could not see me blushing in the dark.

"Hey, I have to get home now. I'll come by here tomorrow morning before I go looking for them. Don't tell anyone, not even your mother, or she'll try and stop me."

I nodded as he turned to leave. So he was really going to go through with it!

"Wait!" I called after him. "Let me come with you."

But Martin had already disappeared into the darkness.

Rosanna

Chapter 28

June 28, 1863 near Chambersburg, Penn

Two weeks have passed since my return to the regiment. A dozen times a day something reminds me of John, and I feel again the pain of losing him. It subsides only when I lose myself in my work. And goodness knows there is plenty of it. Even during the summer months, disease runs rampant among men weakened by two years of unremitting duty under poor conditions.

It is strange to be in Pennsylvania as the enemy, when I intend to harm no one. The region looks so prosperous, compared to the devastation in Virginia. I wonder if part of Lee's motive for invading the North was to feed his hard-up soldiers. Indeed, our men rob empty houses and steal chickens and food, despite orders to the contrary. Some do it from desperation, others with a spirit of revenge I cannot condone. No wonder the citizens of Chambersburg regard us sullenly. Mrs. Throckmorton and I have had some success in persuading them to provide from their gardens and pantries in exchange for a guard posted to prevent worse damage to their property. Meanwhile the officers are trying to restore discipline by rounding up deserters and stragglers. They brought a very inebriated Hiram Watt back to camp. He seldom drank while my husband was his friend, but without John's moderating influence, Watt has fallen in with worse company. Sadly I must no longer associate with him, out of concern for my own reputation.

I cannot stop thinking about the road through the South Mountains that would take me to Gettysburg in hours. Margaret and Lizzie cannot know that I am only twenty-five miles away. Dare I attempt to visit them while we are camped near Chambersburg? What a surprise it would be!

June 29, 1863 Chambersburg

Still we wait. Rumors change from hour to hour. I had thought Harrisburg was Lee's destination. But he appears to be biding his time here, waiting—with growing impatience—for General "Jeb" Stuart and his cavalry to return and tell him where the Union army is. Is the great General Lee really so blind without Stuart?

Tomorrow I will ride to Gettysburg, on the pretext of looking for medicinal herbs in the woods around Cashtown. I long to see my sister and Lizzie again! I wonder if they think of me fondly, as I do them.

June 30, 1863 Chambersburg

There has been no sign of Stuart, but Lee has discovered by other means (a spy perhaps?) that the federal army, with a new commander, is near Frederick, Maryland—closer than he thought. But everyone deems this new Union general—I don't even recall his name—as weak and inexperienced as all the others.

According to General Gordon's wife, usually a reliable source, General Heth's division will set out in the morning for Gettysburg. Reportedly a warehouse full of shoes waits there, and only a small contingent of Union cavalry guards the town. This sounds like a mere rumor to me, for to my knowledge, Gettysburg has no more than the usual number of shoemakers. In any case, I would not risk a confrontation over a few pairs of shoes! But the generals and their spies undoubtedly know better.

Our company will remain in the rear with Pickett's division. If Heth's men encounter the cavalry, there will probably be a small skirmish not rising to the status of a battle. Dr. Walker has ordered us to prepare the hospital here for possible casualties. Therefore I must postpone my plans to ride to Gettysburg.

Lizzie

—◆◆—

Chapter 29

I woke up with my cotton nightdress clinging wetly to my chest and legs. In the wide-open window, the curtains barely stirred. But birds still chirped and trilled. It was Wednesday, the first of July. I knew that Ben and Amos had not returned in the night. I rolled quickly out of bed, washed my face in the basin, and dressed, all the while listening for Martin. A distant *pop-pop* came to my ears, like the sound Clara made with her lips when she pretended to be a fish. It could have been someone chopping wood or nailing shingles to a roof. I twisted my hair and pinned it high off my damp neck.

Downstairs Mama and Grace leaned over the kitchen table kneading masses of bread dough. Grace's belly, now the size of a watermelon, got in her way. Several bowls of puffy dough awaited a second kneading. Why were they making so much bread?

"Has Martin come by yet this morning?" I asked, striving for a casual tone as I poured a cup of bitter coffee. "Shall we open up the shop?"

"No," said Mama tersely. "And no."

I decided that Martin had probably come and gone without anyone seeing him. Then the popping noise sounded again, a little louder, like the cracking of pins and balls against each other in a game of bowling. I looked at Mama, suspecting the truth.

"The battle started just after daybreak," she said.

"Where?" I asked, feeling my stomach go sour already.

"To the west, more than two miles away. We're not in any danger here."

"Two miles—why, that's close! What should we do?"

"Work as usual. It's wash day," Mama answered, her hands still mired in dough.

With a growing sense of dread, I began my chores, fetching enough wood to stoke the oven for the entire day and pumping buckets of water for the washing. From time to time, we paused to listen at the front door, hearing muffled explosions and rifle fire to the west. At least, I thought, Martin would have headed east, possibly before the fighting began. Then there came a sound like a high-pitched scream, followed by a sharp and splintering blast somewhere nearby.

"It sounds like a building was hit!" I cried. "Are they shelling the town?"

At that moment our neighbor, Mrs. Klinger, ran out into the street carrying a valise.

"Sarah! Where are you going?" shouted Mama through cupped hands.

"To my daughter's house, away from this!" she cried.

"Why, her daughter lives only four blocks away," I said to Mama.

"Sarah, stay! You'll be just as safe in your own home," Mama cried, but it was too late. Mrs. Klinger disappeared around the corner of Liberty Street.

"Shouldn't we leave too, Mama?" I asked.

Instead of replying, Mama waved her arms to gain the attention of a Union officer riding by. He reined in his horse and shouted, "Go into your homes and stay there!" before galloping on.

We obeyed, and Mama locked the door and began to shutter the front windows.

"Lizzie, gather all the spare bedding and take it to the cellar, along with candles, lamps and oil, a chair for each of us, and pillows for Grace."

I rushed off to obey her. As I was pulling the coverlet from my bed, I heard another volley of artillery fire, followed by screams. I dropped the bedding and dashed down the stairs to investigate.

In the street Margaret stumbled down from a cart while Clara stood in the back screaming and covering her ears. Jack had jumped down into the street, where he spun around like a dervish. The horse whinnied and pawed the ground, ready to bolt, and the boxes and bundles piled atop the cart threatened to tumble to the ground. Margaret flung herself into Mama's arms, sobbing.

"What in God's name are you doing abroad! And with the children?" cried Mama. "That stray shell could have struck you. Now get inside."

Grace rounded up Jack and Clara while I tied the nervous horse to the fence. Inside, Mama held the smelling salts under Margaret's nose, but my cousin brushed the vial away and began to talk rapidly.

"Aunt Mary, I know it looks crazy, my coming into town when everyone with any sense is running the other way. But this morning when I went over to see Georgia's new baby, she said there were reports of fighting on Oak Ridge, near the seminary. We couldn't hear anything, but when I went back home I saw soldiers coming up the pike and marching east over the fields, taking down fences in their way. They were headed for Oak Ridge all right."

"Whose soldiers?" Mama asked patiently.

"Why, our troops, of course."

"Then, that's good news. They'll push the rebels back to Cashtown. So why did you panic?" I said.

Margaret bristled. "It looked like a battle was fixing to break out right in front of my house. You would have been in a state, too. Then some officers rode up, along with a general who said his name was Reynolds. He came into the house, and I gave him bread and coffee, and Clara even sat on his knee and played with the brass buttons of his coat. He was so polite—and calm, not at all like a general heading for the battlefield."

Margaret paused to sip the coffee Grace had poured for her. Her hands trembled a little. The yeasty smell of fresh bread filled the kitchen.

"Go on. What happened next?" I urged.

"Well, General Reynolds said if I had someplace to go within town, I should leave for it now. It was almost an order! He said he wanted to post a lookout at my house because the two roads converge there. I couldn't refuse him. I said I wanted to bring the portraits and silver along, so he called his aides to load everything on the cart. But the sewing machines were so heavy, and we were so rushed, I was able to bring only one."

I didn't see why Margaret had to bring anything at all with her. It took us almost an hour to unload the cart, and I nearly cursed when the sewing machine was set down on my foot. Limping, I led the horse and cart into the alley behind the house, where Jack helped me coax the nervous creature into the shed.

When another shell exploded nearby, rattling the windows, Mama ordered everyone to the cellar. No one objected. Laden with blankets, food, and water, we descended the narrow steps. The laundry would not get done that day. The fire in the oven would burn down to embers, since no one would be cooking dinner. We were silent, not even speculating how long we would have to remain underground.

Throughout the afternoon, the earth rumbled and shook around us like a volcano about to erupt. By the flickering light of an oil lamp Mama read her Bible. Margaret mended clothing, her fingers fluttering nervously. Jack and Clara were restless, so Grace sang them a hymn about Moses that finally put them to sleep. I had nothing to read but an old almanac. The irrelevant weather predictions and bits of lore were oddly comforting. During a lull in the fighting, I thought I heard the faint strains of a band but could not make out the tune.

I glanced over at Grace, her black skin glossy in the faint light, her expression placid. Something about the semidarkness made me bold.

"Grace, how did you come to know Amos?" I asked softly.

A long moment passed, while she seemed to be weighing whether or not to reply.

"I was the new slave at the plantation where Amos lived," she finally said. "His mother was dyin' from grief since Mastuh McCarrick sold all her childern. One night I went wif the mistress to help nurse her, an' I saw the kindness in Amos's eyes. We was both full of sadness then."

"What were you sad about?" I asked.

Grace shook her head. So I prompted her on to a happier topic.

"Then you and Amos got married by a preacher who came along doing baptisms?"

"How do you know that?" she asked, sounding surprised.

"Amos told me. Then he said you were sold away. But he didn't say why."

"My mistress had some good in her an' a lot of meanness," Grace said, shaking her head. "When she found out I had married Amos, she went into a fury. She said that I, bein' a house nigger, had debased myself by marryin' a field nigger. You see, she wanted to decide who I married, maybe keep me from havin' a husband at all, so's I could take care of her forever."

"But what could she do if you and Amos were already married?" I asked.

"She broke us up by havin' her husband sell me to that crazy Mastuh Johnston."

"So that's how she punished you for defying her. Now I understand." I touched Grace's sleeve. "I'm sorry," I whispered. She didn't pull away.

"If I'd've just waited a bit to marry Amos, I'd've been free, too. But I guess I was too much in love." She said this without regret or bitterness. "An' it don't matter now, anyhow."

After a moment I asked, "Do you have brothers or sisters?"

Grace pressed her full lips together tightly.

"Don't ask me no more. I'm tired now." A look of pain crossed her forehead, and she closed her eyes.

A sudden barrage of artillery made the jam jars rattle on the shelf and shimmy to the edge. I leaped up and caught one just before it hit the dirt floor near where Rosanna's scrapbook lay hidden.

Lizzie

Chapter 30

Eventually the guns fell silent, and Mama and I came up from the cellar to have a look. Hearing muffled shouting in the streets and the pounding of feet, we cracked open the shutters on the parlor window and peered out. Union soldiers filled York Street, running pell-mell toward the east, chased by rebels. Shots rang out. A man slammed to the ground just outside our gate, a crimson flower of blood blooming from his back. My hand flew to my mouth and a horrified cry escaped me. Margaret had come up behind me, and at the sight she sank to her knees and gently fainted. I could not take my eyes off the scene in the street. I saw a horse shot from beneath its rider, who was thrown backward into the street as the animal reared up. A high-pitched and wavering yell echoed between the houses, seeming to come from every direction at once. Within minutes, the chaos passed and the street was quiet again.

"Mama, does this mean the battle is lost?" I whispered.

"I don't know, but that man needs help," she said, moving swiftly to the door. Before I could seize her dress to stop her, she had flung it open and was outside. The sharp smell of burned gunpowder drifted inside, stinging my nose.

"What are you doing, Mama? Come inside!" I called. Behind me,

Margaret stirred. Mama knelt beside the soldier who had been shot in the back and spoke to him. He tried to sit up but failed.

"Lizzie, help me!" she shouted.

I tried to obey her but could not get beyond the open door. I felt as if I had been ordered to dive into a flooded river. All my muscles tensed and refused to move.

"Hurry!" urged Mama.

Seeing her crouched in the street without any protection finally stirred me into action. But once outside, I paused again as if stricken. Half a dozen soldiers lay in the street, blood pooling around them. A few stirred and groaned, still alive, while others lay motionless, already dead. The ground was littered with hats, blankets, knapsacks, mess kits, and canteens dropped by the fleeing troops. A soldier staggered around the corner of Stratton Street, carrying a man over his shoulder like a rolled-up rug. He climbed the steps of St. James Church, then disappeared. The intersection filled with Union soldiers again. An officer on horseback tried to herd them like cattle.

"To the Hill! Cemetery Hill! Take the heights and hold them," he shouted.

"Lizzie!" Mama called, her voice sharp and urgent.

I sprang to her side. "You've got to come inside. You'll be trampled or shot."

"No. Help me carry him into the house. You lift his legs."

I glanced at the soldier. His eyes were closed and he gasped for breath. I lifted his feet, and together Mama and I half carried, half dragged him into the house and laid him in the hall.

Margaret had revived but still looked pale.

"Aunt Mary! What are we to do with him?" she asked hoarsely.

"We will stop his bleeding and keep him alive, that's what." Mama took off her apron and tore it into strips, then heaved the man onto his side and pressed the material into the wound. The sight of his blood running over her fingers made my stomach churn. I had to turn away and try very hard not to throw up.

"That's the best I can do for now," said Mama, regarding the roughly bandaged wound.

Margaret took a scrap of cloth and began to wipe up the blood streaking the floor.

"Never mind that now," Mama told her. She leaned back on her heels with a sigh. "We'll never get him down the stairs. He'll have to lie here. Margaret, fetch a mattress from the cellar. And tell Grace to keep the children down there with her."

Margaret dropped the cloth and hurried away.

"Are you all right, Lizzie?" Mama asked. "You look pale."

"I'm a little shaken up," I admitted in a wavering voice.

Mama's hands were not even trembling. I didn't know she could be so brave. I forced myself to look at the man's face. His eyelids fluttered and his forehead was twisted with pain, but he didn't groan or complain. I took his canteen and held it to his dry lips while he drank.

"Try to rest now. The bleeding is not so bad now. You'll be fine," I said, wondering if I were telling an unforgivable lie. I looked up at Mama. She nodded. I had done all right.

We had eased the soldier onto a straw mattress and Margaret was rebuilding the fire to heat water for broth when the kitchen door burst open and two soldiers stumbled into the house, clutching rifles with glinting bayonets.

Margaret screamed and began to fumble about the sideboard, sending bread pans crashing to the floor, until she laid her hands on a knife.

"What is it now?" cried Mama, running into the kitchen.

"For gosh sakes, Margaret, put down the knife!" I cried. "They're our soldiers." Though torn and crusted with dirt, their uniforms, I could tell, had once been blue.

"Thank you, miss," one of the men said to me, removing his tattered slouch hat to reveal a head of wispy hair. The other man leaned against the table, groaned, and slumped into a chair. Margaret dropped the knife into a drawer.

"Ladies, we regret this rude manner of entering your house," the first soldier said with exaggerated politeness. "Might we bide some time here? Our alternative is to be taken captive by the rebels, and that ain't our preference."

I hoped Mama would say no. What if the rebels came again and found them and Grace, too? We were all in terrible danger now.

"You see, my buddy here is wounded, so we can't exactly outrun the Johnnies," he added, nodding to his companion.

"You may stay until it is safe to go," said Mama. "My husband has been captured by rebels, and I would spare others that fate."

She motioned to me to lay out food on the table. The soldier with the wispy hair introduced himself as John Ray, and his friend as Noah Zimmer of the 147th New York Infantry.

"Let me see that leg, Mr. Zimmer," Mama said.

"Goddamn horse stepped on me." Zimmer gritted his teeth. "Sorry, ma'am, about the swearing," he said, taking Mama's frown for disapproval. She took off his shoe and cut away his pant leg at the knee. I watched, ready to avert my eyes, but there was no blood.

"Looks and feels broken all right," Mama said. "Lizzie, bring me two short planks—those shelves will do. Margaret, tear up that sheet."

As John Ray held the pieces of wood in place, Mama wrapped Zimmer's leg in a splint. Then she took a jug from deep in the pantry and poured out a dark amber liquid. The sharp smell of spirits filled the room. My eyebrows shot up.

"I keep this for medicinal purposes," Mama explained, glancing at me.

Zimmer downed the whiskey in one gulp and his eyes pleaded for more.

A sudden explosion made the windows rattle and jarred me from silence.

"What *is* happening out there?" I demanded. "If you need to hide here, does that mean the rebels won the battle?"

"It's hard to know exactly, miss. We couldn't hold 'em on that ridge to the west, so we had to fall back through town. I think what you just heard was one of our guns near the depot aimed at the rebs to the north."

"They're coming from the north, too?" My voice rose and quavered.

"Damn murderin' redneck rebels is everywhere," grumbled Zimmer, gritting his teeth.

"It's not a good situation," admitted John Ray. "You see, we lost General Reynolds early this morning."

"General Reynolds?" Margaret cried out. "But he was at my house this morning and I served him coffee. He was such a gentleman. You must be mistaken!"

"I wish I were, but it's the truth," said John Ray. "And now, if you take my advice, you'll leave here before the fightin' picks up again. We had to give up some ground, but we ain't beaten yet. Mark my words, tomorrow this town will be whizzing with bullets."

"Mama, Mama, who's here?" came Jack's voice as he and Clara burst out of the cellar. Margaret seized their hands and I stepped into the doorway so they would not see the wounded soldier in the hall.

"It's all right, Grace," Mama called down.

John Ray regarded Jack and Clara with dismay. "Ma'am, this'll be no place at all for children." His eyes widened further as Grace emerged from the cellar. "Nor for contraband, neither. Heck, I'd've never burdened you with our presence if I'd known there were children and Negroes here. We ought to go now, Zimmer."

I was relieved to see him shove his hat onto his head and Zimmer heave himself to a standing position, using his rifle like a crutch.

"Wait," said Mama, holding up her hand. "Mr. Zimmer, you are not going anywhere on that leg. Mr. Ray, help him down into the cellar."

After considering Mama and each other for a long moment, John Ray and Noah Zimmer obeyed. Wide-eyed, the children trailed them down the steps. Grace stood looking into the front hall where the wounded soldier lay.

"We must fetch Dr. Horner to get that bullet out," Mama said, following Grace's gaze. "Lizzie, will you go?" She put both hands to her forehead. "I've had too much excitement."

I swallowed hard to keep down the fear rising in me.

"I'll come with you," Margaret offered, and I felt a rush of gratitude. But we were hardly on our way when Margaret quailed at the sight of a dead horse lying stiffly on its side. Flies the size of June bugs buzzed around its flanks. Its blood was turning the dust in the street to mud.

"Just look away and keep walking," I said, but Margaret still hesitated.

"Dr. Horner lives on Chambersburg Street, beyond the Diamond," she said. "Do you think we ought to go that far?"

I also had my doubts. I had no wish to encounter rebels in the street. What if they questioned us? We would have to lie or betray everyone in our house.

"Let's try the church first," I suggested. "I saw a wounded soldier go inside earlier. Perhaps there is a doctor here."

The steps of St. James Church were spattered with blood. The door opened with a creak. Inside, the setting sun touched only the upper windows, dimly illuminating the forms of soldiers lying in the pews. The familiar odor of beeswax was tinged with the acrid smells of sweat and blood. I heard an unexpected sound: dice rattling in a tin cup and clattering on the wooden pew. The sound echoed from the plastered walls and vaulted ceiling. Two stretcher bearers eased a man into a pew and left again in a hurry.

"Is there a doctor here?" Margaret called out in a hesitant voice. A ragged chorus rose in response.

"Nurse? Over here. Water, please!"

Margaret and I looked at each other helplessly.

"What do we do now?" Margaret whispered.

"Pastor Essig? Are you here?" I called.

The pastor's familiar gray head appeared over the top of a pew. We hurried over to him, then stopped abruptly, for he was covering a man's face with a blanket. Then he stood up and held out his hands to grasp ours. I realized he had just prayed for a dead man, and now he calmly welcomed us. But when he heard that we needed a doctor for the wounded soldiers at our house, he shook his head sadly.

"You see there is no doctor here yet. I can only pray that one will soon arrive. We need those bandages the good ladies rolled and sent away to the front. And now we need their help with the injured." He gestured around him. "The soldiers at your house are the fortunate ones. Just take care of them, and pray for them."

I glanced toward the covered body on the pew and thought of the soldier lying in our hallway.

"But what if he dies?"

"Then his soul is God's," Pastor Essig said simply.

Unfortunately I didn't share the minister's faith at the moment. I wanted to challenge God. Did he hate war or welcome it for all the souls it brought in? Did he accept into heaven the souls of men who had killed other men in defense of their country? Were the Union and Confederate dead judged equally in that regard? But I sensed that even Pastor Essig did not have the answers to my questions.

"Pastor, what do you know of the day's events?" asked Margaret.

"I was at the seminary this morning and from the cupola I watched the battle unfold," he said. "What an awesome and terrible sight it was. But I came down quick enough when a minié ball struck the stone just inches from my head. The wounded were pouring into the building already."

"Is it safe for us to stay in town with Aunt Mary?"

He shook his head. "The soldiers coming in here say there are rebels to the west, the north, and northeast. Both sides are putting up defenses and barricades. The only clear direction now is to the south. You ought to leave if you can. Tomorrow every church in Gettysburg will be a hospital. Now, go in peace," he said without irony.

I felt anything but peaceful as Margaret and I left the church and went home to tell Mama the minister's news. Her face was drawn and pale.

"I can't think what to do," she said dully. "I don't know what is best."

"I have an idea," I said. "We can go to the Weigels' farm. It's about three miles to the south on Taneytown Road, far enough from the danger here. Mrs. Weigel even invited us."

"Yes, I remember," Mama said, perking up a bit. She looked questioningly at Grace.

"We be in danger no matter what. I stay—or go—with you all," said Grace.

So Mama packed a satchel with some food and water while Margaret and I gathered up blankets and clothing. I didn't know how long we would be gone. A day? A week? John Ray hitched the horse up to the cart, helped Grace climb in, and lifted Jack and Clara over the sides. Mama made sure Grace was cushioned by plenty of straw and hidden under blankets.

"Remember, now," said Mama to the children, "your job is to keep Grace a secret. It's like a game, but more important."

"You drive, Lizzie," said Margaret. "I can barely control this beast. I'll sit beside you. Aunt Mary will be more comfortable riding in the cart."

I took the reins, but John Ray told us to wait. He went inside and came back with the rifle and cartridge box that belonged to the wounded soldier.

"I don't think he'll have occasion to use this anytime soon," he said, handing it to Mama.

"Heavens, I could never fire that thing," she said. "Show Lizzie how to use it."

I gulped. I couldn't believe I had heard my mother say that. John Ray turned to me and held out the rifle.

I thought, if the soldier in the hallway would not need his rifle, did that mean he was going to die? I hoped Pastor Essig would send a doctor to care for him. I reached for the rifle. It was heavy, but smooth and cool to the touch. I was afraid of it.

"If anyone offers you trouble, miss, just lift it to your shoulder and aim, but don't actually pull the trigger. She's not loaded. The recoil would give you quite a bruising, maybe knock you flat."

I lifted the rifle, the butt against my right shoulder. I had to slide my left hand down the barrel to support its weight.

"That's right. Just act like you're going to fire it and that should do the trick. And don't worry. No decent soldier, not even a reb, should harm a lady."

I laid the rifle across my lap, but it wanted to slide off, so I sat on it instead. It dug into my thighs uncomfortably. I tucked the cartridge box under the seat.

"You'll see soldiers settin' up barricades, but they'll let you by," said John Ray. I nodded. Then he said to Mama, "Let me help you up, ma'am."

"No, thank you. I won't be going."

"What do you mean, Mama? Of course you are coming!" I said. "It's not safe to stay here."

"Someone has to care for these wounded men and keep the rebels from destroying our house." She tried to smile.

"Aunt Mary, John Ray can take care of the other two," Margaret said. "And don't worry about the house. That's not important."

"I know." Her smile faded. "I just have a feeling—I need to be here if—when—Ben comes home. He can't come back and find that we've all gone away."

"But we must stay together," I protested, hardly listening. "If you don't come along, our whole family will be separated—you from me and Ben, Papa from Luke and all of us. None of us together—" I broke off in tears.

Mama squeezed my arm with surprising strength.

"We will be together again one day. But for now, you must do this alone. I know you can. God bless you." She slapped the horse's rump and he lurched forward.

Dismayed, I simply let the beast pull us through the alley and onto York Street, past the dead horse and into the intersection with Stratton Street. To the north, a dozen or more rebels stood in the street near the train depot. They paid us no mind. I looked back. Mama had gone inside. I drew on the reins until we stopped.

"I can't do it, Margaret," I whispered. "I just can't leave Mama here alone. You'll have to go without me, too."

Margaret wrung her hands. She looked at me, and I saw that familiar furrow between her brows that reminded me of Rosanna.

"No! Lizzie, I'll lose my head. Why, this morning I frightened my own children, I was in such a state of hysteria."

"What should we do, then? Grace and the children have to be taken to safety, but I don't want my mother left alone."

Margaret climbed down from the wagon.

"I will stay here with your mother, Lizzie." She stepped on a spoke of the wheel and peered over the side of the cart. "Good-bye, darlings! I will see you shortly. Remember the game!"

I sat there, speechless, the rifle hard under my legs, the reins limp in my hands.

"Go, Lizzie," she said earnestly, causing the furrow between her eyes to appear. "I trust you."

And she ran off. Just like Rosanna.

Lizzie

Chapter 31

At first I was so angry I almost climbed down from the wagon and refused to go to the Weigels' myself. I seethed, my legs clenched against the hard rifle. But soon I had to forgive Mama, knowing how anguished she was about Ben. I realized that Margaret had also made a difficult choice, knowing that her skittish reactions might endanger her children. This was no time for me to be selfish and scared, for the safety of Grace, Jack, and Clara was now in my hands alone. I would prove that I could be trusted. I smacked the reins hard and the fool horse jumped sideways, almost throwing me off the seat.

I decided to avoid the main thoroughfares, so I turned south on Stratton Street, only to come upon a Confederate search party banging on doors. They were intent upon their business of rounding up prisoners and thus ignored us. But ahead of me the intersection was barricaded, forcing us to halt. A surly bunch of rebels leaned on their rifles and made no move to let me through. I was afraid to ask them, so I turned into an alley. It was dusk, and shadows obscured the way, yet I welcomed the darkness. I thought we could slip through it unseen.

I did not see the three corpses until the horse balked and came to a halt. I climbed down to lead him on, almost tripping over the bodies. Perhaps I could have dragged them out of the way, but I couldn't bring myself to touch them. Instead I tried to persuade the horse to back up.

"Why are we stopping?" came Jack's small voice from the back of the cart.

"Hush! Remember the game, no questions," I warned.

The horse refused to move. My courage was ebbing fast. We had barely begun our journey and we were stuck in an alley. I begged the stupid horse to back up.

"Stay calm now, Lizzie," came Grace's soft voice.

Jack stood up and regarded my predicament, then climbed into the driver's seat.

"Won't anyone obey me?" I said, practically whining.

"This sometimes works. Buster!" he called, clucking softly and patting the horse's rear flank. To my relief, Buster finally began to back up, freeing us from the alley.

Now I would have to go down Baltimore Street after all. As I drove through the Diamond, I saw rebels rolling a keg out the door of Gillespie's Grocery. They bashed open the barrel with their rifle butts and proceeded to eat the salted fish inside, heads and all. Shops and houses with broken windows and doors hanging on their hinges gave evidence that Confederate looters were busy. I saw a house with a red cloth fluttering from a window and realized it was a makeshift hospital when I saw two men with a stretcher disappear inside.

At Middle Street, another barricade blocked the way. This one, too, was well guarded. But I had already decided what to do. I drove right up to it before drawing on Buster's reins.

"Let me through, please!" I shouted over the wild thumping of my heart, hoping my voice didn't sound shaky.

One of the guards, a stocky, rough-faced man, came over to the cart and stood with his legs apart.

"Why should I let you by, missy?" he asked in a languid voice.

"This is my town. I live here."

"No, it's our town now. You kain't pass here." He reached up to grab Buster's harness but the horse jerked his head aside.

My mouth was dry. It would be foolish to try and and break through the barricade, even though Buster was strong enough.

"I have important business, sir."

"Oh, indeed. Jus' what is yer business, little lady, that it has to be done now?" he asked in a mocking voice.

Figuring that that most men wanted nothing to do with women's emergencies, I took a deep breath and launched into my story.

"My sister is having trouble giving birth and she needs my help!" I said. "You see, she's built very narrow. I'm afraid she and the baby will both die if I don't get there soon. She lives on Taneytown Road, so I must go this way."

From his hard look, I don't think he believed me. Why would I need a cart for such an errand? I was afraid he would search me and find the rifle, or peer into the cart and discover Grace. I was considering whether to make a dash for the barricade when another guard strode up, wearing the gold braid of an officer on his sleeve. My hopes sank; we would be searched and detained for certain.

"Jake! What're you up to now?" he asked roughly, then turned to me and said politely, "Is this man botherin' you, miss? 'Cause if he is, I'll have the rascal taken out an' shot. Allow me to escort you through myself."

Too surprised to protest, I let him take the reins from me. Jake scuttled, ratlike, to open up the barricade, and the next thing I knew, we were on the other side. The officer tipped his hat to me and growled at Jake, who protested, "I was jus' lettin' the lady through, sir."

I let out my breath in a sigh of relief, then smiled in triumph.

As Buster ambled toward the outskirts of town and began to climb the hill leading to the cemetery, I had an eerie sense of being watched. It was easy to imagine that the dusky shadows hid an entire army. Then the gleam of a rifle barrel in a second-story window of the tannery caught my eye, and I made out the shape of a man on the sloping roof. Sharpshooters. They could hit a target a mile away, I had heard.

Hoping that Jack and Clara and Grace could hear me, I said in a low voice, "It's very important now that you stay perfectly still until I say so. I'm going to cut through Evergreen Cemetery to Taneytown Road."

"No, I want to get out now!" said Clara, beginning to fuss.

I heard Jack call her a baby. Clara wailed even louder. Grace's voice came, a soothing murmur. I urged Buster on faster, expecting at any moment to be shot at.

"I want Mama," Clara cried again, and began to kick the sides of the cart. I seethed with irritation at the girl. Finally, Grace was able to quiet her.

We had left behind the houses on Baltimore Street and the cemetery gateway was in sight when a strange medley of sounds reached me. I drew up Buster and listened. I realized I was hearing the clanging of shovels against rock and the *thwack* of ax blades biting into trees. In the fading light I could see men building low mounds of dirt and piling fresh-cut logs on the slopes of Cemetery Hill and Culp's Hill. I remembered the Union officer shouting "To the hills!" and guessed that our soldiers who had retreated through Gettysburg were building breastworks to defend their position.

Seeing the preparations for battle made me nervous. I shook the reins vigorously but the horse balked and tried to move sideways, as if someone were restraining him.

"Who's there? Let go of my horse!" I cried out in a panicked voice.

I started to rise up, then remembered the rifle and stayed seated, tensing my legs around it. Then I saw them: two men in faded brown jackets, wearing caps with the Confederate insignia. One of them held firmly on to Buster's bridle.

"Leave me alone," I demanded, trying to keep my voice steady. "And let go of my horse."

"You listen to me, miss. We jus' need a short ride through that cemetery there," said the taller of the two men. "We're scoutin' aroun' this here area, an' you come along at the right time to help us." He smiled, revealing teeth stained with tobacco.

"Go away. I've got my own business."

In reply, the man held up a large pistol. For a moment I truly believed he would shoot me. He was a soldier after all, and no doubt accustomed to killing.

I heard myself say, "If you kill me, who will drive you through the cemetery?"

"That's right," he said, tucking the pistol into his belt. "I knew you'd come to see it my way."

"Wa'll lookee what we foun' back here!" said the second rebel, and I realized with horror that he had climbed into the cart. "Two wee 'uns and their mighty big mammy. What'll we do with them?"

"Why, shoot 'em, if they give us away. D'yall hear that?" He vaulted over the side of the cart. "Now drive, young lady."

Instead I whirled around, taking care to keep the rifle from falling off the seat.

"If you harm a hair of any of their heads, I'll scream until the whole Union army comes to take you prisoner!"

The second scout laughed. "Ain't she a feisty one!" he said. "Like a wildcat protectin' her young."

"You scream or holler an' it's the end of your children and their mammy," said the other, brandishing his pistol again. "Now sit down and drive like nothing is wrong."

My hands and arms shook like I had the palsy. But I took the reins and Buster started up again. We drove under the arched gateway and into the cemetery. The gatehouse was brightly lit, and officers stood around eating, smoking, and talking intently. One of them leaned against the old sign that read *All persons found using firearms on these grounds will be prosecuted with the utmost rigor of the law.* The story was that two rivals had once dueled with pistols in the cemetery, and the town council, outraged that the peace of the dead had been violated, erected the sign. Now the cemetery was filled with soldiers carrying firearms and bristling for battle.

A guard approached the cart and signaled for me to stop.

"Evening, miss." He touched his cap. "What's in the wagon?"

Unable to lie or tell the truth, my tongue was tied.

"I'll have to take a look," he said.

Panic rose in me like floodwater. Just then Jack's head popped over the side.

"It's me and my little sister. She's asleep." His voice was pitched high with excitement. "That's my auntie driving. We are trying to find Taneytown Road. Mama sent us on this adventure to get us away from the rebels in town."

The soldier laughed, ruffled Jack's hair, and waved us on.

"Good boy, Jack," I murmured. "There's candy for you when this is all over."

I was desperate to get through the cemetery before anyone else confronted us, but army wagons, artillery carts, and soldiers crowded the gravel trail, forcing us to creep along at the pace of a turtle. The boughs of evergreen trees drooped in a ghostly way over the path, the glow of campfires lighting them from beneath. Soldiers lounged against the gravestones, polishing their rifles or sleeping. Another picket approached the cart. If he discovered the spies, I wondered, could I be charged with treason for aiding them?

Although my heart banged in my chest, this time I kept my wits about me. I explained that I was taking a shortcut to the Weigel farm to wait out the battle. It was half of the truth.

Jack started a rapid one-sided conversation with the soldier. "Is that a real gun? Can I touch it? Can I have your cap? My sister's asleep in here. You'd better not wake her."

"Move on through, now," the picket said, looking tired. "This ain't no place for women and children."

"Yes, sir," I said, jiggling Buster's reins to hurry him along.

Fragments of conversations drifted to my ears: "General Meade's just arrived. He's with General Warren and Sickles in the gatehouse. . . . We may have taken a beating today, but we're on good high ground here. . . . Crawford and the whole Fifth Corps are on their way from Hanover. We'll have those Johnnies outnumbered tomorrow! . . . The roads are jammed with our infantry falling over one another to get here first. . . . Tell 'em to slow down. It ain't a footrace; it's a damn war."

Though I was eager for news, I also knew that every remark was being overheard by the rebel spies. So I slunk through the Union ranks, feeling like a traitor. When the path began to circle around again, I drove down the opposite side of the hill, past the sharp palings of the new breastworks. The cart swayed and bumped down the rocky slope, but I heard not the slightest moan from Grace. I drove through a field until I came to a break in the fence and guided the cart through it. I had to wait while a Union artillery regiment passed by, the caissons rumbling on the hard, dry road. Were these to be my last moments alive, sitting along the Taneytown Road in a cloud of dust eerily lit by moonlight, before the rebels shot me? When the last wagon had rolled by, I drove through a muddy ditch and up the precarious rise onto the roadway itself, where I reined in Buster.

I don't know if it was anger, plain terror, or relief at being still alive that made me bold to the point of foolishness. I stood up, picked up the empty rifle, and aimed it at the cart.

"You've had a long enough ride. Now get out," I said.

Lizzie

Chapter 32

I heard a rustling in the straw and Jack peered over the side of the wagon. He was wearing a Confederate cap.

"Don't shoot me, Lizzie!" he said in a high voice.

I kept the gun as steady as I could.

"I'm talking to those two rebels," I said.

"Oh, they're gone!" Jack said. "They jumped out. Look, they gave me this cap for being so good."

My arms and shoulders went limp, and my grip on the rifle sagged.

"Thank God! Are Clara and Grace all right?"

"Clara's sleepin'," came Grace's low voice. "They did'n' hurt us none."

"That was a dandy adventure, Lizzie!" said Jack, tugging on his new cap. "I can't wait to tell Mama!"

"Don't tell anyone we helped a couple of rebels!" I warned him.

"But we were kidnapped. And you acted like a hero!"

I sighed, knowing Jack could never keep the night's events a secret, and slapped Buster with the reins. It was nearly midnight when we reached the Weigel house. In the dark it looked like all the other stone farmhouses along Taneytown Road, but I recognized it because it stood at an angle to the road. Lights glowed in all the windows as if a party were going on. I wondered if Martin was home. I climbed down from the cart. My muscles were as wobbly as gelatin and my head ached.

"*Wer da?*" called Mrs. Weigel from the doorway. "Lizzie! I thought you would come, but not so late. *Es is fast Mitternacht.* You have Margaret's children with you! *Komm, meine Kinder.* Bring your blankets with you. Where is your *Mutti*? And Margaret? They have not been hurt?"

"No, they stayed home," I said, too tired to explain further.

"Did you hear, *die Ungeheuere,* the rebel monsters, they set fire to the McLean home today. *Kleine* Amanda and her poor aunt, *sie reissen aus,* they ran for their lives!"

I wished she hadn't told me that. But I noted the Weigels' house was made of rough-hewn stone, like a fort.

I helped Grace climb down from the cart. She held her belly and grunted with the effort.

"*Ach . . . mein Gott!*" said Mrs. Weigel in a tone of surprise, and fell silent.

Up that moment, I had been intent on getting to safety. I had not considered that Mrs. Weigel might turn Grace away. What would I do then?

I swallowed hard and put my hand on Grace's shoulder.

"This is our hired man Amos's wife, Grace. She needs to lie down somewhere and rest," I said.

Mrs. Weigel frowned and gazed around, as if considering where to put Grace. The moonlight shone on the garden, where melons ripened on the ground among vines and leaves.

"Then bring her inside," she said at last, holding the door open for all of us. Clara stumbled in, half-asleep, while Jack strode like a little man with the rifle and cartridge box. I motioned for him to put them in a corner of the parlor. Mrs. Weigel didn't notice, she was so busy chattering.

"I put you all in the same room, *ja*? Frieda Baumann and her Annie came this morning. Then Frieda went back home because she was afraid the house would be *geplundert* and their furniture wrecked."

"Why, the Baumanns live on Middle Street, which is barricaded now. The rebels have taken the whole town," I said.

"*Liebe Gott!* I said she was foolish. But Annie, she would not go home with her mother. She wanted to stay and help with the soldiers. *Ach*, how they argued! But she is no more *eine kleine Mädchen*. You, too, Lizzie, are all grown up. You are more like your mother all the time. *Ja*?"

I smiled wearily, not minding the comparison. "So there were soldiers here too?"

Mrs. Weigel raised both her hands. "All the day we cooked and pumped water for *tausend und aber tausend Soldaten*, their throats dry with dust from the long marching. *Komm, komm*. Sit down." She poured broth for me and for Grace, then prattled on, preventing me from asking where Martin was. "And from the direction of town came the ones with terrible wounds, some of them almost dead. *Ach*, how I do run on. The children, are they asleep already? Grace, can you climb the stairs? *Du liebe Himmel*, goodness, that baby is low in your belly. Well, this is as *gut* a place as any, with the doctors out there in the barn."

"What do you mean?" I asked, barely listening. I was just glad that Mrs. Weigel had decided to welcome Grace after all.

"You look tired, Lizzie. Follow me." She led Grace and me into a room with a stripped-down bed and a mattress on the floor. A wash basin stood in the corner under a cracked mirror. Jack and Clara were already asleep on a rolled-up rug. "*Deine Mutti*—is she well, your mother?"

"She is worried. We haven't heard from Ben and Amos in over a week, and I'm afraid . . . they've run into . . . rebels." My voice caught like cloth on a thorn bush.

"*Sei nicht nervös*. Don't fret yourself, Lizzie. Your Benjamin is a clever one and he can run fast. Oh, to be young and swift again! *Gute Nacht*. Now, go to sleep. *Und Gott sei dank,* thank him that you are alive and with all your limbs. Here, you must use your own blankets. All the beds we took apart to use in the barn. Don't fall asleep before you put out the lamp."

My eyelids flickered. Her words made little sense to me. Why did she keep referring to the barn?

"Wait, Mrs. Weigel. Did Martin—go anywhere today?"

"Goodness, no! Would I let my boy leave here with a battle going on *direkt vor der Nase*, under our very noses?" She turned and left the room.

So Martin had not kept his word. No one would be searching for Ben and Amos now. My disappointment, however, was tinged with relief that Martin would not also be in danger. I couldn't bear the responsibility for that, too. I lay down and thanked God that we had arrived safely at the Weigels', but the words were like ashes in my mouth. I might be safe for the moment, but what about Amos and Ben? Papa and Luke? Mama and Margaret? And what about the thousands of soldiers, gazing sleeplessly into campfires in anticipation of the next day's battle? How many of them would die? With a sigh I rested my cheek on a folded quilt that smelled of Mama's lavender water and, despite my overwhelming worries, soon fell asleep.

Rosanna

———◆———

Chapter 33

July 1, 1863 Chambersburg

Awakened early this morning to the noisy preparations of General Heth's men, which resolved into the measured tread of marching, led by fife and drum. For a moment I considered saddling Dolly and galloping to warn Margaret, Lizzie, and everyone to flee to safety. Alas, such an act would make me a traitor!

Mrs. Throckmorton brought me some coffee, a rarity obtained from a sympathetic grocer in the town. "I know you have relatives in that town," she said, nodding over her shoulder. "I'm sure they will not be harmed."

Sipping the warm, bitter coffee, I began to tell Mrs. Throckmorton about Margaret, how I missed her though she hated rebels, how Jack and Clara used to hug and kiss me. I told her how much I regretted hurting my best friend, Lizzie, by leaving so suddenly. I confessed like the Catholics do to their priests. "I fear I will never see them again in this life," I concluded, beginning to weep. The sobs seemed to echo in the emptiness within me left by John's death.

"I understand, dear," said Mrs. Throckmorton, taking my hands in her big, fleshy ones. She said one of her prayers full of "thees" and "thou" and "O Lords" and "darkness" and "light." The stream of words did have a soothing effect.

It is now the blackest hour of the night, no longer the first day of July but not fully the second. Late in the afternoon casualties began to arrive from Gettysburg. Apparently every farmhouse and barn between here and Cashtown overflows with wounded. They came in ambulances and ordnance wagons that had been emptied of ammunition. What minié balls and shells began, often the journey completed. Crowded into wagons and driven over rough, bone-rattling roads, many died from pain and blood loss. It should not have been necessary to carry the wounded so far to receive care. But when I demanded of Dr. Walker why there was not a better-equipped hospital near the field, he had no answer.

Among the wounded, poor Mrs. Throckmorton discovered her own husband. A shell fragment had disfigured his face. But the brave woman merely crossed herself and went to work on him with the same determination she lends to all her patients.

My sorrowful case was an artillery gunner suffering from burns. His companion who carried him in said that a shell had struck an ammunition box, exploding its contents. The man's skin was black and charred, his hair and beard burned away. Only his upper face, which he had shielded from the blast, remained untouched. He could not even talk though he was conscious. I asked Dr. Walker for a dose of the scarce morphine, which he allowed, seeing the man's terrible suffering. I had to dissolve the pill in water and dribble it into his mouth. Because his hands were covered with burns, I could touch only his forehead while he quietly expired.

A strange thing happened as I sat beside him, tears running down my cheeks. The emptiness inside me began to fill up, as if a warm liquid were flowing into all my limbs and stirring my heart. A feeling of serenity, even courage, took possession of me, overcoming grief and despair. Can it be that the spirits of the dead have the ability to strengthen the living? Perhaps that is how they earn their reward.

July 2, 1863 Chambersburg

After a brief rest, I arose to find today's plans in motion and yesterday's events clarified. General Heth met with unexpected resistance, but aided by General Ewell's corps, caused the federals to retreat through Gettysburg. However, Ewell did not press on to a victory, a failure for which he is already being maligned. The federals have lost about seven thousand men, including three thousand prisoners. Our losses were somewhat less though our numbers were more, about twenty-five thousand men who fought to their twenty thousand.

Today the remainder of Lee's army here in Chambersburg will march to Gettysburg to complete yesterday's unfinished business. As I write I can hear General Pickett, full of confidence, exhorting his men to glory in battle. With a victory, the path to Washington will lie open, and once that city falls, the war must end.

While Mrs. Throckmorton and I were helping load the hospital wagons, Dr. Walker surprised us by declaring that the women would remain in Chambersburg. He said he was obliged to make haste and that he had enough orderlies among the convalescents to assist with the wounded.

"I respectfully disagree, sir," I found myself saying. "Had there been trained nurses nearer the field yesterday, many of our men might have been cared for sooner. Whose orders are these?"

"General Lee would wish the ladies out of harm's way," he replied gruffly.

"Then let General Lee command me himself," I said (knowing the general has bigger fish to fry). Mrs. Throckmorton's eyes grew round.

"My dear Mrs. Wilcox," replied Dr. Walker, striving for patience, "I have learned to value the skills that women bring to nursing. But today's encounter will be a terrible one. I cannot vouch for your safety."

"I no longer care for my safety," I replied. "How can I hold my life dear when others are willing to lose theirs?"

"Then go! Put on a uniform and march, for all I care! Do what you will," he shouted, waving his arms to dismiss me.

"You are a brave girl! Go, and do my share as well," said Mrs. Throckmorton, who was willing enough to stay behind with her husband. Fortunately, he is likely to live.

Tom then brought Dolly to me. I noticed how healthy she looks, thanks to his care. He took the news of my going without a flicker of surprise or disapproval.

"I be nearby you, Miz Wilcox," was all he said.

I do not always understand my actions. While I did not precisely ask to accompany the medical corps, everything I said conveyed a will to do so. But why am I so determined to be at the scene of today's battle? I cannot hope to encounter Margaret or Lizzie there. Is it some reckless impulse that stirs me? What sorrowful consequences may result? Whatever they may be, I will face them with calmness and courage.

Lizzie

Chapter 34

The first thing I heard when I awoke was a cock crowing as if trying to raise the dead. More faintly, birds twittered. Downstairs in the kitchen, pans clattered on the iron stove. Lying on the familiar quilt, I drifted in and out of sleep. Had I simply imagined the terrors of the day before? Surely they had been a dream, and I was about to open my eyes to an ordinary, peaceful summer's day.

But when I sat up and saw Jack and Clara sprawled on a pile of blankets and Grace curled up on a straw mattress, I knew yesterday's events had been real. My arms ached from driving the cart and my legs were bruised from sitting on the rifle. I stumbled to the washstand and splashed water on my face. With my fingers I combed and rebraided my hair. I could hear in the distance the beat of a drum and a fife trilling above it like the sound of hope. I smoothed my dress, rumpled from being slept in, and hurried downstairs.

In the kitchen Mrs. Weigel and two other women chattered in German while mixing and kneading dough with vigorous thrusts of their sturdy arms. The sideboard was piled with mounds of small cakes. Mrs. Weigel introduced me to her sisters-in-law. Bonnie Weigel was stooped and gray haired, while Louisa was a heavy woman with a thick brown braid down her back.

"Drei Frauen Weigeln in einer Küche," Louisa Weigel said, and they all laughed. I didn't understand the joke, but I smiled anyway. "Eat a cake," she said with a thick accent and nodded in the direction of the sideboard.

Nibbling on the sweet, crumbly bread, I went onto the front porch and nearly choked with surprise when I came face-to-face with Martin. He took a step backward.

"Ma told me you were here. I was waiting for you to get up so I could talk to you," he said. His hair was rumpled and he looked tired.

"Where were you yesterday?" I asked, unable to keep the disappointment from my voice. "You promised—"

"I know. I'm really sorry," he interrupted. "I was ready to leave, but everything started to happen here." He gestured with his arm, and I peered around him to see what I had missed in the darkness: soldiers in bandages lying on the ground and leaning against the barn a mere thirty yards from the house. A flag marked with a red cross hung from the hayloft.

"A field hospital!" I said with quiet amazement. "In your barn?"

Martin nodded. "Early yesterday morning officers came by looking for a location a safe distance from the fighting. The barn's three times the size of the house. So we cleaned it, and all day Pa and I made cots out of old boards and fence planks. They filled up as fast as we could hammer them together."

"No wonder you're tired."

"You don't look so fresh yourself." He regarded me with his head tilted to the side.

I reached up to smooth my hair and looked down at my rumpled dress. Why did Martin always see me at my worst?

"Annie Baumann's here, too," he went on quickly. "She and I were up most of the night. Cleaning up, changing bandages, that sort of thing. She's a hard worker."

At the mention of Annie, jealousy pinched me. I crossed my arms over my chest.

"Lizzie, I would have gone, but it was impossible," said Martin softly. "I'll make it up to you somehow."

"I'm afraid it's too late," I said in a choked voice, and turned to go inside. But Mrs. Weigel met me at the kitchen door and sent me back out with a platter of cakes and an iron kettle full of hot black coffee.

"*Die Soldaten* are still coming up from Taneytown. They have been marching *die ganze Nacht,* all night, perhaps asleep on their feet. They need *Kaffee.*"

As I stood near the road, soldiers dropped from the ranks, lined up, and took the cakes, one by one, until they were gone. Clumsily I ladled coffee into their tin cups, apologizing when I spilled some onto their fingers. Every soldier tipped his cap, thanked me, or merely smiled gratefully.

"Where are you from?" I asked a man with graying hair who reminded me of Papa.

"We're the 17th Maine Infantry, miss."

This proved an easy question, so I asked it often. The soldiers were from as far away as New Jersey, Michigan, and Illinois. Their speech varied, as did their uniforms, with different shades of blue and styles of jacket: single-breasted, double-breasted, braided, and plain. Some soldiers wore badges on their caps, white gaiters over their shoes, or wide trousers gathered at the ankle. But they all carried rifles and knapsacks, bedrolls and clanking mess kits. They all sweated until tiny rivers of dirty water dripped from their cheeks and soaked their jackets, leaving dark stains and a rank smell, as if they hadn't bathed in weeks.

The strangest sight was a company dressed in wide red pantaloons, cropped jackets with elaborate braid, and red caps with gold tassels. They looked almost like pictures I had seen of circus performers. With them marched a woman with long dark hair, wearing a bright red skirt over trousers. A wide-brimmed hat partially hid her face.

I thought of Rosanna and dropped my ladle, which splashed into the coffee.

"That's French Mary. She follows the 114th Pennsylvania, what call themselves Zouaves. She sells cigars and hams and best of all, whiskey," explained a soldier waiting for coffee. Indeed I saw that she carried a small barrel slung across her chest.

"Are there other Pennsylvania regiments coming? My brother is in the First Reserves; have you seen them?" I asked him.

"I don't know exactly who's behind us," he said with a shrug.

A soldier chewing on a large plug of tobacco spoke up. "Golly, girl, the whole durn army's heading here by one road or another." He smiled and I saw that he was missing a few teeth.

It would be an impossible coincidence, I thought, to see my brother marching to Gettysburg along this road. I was pretty sure he was still in Virginia.

As I watched black iron cannons being hauled by teams of horses, there was a sudden explosion and a man was thrown into the air. He landed in a wheat field next to the road. The horses bolted, leaving behind flaming pieces of a wagon and a wooden chest that spilled its load of long, rounded shells. As the man was carried past me toward the porch, I saw his blackened face and felt sick. On the road, the artillery regiment rumbled onward as if nothing unusual had happened.

Mrs. Weigel called for my help with the wounded man. I tried not to look at him. I heard him say, "It is because I forgot to read my Bible today. What will my poor wife say when she hears of this?"

"I'll run the coffee and cakes to the barn for you," I said, taking the tray from Mrs. Weigel.

She leaned over the injured man and said, "You are lucky, *ein Gluckspilz*. It was mostly smoke."

As I approached the barn, trepidation slowed my steps. What awful sights would I find inside? Would I have to step over dying men to find Martin? Just then the door swung outward, nearly knocking me over, and two orderlies hurried out with a stretcher.

"Martin!" I called into the dim cavern of the barn. He came out blinking into the sunlight.

"I've brought some coffee and cakes from your mother."

He gobbled down three cakes in three bites. Then I noticed his shirt and trousers were splattered with blood.

"What happened to you? Are you bleeding?"

"No, I've been assisting the surgeons." He gulped the coffee. "They needed someone to hold the patient while they—they—well, there's a lot of men who are pretty badly wounded."

"I know. We took one into our house yesterday," I said, shuddering at the memory. "Did you hear the explosion just now? There's an injured man on your porch." I looked behind me and saw that the orderlies were already tending to him.

"It's terrible, Lizzie," said Martin, taking another cake. "There are at least a hundred men here now. Some of them won't make it."

"Let me come in and help," I said, steeling myself. "If Annie Baumann can handle it, so can I."

"Lizzie, it's not a pleasant sight—"

Determined, I brushed past Martin and stepped into the barn. The first thing I noticed was the smell, like beef rotting in the heat. When my eyes adjusted to the gloom, I saw men laid end to end on blankets, rough cots, and piles of straw. Annie stepped between them, carrying a basin of water. My gaze traveled to an open stall that had been swept clean. Inside was a table, and on it lay a man, a sheet of blood-splashed canvas partly hiding him from view.

"No, no!" he pleaded until an orderly placed a cloth over his face. He slumped, unconscious. Then I saw the mangled arm hanging down, and before I could even look away, a surgeon applied his saw and with a few swift strokes severed it.

I swayed on my feet for a few seconds while bright stars appeared in my gaze. Then everything went black.

Lizzie

Chapter 35

When I opened my eyes, I was lying on the ground outside the barn. My face and hair were wet. Martin and Annie stood over me, Annie holding an empty basin.

"You fainted. Martin had to carry you out," said Annie.

Humiliated, I rolled onto my side and covered my face with my hands.

"I'm sorry I had to soak you," she added. On the contrary, I was sure she had enjoyed it.

"I tried to stop you from going in," Martin said feebly.

Without a word I got up and went back into the kitchen. I decided to stay there the rest of the day. I found an apron and used it to pat my hair and face dry.

"Why don't you all sit on the porch, where it's cooler? I will watch the bread," I said to the Weigel sisters, whose faces were ruddy with perspiration.

Smiling gratefully, they traipsed from the kitchen. I could hear their voices drifting in from the front porch, English words mixed with the unfamiliar German. Their rocking chairs creaked in rhythm, and Jack and Clara's marbles clicked on the wooden porch. I marveled that such ordinary activities could continue while men were dying in the Weigels' barn or waiting in the streets and fields of Gettysburg for fighting to break out. It was nearly noon. I took three loaves from the oven. I thought of Mama, in our house with Margaret and three soldiers, and wished she had come with us.

I didn't hear Martin come into the kitchen until he cleared his throat. He had changed out of his blood-spattered clothes.

"I cleaned up before I came in." His hands disappeared into his pockets.

"I see. You didn't have to do that for me. I mean, I won't faint again."

"Well, I was starting to smell bad," Martin said, wrinkling his nose. "Are you feeling better?"

"Wouldn't you think I could tolerate the sight of blood? I'm a butcher's daughter!" I punched my fist into a bowl of dough and watched it slowly deflate.

"Don't be so hard on yourself. The first time I saw a man lose . . . the surgeon take . . . well, I barely made it outside the barn before I threw up. Annie, I saw her crying a lot yesterday. But you get used to it. You have to close down your feelings."

Martin fell silent, and I couldn't think of anything to say.

Then he sniffed. "Is something burning in here?"

The oven was smoking. I jumped up, flung it open, and extracted a tray of small cakes I hadn't realized were still inside.

"Well, now I feel completely useless!" I said, eyeing their blackened crusts and waving the smoke away. But Martin was smiling. Then we both began to laugh.

"I'm getting out of here before the bucket brigade rides in! Tell my ma I'm going to try and get some sleep. Don't wake me unless the house is on fire," he said with a wink.

I picked up one of the cakes and threw it at him, but he ducked out of the kitchen and it hit the door frame instead, scattering little burned flakes. I hadn't seen Grace coming down the stairs, she moved so slowly.

"That's no way to behave in a kitchen that ain't yours!" she said sharply. She leaned on the back of a chair for support.

"And you shouldn't be walking around," I said.

Grace sat down gingerly and said in a low voice, "I saw the way you smiled at him. Now I knows why you was so eager to get here."

"No, you don't." I tried to keep a bland look, setting some bread and jam before her.

"I can't eat nothin'," she said, pushing it away. "I'm full of aches and pains after that bumpy ride las' night. My belly's as tight as a drum."

I stared in amazement at Grace's huge hump. The gathers of her skirt spread over it like a tent.

"How long until the baby—," I began, then broke off, hearing the pounding of horses' hooves and the excited voices of the Weigel sisters.

"Better not be rebels coming, 'cause I can't move fast enough to hide from 'em," said Grace wearily.

I ran outside to see four horses stirring up clouds of dust. Their riders wore blue coats with brass buttons. One of them dismounted at the porch steps and introduced himself as Gouverneur Warren. It was a strange name, I thought, but even more impressive was his title: brigadier general and chief engineer of the Army of the Potomac.

"Governor Warren? Governor of what state?" asked Bonnie Weigel, who was hard of hearing. Louisa motioned for her to be quiet.

"*Wilkommen, Herr* General Warren," said Mrs. Weigel proudly. "Welcome to this house, built by my husband's father with his own two hands."

General Warren nodded politely. "It's a fine house, ma'am. General Meade has sent me to survey the area around these hills."

"You're not planning a battle here, are you?" she asked, narrowing her eyes with suspicion.

"Not precisely here, but it may be close by."

"Is there fighting in Gettysburg still?" Louisa Weigel broke in.

"Just some skirmishing between our troops on Cemetery Hill and the rebels in the town," the general replied, then turned back to Mrs. Weigel. "Mr. Washington Roebling and I request permission to view the field from the roof of your fine house," he said firmly, as if he did not expect to be denied. The aide dismounted and took off his hat.

But Mrs. Weigel shook her head. "*Keine Soldaten in meinem Haus!* No soldiers in my house, shooting from the windows. We have women and children here, and wounded men in the barn. You will only draw fire on us."

General Warren scratched his head and exchanged looks with his aide.

"That is not my intention, ma'am," he replied.

Mrs. Weigel nodded. "Then you may observe. Lizzie, your legs are younger than mine. Show the general the door on the upper landing that leads to the attic and the roof. *Mach schnell.* Hurry!"

While two of the aides remained with the horses, General Warren and Washington Roebling followed me up the narrow stairway. I unlatched the small attic window and they climbed through. Then the aide turned and offered me his hand. Surprised, I took it and clambered up the tin roof, clutching my skirts to keep from tripping over them. I could feel the heat of the metal through my shoes.

The peak of the roof offered a splendid view across Taneytown Road, where fields and scattered groves of trees spread far into the distance. Over this undulating valley I could see ranks of infantry and artillery sweeping northward, with officers on horseback riding to and fro between them.

General Warren looked through his field glasses and made quick, precise sketches on paper. He had wavy hair that receded from his wide forehead; a large, hooked nose; and a bushy mustache that entirely covered his lips. The aide had short dark hair and a smooth face. Watching him as he sorted papers in his leather pouch, I decided he was even more handsome than Frederick Hartmann.

"The hills behind us run north along Taneytown Road, all the way to the cemetery," I said, trying to be helpful.

"Yes, our troops are positioned along that ridge," said the general. "Clear to the cemetery and then around to the next hill."

"That would be Culp's Hill," I said. "I saw them building defenses there last night."

Mr. Roebling gave me a questioning look. I blushed and fell silent, lest I reveal the incident with the rebel spies.

"If you could see that far, our defense would look like a fishhook. A good, tight formation," said General Warren, sounding confident. "Now we can feed these reserves anywhere they're needed along the line."

"Smartest thing General Hancock did yesterday was to order our retreating soldiers to occupy those hills," added Roebling.

"But where are the rebels now?" I asked.

"Along a ridge that runs roughly parallel to this one, about a mile to the west," replied the general. "We can't see them from here because of that hill." He considered the wooded slope behind the Weigel house and came to a decision. "Roebling, take Mackenzie with you up there. There ought to be a signal tower at the top. Note the Confederate troop positions. Move quickly and report back to me here. We meet with General Meade at three o'clock."

Roebling disappeared through the attic window, and General Warren sat down, straddling the rooftop while he jotted notes. I leaned against the chimney, watching him.

"What do you know about these hills, Miss—?"

"Lizzie Allbauer, sir. Well, that's Big Round Top off to the left, and this one directly behind the house we call Little Round Top." A thought had just occurred to me. "General, what if the rebels come right over these hills, or right between them?"

"According to this report, they're too thickly wooded to get troops and artillery to the top," he said, glancing at his papers. "So I don't reckon the Johnnies can flank us here."

"Well, I've never been on Big Round Top, but Little Round Top is mostly bare on the far side. Many of the trees have been cut down for timber," I explained. "We go sledding there in the winter."

General Warren looked at me intently. "So you're telling me . . ."

"It's steep in places and rocky, but it's easy enough to get to by the lane that runs west from Taneytown Road."

The general frowned. "Moving troops into position from that direction, we'd be fully exposed to rebel fire." He looked at the hill, dense with trees. "Wish we could get up there from this side."

"You can!" I cried, suddenly remembering the old logging path we had taken in the winter. "There is a way you can get artillery up there without being seen by the rebels. I can show you."

"General Meade needs to hear this right away," said Warren, springing to his feet. I thought he would jump off the roof in his haste. But instead he squeezed his large frame through the attic window. I slipped through more easily and ran down the stairs to keep up with him.

"Roebling! Where are you, man?" the general shouted.

"They're not back yet, sir," said the one aide who remained.

General Warren paced back and forth on the porch and checked his pocket watch. I knew what he was thinking: that the far slope of Little Round Top lay open, and the battle might belong to whomever could reach it first. My stomach twisted nervously.

"It's nearly three o'clock. I can't wait any longer. Reese, let's go. Come along, Miss Allbauer."

All at once I found myself in front of the general in his saddle. As he spurred the horse, I caught a brief glimpse of an astonished Mrs. Weigel returning from the barn. We galloped along Taneytown Road, and I tried to point out the way leading to the logging path.

"There's no time now. We'll report to General Meade first," Warren shouted.

I gripped the pommel and clung with my knees to the horse. The wind whistled past my ears and worked my hair loose. The general's arm was around me, pressing me to his chest. I felt like a damsel from King Arthur's time. Here I was, on my way to see General Meade and show him a route for his army. What a thrilling story this would make!

General Warren reined in his horse before a small whitewashed cottage. By the flag flying from a pole and the pennants decorating the porch, I took this for General Meade's headquarters. Horses tethered to the picket fence flicked away flies with their tails. Guards stood at attention as General Warren dismounted.

"Reese, send Roebling in directly when he arrives," he said, handing the aide the reins and disappearing into the cottage.

I slipped off the horse's back and stretched my legs. I tried to imagine the scene inside the cottage. When would General Meade come out? How should I greet him? The buzz of insects in the surrounding fields grew more intense and the temperature seemed to rise with it.

"Miss Allbauer!" I jumped as General Warren called my name. He beckoned to me from the doorway and I hurried to him, almost tripping in my excitement.

Inside the tiny cottage, the air was thick with heat and tobacco smoke. Generals and officers, wearing long coats with bright shoulder decorations, crowded around a table piled with maps and papers. The one I took to be General Meade stood up. He was about six feet tall, lean and strongly built. His bushy beard was brown and gray and a pair of spectacles sat on his long nose. He acknowledged me with a nod.

"General Warren informs me that you know the west-facing side of this hill to be clear and unforested?" he asked in a brisk voice, his finger resting on the map. "Are you quite certain of that?"

"Yes, sir." My voice came out as a squeak. "Yes, sir," I repeated, louder.

"Please show me the location of the path you say is passable."

I peered at the map, trying to make sense of its jagged lines, arrows, crosses, and jottings. I located Taneytown Road and the lane that ran westward by Little Round Top toward Mr. Rose's wheat field. The two hills were drawn as circles of little marks like sunbursts. My finger hovered, trembling, as it sought the spot where the logging path led to Little Round Top. General Meade tapped the edge of the map. I felt myself grow flustered.

"It's somewhere between this creek and the road. I can't tell exactly from this map," I said in dismay. "But I can take you there."

Meade's sharp eyes regarded me and the brows above them bristled. I didn't look away. He was about to speak when Washington Roebling strode into the room and spoke into General Warren's ear.

"General Meade, sir, pardon my interruption," said General Warren, stepping forward. "My aides Mackenzie and Roebling have just returned from the smaller hill. It indeed affords a wide vantage of the field. But there is a problem, sir. Our line is no longer straight. General Sickles has moved his men forward into an orchard along the Emmitsburg Road, leaving a gap in the line. We're vulnerable there."

"Damn Sickles!" exploded Meade. He turned to Roebling. "How did you get up that hill? Did you come across any kind of road?"

"No, sir, I just hacked my way through the brush. That's why I'm late, sir."

General Meade pursed his lips tightly and returned his attention to the map. I stepped back as the officers gathered around the table and began to debate how to reinforce the line broken by Sickles. General Meade made bold marks on the map with a pencil and issued terse orders. One by one the generals saluted and left the cottage. I thought I had been forgotten until I heard Meade's final sharp command.

"Warren, take the lady to the hill called Little Round Top. Find that road and determine if it's suitable. Meanwhile I will pay a personal visit to General Sickles and discover why he flouts my orders," he added testily.

Moments later I was again in Warren's saddle, galloping down Taneytown Road in a flurry of flags, with grit in my mouth and the pounding of hooves in my ears. I wished everyone I knew could see me, Lizzie Allbauer, in the company of the commanding general of the Union army and all his aides!

We came to the road that led to the peach orchard, and General Meade and his party broke off to meet with Sickles. General Warren slowed his horse and I began to look for the logging path. The three aides followed us. We crisscrossed the shrubby ground at the base of the hill and splashed through the creek north of the Weigel farm as I grew more and more confused.

"I know it's directly by this creek, but the land looks different in the summer with all the bushes and the trees full of leaves," I tried to explain. "In the winter you can see it clear as anything."

Just then the booming of artillery began. I cringed and gripped the horse's mane.

"Well, we don't exactly have the luxury of waiting until winter," said General Warren crisply. I felt his muscles tense as he called out, "Turn around, men! Let's look farther to the south."

I knew the path was not in that direction. But General Warren had lost confidence in me. Holding on to the pommel and leaning to the side, I craned my neck to look behind him. Then, at last, I recognized a large pitted boulder.

"No! Turn back. I see it now," I cried, pointing to the rock. Warren's aides jumped from their horses and, slashing at the bushes and brambles with hatchets, soon exposed the road. It was overgrown with tall grass but easily wide enough for wagons. We rode up the hill, and when the path ended we continued on foot to the top. The woods ended in a clearing marked with huge boulders that looked as if they were tumbling down the opposite slope. General Warren and his aides stepped out onto a wide, flat rock, and after a brief conference, one of the aides saluted and left.

Curious to see where the battle would unfold, I ventured from the shelter of the trees onto the flat rock. A wide and deep landscape stretched before me, alive with movement. At the base of Little Round Top flowed Plum Run, and beyond the creek, in a field enclosed by trees and strewn with boulders, soldiers scurried like ants, moving the smaller rocks and cutting trees to make breastworks. As my eye traveled north, I saw the narrow lane from Taneytown Road clogged with horses pulling artillery. Union soldiers spilled from the roadway into the valley like water after a flood. Beyond, the road passed by a wheat field that looked like a gold flag spread on the earth, dotted with moving specks of dark blue.

"What you're seeing is the left flank of the Union army, the end of the line that extends nearly three miles," General Warren said with a grand gesture of his arm.

"It makes me proud to see them, sir," I said. But I wished the scene would suddenly freeze into a painting, without a single shot being fired.

On the ridge beyond Emmitsburg Road, a series of flares followed by white puffs of smoke caught my eye. Seconds later the booming reached my ears, and I realized those were enemy cannons, nearly a mile away. The Union cannons fired back.

"The rebels'll try to do as much damage as possible with their artillery before engaging the infantry," explained Mr. Roebling. "Look for yourself."

He handed me his field glasses, and I gasped as the scene leaped directly before my eyes in precise detail. I saw a shell burst amid a herd of unlucky cattle standing in the creek, which began to flow red from their blood. I watched a team of artillerymen load a cannon, light the fuse, fall back, and the great iron gun rock as it recoiled with the blast. I saw a man idly smoking behind a pile of rocks and several soldiers struggling to move a wagon with a broken wheel.

"Follow that lane beyond the wheat field and you'll see where Sickles has put himself, sticking out like a sore thumb," Roebling said, stooping slightly and directing my gaze with his outstretched arm.

My face inadvertently brushed against the rough nap of his sleeve, and I smelled the sharp tang of wool and sweat, but I didn't draw back, so intent was I on the scene. There they were, the wayward troops, occupying a peach orchard on a rise along the Emmitsburg Road, and separated from the rest of the line by a wide gap. A sudden burst of artillery fire came from the orchard.

General Warren erupted like an angry cannon.

"Now that damn fool Sickles is provoking the rebels! They're going to attack before we're ready and collapse the line there." Roebling went to the general's side just as another aide called out, "General, look! The rebels' right flank is getting mighty close."

Using Roebling's glasses, I peered along the distant ridge until I could make out the gray soldiers moving toward the Emmitsburg Road about half a mile south of General Sickles's men in the peach orchard. My hands began to shake, making the scene jump wildly. I went over and gave Roebling his glasses. He took them without even glancing at me.

"Damn, I didn't know they were this far south! We need men up here now," said General Warren. "Mackenzie, get this message to Meade at once," he said, scribbling a note and giving it to his aide.

I knew I ought to run back to the Weigel house and take refuge inside its fortlike stone walls. But the unfolding battle had seized my attention, rooting me to the spot against my better judgment. Artillery fire now came from all along the distant Confederate line as foot soldiers dashed toward the Emmitsburg Road. I could faintly hear them yelping like a pack of hunting dogs. Cannons in the wheat field and the boulder-strewn meadow flared in reply, and the rebels began to drop in their tracks. I covered my ears against the deafening noise. Soon smoke obscured the field, and I knew only that a blue and gray mass of men had melted together below me.

General Warren paced back and forth on the large rock. "Damn Sickles forever!" I heard him say as the rebel guns pounded exposed troops in the peach orchard. I couldn't blame him for cursing. It looked as if the Union line might give way, letting the enemy sweep through the entire valley.

"Good God, Miss Allbauer, what are you doing here still?" Warren shouted at me. He was immediately distracted again. "Roebling, I think Law's brigade is heading straight for that hill. I don't know if our sharpshooters down there can hold them off." He motioned to where the end of the Confederate line was approaching Big Round Top. "We've got to hold them there." He pointed to the rocky field below, where hundreds of our soldiers hunkered down behind breastworks shooting at the rebels. Already bodies lay scattered on the ground.

"We call that the Devil's Den," I said, but my voice came out as a hoarse croak and no one heard me.

"If our men break and run from there, the rebels will be all over this hill, and once they get their batteries up here they'll destroy this whole end of the line," said General Warren grimly. "It's darn near too late."

I had decided it was time to take myself back to the Weigels', when Mackenzie returned, reining in his foaming horse just short of the big rock.

"General Warren, sir!" he called out. "Meade has ordered General Sykes to cover this hill immediately. Colonel Strong Vincent is moving four regiments into place along the southwest slopes even now."

The name *Strong Vincent* sounded familiar. I tried to recall where I had heard it.

"Now we have a fighting chance!" cried Warren, striking his fist into his palm. "Miss Allbauer?" he called, striding over to where I stood. "Allow me to thank you for your service to the Union today. Your information regarding this hill has been most valuable. I believe we can now keep the rebels from flanking us here."

"You're welcome, sir." I smiled, glowing with importance, then forced a more sober expression, considering the serious situation. "And good luck today."

"Roebling, take this young lady home or else give her a rifle, for we'll be in the midst of it here before long."

"Who is Colonel Strong Vincent?" I asked Roebling as we mounted his horse.

"He and his men arrived from Hanover this morning. They have been in reserve all day, so they're rested up now and ready for action. Good thing, because a lot depends on them."

He steered his horse to the side of the logging road to make way for a group of horsemen. The lead rider carried a banner printed with a square blue cross with flared ends. Roebling and the officers saluted each other.

"That was General Crawford and Colonel Vincent," Roebling said to me. "With the vanguard of the Fifth Corps."

Finally I remembered the letter from Luke. *Our regiment is in the good hands of Colonel Strong Vincent, his courage matches his name.* Despite the day's heat, I felt a cold flash of fear.

I twisted around in the saddle to face Roebling.

"My brother Luke is serving under Colonel Vincent."

"Well, indeed!" he said with a smile. A lock of dark hair fell over his forehead. "Then he'll be fighting good and hard to hold this hill and keep the rebels out of your backyard, won't he? He'll want to make you proud of him."

Lizzie

Chapter 36

Mr. Roebling deposited me at the farmhouse, tipped his hat, and galloped away again. With him went all my sense of security, all my pride in having helped the Union generals strengthen their defenses on Little Round Top. All I could think of was that my brother would soon join the battle, and if anything were to happen to him, it would be my fault.

"*Gott in Himmel!* I was worried to death about you!" I heard Mrs. Weigel cry out. "Where were you? *Nein*, tell me later. Go to the cellar where it's safe."

I glanced toward the barn, hoping to see Martin, while Mrs. Weigel shoved me toward the house.

"What would I tell *deine Mutter* if you hadn't come back?" she scolded.

"You saw me go with the general. I was not in danger," I said, annoyed by the fuss she was making.

In the cellar, Louisa and Bonnie were knitting by the light of an oil lamp. Grace, in a rocking chair, looked at me and raised her eyebrows. The sisters peppered me with questions, but I didn't feel like talking. I admitted that I had seen General Meade and that there was fighting in the valley. I did not tell them everything I knew, and what I left unsaid weighed on me like a lie.

"Well, Little Round Top stands safely between us and the battle, *Gott sei dank*," said Mrs. Weigel.

"But what if the cannonballs come over the hill and explode here on the roof?" asked Jack, sounding more eager than afraid.

"They can't shoot that far," I replied, though I was not at all certain. The sounds of artillery rumbled through the ground, entering my very bones. Clara covered her ears and whimpered. Hadn't we left Gettysburg to avoid this?

I sat on the floor and let its coolness seep into me. My dress, damp from sweat, now felt cold on my skin, and I shivered. I picked up a toy that the children had been playing with, a maze of angled tunnels made from tin and supported by wooden struts. I dropped a marble in the funnel at the top and tipped the frame this way and that, watching the marble tumble downward. I tried to manuever it away from the wooden trap at the bottom and out the chute instead, but again and again the marble rolled into the trap.

Louisa Weigel cleared her throat reprovingly. I looked up to see that she had opened the Bible. With a sigh I put the toy aside and folded my hands in my lap.

Louisa leaned close to the pages and read aloud. "*Your hand will find all your enemies. You shall make them as a fiery oven in the time of your anger; the Lord shall swallow them up in His wrath and the fire shall devour them.*"

"*Liebe Jesu!* Sweet Jesus, read something else," said Mrs. Weigel.

"The fall of Jericho, perhaps?" Louisa suggested.

"No, *ein Familiengeschichte*, a story to take our minds away from battle. Perhaps Noah and his ark—"

An explosion made us all start and scream. It sounded like the house itself had been hit.

"I was right!" shouted Jack.

Mrs. Weigel jumped to her feet.

"*Gott in Himmel!* I'm fetching that boy in here right now!" she said, as if Martin were at fault for playing with fireworks and needed to be punished.

I heard the pounding of feet overhead, and Martin appeared at the cellar door.

"That was a close one," he said. "Tore up the field beside the barn. Pa made us come back to the house." He ducked to avoid the overhead beams, and a pale-looking Annie followed him down the stairs, steadying herself with a hand on his shoulder. Her hair no longer hung in neat ringlets, but was tied underneath a headcloth like a servant's.

"*Wo ist dein Vati?*" Mrs. Weigel demanded of Martin

"*In der Scheune, natürlich.* Papa is taking down the stalls in the barn and using the wood to build more cots. He says he is not afraid for himself."

Mrs. Weigel threw up her hands and began to complain in German. Martin came over and sat next to me, his long legs sprawled out in front of him.

"Where have you been all day?" he asked.

"If I told you, you would never believe me," I said, even though I was eager to tell him. Was I actually flirting?

"Try me. If you can look me in the eye, I'll believe everything you say."

Was Martin now teasing me? I couldn't see his expression because he was in the shadows. So I shifted, letting the dim light from Louisa's lamp fall on his face. Then I told him about meeting General Warren and General Meade and showing them up the logging path. Our faces were less than a foot apart, but I was too intent on my story to let myself become flustered.

Martin's eyebrows lifted until horizontal lines crossed his forehead.

"And *you* got to see General Meade and the battlefield because I was *asleep*?"

"Well, you said not to wake you unless the house was on fire," I reminded him.

"And the reserves are on their way to the field now?"

I nodded and whispered, "I'm worried about Luke."

"And Sam Pierpont and all the other fellows. Out there fighting while I'm hiding out in a cellar." Martin leaped to his feet and bounded up the cellar stairs before I or his mother could stop him. The door slammed behind him.

"Martin?" Mrs. Weigel's voice trembled. A look of pain crossed her face. She started to get up but changed her mind and sat down, squeezing her eyes shut. Louisa patted her hand.

Annie scuttled over to me on her hands and knees.

"I saw you two whispering together. What happened? He likes you, you know. Did he try to kiss you and you wouldn't let him?"

I glared at Annie. "Don't be a fool. His mother is right over there."

"Well, if the boy I liked was sitting here, I wouldn't go and say something to make him run off like that."

"I didn't," I protested irritably. I decided not to tell Annie that my brother, the boy she supposedly liked, was fighting nearby.

"Luke is still writing to me, you know," said Annie. "Rosanna hasn't written at all, but she and I can swap nursing stories when she comes back—"

"She'll never come back to Gettysburg," I said knowingly.

Annie sighed and slid down until she was lying on her side, her head resting in the crook of her arm. I worried about Martin. Where had he gone so suddenly, and why?

"Lizzie, remember that huge flag we made at the beginning of the war?" Annie said, touching my arm. "I also thought it was a bit useless. But I didn't say anything because I wanted to be Rosanna's friend. And then I didn't even help her finish it."

Annie's confession astonished me. "That was a long time ago. Let's just forget—" I heard a grunt and looked down to see that Annie had fallen asleep with her mouth wide open.

A lull came in the fighting. Jack and Clara fell asleep alongside Annie, and the rest of us ventured upstairs. Mrs. Weigel cleaned up a batch of bread dough that had risen beyond the bowl, spilled onto the table, and begun to dry out. I went outside to get fresh water from the pump near the porch. I figured that the rebels had been driven back, for if they had taken the hill, they would now be swarming the Weigel farm. Shadows crept across Taneytown Road until the sun lit only the distant fields, where white specks indicated the tents of a camp.

A sinking feeling came to me. Martin had gone off to join the soldiers there! He was ashamed of being at home while most young men were away fighting. It dismayed me to think that he was just like everyone else who thought that to be a man you had to be carrying a rifle in a war. "Please don't get hurt!" I whispered.

"Ain't gonna be long in comin' now," Grace said, interrupting my thoughts. Her words sounded like a prophecy of doom. Then with a start I realized she was referring to her baby.

"How can you tell?" I asked. "Don't first babies come slow? Mama says Luke took forever and a day being born but I came out right after."

"Feels like a rope tied aroun' my middle."

"Grace, just tell me when you need a doctor and I'll fetch one."

"You think the doctor will leave dyin' soldiers to help a Negro gal have a baby?" Her tone was sharp, but not bitter.

"The Weigel sisters can help. A farmer's wife always knows about giving birth," I said.

I thought I heard Grace say, "I'll bear it out myself," but an empty artillery wagon rolled by at that moment. A few tattered soldiers stumbled toward the barn on makeshift crutches. The wounded were coming from Taneytown Road.

"I dreamed las' night that Amos and Ben were somewhere safe," Grace said softly.

Gazing out over the fields again, I nodded. "In your dream, was Luke with them?"

"No. Why you ask?"

"Because he might be out there now," I said. "Oh, Grace, I showed the generals a path up Little Round Top, so they could hold back the rebels from coming over these hills."

"Why, you are some kind of hero, Miz Lizzie," Grace said with a smile.

I shook my head. "No! Luke's regiment was one of those called to the battle. If something happens to him, it will be my fault!"

A hospital orderly came to fetch a bucket of water and we watched in silence as he pumped it and left again.

"I never tol' you 'bout my brother," Grace said. She eased herself down onto the porch steps.

Full of curiosity, I sat down beside her, focusing all my attention on her face. She looked beyond me, into the past.

"Befo' I belonged to Mastuh McCarrick an' met Amos, I was a house Negro at a rice plantation. I looked after the young 'uns of Mastuh Shelby an' his missus. I also took care of my sister's boy, Nate, who was raised in the big house too." Grace paused. "Nate, he had lighter skin than my sister an' had Mastuh Shelby's blue eyes. You understand?"

I nodded, for I had heard of plantation owners fathering children with their slaves.

"I loved Nate like he was mine. When my sister died of a fever, I was all the boy had."

"What about your brother?" I asked.

"Cyrus. He hated Mastuh Shelby for what he did to our sister an' swore he'd run away. I begged him not to. I was scared he'd be caught by the dogs and tore to pieces." Grace took a deep breath. "Then Mastuh Shelby heard that Cyrus were plannin' an uprisin'. He demanded I tell him ever'thin' I knowed an' he'd go easy on Cyrus. He said if I lied to him he'd sell Nate an' I'd never see the boy again."

"What did you do?" I prompted. "Was your brother really planning a revolt?"

"He was, along with some others. I tol' my mastuh where the guns was buried in the bean patch and rifles in the cemetery. But he went back on his word. He whipped Cyrus with a cat-o'-nine-tails till the blood run like a river, then hanged him from a tree. Said it was a lesson to anyone even thinkin' 'bout risin' up."

"Oh, how awful!" I reached toward Grace, but she leaned away from me.

"I betrayed my brother. Because of me, he was killed. An' I live with that like a stone aroun' my neck," she said in a hard voice, without self-pity. "Lizzie, don' you regret what you done. Your brother is fightin' in a noble cause."

"It wasn't your fault that your master lied, Grace," I said, trying to offer some comfort in return. "At least you had Nate."

"No, I didn't. Mastuh sold him anyway. He sold his own son!" Her voice rose with anguish. "So I ran away, not carin' if I lived or died. But I was caught an' taken back to Mastuh Shelby, who gave me forty lashes, then sold me to Mastuh McCarrick."

"I'm so sorry, Grace," I whispered through my tears. At last I understood the reason for Grace's cool, reserved ways. Why she never talked about her family. And why she simply had to believe that Amos would find his way back. He was her savior. She had no one else.

I went to the pump and splashed water on my face, then wetted a corner of my apron and, crouching down, began to dab Grace's face with it. She closed her eyes and did not resist my touch. The curves of her face were more gradual than my own, and her dark skin gleamed.

"Grace," I said, "I've hated the war from the beginning." I wiped her neck and she bent her head to the side. "But now I am proud of what Papa and Luke are fighting for."

"Thank you," she murmured. She patted her face dry with her own skirt.

Out of the corner of my eye, I saw something move. I stood up to get a better look and noticed, at the edge of the grassy field that sloped into the wooded hillside, five or six rebels emerge from the brush. They held rifles across their chests and ran, hunched over, toward the house. A scream rose to my throat but stuck there. I moved in front of Grace. More gray-clad soldiers sprang from the bushes like rabbits. As they crossed the field to my right, a fife and drum sounded on my left, but the barn blocked my view of the approaching band. Were they leading more rebels? A standard-bearer suddenly ran into view from behind the barn, waving a tattered blue flag with a yellow fringe and a familiar seal. I recognized the flag of the Pennsylvania Reserves.

I found my voice and released a shout as a company of blue-clad soldiers ran between the Weigel barn and the foot of Little Round Top, trying to cut off the rebels. But when the shooting erupted not a hundred yards from where I stood, I dropped to my hands and knees and pulled Grace with me into a corner of the porch. The low stone wall barely shielded us. Grace curled into a ball, her arms around her stomach. The sharp rifle fire made my ears throb with pain. I longed to see if Luke was among the soldiers but dared not lift my head to look.

The skirmish lasted only a few minutes. After the last shots had been fired, I peered over the ledge of the porch. Two rebels lay face-down in the grass and a third had fallen backward, his arm flung over his head. Another dragged himself toward the barn. The Pennsylvania soldiers had disappeared into the thickets of Little Round Top, and I guessed by the scattered rifle shots that they were chasing the last of the rebels back over the hill.

"Help me up, Lizzie. I'm goin' inside," said Grace. "You best come too."

"I will, in a minute."

But with the danger past, every ounce of strength had flowed out of me, and it was easier just to sink down onto the porch. So I sat there with my back against the stone house, thinking about the men who lay dead only yards away from me. Somewhere in the South, a girl my age would learn that her brother had been killed at a farmhouse near Gettysburg, and a mother would weep for her son. I wanted my papa and Luke to come home alive. Didn't these soldiers also deserve to live?

An orderly finally came out and dragged the three dead rebels away. Dusk gave way to darkness and the fireflies began to flicker randomly, like tiny soundless explosions. Still I sat, not even bothering to wipe away the tears that rolled down my face and tickled my neck as I thought of my family. We had been thrown like grain to the four winds. Would we ever find our way together again? And where was Martin? Had he now joined the ranks of soldiers who might never return alive, leaving behind only women to mourn them?

Rosanna

Chapter 37

July 2, 1863 camp south of Lutheran Seminary, west of Gettysburg

The army made slow progress toward Gettysburg, so I was able to pick a large sack of blackberries without falling behind. I was also lucky enough to find a satchel thrown down by some overburdened soldier, containing a decent pair of field glasses. I expect they will prove useful.

It was nearly dusk when I saw the first evidence of battle, the smoldering remains of a barn and a house with only the brick chimney left standing. We crossed Willoughby Run, all mud and murky water littered with the debris of battle. Dead horses blocked the road, and a thick cloud of fat blueflies swarmed around them. Though I held a handkerchief over my nose, it was not enough to keep away the stench. At least the dead and wounded men have been removed from the field.

Above the trees I could see the cupola of the Lutheran Seminary crowning Oak Ridge. But I was denied my much-anticipated view of the town beyond, for I was obliged to follow the troops as they bore southward behind the ridge. It was dark when I reached the grove of trees that served as a camp. Tom had already put up a tent for me using saplings and canvas. It was thoughtful of him, though I do not expect to sleep much tonight.

I helped the cook dish up supper for the men of John's company. The stew featured some chickens that Hiram Watt claimed to find running loose. No one believed him. I mixed some berries with a little sugar in a frying pan and, pouring a thin batter over them, cooked it on the coals until the berries bubbled and sent up the most divine smell. I made several batches of this cobbler and the men licked every bit of it up.

Reports of today's battle come in fragments. The federals hold Culp's Hill, the cemetery, and the hills all along Taneytown Road. Their General Sickles was shot through the leg and forced to yield his ground, while our General Barksdale was mortally wounded. Though our losses were great, the men anticipate a victory tomorrow, for General Pickett inspires them with his bravado and fierce energy. I judge him quite handsome, with his wavy beard and long, curling hair. But he is said to be completely enamored of the young beauty to whom he is engaged.

This afternoon General Jeb Stuart and his cavalry finally arrived on the field, several days later than expected. Stuart's raids around Carlisle (Pennsylvania) netted a hundred or more wagons and teams, but Lee is not impressed. He wanted Stuart to scout the enemy's location. I heard one officer say that had Stuart arrived even two days earlier with the needed information, Lee could have pulled his army together, surprised the federals, and victory would already be ours. Possibly the battle would have occurred at some other place, sparing Gettysburg. But such speculation is pointless.

A while ago battle resumed about a mile to the east. What kind of fury makes men blaze away at each other in pitch darkness? All fires in camp were put out so that our position would not be revealed. In the dark I nearly tripped over men who had fallen asleep where weariness overtook them and lay in positions resembling death itself. Shaken, I returned to my tent and began to repack my haversacks with bandages, iodine, and whiskey, when Tom appeared out of the darkness and crouched next to me.

"Are you fixin' to leave?" he asked.

I said I was only preparing for tomorrow and admitted to being frightened.

"We're in the lion's den all right, an' no one but God Almighty can keep us from his jaws," he said, shaking his head. "You find somewhere safe to stay during the battle. Mastuh John would wish it."

"I won't do anything foolish, Tom. But I'm not going to hide. I aim to keep as many men as I can from dying."

"An' I'll be nearby, handlin' a team o' horses with the artillery."

"Why, Tom?" I asked. "Why are you staying? You are free to go."

"Same as you, Miz Rosanna, I made a choice. I decided to help them that have been good to me."

Tom's words brought tears to my eyes. No less than John, he was an honorable gentleman.

"I have a favor to ask, Tom," I said, showing him my journal. "I always carry this book with me. It will be in my knapsack. If something should happen to me, please take it to my cousin Lizzie Allbauer in Gettysburg."

He promised and we parted, offering no false assurances for tomorrow. So in the event that I never write here again, these last words are for you, Lizzie, penned in my canvas lean-to in this copse of trees, and lit by the guttering flame of my small lamp:

You have been my dearest friend. I love you and daily regret the circumstances of war that have separated us. I know you will forgive all my frailties. Remember me, Lizzie.

Lizzie

Chapter 38

I was dreaming about rocking in a boat on a dark sea. Someone was calling my name and shaking me. I opened my eyes. It was dark and I was still on the Weigels' front porch. My cheeks felt stiff with dried tears and my head hurt from leaning against the rock.

"You scared me, Lizzie, lying here and not moving."

"Martin? Is that you?" I sat up, blinking, then recognized his shape more than his face. "So you didn't run off!" I said, sighing with relief.

"Why would I do that? You must have been dreaming," said Martin gently. "But try to wake up now."

"Why? What has happened?" I said, struggling to sit up. Worry filled me. "Is it Luke?"

"No, but we really need your help, Lizzie. Even if you just go around with a bucket of water. You don't have to come into the hospital."

That's when I saw the wounded men lying in the yard and propped against the house, dozens of them, and heard their moaning.

"Where did they all come from?" I asked, still dazed with sleep.

"From the battle on Little Round Top, mostly."

"Of course I'll help," I said with a sick feeling. "Let me find a lamp."

In the kitchen, army nurses were preparing coffee and broth while Bonnie Weigel stirred the pots and Louisa stoked the oven fire.

"*Louisa, was machst du? Das Brot wird gebrennt werden!*" cried Martin's mother, opening the oven door and fanning away the smoke. "There you are, Lizzie. I sent the children upstairs. *Es ist schrecklich!*— too terrible for their eyes. They should have stayed in town!"

I went to check on the children and found Grace pacing the hallway, grimacing.

"Do you need a doctor now?" I asked in alarm.

"No, I be fine. Go 'long with you now," she said, waving me away.

I found a lamp and went back to the kitchen, where someone handed me a pot of broth. I stepped off the porch carrying the heavy pot and stumbled over a man lying on the ground. His arms were crossed over his stomach, and his eyes were closed. The smell of sweat and rancid blood rose from him. Buzzing flies settled on his clothes. I thought of the back room of the butcher shop at the end of a busy workday. The man stirred. I crouched beside him.

"What can I do for you?" I asked timidly.

"Nothing. I'm dying," the man replied. He lifted his elbows enough for me to see his torn flesh and glistening innards. I let out a cry and fell back on my rear. Afraid I was going to be sick, I squeezed my eyes shut tightly.

"I'll have something to drink, miss."

My eyes flew open. A man with a bloodied sash wrapped around his head was beckoning to me. I scrambled over to him.

"An' a little smile with that, if you please. That's better."

Embarrassed that he had seen my reaction to the dying man, I gave him a big smile as he requested. After I dribbled broth into his mouth, he lay back with a deep sigh. I moved on to another soldier, having realized it was easier if I looked into their eyes, not at their wounds. When I saw someone badly injured, I called out to one of the surgeons, who came over to determine whether the man should be operated on. Then Martin or his father would carry him into the hospital.

Some of the men told rambling stories like they were fevered. One man swore he could have walked across the wheat field without touching the ground, the dead lay so thick there. I heard that General Sickles had lost the peach orchard and been shot in the leg at the Trostle farm, where dead horses lay in heaps.

It was a soldier from Maine with a gash in his leg who told me about the battle's climax, the struggle for Little Round Top. The rebels had attacked again and again and had almost won the hill when the few remaining defenders fixed their bayonets to the end of their rifles, charged the rebels, and sent them flying in retreat. One more rebel attack, he said, would have done them in. But they had held on to the hill and kept the Union's southern flank from collapsing.

I asked an ambulance driver waiting by the barn if he had seen or heard anything of Luke's regiment.

"The First Pennsylvania Reserves, Thirtieth Regiment?" he repeated thoughtfully. "I b'lieve they're the ones still standing watch over the batteries on the hill. Lyin' down rather, if they're smart. Them rebel sharpshooters are like coons, they can see in the dark."

The news that Luke's regiment was standing guard on Little Round Top filled me with hope. He was nearby, protecting us. Then a darker thought occurred to me.

"Have you brought in any casualites from that regiment?" I asked.

He shook his head. "Sorry, miss, but I've come back empty-handed. It's too dangerous to pick up the injured because pickets on both sides are firing wildly at anything that moves."

All at once I feared that Luke might be lying in the woods, wounded and in danger of losing his life during the night. Numbly I went back into the house, where Mrs. Weigel was nursing two wounded officers in the parlor. One gritted his teeth while she bandaged his chest. The other propped his legs on the good settee, still wearing his boots. His head was wrapped in what looked like an old apron, and he smoked a cigar that filled the room with thick smoke. The sight was almost comical, but I was too worried about Luke even to smile.

"Lizzie, take a pot of broth to the *hungrige Menschen* by the shed," called Mrs. Weigel.

"Yes, ma'am," I said.

In the kitchen, a single pot of thin broth simmered on the stove. There were no potatoes or onions left, so I stirred in some flour to thicken it. With the pot in one hand and a lamp in the other, I made my way to the shed. I ladled broth into a tin cup and handed it to a man half reclining on a bedroll. He inserted the cup under his long brushy mustache and sipped loudly. There was something familiar about his powder-blackened face. He raised his head and the light shone into the unmistakable blue eyes of Frederick Hartmann.

"Why, my dear Miss Allbauer, what a pleasure."

"Mr. Hartmann? Is it really you?" I said stupidly.

"The same." He nodded. "Although you're taller since I last saw you."

"That was—last October. I haven't grown that much. Anyway, how can you tell if I'm taller if I'm not even standing up?" There I went, sounding coy again.

"Not only taller, but prettier, and witty, too," he said, winking at me.

I knew why Margaret was so sweet on him. Quickly, to cover up my confusion, I said, "Are you hurt? Let me find a doctor to look at you."

"No, I don't need a sawbones," he said with a wave of his hand. It shook, however, as he lowered it to his chest. "I hope to live a while longer."

I looked him over and was relieved to see he was all in one piece.

"Well, can you get up and come inside then?"

"Not quite. I took some shrapnel in my back. The bleeding's stopped, but my legs are still numb. I don't need anything but another cup of that broth."

"How long have you been here? Where's your horse?" I asked, refilling his cup.

"Running wild somewhere, like I wish I was. Our cavalry just came up from Emmitsburg and caught the end of today's battle. Those rebels almost got the better of us. But enough about me. I'd rather talk about you. And your lovely cousin, Mrs. Roth, of course."

So I told him all about Margaret. When I described her grabbing the kitchen knife to fend off the soldiers, he tried to laugh but it turned into a groan.

"Now, don't let me keep you from your work any longer, Miss All-bauer. But promise you'll come by in the morning with some ink and paper. I'd like to write a letter to Mrs. Roth."

"Of course. And I will bring you some hot porridge too. I'll make it myself."

"My dear Miss Allbauer, you have given me something to live for." He sighed and closed his blue eyes.

It was reassuring to see that a man could be injured in battle and remain so jaunty. I doled out the rest of the broth cheerfully until the pot was empty. It was surely long after midnight when I trudged up the stairs to bed, bone weary. I eased the door open. Jack and Clara were fast asleep on a mattress on the floor.

At the sight of Grace, however, I froze. She crouched on the floor, clutching the bedstead. By the light of a candle burning on the wash-stand, I saw beads of moisture on her forehead. Sweat had soaked her dress, which was gathered up under her arms. She grimaced, showing her teeth, and a deep groan escaped her. Her eyes were closed. She did not know I was there. Her knees trembled and her huge belly almost touched the floor as she strained. She had folded a rug beneath her to catch the blood and water that spilled from between her legs.

"Grace, hold on, I'll get a doctor," I said, but at that moment she groaned again, gave a great heave, and a glistening baby slipped from her body into her own hands. She eased it onto a folded blanket, wiped it clean with her skirt, and sucked the fluid from its mouth and nose. The baby gasped and gave a thin cry. Grace slumped over and let out a sigh.

"How can I help?" I said, finally venturing into the room.

Grace looked up, not showing any surprise to see me. Her whole body shook with exhaustion. She motioned weakly toward a pair of scissors lying nearby. I picked them up and cut the baby's cord and tied it with string. Clumsily I wrapped him in a clean apron. Grace had obviously prepared everything beforehand.

"You have a boy," I whispered, placing him in her arms.

Grace's eyes brimmed, but she smiled.

"His name is Lincoln," she said proudly, her tears spilling onto the baby as if baptizing him.

Lizzie

Chapter 39

Grace wouldn't allow me to fetch a doctor or disturb the Weigel sisters. So I brought up a bucket of water and helped her clean up and put on an old dress I had found by rummaging in a hall cupboard. The baby started to cry, waving his tiny fists, but Grace put him to her breast and he was quiet. I made Grace lie in the bed, while I slept on the floor and did not stir until morning, when the light coming through a crack in the shutters fell on my eyes.

Grace was still asleep, curled around Lincoln as if he were still inside her. The air in the room was stale, so I opened the window, but the air outside was no less thick and humid. I heard the clank of mess kits, the sound of a fiddle, and the eager voices of Jack and Clara down in the kitchen. From a distance came the booming of artillery.

I got up to relieve myself and found the privy so full that it made me gag. On the way back I had to avert my eyes from a soldier crouching near the fence with his trousers down. When I went to pump water to splash on my face, not even a trickle came out. Martin passed by with a yoke over his shoulders, carrying two full pails of water.

"Well's dry. We're fetching water from the creek," he called.

I decided to wash up later, after I had taken porridge to Mr.

Hartmann, along with ink and paper so he could write to Margaret. I would also tell him the good news about Grace's baby.

"Lizzie, do you think you could find some linens?" came Annie Baumann's voice. "We are plumb out of bandages."

Tired half-circles looped under her eyes. She looked as if she had not slept at all.

"I don't think there's a single piece of cloth left in the house," I said.

"Well then, we'll just have to reuse the soiled ones," she said.

"That's disgusting," I blurted out. "Give them to me and I'll wash them out in the creek." The job did not appeal to me, but it had to be done. I followed Annie and saw the surgeon's table sitting outside the barn with a canopy over it.

"Why is this out here?" I asked.

"Because the light is better, and the air can circulate freely, which is more wholesome," said Annie, sounding knowledgeable. "Stay here and I'll get the bandages."

A man climbed onto the table, holding one hand close to him. He was smiling and appeared to be joking with the assistants. The surgeon opened his case and examined his instruments. Annie came back and set the box of soiled bandages on the ground.

"This isn't a serious case. Just a few fingers," she said. Then she added in a whisper, "He's a handsome one, too, and not married. I think he fancies me!"

"Wait, I thought you liked my brother."

"Ye-e-s," she said. "But this one's an *officer*."

"Annie Baumann, how dare you think you're better than my brother?" I jammed my fists against my hips. "You know, I was beginning to think that I had misjudged you, but now I know I had it right all along. You *are* an insufferable snob."

I grabbed the box of bandages and marched off without looking back. At the creek I splashed cool water on my face, then plunged the bandages into the water and watched the blood dissolve and swirl away. I used a rock to scrub the remaining stains until the bandages were mostly clean, then laid the wet cloths on rocks and bushes in a sunny clearing. I felt a twinge of hunger and decided a bowl of porridge with some berries or sugar would taste grand.

I leaped to my feet. I had forgotten Mr. Hartmann! I ran all the way back to the shed. At the spot where he had lain, there was only a rumpled blanket and a tin cup.

"Where . . . did he go?" Panting, I appealed to a man lying nearby. "Last night I sat and talked to a man right here." I pointed to the spot.

"They come with a stretcher real early and took some fellow away. He wasn't moving," the man said. "Asleep in Jesus, I reckon."

"No, this man wasn't dying," I protested. "He told me he wasn't badly hurt."

"Well, I sure am. Can you get me some morphine?" he begged.

I shook my head, then glanced around. Of course! He had been taken to see a doctor. I ran into the barn, almost colliding with Annie. Though she was the last person I wanted to see, I grabbed her arm and began describing Mr. Hartmann.

"Please help me find him here," I pleaded with her.

"Why, is he someone you fancy?" she asked coolly.

"No! Is that all you ever think about? He is my cousin Margaret's beau."

"Ask the assistant surgeon over there," she said, pulling away from me.

I waited while the surgeon checked his list. He shook his head. I asked him to check again.

"I record each soldier's name, rank, and injury when he is admitted to the hospital. He's not here, miss."

I turned and shouted into the thick, putrid air of the barn, "Frederick Hartmann? Are you here? It's me, Lizzie!"

The surgeon took my arm and propelled me from the barn.

"I'm sorry," he said.

I stood blinking in the sun. What if the numbness in Mr. Hartmann's legs had gone away and he had walked off to rejoin his regiment? I set off along Taneytown Road, asking the soldiers I passed if anyone had seen a cavalryman with blue eyes and a big mustache. They all shrugged or shook their heads. Soon the futility of my search struck me. I had as much chance of finding him as I did a single leaf in the autumn woods.

I sat down on a rock and ground the heels of my hands into my eyes, berating myself for breaking such a simple promise. How could I have been so distracted by the stupid bandages? Now Frederick Hartmann was gone. What must he think of me? I trudged back up the road, hearing the intermittent firing of cannons somewhere near Culp's Hill. I wondered how many tons of gunpowder, lead bullets, and cannonballs had been used in the last two days, and how many thousands of men had been injured or killed. At least Mr. Hartmann was alive somewhere. Martin would help me search every cot and corner of the barn until we found him. Buoyed with this small hope, I picked up my pace.

Along the road near the Weigels' drive, I saw the stack of boxes. Long and narrow, they were made of rough pine and scrap lumber. They had been placed there recently, for they were not yet covered with the dust stirred by the passing traffic. I counted ten of them. With a start, I realized they were coffins, and I knew in my heart that Frederick Hartmann hadn't wandered off—he was dead.

I walked down to the creek and scrubbed bandages until my fingers were raw and my hands and arms ached. When Martin came up to me, I tried to hide the tears that slipped silently down my cheeks.

"There you are, Lizzie. Stop what you're doing for a minute. Listen."

Two redbirds called to each other from the branches of a nearby tree. Crickets chirped lazily. The leaves overhead rustled. The wet cloth in my hand dripped into the water.

"The fighting has stopped," he said.

"Then I can go home," I said, thinking of Mama. But then the face of Frederick Hartmann came to mind, and I started to sob loudly.

"Great golly," Martin said. He shifted from one leg to the other. "Why are you crying?"

"A soldier . . . died . . . because I didn't feed him!" It took me a while to choke out the words

"That happens, Lizzie. There are too many of them for us to help."

"But I knew this one. He was our friend. He helped rescue Grace, and he was in love with Margaret." I stared into the water. Upstream, someone was stirring the creek, for it flowed by murkily. "Of all the men who were killed yesterday, only this one makes me cry," I mused. "Isn't that selfish?"

"Maybe you are crying for all of them," he said.

"Well, I'll stop for now, because it sure doesn't do any good," I said, trying to smile. I didn't want Martin to think I was one of those weepy, emotional girls.

I sat down on the trunk of a tree that had fallen across the water. Martin sat next to me and the tree bounced gently under our weight. I gripped the trunk with my legs, afraid I would lose my balance. Then Martin put his arm around my back and rested a hand on my shoulder. I felt myself relax against him. His other hand reached for my right hand and gave it a squeeze.

"Lizzie, you can't worry about the dead. You have to think about the living."

Martin turned his head toward me and took a breath as if he intended to say more. His face was inches from my own. Tensing, I sprang up from the log.

"That reminds me, Grace had her baby last night!" I exclaimed.

Good heavens, had Martin been about to kiss me? I was thinking.

"I know, I came to tell *you*," he said.

"Well, I want to see how she is doing," I said, gathering up the bandages that were dry.

"My ma and aunts are fussing around her and the baby like they are African royalty. Let's stay here a bit longer," he pleaded.

I was afraid to sit down on the log again. Martin would know I wanted to be kissed. So I gathered up the bandages that were dry and started back to the house. With a sigh, Martin followed.

I found Grace lying in the bed, nursing the baby, who had a wrinkled face and fuzzy black hair. His toes looked like tiny peas inside a freshly opened pod. Grace looked up, beaming, until she saw my tear-streaked face.

"You been cryin', Miss Lizzie," she said. "What's wrong?"

"Nothing, I'm just tired," I lied. I could not tell her about Frederick Hartmann and cut into her joy. "The fighting stopped. I'll take you and the baby home today, so Mama can look after you."

Grace shook her head. "First you bounce me down here an' brought on this baby, an' now you want to bounce me home again, sore as I am? No, we stayin' here. But you go on, and if Amos is back—"

"I'll give him the news, of course," I said.

I went to the kitchen to tell Mrs. Weigel that I was going home. She and Martin were drinking coffee and eating flatbread, for the yeast was used up.

"Going back to Gettysburg! With soldiers and rebels everywhere shooting at each other? *Martin, sie ist verrückt!*"

I guessed that Mrs. Weigel believed I was crazy, and Martin looked as if he agreed with her.

"The fighting seems to be over now. And Grace needs clean clothes and linens for the baby," I said.

Mrs. Weigel gave a dismissive snort. "That baby needs nothing but his mother."

"Well, I want to see *my* mother. And Margaret will be worried about her children."

"You cannot take the little ones! It is not safe yet."

"Well *I* am going. You can't stop me!" I tried to sound firm but my voice wavered.

Martin pushed back his chair and stood up.

"How about if I go along, Ma? I'll see her home and then come back. The rebels won't waste their ammunition on us."

I stared at Martin in surprise, while he watched his mother, waiting for her decision. She pursed her lips, frowned, and shook her head, but finally she gave in. She spoke sternly to Martin in German, and he replied in a reassuring tone, kissed her on the cheek, and dashed out.

Mrs. Weigel grasped me by the shoulders. "Be careful, Lizzie dear. Greet your *liebe Mutti* for me." Then she embraced me as if she thought she would never see me alive again.

Lizzie

Chapter 40

I retrieved the rifle John Ray gave me and slung the cartridge box diagonally across my chest so that it rested on my hip. I was standing in the drive when Martin reappeared with a knapsack and two canteens filled with water.

"Bad news," he said. "The cart you came in is being used as an ambulance, and your horse ran off."

"Then I'll walk," I said, taking a canteen from Martin and fixing it to the leather strap of the cartridge box. Martin tied the other one to his belt.

"No, don't," I said gently. "I'm going by myself. I'm not very useful here, but you are badly needed."

"I want to come with you," he said.

"Then you would have to come back alone. I can manage on my own," I insisted. I lifted the rifle over my shoulder as Martin's eyes widened in alarm. "Don't worry, I don't even know how to use it."

"Well, you'd better learn," he said, a bit sharply. He took the gun from me and whistled. "This is no squirrel shooter. It's a Springfield. Where'd you get it?"

"From a soldier lying in Mama's front hall." I told him about John

Ray and Zimmer, too. "Seems like that happened two weeks ago, not two days ago."

Martin continued to admire the rifle. "Don't tell Ma, but a sergeant showed me how to load these. Hand me a cartridge and a cap."

I fumbled in the pouch and drew out a wrapped cartridge about the size of my forefinger and a cap smaller than a thimble. Martin bit open the cartridge and spit out the paper.

"This here contains powder and a ball. You ram it into the barrel using this rod, then lift the rifle to firing position. Now insert this little percussion cap. Cock the hammer, and aim." He squinted down the barrel. "You do this for each shot. A quick soldier can get off three shots every minute."

Martin's long fingers worked nimbly. The muscles in his forearm stood out beneath the skin. I had trouble concentrating on his instructions. He handed me the gun and I shouldered it as he had.

"Don't fire it now!" he warned, laying a hand on my arm.

I lowered the gun and took a step away from him. "I'm not stupid," I said, while my heart beat faster with excitement.

"Lizzie, back there by the creek, I only meant to comfort you, not to scare you," Martin said softly, his eyes pleading.

"I wasn't scared," I said, but that was a lie. I couldn't even meet his eyes.

"Here, before you go, take this," he said, setting his hat on my head. It was too big for me, but it was wide-brimmed and shaded my face from the sun.

I thanked him and walked away quickly. It was about noon. Home was five miles up the road. I figured it would take me less than two hours to cover the distance. But the going proved rough, with all the debris scattered on the road and the ruts that threatened to turn my ankles. The sun beat hotly down and I was grateful for Martin's hat. An ambulance pulled by two weary horses passed me, and the dust almost made me choke. A soldier riding in the back, his arm in a sling, tipped his cap to me and I waved back. To my left, the green hills of Cemetery Ridge rose up, and I wondered if the Union soldiers were still entrenched there, or if they had moved on in the night.

North of the Hummelbaugh homestead, I saw a group of soldiers in dirty blue jackets approaching on the road. Their officer was using his rifle to prod a man who shuffled before him with his head down. I yielded the road and waited for them to pass.

"Hey there, Billy, you don't fool me none," called out one of the soldiers, whose face was almost hidden by his huge beard. "Take off the skirt!"

When I realized the soldier was addressing me, I was afraid they meant to harm me. So I climbed over the stone fencerow and ran across a field. The rifle, cartridge box, and canteen banged against me, slowing me down. I looked back and the bearded man was close behind me.

"Stop or I'll shoot ya!" he yelled. "Put down yer rifle!"

I stopped, let the rifle drop, and reached up instinctively to protect my head, knocking off Martin's hat.

"Why, I'll be durned, it's a lady!" he said. Another soldier ran up and grabbed the bearded man and cuffed him.

"Beg yer pardon, miss. Bernie here's an idiot."

"Ow!" said Bernie, shrugging off the other soldier. "We thought you was a straggler or a deserter, like that cowardly bag of bones we found in yonder shed," he said by way of apology.

The second soldier picked up my rifle and escorted me back to the road, where the officer waited.

"Corporal Bingham. Third Minnesota." He introduced himself without taking his gun off the captured deserter. "Don't think they're allowin' women into the army just yet. Shouldn't you go home, miss?"

"I am going home. I live in Gettysburg."

"Then be careful. There's still rebel snipers up there. If you're determined to go, be sure and take off that hat before you get near. Let them see that long yellow hair of yours, so they don't take you for one of us."

"Yes, sir, thank you," I said.

"No hard feelings, miss?" asked Bernie. Looking contrite, he held out a square biscuit. I took it with a small nod. The soldiers began to move on, shoving their reluctant captive before them, but the corporal hesitated.

"I'm not sure you ought to be toting that rifle," he said to me.

"Sir, I may come upon someone who intends to harm me," I replied, looking pointedly at Bernie. The officer laughed.

"If you do, be sure you don't shoot yourself by mistake," he said.

A bold impulse, or maybe it was a foolish one, made me raise the rifle, cock it as Martin had shown me, and take aim at a boulder about fifty yards away. Bracing for the recoil, I pulled the trigger. The crack of the rifle made my ears ring, and the butt struck my shoulder hard, but the bullet hit the rock, leaving a charred black spot. The officer raised his eyebrows and whistled.

"I see you can take care of yourself," he said. "We'd better skedaddle, men."

When they had left, I realized that my knees were shaking uncontrollably. I had actually fired a rifle! Even more amazing, I had hit my target. I ran my hand down the barrel, which was still hot. Slowly it cooled, and I reloaded exactly as Martin had shown me.

When my legs felt solid, I set out walking again. I was hungry and realized I had not eaten anything all day. So I took a bite of the biscuit the soldier had given me and almost broke a tooth. So this was the hardtack Luke had written about! I took a sip of water and held it in my mouth until it softened the biscuit so that I could chew it. The heat grew more intense, and sweat tricked down my back and between my breasts until my dress was soaked. I was halfway home. What would I do if Mama and Margaret were not there?

In a field beside the road, Union soldiers on horseback circled a hundred or more gray-clad soldiers, rounding them up like cattle. The men, weaponless, trudged with their heads down. Thinking of Papa, I pitied them, even if they were rebels. Then it dawned on me that the sight of so many prisoners must mean that the rebels had lost the battle. Filled with hope, I quickened my pace. My heavy rifle felt as light as a toy.

Then, with no warning, an explosion tore the silence, followed by another and another, like a giant boulder rumbling down a hallway in the heavens. Instinct drove me from the open road to the protection of a stone wall running alongside it. I pressed my hands against my ears and peered up at the hills, expecting to see trees and rocks tumbling down toward me. Then the answering fire came and it was, if possible, even louder. I saw smoke rising over the treetops and realized that the guns on Cemetery Ridge were firing back at the rebels. The ground rocked as if it would break open and swallow me. Then from out of the cumulative thunder came a whirring sound, ascending to a shriek, followed by a loud crack. I felt the stone wall shift and dirt and pebbles rain on my back. When I dared to look up again, I saw that an oak tree not fifty yards away had been broken in half like a stick of firewood, leaving a jagged trunk. The top of the tree lay on the ground, its branches still shuddering from the impact.

I scrambled to my feet and ran as if pursued by demons.

Rosanna

Chapter 41

July 3, 1863 camp south of Lutheran Seminary,
west of Gettysburg

I awoke this morning to a vivid and bustling scene of preparation for yet another day of battle. A fifer merrily played "Dixie." An infantryman drank his ground chicory "coffee" and adjusted his knapsack with an air of purpose. His rifle shone, ready for use. Officers tied on gold sashes, their buttons and braid gleaming in the morning sun. Their horses stood by, groomed and saddled. Expectation charged the air, masking the fear, the exhaustion, the uncertainty. Some men knelt and prayed for victory, for deliverance, or for luck. For their lives.

As soon as I had combed my hair, I reported to Dr. Walker, from habit and a sense of deference. The medical corps appeared ill-prepared for battle and Dr. Walker helpless to remedy the situation.

"I have enough orderlies to staff the hospital and ambulances. What I don't have is an assistant surgeon, someone to do battlefield triage," he lamented.

"I might be of use. I have a medicine kit, bandages, and a horse," I replied. "And some skill in diagnosis."

"My dear Mrs. Wilcox," he said with irritation, "you overestimate your usefulness." Then, seeing how his words stung me, he mumbled an apology, and with a tired wave of his hand, said, "Do what you wish. But I cannot be responsible for you."

"Then, sir, I will be responsible for myself," I said, and turned to leave.

"Wait!" he called and began to rummage through some crates until he came up with a piece of canvas marked with a red cross. "If you must be in the way, this might keep you from getting shot at."

I fastened the canvas to my haversacks and fixed them behind Dolly's saddle. Then I rode to where John's regiment had taken up position in the hollow of a field near the house of a Henry Spangler. Like a passport, the red cross on Dolly's flank allowed me to move freely among the men. I dispensed iodine for cuts, balm for a powder burn, and bound up an ankle sprained on the uneven ground.

By listening and observation, I learned much about the situation of the two armies. Our soldiers hold this entire ridge to the west of Emmitsburg Road, supported by 160 guns placed in batteries as far as the eye can see, iron beasts with their mouths facing the enemy. The Yankees occupy a ridge about a mile away and are hidden by the trees. Their batteries cluster in the center. Lee believes that Meade has strengthened his flanks, expecting an attack there. So he plans to strike at the center and break the Yankee line in two. Yet what if Meade's center is stronger than Lee suspects, and his flanks encircle and crush Lee instead? What a terrible responsibility it must be to plan a battle. Ordinary men would shrink from making decisions when so many lives are at stake. Generals must be a different caliber of men.

It is noon, and I have retreated to a sheltered spot until my services are needed. Like the newspaper correspondents in their battered suits, I write and peer through my field glasses. I see men pelting each other with green apples from the Spanglers' orchard. I guess it is better to throw them than to eat them and be cramped and sick. Now General

Pickett's troops are moving forward, forming a line several men thick at the edge of the woods, behind the artillery. Officers on horseback gallop between the batteries where the teams of cannoneers wait at their positions.

1:30 p.m. A terrible artillery barrage is underway. Two blasts from our guns to the south triggered a succession of explosions like the banging of a stick along a picket fence, magnified ten-thousandfold. The hellish noise persisted for many minutes, until thick clouds of smoke obscured everything, even the gunners themselves. Now the Yankees return the fire. Through the smoke, flashes of flame reveal their cannons' mouths. The air grows acrid with smoke and powder, making my eyes water.

A grim-faced General Longstreet rides by with his officers.

Looking through my field glasses, I see a caisson explode, hurling balls of flame and splintered wood. A gunner lies on the ground. Tom holds the restless horses. An officer points to the gun, which has fallen still. He is making Tom take the post of the injured gunner! I watch Tom climb astride the ammunition box. He hands the round iron ball to a second gunner who rams it into the muzzle, while a third lights the fuse. Then Tom jumps to the ground and pulls a lanyard and the gun discharges its deadly load, recoils violently, and disappears behind the smoke.

Two orderlies with stretchers join me, waiting for a lull in the fighting. One is Thomas Langan, whom I recognize from John's regiment.

"Do they keep firing until all the guns are destroyed?" I shout, but Langan seems not to hear me. He gestures and shouts. I believe he is trying to tell me that when our guns have taken out theirs, our foot soldiers can advance and seal the victory. Oh, I pray for the end of this battle and freedom from this horror!

Lizzie

Chapter 42

As I dodged the ankle-turning ruts, another shell overshot its mark and exploded in a field behind me. There was nowhere to take cover, so I kept running until I came to General Meade's headquarters. The beams supporting the porch had been shot away and the roof sagged dangerously. The flags were gone, and a glance in the windows confirmed that the place was abandoned. A bleeding horse lay on the ground, neighing pitifully while straining the rope that tethered it to a tree. I pulled the the knot until it came loose, and the horse dropped its heavy head to the ground.

I kept on going. My feet throbbed with pain and my throat felt parched. I tossed away the empty canteen, but kept the rifle, though it banged against my side with every step. I struck out over the fields to avoid a regiment of bluecoats coming toward me. It was about six hundred yards to the Baltimore Pike, from which I could see Culp's Hill. Its sides had been stripped to build defenses that sheltered a line of guns. The trunks of trees were gouged and spotted with black holes. Some had their limbs torn off as if by an angry giant. Men were carrying the wounded to ambulances that blocked the road.

"Is Culp's Hill still ours?" I called out to one of the drivers.

"It sure is! We sent them Johnnies running," he said. "They've retreated toward Hanover Road."

"That means this end of the line held up!" I exclaimed, remembering General Warren's description of the fishhook-shaped defense.

"Don't count your chickens yet, missy. Meade's still got his hands full over yonder." He indicated Cemetery Ridge. "There's probably six thousand of General Hancock's men along the ridge, and Lord knows how many Johnnies facing 'em, and they're not about to shake hands and call it a day yet."

"General Meade hasn't been injured or captured?" I asked, worried.

"No, not so far as I've heard." The driver spat a stream of brown juice into the road. "But they don't tell us the half of what's going on. So, what's your business?"

"Just tell me, can I get into town safely?"

"Sure. Climb up, and you can ride along that way, once I'm loaded up," he offered.

But I was too eager to get home, so I thanked him and hurried on. At the edge of town I saw a house with its windows broken and the jambs riddled with bullet holes. Remembering the corporal's warning about snipers, I took off Martin's hat and shook out my hair. But the street seemed deserted, with no soldiers or townspeople in sight.

Then I noticed a small boy sitting on a low stone wall along the street, his head in his hands.

"Hello? Are you all right?" I said.

The boy looked up. It was Ginnie Wade's eight-year-old brother.

"Harry? Don't you live on Breckenridge Street? Why are you down here all alone?"

"This is my auntie Georgia's house," he said.

"Does your mother know where you are?"

"She's here. We all are."

"Ginnie, too? Tell her to come and visit Lizzie in a few days. I have so much to tell her, but I have to get home now."

In reply, the boy only whimpered.

"Harry, come inside this minute! It's not safe out there." Ginnie's mother appeared at the cellar door. Her face was red and swollen. "Why, is that Lizzie Allbauer?"

"Yes, Mrs. Wade," I said, going up to her. "What's happened? Is someone ill?" I thought of Georgia's new baby. Sometimes, I knew, a baby would seem perfectly healthy and then just get sick or even die for no reason.

"No, it's my poor Ginnie!" she wailed, dabbing her eyes. "She came to help Georgia with the new baby, and then we all came because of the fighting in town. But the rebels hiding around here started firing, hitting the house over a hundred times. One bullet struck the bedpost and barely missed Georgia. Then this morning, Ginnie got up early to make bread."

Another sob escaped Mrs. Wade and I touched her shoulder in sympathy. But why hadn't they all stayed in the cellar?

"Ginnie was kneading the dough when a bullet came right through the door. Lizzie, hurry home now, before—"

"Ginnie was shot?" I interrupted. "But will she be all right?"

"Lord, no," Mrs. Wade wailed. "It struck her in the heart and she died that moment."

I ran the rest of the way home, imagining the worst: our house in flames and Mama and Margaret killed for harboring soldiers. Tears stung my eyes at the thought of Ginnie's death. I ran past the barricades that had stopped me two nights ago and now lay broken in the street. Past the

Methodist church, where wounded men leaned against stones in the burial ground. Past St. James Church, where men unloaded boxes from a wagon marked "U.S. Sanitary Commission." Our house was now in sight. I thanked God it looked exactly as it had two days earlier. I tried the front door but it was locked. Not a sound came from within. I went around to the kitchen door. A bucket of dirty water stood next to a pile of kindling. Was this a good sign or a bad one? I tried the latch, and it, too, held firm.

"Mama? I'm home. Margaret? It's me, Lizzie," I shouted, thumping on the door. I thought I heard footsteps and saw the curtain in the kitchen window move. Then the door opened, and I fell into Mama's arms.

"Oh, bless Jesus, my prayers are answered again!" she cried, covering my face with kisses. Over her shoulder, I could see Margaret, her eyebrows raised in a mute question.

"Jack and Clara are safe at the Weigels'," I said, and she sagged with relief.

The next few moments were a blur. I heard footsteps coming up from the cellar steps and expected to see one of the soldiers. But instead, bounding through the doorway, came my brother Ben, and behind him, a broad smile on his dark face, stood Amos.

Then we were all crying and talking at once. I told Amos that he was a daddy, and he hugged me so tight I couldn't breathe. Ben wanted to know where I'd gotten the rifle. Mama scolded me for leaving the Weigels', but Margaret defended me. I asked about Ben and Amos's journey, but first Mama wanted to hear about the battle, for they had been living in the cellar without news for almost three days.

I thought about what I should tell them and what I should spare them. I said there had been fighting on Little Round Top, but I didn't mention that Luke's regiment was called to defend the hill. I described meeting General Meade but didn't say that I had seen men blown apart in Plum Run Valley. The spies in our wagon, the stack of coffins beside the road, the death of Ginnie Wade—these I kept to myself, for the time being.

"What happened to the soldier in the hall?" I asked Mama.

"He didn't last the night, God rest his soul. I must write to his family."

I was not particularly saddened by the news. Perhaps I was fresh out of tears, as I had cried so many of them lately.

"Everyone back to the cellar. There may still be snipers around," Mama ordered, and we traipsed reluctantly down the stairs. In the basement, Noah Zimmer sat with his bad leg resting on a stool.

"Brave little lady, I hear," he said when he saw me. "Wish I could get out there and chase them rebels like you been doing."

"Where's your friend, John Ray?" I asked.

"Went back to the regiment. I tried to go too, but your ma wouldn't let me. So I reckon I'm stayin' here. Least I'm not getting shot at."

I turned to Amos and Ben. "Now tell me everything that happened to you."

"Well, getting to York was the easy part," said Amos, stroking his chin.

"I drove the wagon the whole way," boasted Ben.

"Only took us two days, spite of the rain. But when we pulled up, the butcher wouldn't have nothin' to do with me. He said I done stole Mr. Allbauer's stock and he ought to call the constable. 'If I stole it, how come I'm bringin' it to you for safekeepin'?' I asked, but he wouldn't listen."

"I never trusted that Mr. Schupp," I said.

"When I told him Mama sent us, he called me a lying pipsqueak," said Ben.

"We will never deal with him again," said Mama.

"Then I remembered that Mama had an uncle Herman who lived near Wrightsville," Ben went on. "It took us a whole day to find him, but he said he'd keep the stock."

"What good thinking, Ben!" I said.

"We waited there a couple of days, 'cause we heard there were rebs in the area. But we knew everyone would be worried the longer we stayed away, so we decided to come home. That's when our adventure really started."

"Passin' through Wrightsville on our way back, we landed in the middle of wagons an' refugees all jammed up on the turnpike. The rebs were comin' up behind them an' the local militia was guardin' the bridge in front of them. No one could cross the river. People shouted at us, 'You're crazy to be headin' to York. The rebels have taken everythin' in it!' Well, we were glad we didn't leave the livestock there." Amos chuckled.

Now Ben interrupted, too excited to stay quiet.

"Then the whole Confederate army filled the road, and me and Amos hightailed it for the bluffs along the river. We could hear fighting, but we couldn't see anything with all the buildings and warehouses in the way. Then we heard great whooshing and crackling and saw that the bridge was on fire. Whenever a piece broke off and fell into the water, it sizzled and sent up steam and smoke."

"But why would the rebels burn the bridge?" I asked.

"It wasn't them who burned it," said Amos. "It was the militia, to keep the rebs from gettin' to the railroad on the other side. But then the fire spread to houses and buildings near the wharf, an' we saw somethin' unforgettable." He shook his head.

"The rebel army turned into a fire brigade!" shouted Ben. "The soldiers joined the townspeople, passing buckets and pots of water from hand to hand like they were trying to save their own houses."

"Can you believe that?" said Mama, touching her hand to her heart. "Helping each other, not like enemies but like brothers."

"That night," Amos said, "we slept in the woods. Monday we started to pick our way back toward York, stayin' clear of the main roads. But it commenced rainin' hard an' Ben here was shiverin', so we holed up in a barn somewhere near Hunterstown."

"I wasn't sick," Ben protested. "Just tired. And hungry."

"We figured the farmer wouldn't grudge us the shelter or a few potatoes from his garden. But we was pretty wrong about that." Amos winked at Ben.

"What do you mean? What happened?" I prompted.

"We woke up the next morning with rifles in our faces!" cried Ben, hoisting an imaginary gun. "A farmer sood there with two rebs who itched themselves like they were full of lice. The farmer told them Amos was a runaway. One of the soldiers said, 'We'll take care of him,' and gave the farmer some money."

"There you have it!" interrupted Margaret, indignant. "I've always said the country around here was filled with copperheads and secret slavers."

"I told them over and over that Amos was a free man. One of them finally said, 'I b'lieve you, son, but you know I jus' don't care. He b'longs to me now an' he'll fetch a good sum,'" said Ben, imitating the soldier's drawl. "They tied up Amos and argued about whether I'd try to run away and rat on them, till they decided to tie me up too. We sat all day listening to those two no-counts jawing and boasting. They commenced drinking, and Amos whispered to me, 'When they fall asleep, we got to get away somehow.' But I couldn't even reach my pocket knife."

Ben paused and lifted his hands in a gesture of helplessness. He was clearly enjoying having everyone's attention.

"Go on, tell us how you managed to escape," I urged him.

"Well, Amos was worried about me being sick, so I decided I would act like I was. I started coughing and shaking and added some moaning, too. The rebels were looking scared I was going to die on them. 'We don't want him anyway, just the nigger,' they said, and untied me. 'Go up to the farmhouse, boy, and tell the missus to take care of you.' And they booted me out."

"I'll watch for that trick next time you're trying to get a day off school," Mama said, ruffling Ben's hair.

"So there I was, standing outside in the dark, wondering what to do next. I decided I'd wait until they fell asleep and then go back in and cut Amos free. When I heard them snoring, I tried the door but they had bolted it from the inside. So I crept all around the barn but there was no other way in. It was all made of stone. Then I nearly tripped over a shovel lying in the weeds, and that gave me an idea. I dug a hole outside the barn door. The ground was soft, and after a while the hole was a couple of feet deep and about four feet long. But because of the rain, it kept filling up with water and mud."

"I could hear you were up to somethin' out there," said Amos, smiling.

"I waited there, hoping for the rebs to come out and, you know, relieve themselves. I was about to bang the shovel on something to get their attention, when the door creaked open, and I barely had enough time to flatten myself against the side of the barn and hope he couldn't see me."

"Clever-ass boy," said Noah Zimmer, clapping his hand against his thigh. "Sorry, ma'am, I mean he's a right smart boy."

I saw an amused smile play around Mama's lips.

"I saw the reb swaying like he was drunk and trying to unbutton his trousers," Ben said. "Lucky for me, he wasn't carrying his rifle. He stepped right into the hole and fell over, face-first in the mud. A few seconds later the other one stumbled out with his rifle and fell on top of his friend. They started cursing mightily."

The thought of two drunken rebels tangled in a muddy hole made me explode with laughter. Mama and Margaret and Amos and Noah Zimmer all joined in, and Ben sat there beaming at us all. I had a new respect for my little brother.

"Next thing I know this boy cuttin' my hands free wif his knife," said Amos. "While I set to work on my ankles, he stood at the door wif that shovel raised. 'Ah busted myself!' groaned one reb, an' the other cursed, 'My dang rifle's all muddy!' Once my feet was free, I grabbed the other soldier's rifle an' we jumped clean over that hole. The horse weren't where we'd tied him to a tree. So we jus' took off runnin'."

"Some folks have all the fun, while the rest of us get the sorry luck," said Zimmer mournfully, rubbing his leg.

Amos related how they had gone several miles on foot before stopping to build a fire and dry off. Then on Hunterstown Road, they had come up behind Confederate troops on their way to Gettysburg. They had hidden in an old shack all day, hearing the distant, sporadic fighting. That had been Wednesday, the first of July.

"At night," said Amos, "we tried to sneak home by moonlight but there was too many rebel patrols around, so we went back to our hidin' place. We was mighty hungry, so Ben poached a knapsack right off a sleepin' Johnnie, an' we had ourselves a feast of rancid bacon and worm-eaten cornbread. We tried again las' night and was able to sneak through without the rebs catchin' us."

I saw by the hollows under my brother's eyes that despite his plucky storytelling, he had been desperate to find his way home again.

I put my arms around him to let him know I understood, and he did not pull away.

Then Mama had me come upstairs with her to put together some supper for the six of us. But I found she didn't really need my help.

"You're not telling me everything, Lizzie," she said with a worried look. "We could hear the artillery fire, you know. I regretted sending you down there and never stopped praying."

"I worried about you and Margaret, too. But I am home safe, and so is Ben." I smiled, but I couldn't fool Mama. She kept searching my face.

"Tell me, Lizzie," she prompted again.

I could no longer hold everything inside. "Ginnie Wade," I began, my voice breaking already. "She was killed by a stray bullet, standing in the kitchen of her sister's house."

Mama let out a moan and leaned on the sideboard. From the cellar came muffled voices and the sound of Margaret's laugh.

"And Mr. Hartmann is dead. It's a long story for some other time. I didn't want Margaret to find out."

"Not now anyway," Mama agreed, her voice a hoarse whisper.

"But that's not all. Mama, yesterday the reserves were called into battle. I saw their flag. Luke was at Little Round Top. I don't know if anything happened to him."

I had been so afraid to tell Mama this, but she did not react as I had expected.

"He's that close by?" she said, her eyes wide. "Why, tomorrow we'll ask at every hospital until we find out if he is hurt. If so, we will bring him home."

Mama seemed buoyed by hope. After all, Ben and I had returned to her. But I knew that locating Luke would not be an easy task. There were makeshift hospitals in barns, churches, and houses all over the county. To search them all would be impossible.

But I said, "Yes, Mama. That's what we'll do."

I recalled my desperate search for Mr. Hartmann.

What if we don't find Luke—alive?

Rosanna

Chapter 43

July 3, 8 p.m.

My pen is heavy with the weight of this tragic history. Writing is a struggle. But words are all I have to paint the horrors of this day.

The artillery barrage this afternoon lasted two hours but seemed endless. From time to time the guns stuttered into silence, only to roar again to life. My ears were deafened and my nerves frayed from the constant thunder. Even the horses were driven mad and broke from their tethers, plunging riderless through the fields until many were struck and killed. I watched a team of gunners struggle to reset their cannon as it sank into the soft ground with each recoil, sending missiles beyond their targets on the far ridge. A sudden blast threw the gunners to the ground, where they lay unmoving. I started forward with my satchel of medicine. Langan grabbed my skirt but I shook him off. Death was claiming good soldiers every minute, and my life was no more precious than theirs.

I ran through the knee-high grass toward the line of flame-belching cannons, stopping only to let a caisson loaded with ammunition roll by. Its driver gave me a startled look. Langan and the other fellow had followed me, and they quickly bore away the gunner with the worst wounds. I supported a second one as he hobbled back to the grove of trees, and the third was able to crawl to shelter. I treated their blistered skin with tallow. Langan brought soldier after wounded soldier to my triage station, where I dispensed what aid I could, so intent upon my work that I barely flinched when a Yankee shell hit the ground nearby. It dislodged great clods of earth but fortunately did no further harm to my patients.

I looked up to see a man walking slowly toward me, a large piece of iron shrapnel protruding from his breastbone. To my astonishment, he was not even bleeding. His mouth opened and closed as if he were trying to speak, and he pointed to his chest. I thought of a statue of Christ holding his heart that I once saw in the Catholic church in Richmond. I touched the metal, but realized that if I tried to remove it, he would probably bleed to death. Langan had already gone, so I advised the man to take himself to the hospital. It pained me not to be able to help him.

It was about midafternoon, judging by the sun's decline, when the situation on the field began to change. First the artillery fire sputtered. Officers and couriers galloped back and forth behind the guns with a sense of urgency. Langan asked to borrow my field glasses.

"I see Longstreet conferring with his artillery commander," he reported. "We must be almost out of ammunition. If we don't attack now, our men will be going forward without any covering fire!" He seemed very agitated.

"I don't understand. If there is no more ammunition, how can the battle go on?"

Langan didn't reply. He continuted to scan the field.

"The Union batteries are pulling back. They've stopped firing. By God, what is Longstreet waiting for?"

Just then General Pickett rode by on his black horse, shouting, "Up men, and to your posts! Don't forget today that you are Virginians!" The infantry began to move forward from the woods. The standard bearers of every regiment and company raised their colors. Seeing the blue flag of Virginia waving in the hot breeze, I joined my voice to the rising cheer. Then the thousands of men, forming an unbroken line almost a mile long, began their advance. The sun was at their backs, casting long shadows before them and glinting off their bayonets and rifle barrels. They advanced in silence. Their ranks parted as they approached a battery of guns or a dead horse, then closed up again, like a river flowing around a rock.

Long minutes passed before the artillery resumed their covering fire, and the men advanced with the sound of their own guns at their backs. They did not look back. I watched the inexorable tide flow down the grassy slope. The soldiers marched with steady, measured steps over the mile of open ground. No one cheered any longer, and my excitement at seeing their march commence turned to dread as they neared the enemy's lines. I realized that the artillery bombardment had been only a prelude to this more deadly stage of battle.

When the leading column had traversed half the distance between the two lines, the Yankee guns opened their fire again, raining shot and shell upon our brave soldiers. Though they fell like ninepins, the line moved on. Those on the flanks lagged a little, and the straight line took the shape of a crescent. Like a blunted arrow our soldiers converged on the center of the Yankee line. Fire from Yankee guns raked them from the side, and dozens fell, disappearing in the tall grass. As the men slowed down to climb over the fences along Emmitsburg Road, Yankee sharpshooters picked them off. But the lines re-formed, and the men advanced at a doubled pace, uttering battle cries that floated back to us on the wind.

Then, as Pickett's brave Virginians came within a hundred yards of the enemy's breastworks, the Yankee rifles fired simultaneouly with a deafening crack, and the minié balls did their precise and deadly work. In the open fields, men fell like wheat cut with a scythe, but the remainder marched on, undaunted by the certainty of death.

I could no longer bear to watch, but laid down my field glasses, and the scene became a distant blur of movement and smoke. I busied myself treating wounds while for an hour the clash continued. Then the sounds of battle subtly changed, and peering through my glasses again, I saw our men stumbling, running, and crawling away away from the point of battle. Some held up handkerchiefs or caps as if they were surrendering. Yet others persevered, gaining the wall and fighting up the hill until they were driven back with bayonets. Soon I had little doubt that the valiant Virginians were in full retreat.

Alas, my disappointment was nothing compared to that of the soldiers who straggled back, their bodies broken and defeat written on their faces. Among them I looked for Tom, but in vain, for every man's face was blackened with dirt and powder. Hiram Watt stopped, seeing that my aid station was overwhelmed, and helped Langan carry the wounded to ambulances. As I write, hundreds of bodies still lie on the field and the stretcher bearers pick their way among the fallen, seeking those who have a chance of living. The others, they leave to die.

July 3, 11 p.m.

An hour ago I set out across the wide field to look for Tom. I carried my satchel of medicines, a canteen of water, and a lamp. Only a few crickets chirped feebly in the grass. All the other creatures of the field had fled, or were stunned into silence. Blood soaked the trampled earth, and bodies lay scattered and broken in death. Oh, the wastefulness of war!

As I came to the fence near Emmitsburg Road where so many brave Confederates fell, I heard a weak cry for help. It came from a slight fellow, no more than a boy, lying with his head on the chest of man with a graying beard. Crouching down, I determined that the bearded man was dead. The cap had fallen from the youth's head, revealing curly black hair and fine features. He opened his eyes, which were filled with tears. I asked him if he was hurt.

"It's broken. Oh, my heart," he murmured.

Thinking he had a chest injury, perhaps a fractured rib, I turned him on his back and unbuttoned his jacket. Amazed, I beheld—a woman! Blood from a wound to her chest smeared her breasts.

"Who are you?" I gasped. I had heard of women pretending to be men in order to fight, but I had never met one.

"Kate O'Neill," she said, grimacing in pain.

"I must get you to a hospital. If you can stand, perhaps I can carry you."

But she refused to leave the man, even after I gently informed her that he was gone. I asked if he were her dear father or an uncle.

"No, he was my husband," she sobbed. "We were married two years ago. We came over from Ireland together. All my family is dead. I can't live without him."

The strain of talking and weeping caused her to bleed even more. I saw that her wound was mortal after all. Murmuring some words of comfort, I placed her on her side so that she could see her husband's face and I held her hand. It was only a short time before she joined him in death. Alas, the sight of the lovers released my sorrow for John in great wracking moans and choking sobs. Anyone who heard me would have thought I was dying too.

Now Kate O'Neill's brave sacrifice has moved me to write, which calms me though I sit amidst the dead. Most people consider dying for love to be a noble deed. And yet, how unnecessary it is! What, then, is worth dying for, if not love? Is freedom worth dying for? The reunion of our divided nation?

Whatever is good, let us live and work for it, not die in its name, for that

Lizzie

———

Chapter 44

Someone in the street was shouting, "The rebels are in retreat! They're leaving!"

I jumped out of bed and threw on yesterday's sweat-stained dress, hollered to Mama, and dashed outside in time to see a Union patrol escorting half a dozen rebels tied together by the waist. They halted in front of our house.

"One of these fellers were hiding in your shed back there," the captain said to me. "We found this on him." He held out a box I recognized. It was the family silver.

"I'll take that, thank you." Mama had come to the door. She opened the box and glanced at the contents. "There are three spoons missing."

The captain grabbed the rebel who had stolen our silver and emptied his knapsack onto the ground. He made the man pull out his pockets, but the spoons were not there.

"Bates!" the captain shouted, staring directly at a fair-haired man in his own patrol. For a tense moment, no one moved or spoke. Then Bates dropped his arm and with tinkling sounds the spoons fell from his sleeve. He handed them to the captain, who handed them to Mama, then turned and cuffed Bates on the side of the head. For some reason, I felt sorry for Bates.

The patrol moved on. I turned to Mama.

"Why are you so calm? That rebel snuck into the house last night and stole the silver and we didn't even know it!"

"He did not break into the house, Lizzie. I hid the silver in the shed, figuring it would be safer there."

I heard drumming and the strains of "Yankee Doodle," and Mama and I hurried to the Diamond, where we could see a band leading a column of blue-clad soldiers into town. A great cheer went up as the Confederate flag was pulled down and the Stars and Stripes hoisted in its place.

It was our Independence Day, the 4th of July.

By now a small crowd had gathered and news of the victory spread. Twelve thousand Confederates had charged down from Seminary Ridge into Meade's unbreakable line, and almost half of those rebels had fallen. All this had occurred while I was enjoying my reunion with Ben and Amos.

We saw Mrs. Wade in the crowd with a somber-faced Harry. Mama embraced them, and Mrs. Wade said that Ginnie would be buried in the garden for the time being.

When the band stopped playing, Mr. Kendlehart stood up to give a speech. He looked as if he had slept in his clothes. More likely, he hadn't slept at all. No sooner had he begun speaking than he was interrupted by someone on his council. They held a brief conference.

"Folks," Mr. Kendlehart said, "I have been advised that it is not wise to be abroad in the streets. The rebels have not withdrawn from Seminary Ridge, and their marksmen are still firing on our soldiers in the west side of town."

Anxious murmuring ran through the crowd. Someone said the rebels might charge down from Seminary Ridge and try again to take the town. The soldiers who had marched so gaily to the Diamond were already erecting barricades along Chambersburg Street. A soft drizzle began to fall on the dusty streets, and the sky that had been so clear at daybreak was now a solid mass of gray clouds. People began to hurry home, locking their doors behind them and closing their shutters.

Weary dread filled me at the thought of enduring another day of noise, fear, and uncertainty. I wanted to climb into bed and forget everything. Amos had to forego his plans to fetch Grace and the baby home. Margaret sat forlornly, no doubt thinking of Jack and Clara. And perhaps of Frederick Hartmann. Then the storm broke, and by midafternoon, rain was falling heavily, drumming loudly on the roofs and running in muddy streams down the streets. Thunder and lightning raged in the sky. If there was a battle west of town, we couldn't hear it.

In spite of the storm, Ben went to check on the butcher shop and Mama took bandages and bread to the hospital at St. James Church. Meanwhile I neatened the cellar and brought up the bedding. Noah Zimmer made sorry jokes every time I went down, and I began to wish we could send him to a hospital somewhere. Ben came back, soaked and dripping, and reported that the livestock pens had all been pulled down to build barricades, but nothing else had been damaged.

I knew I should scrub the kitchen floor, but I was too tired. The front hall, too, was crossed by muddy footprints. Standing on the spot where the soldier had lain, I felt a twinge of superstition and opened a window to allow his spirit to drift out. The drumming rain and the steady ticking of the parlor clock drove me to lie down on the sofa. Tomorrow, we might open the shop. Later Amos could rebuild the pens. But now I would sleep. How pleased Papa would be to come home to a thriving business! I imagined him smiling and lifting me in his arms, swinging me back and forth like a little child. *Tick-tock, tick-tock.* In my dream, I was at a party with people shouting and laughing. Jack and Clara jumped up and down. Someone was shaking me, but I was too heavy and couldn't move my limbs.

I opened my eyes. Jack was shoving me and telling me to wake up. Margaret knelt on the floor, with Clara clinging to her neck. Amos stood in the hall with his arms around Grace, who was holding her baby. This was no dream. I sat up, feeling like Rip van Winkle.

"How did you all get here? How long have I been asleep?"

"Just a few hours," said Margaret.

"You won't believe the surprise we have for you, Cousin Lizzie!" interrupted Jack.

"I don't believe *this*," I said. "But how—?"

"Guess how many dead horses we saw along the road?" Jack wrinkled his nose. "But Luke showed me how to breathe into my sleeve, like this."

"Who? Luke?" I asked, looking around in disbelief. A soldier with long hair and the start of a sandy beard stood in the parlor doorway, his arm around Ben. He was taller than Mama, who stood beside him, smiling in a dazed way.

"How about a proper greeting, Lizzie?" he said, holding open his arms.

"Luke! I'm not still dreaming, am I?" I hugged him, laughing and crying at once. "You look so different. Your shoulders are so big!"

"You've grown a heap, too, Lizzie," he said, looking me up and down. Though he smiled, his eyes looked weary and pained, like they belonged to an older person.

"Where is your bugle? Play it for me," demanded Ben.

"Sorry, but I swapped it for this rifle, which is a durn sight more useful."

"But how did you all get here?" I asked, still confused.

Luke replied, "I was carrying a buddy whose leg was all busted up, and we stopped at this farmhouse because we smelled fresh bread, and there were Jack and Clara on the porch. I said, 'How'd you all like to go home today?' So we flagged down an ambulance for my buddy, and Clara and Amos's wife and baby rode courtesy of the U.S. government, while me and Jack walked."

"The nice man in the am'blance showed me a picture and said I was just as pretty as his girl!" said Clara.

"But won't you get in trouble for leaving your regiment?" I asked Luke

He shrugged. "Some of the men got leave to visit their folks in town, and when the rest of us heard, we took off too. I'm going back, of course. I've got to, Ma," he said, looking regretful. "Tomorrow morning we go after Lee's army. They're already starting to slink away like whipped puppies." He said this without gloating.

"Did you see Annie Baumann?" I asked carefully. "She is working as a nurse in the Weigels' barn."

"Gosh durn it, no," he said. "I was hoping to see her here in town."

"Luke's in love with a girl," Ben began chanting, but Luke only laughed at him.

"Who's Lizzie in love with?" he asked Ben.

"No one!" I said quickly.

"Martin Weigel!" shouted Ben, darting away before I could grab him.

"That skinny farm boy?" said Luke in disbelief.

"You're not the only one who's changed in two years," I said, feeling defensive of Martin.

"Come and eat something, Luke," called Mama. "I dug deep in the pantry and found some potatoes for the soup." She put a bowl in front of Luke and we watched him eat. "You're so thin," she said, cutting a generous slab of butter for his bread.

"That's not fair," I said. "We only get a teaspoon of butter each day."

Mama sighed and started to scold me, but I interrupted her with a laugh.

"I'm teasing! Here, Luke, have some more. And tell us everything that happened to you the last few days. You were on Little Round Top."

"How did you know?" he said between bites. "I hardly knew where I was."

"I showed General Warren the road on the east side of the hill, and I was on Little Round Top when the battle started Thursday."

"Gosh, you're the one with the story to tell!" said Luke with his mouth open, showing his half-chewed food.

Mama raised her eyebrows at me. I hadn't told her everything after all.

"Luke, don't talk with your mouth full," she said.

"Sorry, Ma. Well, we marched thirty-five miles on Wednesday, then bivouacked about a mile east of Cemetery Ridge. I fell asleep until Thursday afternoon, when we were called up and hustled into place behind a stone wall on that hillside, and I stayed there all night and all yesterday."

"Did you see the Confederate charge yesterday?" Mama asked.

"Ma, a soldier can't see nothing on the battlefield. You don't know the plan. You just go where they tell you. All you know is the fence in front of you, or the ditch where you're lying. Half the time, you don't even know where the enemy is."

"So that's why the generals stand above the battle and give orders," I said, thinking of the view from Little Round Top.

"Well, for their own safety, too. But no, I didn't see the charge, didn't hear until today that it was practically a massacre." Luke finished chewing his mouthful of bread. "After it was over we got the order to clean out the woods in front of us, so we drove the rest of the rebels through Rose's woods and a wheat field full of bodies. We captured a passel of prisoners, a heap of muskets, and the colors of a Georgia regiment."

"How many rebels did you kill?" asked Ben, who had come into the kitchen.

"You don't stop to count," Luke said, a grim look on his face.

Mama pointed her finger, and Ben left the room sulking.

Luke shrugged. "That's all. I was lucky. Others weren't."

I could tell he didn't want to talk any more about the battle. He fiddled with his knife. Something was still weighing on his mind.

"Any news from Pa?" he finally asked.

Mama shook her head. "Are prisoners even allowed to write letters?"

"I don't know," Luke said.

"Are you sure he wasn't wounded?"

"Ma, I'm sorry!" Luke said, covering his face with his hands. "I know I promised I wouldn't come home without him, but—"

"Hush. There's nothing you can do. It's not your fault." Mama said, stroking his hair. "I just wish I knew where he was."

"Soldiers captured in Virginia often get sent to Belle Isle Prison, near Richmond. It ain't such a bad place, I hear," said Luke.

"Richmond! Why, I'll write to my brother now. He works for the Confederate government. He can use his influence to find your father," said Mama, springing up.

Luke and I were left alone. He toyed with the remainder of his food.

"So, how's school?" he asked.

"I don't even go to school. I've been too busy at the shop. Mama lets me make most of the decisions."

"I would have made a mess of Papa's business in two months," sighed Luke. "So, you're not still mad at me for leaving?"

"After two years? No, I finally got over it . . . sometime last week."

Luke snorted. "That's funny, Lizzie! I don't remember you having a sense of humor."

"If you don't laugh sometimes, you'd always be crying, these days,"

I said soberly. "Luke, I learned this morning that Margaret's beau died. She doesn't know yet."

"I was on burial detail this morning, Lizzie," Luke began in a low voice. "I shoveled dirt on fellows who were alive just two days ago. In some places, the bodies lay so thick we had to just dig a trench right there and bury them all together. No one even said a proper prayer over them." He exhaled raggedly and ran his hand through his hair. "I ain't saying I wish I'd never enlisted. Hell, I'm glad we won this battle. Maybe we'll win the war now. But North and South ain't never going to be one country again. Who can forgive all this killing? And can anyone tell me what in the bloody hell—I mean, what in the heck are we fighting for?"

My heart went out to my brother. I had never seen him so distressed. Fortunately Ben staggered into the kitchen carrying a load of wood, sparing me from having to answer Luke. Amos was behind him with a bucket of water. Grace came up from the cellar with the baby wrapped in a small colorful quilt.

"Time to give mah son his first bath," said Amos with a proud grin.

"What's his name?" asked Luke with some effort.

"Lincoln," said Grace. "After the president." She tilted the baby so that Luke could see his round, scrunched-up face.

"What do you say we call him Lincoln *Benjamin*," said Amos, "on account of this boy who kep' me from bein' sold back into slavery."

Ben's eyes lit up with pleasure. Luke looked back and forth between them, confused.

"That would be great! It will be like having another brother," Ben said. Then he turned to Luke and added, "It'll make sense once I tell you all the adventures Amos and I had."

I put my hand on Luke's shoulder. "Does this answer your question?"

Lizzie

Chapter 45

The next morning, the streets were free of stray rebels. It was Sunday, but there were no services, for every church in town was full of wounded soldiers. So Mama gathered everyone into the parlor for prayers. Even Noah Zimmer hopped up the stairs on one foot to join us.

Mama held the family Bible tight and just prayed from her heart, "We thank you, Lord, for restoring our loved ones to us. Your blessed mother was not so full of joy as we in this room."

Margaret, Grace, and Mama were in tears. Grace murmured "Amen," and we all echoed her.

After prayers, Luke and Amos made a handcart from a broken wagon they found in the street and loaded it with some of Margaret's things. Luke wheeled the cart to her house on his way to rejoin his regiment, and I went along, too. Margaret held the children's hands firmly to keep them from exploring the debris-scattered street.

Near Middle Street we met Mrs. Brodhead, who was in a talkative mood.

"I've been in my cellar for four days," she said. "We were in the thick of it the whole time. I declare, I worried away a good ten pounds of flesh. I thought those rebels would never go away. Now I'm on my way to help at the church."

"Yes, indeed," said Margaret sympathetically, "you did have the worst of it there on Chambersburg Pike."

We crossed the street to investigate a sort of celebration outside the newspaper office. The telegraph was still broken, but a merchant returning from Harrisburg had brought the news: Vicksburg had fallen to General Grant. Luke let out a loud whoop.

"The tide has turned!" proclaimed Margaret with more than her usual zeal.

"Surely the war can't go on much longer, after two such victories," said another bystander, and people nodded in agreement.

After we unloaded Margaret's belongings and determined that no stray rebels lurked inside the house, it was time for Luke to go.

"This time you have to say a proper good-bye," I said. We hugged each other tightly, and I said, through my tears, that I was proud of him. He was too choked up to reply. I stood gazing after Luke long after he had disappeared from view.

I returned to find Margaret picking up shards of glass in the dining room. A bullet had broken the window, shredded the draperies, and lodged in the opposite wall, cracking the plaster over her sewing machines.

"That's not the only one," said Margaret. "Both sides of the house were hit. There's a bullet in the parlor mantelpiece, too."

"Thank God you weren't here," I said.

"Yes. Oh, poor Ginnie Wade—and Georgia, and Mrs. Wade," Margaret murmured. "Will you stay here tonight, Lizzie?"

"Yes, I told Mother I would."

"Then let's get to work," she said, dusting off the sewing machine. "Time to make bandages instead of trousers. Lizzie, start in Rosanna's old room and gather up the extra linens."

I went upstairs and opened the door to Rosanna's room. There was the bed, mounded with pillows, where I had last seen my cousin weeping at the news of Henry Phelps's death. I put my cheek against the pillows, but of course Rosanna's scent was long gone. Her favorite book of poems still rested on the bedside table, collecting dust. I opened it up to the ribbon marker and read a verse she had marked with a pencil: *O for the touch of a vanished hand and the sound of a voice that is still.* There was no anger left in me, only a sad longing for something that was past. I wondered where Rosanna was and imagined her wearing a black crepe dress and weeping as she followed the Confederate army somewhere deep in the South. I started to pull the quilt from the bed but stopped. I smoothed it back in place, resettled the pillows, and closed the door again. In the hall cupboard I found some spare linens.

The rest of the day I spent cutting linen into strips while Margaret stitched up the edges. Clara played with the scraps on the floor, and Jack pressed his face to the window, complaining because his mother would not let him play outside.

"Thank you for staying, Lizzie. I know this is dull for you."

"I don't mind it," I said. "I've had enough excitement."

"I'll say. Taking Grace and the children to the Weigels' and coming back, right through the battle lines, toting a rifle, just to be sure we were safe! Jack told me about the rebel spies, too. You are indeed brave, Lizzie. I'm too scared to even touch a gun, but I've no doubt you would kill a man to save one of us."

"Perhaps I would," I mused. "But let's hope I don't have to. Because I left the rifle at mother's." Margaret and I both laughed.

"Look who's here!" cried Jack, dashing from his post at the window to open the door. There stood Ben, covered in mud. He carried a knapsack, which fell to the floor with a heavy thud as he eased it from his shoulders.

"What do you have there? Where have you been?" I asked.

"Hunting for relics," he said, his face shining with excitement.

Margaret and I exchanged confused looks.

"Souvenirs—of the battle," he explained.

"You've been out on the battlefields?" I shook my head in disbelief.

"Sure! All around Culp's Hill. Lots of people are there picking up souvenirs. They've come from everywhere."

"But aren't there bodies still on the field?" asked Margaret.

"No, they are mostly buried. But there are dead horses still lying around. It smells ten times worse out there than the critter that died behind the kitchen wall last year. Remember that, Lizzie? But look what I found!"

Ben opened his bag and withdrew a Confederate cap and fringed cavalry sash, a pipe and tobacco pouch, several chunks of shrapnel, a framed print of a woman and a baby, and a bowie knife. Jack clamored to touch the knife, but Ben held him back. He placed some misshapen metal pellets in my hand. I was too astonished to speak.

"Minié balls. They get bent from the heat when they strike a rock or tree," Ben explained. "Look, these two are melted together. They must have hit each other in midair. But here's my best find!" He unwrapped from a blanket a twelve-pound cannonball.

Margaret gasped and I finally found my voice.

"Whatever possessed you, Benjamin Allbauer? Don't you know how dangerous this could be?" I sounded exactly like Mama.

"Oh, I know. Some boys found a shell lying on the ground, and they were throwing rocks at it, trying to hit the fuse. I would never do that."

"Did it blow up?" asked Jack.

"Yep, finally it exploded. But they weren't badly hurt."

"They might have been killed!" I grabbed Ben's collar and said in my most dire voice, "Don't you ever go back there."

"I think it's shameful, to go playing and digging about where men died for the cause of freedom," said Margaret.

"What will you do with these things?" I asked.

"Well, I can't take them home because Ma would yell at me worse than you are," Ben said, putting his souvenirs into the sack one by one.

"Do you plan to sell them? Did you collect them just for the money?" I demanded.

"I'm not going to sell anything!" Ben cried, clutching the knapsack. The tintype of the mother and child slipped to the floor. "I'm going to keep all of my souvenirs and show my children and grandchildren so that nobody will ever forget this battle!" He was almost in tears.

Margaret picked up the tintype and gazed at it. Then she said gently, "You may leave your treasures here for now, and I will keep them safe."

Ben's shoulders sagged with relief. "Thank you," he murmured.

"Now go straight home," I ordered my brother. "I know you didn't mean any harm, but stay away from the battlefield. Tell Mama I'll be home tomorrow morning, and we'll get the shop ready to open."

Ben left in a chastened mood. The sun was sinking behind the rooftops and the only traffic on Baltimore Pike was the Union soldiers heading south. Drumbeats kept their weary steps in rhythm as they marched on, pursuing Lee's army.

"I hope they aren't leaving us entirely undefended," said Margaret in a worried tone. She began to light one lamp after another. "Let's make it look like the house is full of people."

Jack and Clara went to bed early, but I stayed up to keep Margaret company. I yawned as we stitched and rolled bandages. Then I realized Margaret was shaking me by the arm.

"Did you hear that?" she asked. A *V*-shaped furrow appeared between her eyebrows.

"No," I said. "I must have dozed off."

337

"It sounded like the gate creaking. I think I hear footsteps!"

We tiptoed to the front window, but the lights inside the house made it difficult to see outside. Finally I could make out the figure of a man, his face hidden by a hat.

"It's not a Union soldier. His pants are light colored," Margaret whispered.

"I don't see a rifle. Do you?"

"Look at his hand. Is it a Negro?"

"I think he's alone."

"Oh, Lizzie; what if he's a deserter come to shoot us? It's after dark, so he cannot be up to any good. What are we going to do?"

I wished I had John Ray's rifle to put between us and the stranger. Otherwise I was out of ideas. "I'm thinking!" I said.

"I'll grab Jack and Clara and we'll run out the back door," suggested Margaret.

"No, wait," said Lizzie. "If he has come to the front door of a lighted-up house, he isn't looking for trouble. And there are two of us. Get the fireplace poker, just in case. I'll see what he wants."

With Margaret beside me hiding the poker behind her skirts, I swung the door open and demanded in the surest voice I could muster, "Who's there?"

The man took off his hat and said in a voice deep and soft with the accent of the South, "My name be Thomas Banks, an' I mean you ladies no harm."

I could see that the man was in a pitiful state. One arm was in a sling made from a scrap of blanket that was damp and sticky with blood. Over his other shoulder he carried a haversack with a red cross stitched to it.

"We can't take any wounded in," said Margaret. "You'll have to be on your way."

"I didn' come for myself, ma'am," he said.

"Let's at least get him some water and food," I said, noticing how he swayed as he stood there.

"First tell me, what is your business?" Margaret asked warily.

"If it please y'all, I'm looking for the sister of Miz Rosanna Wilcox."

Margaret let out a cry and the poker clattered to the floor behind her.

"Rosanna! You have news of Rosanna?" I said eagerly. But I didn't want to hear it. It could not be good news, brought by this weary, injured Negro. "Don't tell us she's—"

"Tell me," Margaret said, trembling all over. "I am her sister."

"She's a short ways off." Thomas Banks nodded his head toward the road. "Comin' across the fields was awful hard on her."

Margaret brushed by him and ran out into the darkness, shouting "Rosanna! Rosanna!"

I helped Thomas Banks into a chair and poured him some water. He pointed to the door, as if urging me to go as well. A quick glance in his eyes and I knew he could be trusted, so I left him there and ran outside.

Margaret was standing in the middle of Baltimore Pike, crying and holding up Rosanna, who could barely stand. Her head was wrapped in a bandage, but her familiar black hair sprung from beneath it in wild profusion.

"My side! Oh, it hurts to breathe. Don't . . . make me cry, too . . . dear sister!" Rosanna gasped, grimacing with pain.

I ran up and seized Rosanna's hand. "Is it you? You're really here?" I said, choking back tears.

"Yes, it's me. I think. Lizzie? I don't remember! My head." She groaned and reached up to touch the bandage.

"Hush now, Rosie, let's get you inside and lying down," said Margaret.

"Oh, Lizzie, I've missed you so," murmured Rosanna.

Somehow Margaret and I managed to carry Rosanna up the stairs to her bedroom. We laid her on the quilt that I had smoothed only hours before. We undressed her and checked all her limbs, bathed her as best we could, trying not to touch the bruises. I saw that she wore John Wilcox's wedding ring and a leaden heart around her neck. There was a small wound below her left breast.

"What happened to you?" I kept asking, but Rosanna only shook her head.

"Let her rest now; we'll learn everything later," said Margaret gently, drawing a clean nightgown over Rosanna's head.

But Rosanna seemed worried about Thomas Banks, and only when Margaret promised she would take care of him did she fall asleep. I confess I wasn't much help as Margaret bathed and wrapped the Negro's wounded arm. He explained that he had been John Wilcox's valet but was now a free man. Margaret looked surprised but did not question him further. I went back upstairs, climbed on the bed next to my cousin, and gazed at her familiar features: the full, red lips, now cracked and sunburned, the arched brows over her closed eyes. I wanted to know everything she had been through. I held her hand, rough-skinned and brown, and touched her cheek, then her unruly black hair. Why was she in Gettysburg?

I had so many questions, but what did the answers matter? My cousin Rosanna was alive, and she had finally come home.

Rosanna

Chapter 46

Monday, July 6, 1863

How strange it was to wake up this morning to find myself lying in a soft bed in my old room! Lizzie and my sister brought tea and oatmeal and did not leave my side until I pleaded to be allowed to sleep again. I am scarcely able to move for all my bruises and the pain in my head. But I can still write.

The last thing I remember was kneeling beside Kate O'Neill and her husband. Then came blackness, until I awoke on a cot in a field hospital with Dr. Walker looming over me. My head throbbed and when I tried to sit up, dizziness and sharp pains in my side nearly overcame me.

"You have broken a rib or two and sustained a concussion, but I believe you'll mend." He frowned but at least refrained from expressing his opinion that I had proved to be a nuisance after all. I tried to ask how my injuries had occurred, but my voice came out like the croaking of a frog.

"You'll have to ask that Tom Banks fellow who brought you in," he said. "I've got amputations waiting."

I was relieved to hear Tom was alive. Shortly Tom himself came by and explained that he had been rounding up runaway horses when he heard the sound of weeping and discovered me bent over my journal. As he helped me rise, a bullet struck his arm and passed through, then knocked me to the ground. He carried me to an ambulance, not neglecting my satchel of medicine and my journal.

"You took a bullet that could have killed me, and then you carried me despite your broken arm?" I said in wonder.

"You ain't so heavy, ma'am. I used my good arm." Then he frowned. "Do you think Tom Banks would leave you lyin' there?"

I said I knew he would not. I wondered where the bullet had come from, for the fighting was over. Tom said it might have been a sniper. Or, he surmised, a man died with his finger on the trigger, and when his body started to seize up, it pulled the trigger and his gun went off. What grim luck—to be shot by a dead soldier!

Once again, I owe my life to Tom. As usual, my attempts to thank him only embarrassed him. Nor was he eager to permit Dr. Walker to examine his arm, which was in a makeshift sling.

"Perhaps, if he get the chance. But I'll be goin' now. It ain't fittin' for me to be here talkin' with you anyhow."

"Damn what is fitting. None of this is fitting!" I cried out, thinking of the wounded crawling with flies in overcrowded tents, and the battlefields where blood and mud mingled. But had I really cursed all propriety? My head ached, and I feared my brain was addled.

"What day is it?" I asked Tom, and he replied that it was Saturday, the 4th of July. Independence Day! The federals must be celebrating. But in our hospital was only misery. The rain drummed on the tent and the air inside grew dank and fetid. Rain trickled in, turning the ground to mud. The sense of defeat hung like a sodden blanket over all, hastening the death of many who might otherwise have rallied and lived. Dr. Walker worked without rest until he resembled a walking corpse. And I could do nothing but lie there.

On Sunday, orders came to dismantle the hospital and follow Lee's retreat. There were not enough ambulances and wagons for all the injured men, so many would be left to the mercy of the Yankees. Woe to those unable to walk! I saw a soldier get up from his bed, determined to go along, but his shattered leg collapsed under him, and he fell to the ground, crying, "Don't leave me!"

Dr. Walker stopped to check on me and said that I could not be accommodated on the retreat. Moreover, as a doctor, he did not advise traveling in my state.

"I expected as much," I said. "I would only be a hindrance to you."

We shook hands, and that was our awkward farewell. I believe he wished to say more but was unable, perhaps through extreme weariness and despair.

What would the Yankees do with me? I was hardly going to stay around and find out. I would go to Margaret's house. It couldn't be more than two miles away if I crossed over the battlefields. I found I could walk if I took small steps and sat down often to combat dizziness. My ribs hurt, and my dress stuck to my wound, tugging painfully with every movement. But I had no other choice. I told Tom my plan and he insisted on coming with me. First, however, we had to store up our strength.

By midafternoon nothing remained of the camp save the tent where the injured men lay waiting for death or the Yankees. Even Dolly, to my dismay, had disappeared, and Tom supposed she had been conscripted to haul artillery. Alas, my poor, gentle mare! Tom and I foraged enough provisions from abandoned knapsacks to cook up a stew, which we shared with those who were able to eat. When the day's heat began to subside, we set out across the fields. The monster of war had burned and trampled the earth, scattered chunks of iron and lead, flung fence-posts and wagon parts and dead horses in every direction. We saw no living souls, save a farmer surveying his ruined land. Fresh mounds of dirt marked where soldiers had been crudely put in the ground, and the rain had already uncovered an arm here, a leg there. Except for the sound of our own breathing and the mud sucking at our shoes, it was eerily quiet where two days ago the earth had shaken with hellish thunder. Tom kept watch for unexploded ordnance, and I stopped frequently to rest, so we made slow progress. Finally we reached the point where the roads converged on the edge of town. We waited, concealed by darkness, while Union troops passed by.

We were only a short distance from Margaret's house when a sudden fearful anticipation overcame me and I could go no farther. Tom went ahead while I sat beside the road, trembling. Would Margaret turn her back on me, her rebel sister?

Alas, my brain must have been addled to come up with such a thought. Lizzie and Margaret welcomed me with such joy that I almost forgot my pain. Margaret examined my side and determined that my stays had broken from the impact of the bullet and cut into my flesh, yet they also had prevented greater injury and held my injured rib secure.

"Perhaps soldiers should all wear whalebone corsets," Lizzie joked as Margaret wrapped wide strips of linen snugly around my middle and put a clean gown on me. Then I fell asleep. When I woke briefly in the night, I discovered my dear Lizzie sleeping beside me, her hand resting in mine.

Tuesday, July 7, 1863

Today I ventured downstairs for the first time. My purpose was to treat Tom's wound myself, for Margaret claimed it was beyond her ability. She helped me by removing his sling and wetting the dried bandage until it came loose from the skin. The wound indeed smelled foul and was teeming with maggots, like fat grains of rice. Margaret was appalled, but I explained that the creatures ate the decayed flesh and thus kept the wound clean. Probing with my fingers as I had seen the surgeons do, I felt a fragment of bone and asked Margaret to hand me the small scissors.

"Your hands are shaking, Rosanna," said Margaret. "Tell me what to do." My head had begun to ache again, and my eyes could not focus, so I instructed her how to grip the piece of bone between the small blades. In a few moments, she produced the offending fragment. Tom made not a sound but only grimaced, and my sister deftly stitched the torn skin together.

I've no doubt Tom would have lost his arm had it festered any longer, or even his life. At last I had the pleasure of repaying in part his goodness to me.

Wednesday, July 8, 1863

Lizzie has so much to tell me, and I her, that we talk for hours at a time. I listened with amazement as she recounted her adventures during the battle. She told me about her father being captured in May. Since then they have heard nothing! Poor Aunt Mary. Lizzie also counted up the local boys and men who had been killed or injured, and I realized how wrong I had been to imagine Gettysburg and my cousin untouched by war.

What Lizzie finds most amazing, however, is that she and Luke and I all witnessed the battle, unbeknownst to one another. She concluded that providence made our paths cross so that she could be reconciled with Luke and with me. I thought for a moment before responding that I could credit neither providence nor chance for bringing me to Gettysburg.

"My being here is the end result of many choices. I came of my own will. I believe I wanted more than anything to see you and Margaret again."

"Then you don't mind so much—losing the battle?" she asked.

"No, when I see how the winners also suffered. In war, death is the only victor."

I am beginning to sound like a philosopher!

Thursday, July 9, 1863

I have been walking and taking the stairs for exercise, testing my sore rib by how much it aches when I take a deep breath. I must be getting better, for Jack and Clara no longer give me headaches with their noisy playing.

Lizzie visits me every day after the shop closes. Even then, she is all business. This week the cows and pigs were brought back from Wrightsville, their pens rebuilt, the store restocked. She is a born shopkeeper, with her head for figures and account books. She also has a good heart. She sent a ham to the family of a Gettysburg boy killed in fighting near Little Round Top, to feed the funeral-goers. I hear people are charging steep prices for such common things as a pail of fresh water, a loaf of bread, even a bumpy cart ride to visit an injured soldier. They should be ashamed to profit from the misery and sacrifice of others.

Friday, July 10, 1863

Lizzie came today and, without preamble, said, "I kept your secrets. I didn't tell a soul." And then she handed me my old scrapbook, tied with the red ribbon, and stepped back, as if she were glad to be free of it.

Taken by surprise, faced suddenly with that reminder of my

younger, foolish self, I buried my face in my hands and burst into tears.

"I didn't mean to upset you. Please don't cry," she pleaded. "I thought you would want it back."

I opened the book. An earthy smell rose from its pages. There was John's photograph and his old letters. Love and shame, nostalgia and remorse swept over me. I couldn't stop crying as I paged through the scrapbook. When I looked up, Lizzie was gone.

Sunday, July 12, 1863

Lizzie didn't visit yesterday. Did my outburst yesterday alarm her? Perhaps she was too busy with chores.

This morning I went with Margaret and the children to church. Mrs. Pierpont was there with her son Samuel, who was discharged due to an injury. She greeted me warmly, but the other ladies seemed aloof. I don't care in the slightest for their good opinion. I only went to church for the walk and the chance to talk to Lizzie. As I observed her during the service, it occurred to me that she has no idea how beautiful she is becoming. The childish awkwardness in her is gone, like the spots on a fawn that fade and disappear.

After church Lizzie agreed to walk home with me, but she was quiet, waiting for me to begin the conversation.

"I'm sorry that I burdened you with keeping my scrapbook," I began.

"No, it was my fault for reading the letters," she interrupted.

"I knew you would read them, and I hoped that you of all people would understand me."

"But I didn't understand you at all," she said bleakly. "First, I was hurt that you kept the truth from me—"

"I was ashamed, Lizzie. Surely you can understand why."

"Yes, but I cannot grasp why—forgive me for saying this, Rosanna—why, after John Wilcox caused you to steal, you married him anyway!"

No one but Lizzie had ever asked me such a direct question. I didn't know how to reply.

"My theft tormented us both, but John and I made amends, you know," I said, becoming defensive. "Can't you forgive me?"

"I'm no longer angry, Rosanna. I don't cling to old hurts. And the money—that's not important to me," she said. "But why did you marry him?"

She had laid her hand on my arm so that we both came to a stop. The hot sun beat on my face, but I did not pull the brim of my hat over my eyes. I looked directly at Lizzie and took a deep breath.

"He looked so handsome in his uniform. I was confused and foolish. I thought what I felt was love." These were truths I hadn't dared to utter before.

"So you *didn't* love him?" she asked in wonder.

I paused again as a fuller truth dawned upon me.

"I started loving him the day we were married. I loved him more each day, and with every misfortune that almost took him from me. And I haven't stopped loving him since the day he died," I said.

"Oh, dearest Rosanna!" Lizzie's face crumpled into tears, and she raised her hands imploringly. I put my arms around her, and we stood there in the street, embracing, our tears wetting each other's cheeks. Finally I pulled away, and with my handkerchief dabbed my cheeks and Lizzie's. We smiled at each other.

"I saw Martin Weigel during the service," I said. "I hardly recognized the boy. You didn't tell me he was so attractive, with that wavy brown hair."

"Oh, you think so?" she said in an offhand way.

"He stared at you during the whole service."

"I didn't notice."

"I see you blushing, Lizzie. Now you're the one hiding something from me."

My gentle rebuke prompted a full confession. Lizzie told me what had happened at the Weigels' during the battle. "We almost kissed, there by the spring, but I backed away, and he has hardly said a word to me since then," she wailed. "He could have spoken to me after church, but he took off like there were rebels at his heels."

"That sounds like love to me," I said.

Tuesday, July 14, 1863

While Lizzie and I are reconciled, only time may mend the differences between Margaret and me. Today some item in the newspaper led her to denounce the South for provoking an unjust rebellion. I countered that the South went to war to defend herself against oppression by the federal government.

"The gentleman planters of Virginia are not as oppressed as their Negroes!" she scoffed.

"I grant you that," I said. "But I do not see how you can justify war as a means to end slavery, when more men have died in recent battles than ever died under the yoke of a plantation master."

Without even pausing to consider my point, she shot back, "The Southern rebels began the war, and it is your own rebellious nature that makes you side with them."

"I hate this war as much as you do. It has claimed my husband," I reminded her. It was a struggle to remain civil. "I hope that people of good faith will in time choose to reject the evil of slavery. You might be surprised to know that it was I who persuaded John Wilcox to grant Tom his freedom."

Margaret looked at me in surprise, and our disagreement went no further.

Thursday, July 16, 1863

When I dressed Tom's wound this morning I was pleased to see the tissue looking healthier. I told him I was sure that he would eventually regain full use of his arm. With that, he announced it was time for him to go.

"Will you return to the regiment?" I asked.

"No, ma'am. Without you or Mastuh John, I got no one to keep me safe. They wouldn't mess with me when I was the Wilcoxes' servant, but on my own, I'm just another nigger. I know men who would just as soon send me down South in leg irons," he said grimly. "I heard what almost happened to Mr. Amos."

It had never occurred to me that the steady, capable Tom had relied on John and me for protection. I tried to persuade him to stay, saying Amos would help him find a job. But no, he said, it was time for him to test his freedom. He was leaving to join a regiment of colored troops being mustered at Camp William Penn near Philadelphia.

"Soon I'll be wearin' a blue jacket with the gold eagle of freedom on its buttons," he announced.

The idea of Tom fighting for the Union against the South struck me as a betrayal. I struggled for words to express my disbelief.

"But why? You're free. You can go—to New York, and earn money, say, as a teamster."

"That's right, I'm a free man, an' I wants all my brothers an' sisters to be free, too."

I could not argue with that. I had to respect his choice. But Tom was my link to John, for we both had loved him. He saw that regret in my eyes.

"We sure been through a lot together, Miz Rose. What will you do now?" he asked with sincere concern.

I said I did not know. Indeed I have given no thought to the future.

Tom and I parted. I said that I would always consider him among the finest human beings I had ever known, but I did not carry on praising him, for fear of offending his dignity.

Friday, July 17, 1863

Of late, Gettysburg has been besieged by thousands of visitors and distraught family members seeking news of loved ones killed or wounded here. For three days we had a husband and wife from New York living in the parlor, until they located their son, who was not badly hurt. This heartened us all and took away the sting of so much sorrow. Many who come to town, however, are only gawkers and souvenir hunters who roam the streets all night because all the lodgings are full.

I have been walking into town and back to increase my strength. The streets teem with activity. Fahnestock's store houses the headquarters for the U.S. Sanitary Commission, and wagons full of supplies come and go constantly. Margaret volunteers for the commission, serving soup and coffee to soldiers waiting for trains. Among them are Union soldiers going to hospitals in Washington, D.C., and Confederates being sent to prison camps.

John's regiment must be far away by now. My service there is now a closed chapter in my life. Tom's question repeats itself in my head: what will I do next?

Monday, July 20, 1863

Margaret brought home the news that the Sanitary Commission is erecting a general hospital along York Pike east of town and all the regimental and field hospitals will shut down. Then last night I dreamed about the poor injured man who cried, "Don't leave me!" as the troops decamped and retreated. I woke up with the thought: someone must care for those sons of the South who were left behind after the battle.

I shall inquire at the new hospital when I am stronger.

Tuesday, July 21, 1863

Today Lizzie confided in me something that has been weighing on her for weeks. Margaret's beau, whom Lizzie described as a "dashing cavalier," was at the battle for Little Round Top and the next day died of his wounds. She was still distraught about it as she told me how she had been washing out bandages and forgot to take him his porridge.

"I don't see how that makes you responsible for his death," I said gently.

"And I don't see how you can blame yourself for John Wilcox's death. But we can't help how we feel, can we?"

I sighed, for she was right. "I suppose we women will always feel guilty for things that aren't our fault, simply because we can't change them. If men would take the blame for killing one another, perhaps they'd come to their senses and stop the war."

"Well, maybe so, and maybe not. But how shall we tell your sister about Mr. Hartmann?" asked Lizzie. "The longer I keep this secret, the more I feel like a liar."

"I will tell Margaret myself, when the time is right," I offered.

Later in the day, to test my sister's feelings, I asked her, "Have you heard lately from the gentleman who has been courting you?"

"I have not lost my heart, if that is what you are asking," she said, perhaps thinking of my impulsive marriage. "I am hopeful that he will return."

I saw by her eyes that her affection for him still runs deep. She deserves a good husband. I wish she could be spared the sad news.

Thursday, July 23, 1863

Yesterday while feeding soldiers at the depot, Margaret learned that many Confederate wounded had been transferred to the new general hospital, Camp Letterman. So this morning I dressed myself very presentably in a borrowed dress, wore a clean white apron, and asked Ben to drive me there. I introduced myself to the superintendent and cited my nursing experience, but the stern Yankee gave me a cool reception. Was it my accent? His wife, however, was proud to show me the camp.

The hospital stretches across a gentle hilltop and consists of hundreds of tents in rows, housing almost three thousand patients. At the entrance to each tent hang cedar boughs to ward off insects and cleanse the air. A fresh, untainted stream flows nearby, and a network of ditches carries foul water away from the camp. A depot is being built, with storage tents to hold provisions and supplies that arrive daily. The trains carry convalescents to permanent hospitals in Philadephia or Baltimore, while ambulances bring in the wounded from all around Gettysburg. The hospital is well organized, with dozens of officials and surgeons.

I said to the superintendent's wife that I had not seen, except in Richmond, a hospital better outfitted.

"Our nurses and matrons are well trained, and of the plain and sturdy sort," she replied, regarding my figure with a critical eye. "Mrs. Dix, who supervises the Union army's nurses, does not accept women who are under thirty or attractive."

I would have liked to take issue with Mrs. Dix's views but opted for deference instead.

"Might I assist with the wounded Confederates left behind in the retreat?"

"The rebels are given the same care as our own soldiers, with no distinctions made between them," she said with a firm gesture of her hand. "However, we have one ward of prisoners that is understaffed."

She led me to the ward of four tents, where I expected to find my charges sorely neglected. But I saw that the men, numbering perhaps three dozen, were clean and well cared for. The surgeon was finishing his rounds. A woman with steel gray hair fed a man with no arms. She struck me at once as a diligent and compassionate person. Nurse Spradlin introduced herself. She said her men were a grateful bunch, although the camp at large was not so friendly.

"I've been called a rebel sympathizer and mocked for doing good among the 'butternuts'—the name they give Confederates due to the color of their uniforms, you know. But each one of my patients is as brave as any Yankee," she said proudly.

As Nurse Spradlin described to me the condition of each soldier and the daily routine, she revealed that her father was born in Virginia. I said that I was a Confederate soldier's widow, and as we talked of our lives, I felt that I had found a kindred spirit.

Before leaving, I wrote several letters for my patients, which helped me become acquainted with them. The long day wearied me, and now I must get some rest.

Tuesday, July 28, 1863

Despite its clean and well-run exterior and the able staff, Camp Letterman is home to incurable grief. Each day, new graves dot the cemetery behind the camp, a reminder that the final cost of the battle is not yet tallied. Yesterday a mother who arrived from Alabama in time to watch her son die wept for hours, refusing to let go of his hand. Neither Nurse Spradlin nor I could comfort her, and her piteous cries made all our patients sorrowful. Finally we calmed her with a dose of laudanum and I brought her home to stay for a few days.

Saturday, August 1, 1863

This afternoon I found Margaret sitting quietly in the parlor, her hands resting in her lap. I knelt at her feet and reached up, taking her hands in my own.

"I don't know how to tell you this, sister," I began.

She looked at me, but I could see her thoughts were elsewhere at first.

"What is it? Have you fallen for one of your patients already?" She said this with a smile of sad resignation. Does she still think me so flighty?

"No, this is not about me." I caressed her hand for a long moment. "It's about your Mr. Hartmann. He was injured at Little Round Top. I'm afraid he is—"

"I already know!" Margaret wailed. Her smooth face crumpled with agony. "I found out yesterday, at the depot. Why do you think I've been going there every day? I was hoping, hoping . . ."

I gathered my sister in my arms and brought her down into my lap and we swayed back and forth together, shedding tears on each other's cheeks and grasping one another as if death were trying to pull us apart too.

Lizzie

——◆——

Chapter 47

Gettysburg recovered from the battle like a wounded soldier learning to walk again, step by slow step. First the shops and businesses reopened. Then churches became places of worship again as the wounded soldiers left for the new hospital on York Pike. Eventually all the dead horses were burned, and the air was not so foul smelling anymore. Some farmers replanted their fields, hoping for a mild fall and a decent harvest. People talked cheerfully about life returning to normal again, but we all knew that those three days in July had changed us forever.

One day in the middle of August, Martin came into the shop. I hadn't seen him for weeks. He said, "Hello," then ducked his head slightly as if he were embarrassed. I took a rag and rubbed at an imaginary spot on the countertop.

"Have you come to get your job back? I need someone to help bring in new contracts for slaughtering and curing," I said, trying to sound businesslike.

"Well, no, not exactly." He took off his hat and toyed with the brim.

I wanted to say that I missed him, that it was good to see him.

"Perhaps I could offer you a higher wage."

"I've been rebuilding fences every day," he said, holding up his callused hands. "Some of our neighbors lost all their stock, and the rest of us are still rounding up strays and trying to sort out whose sows and cows are whose. I came to say that I can't work for you, because there's just too much to be done on the farm."

"That's too bad," I said, trying to hide how disappointed I really felt.

"It's going to be a tough winter," he went on. "Almost all the crops were ruined, and farmers around us are afraid to plow their fields, what with all the unexploded shells still lying around. Can you believe it? The battle's over, but it's still possible to get killed around here."

"I know. I've threatened my brother with dire punishments if he goes looking for cannonballs again."

Martin chuckled. He rotated his hat brim between his thumb and forefinger.

"I'm almost done here," I said, putting down the rag. I hoped he would suggest that we go for a walk.

"Perhaps I could ask my neighbors what prices and terms they can manage and try to talk up some business for you. If Amos could drive the stock to market, that might seal the bargain."

"Thank you, that would be very helpful," I said.

Martin shifted his weight to one leg, his hip jutting to the side. He looked confident and manly, until he reached up and tugged at the hair that hung over his forehead.

"You had any news from your pa?"

"No. Mama wrote to our uncle in Richmond, and he wrote back saying there was no record of Papa at Belle Isle or the hospitals. But he allowed there were hundreds of prisoners who were not even processed. That was the word he used. 'Processed.' Like *cattle*. I don't think he looked very hard for Papa. He was always sore that Mama married a Yankee."

"Maybe your pa wrote a letter but it never got through."

"That's what I tell Mama. She's living on the hope that he'll come home as soon as the war is over."

"That won't be much longer, now that we won Gettysburg and Vicksburg both."

"Well, I've heard folks say it might be over now, if Meade hadn't let Lee get away from here after the battle," I said.

"The situation is always more clear when you look back at it," Martin said, fixing his eyes on mine.

What did he mean? I knew what I was thinking: that I should have let him kiss me that day by the stream.

"Do you mean, by clearer . . . the battle?" I asked, my tongue stumbling over the words.

"That too. Well, I should go now," he said, but he made no move to leave.

Just then Mrs. Brodhead and another woman swept into the shop, and whatever Martin and I would have said to each other next went unsaid.

When I told Mama that night about Martin's offer, she laid aside her knitting and folded her hands in her lap.

"I've been considering this matter, too," she said, smiling. "And I have decided to assume more responsibility for the daily operation of the shop."

"Why?" I asked, becoming wary.

"I know how much you regret having to forego your schooling for two years. So I have enrolled you at the Ladies' Seminary for the fall term!" Mama put up a hand. "Don't worry how we will manage the tuition. You have more than earned it."

"I am doing a good job. Why take me away from it?" I blurted out.

"I thought you wanted to go to school and become a teacher," she said, looking hurt.

"I can do that when the war is over. Right now is a critical time for the business. Demand is high, but people are short of money. If we raise prices, we will lose our customers! Father would be crushed if you let—if that happened." I saw Mama's face darken. "It's not that I don't trust you to run the business. But I feel responsible for this family too."

"You can stop trying to prove yourself to me and your father," Mama said sternly.

My feelings boiled over like a pot of jam cooking on a fast fire.

"Do you think I wanted to run a butcher shop? No! But it makes me feel like there's something I am good at, something I have control over. Don't you understand?"

Mama softened. She wasn't holding a grudge for what I'd said.

"I think I do, Lizzie. But I miss seeing you all dreamy, lost in a story. It used to be that all you cared about was having a good book to carry around with you."

"Well, I'm using my head for business now. Storybooks don't seem very useful these days," I said.

"War or no war, children always need teachers. Perhaps you can attend just the literature classes and continue working at the shop. Mathematics might be useful as well. Shall I speak to Mrs. Pierpont about it?"

Mama's offer seemed like a good compromise, so I found myself, at last, a student at the Ladies' Seminary. I was famous, too, for all the girls knew that I had met General Meade, traveled twice through the battle lines, and barely escaped an exploding shell. One girl had even heard that I shot a soldier who tried to molest me, a rumor I quickly stopped. They were less impressed by Annie's experiences, for several of the girls had helped nurse wounded soldiers. But Ginnie Wade, whom most of the seminary girls would never have considered a friend while she lived, was everyone's heroine because of her death. Mrs. Pierpont even had us compose poems for a pageant in her honor.

One day in literature class, Annie showed off a silver ring on a chain around her neck. She swept back her perfect ringlets so that it was visible to all.

"The officer I nursed at the Weigels' gave it to me. He lost only two fingers, fortunately. We're betrothed!" she announced. She seemed to have forgotten that she ever fancied my brother, and I decided it was just as well, for Luke deserved better.

My eighteenth birthday came that October. Rosanna and I decided to have a picnic at Culp's Hill, just the two of us. Mama sent along a chocolate cake and a bowl of thick cream. When I went to Margaret's house to meet Rosanna, she gave me a present, a green silk shawl. Margaret had made a matching bonnet for me.

"It's exactly right for you; it makes your eyes look even more green," Rosanna said, draping the shawl around my shoulders.

"I've never worn anything so fashionable," I said, awed, as she led me to the dressing table.

"Now I'll sweep back your hair, like this." Rosanna wound up my hair, pinned it, and set the bonnet on top.

"But we are going on a picnic, not to a ball. What if these get soiled?" I fingered the lush silk.

"It is your birthday," said Rosanna. "It's no time to be practical."

As we left, Margaret called out, "Keep Rosanna in your sight, Lizzie, so she doesn't run off to Richmond again." I think she was only half teasing.

"We are not going to get on a train for some fancy city, are we?" I asked, regarding my cousin with some suspicion.

"With a chocolate cake and no money? I hardly think so," she laughed.

As we ambled down the street in no hurry, I told Rosanna all about school, about Annie's engagement and the upcoming pageant in Ginnie's memory. We had begun reading Shakespeare, and I described *Julius Caesar* as a great war story about friendship and betrayal. I even begged Rosanna to come back to the seminary.

"Widows do not go to school, Lizzie," she said, affecting the manner of one of the Gettysburg matrons.

"You are hardly older than I am," I pointed out. "And I always wanted us to go to school together. Don't you agree that it would be fun?"

"I have outgrown fun, Lizzie," she said, but she was smiling.

We had gone as far as the Wagon Hotel at the intersection of Baltimore Road and Emmitsburg Road when Rosanna stopped, clapped her hands together, and said, "Well, look who's here!"

It was Sunday, and a few carriages rolled by with folks heading for church or a family dinner. I followed her gaze but didn't see anyone I knew. A man alighted from a horse and hitched it in front of the hotel, where another man was sitting astride the fence. The second man leaped to the ground and took off his hat, and then I recognized Martin Weigel.

"Just the two of us, you said?" I hissed at Rosanna.

"Is it my fault if we happen to encounter a young gentleman on our outing?" she replied, feigning innocence.

"But what will he think of me, decked out like this?" I whispered as Martin approached.

"He will think you the picture of loveliness. Now smile."

So I smiled. Martin looked fine in trousers with a matching vest, a white shirt, and a loose cravat, as if he had been at church.

"Isn't it a grand day for Lizzie's birthday? Why don't you come with us for a picnic? I don't think my cousin would mind, would you, Lizzie?"

Martin took my arm. I didn't mind at all. It was a grand day. The autumn leaves blazed gold and red and yellow, plummeting downward with every gust of wind and rustling loudly underfoot.

I welcomed Rosanna's chatter, though it went right through my ears. I was conscious of Martin's closeness. His grasp was firm as he helped me up the rocky slope of Culp's Hill. Rosanna, too, leaned on him. I was proud of my new shawl and pleased that the bonnet hid my face so he wouldn't see how flushed I was.

In the woods, it was sunless and chilly. We had trouble finding our favorite picnic spot near the stream. So much had changed. Broken limbs hung from trees whose trunks were blackened and ridden with bullets. Breastworks made of earth, rocks, and saplings still stood in a zigzagging line. Here and there were mounds of earth topped by simple wooden crosses. I knew they were the graves of soldiers who had been buried where they fell. Holding my picnic basket, I felt as if I had burst into a church with no thought of praying there. By a mutual and silent consent, we retraced our steps out of the woods and sat down on a warm rock in the sun.

"How could anyone have survived in there, with bullets falling like hail?" I said. It was not a question that had an answer, so no one offered one.

"Did you see all the dirt scattered about? Who would dare to dig up a grave?" said Rosanna indignantly.

"Haven't you heard?" asked Martin. "There is to be a burial ground for Union soldiers beside Evergreen Cemetery. My uncle is on the committee. All the bodies in temporary graves are being dug up and properly buried there."

We talked about the difficulty and unpleasantness of such a task.

Then Martin broke the somber mood. "Isn't this a birthday party? I'm hungry," he said, rubbing his hands together.

We spread out the picnic and shared the tart, red-cheeked apples sent by Margaret. We divided the cake, and Martin ate two pieces for each one that Rosanna and I did. Then Rosanna yawned conspicuously and stood up. She strolled a little ways off, then lay down in the dappled shade of a tree and covered her face with her bonnet. Martin and I were practically alone.

"I'm sorry," I murmured. "My cousin is always coming up with one scheme or another."

"No, this was my idea," said Martin, smiling at me.

I looked at him in surprise. He slid closer to me on the blanket, and we sat as still as two rabbits that have spied a fox.

"I can't see your face," he finally said, reaching over and tugging the ribbon of my bonnet. It came untied.

Startled, I put up my hands to hold it in place.

"Do you like it? It's my birthday present," I said to hide my confusion.

"It's pretty. The green suits you. Let me see your eyes." He played with the ribbon. I lowered my head to allow him to lift off the bonnet. "The shawl looks nice against the pink of your skin," he said, touching my neck. His fingers felt cool. "And the sunlight makes your hair look like gold," he said, smoothing back the wisps that had fallen from the pins.

I was about to melt into a puddle of soft wax. I grabbed his hands and held them between us. He leaned away from me with a sigh, and I let out my breath too. Glancing over at Rosanna, I saw that she had not stirred.

"Look!" Martin freed his hands to point overhead, where a hawk with a broad, white-feathered chest perched on a high branch. As we watched, it swooped to the ground, seized a wriggling snake in its talons, and flew away again, its shadow passing over us.

My own senses sharpened, I heard the thump of walnuts falling from a nearby tree and watched a squirrel turning one in its tiny paws and nibbling away the green husk. Its teeth made a small ticking sound. The browning stalks of coneflowers and goldenrod rustled drily. The goldfinches, who were losing their bright summer plumage, still twittered and hopped among the withered flower heads, picking up seeds.

Martin broke the silence. "I don't ask anything more out of life than what it's given me right here and now," he said with a sigh of contentment.

"Does that include me?" I asked, trying to sound lighthearted, though I was in complete earnest.

"You're *here, now,* aren't you?" he replied, and I nodded. Then he reached into his pocket and brought out a small package wrapped in brown paper.

"For your birthday. It's taken me two months, since I ruined several before I was satisfied."

So he *had* been thinking of me ever since the battle! I held the package. It almost didn't matter what was inside.

"Aren't you going to open it?"

I tore off the paper to reveal a wooden box with a lid that opened with a tiny hinge. On the lid was carved *L. A. 1863.*

"I'll keep this always," I said in a whisper. "What shall I put in here?"

"This memory, first of all," said Martin, reaching over and brushing my cheek with his lips. He stayed there, his breath tickling my skin, silently asking for more. This time I would not lose the opportunity. I turned my face toward him and closed my eyes. Sure enough, his lips, warm and moist, pressed against mine. I opened my mouth just a bit and pressed back. Then, dizzy and out of breath, I pulled free and opened my eyes. Martin was smiling at me. He put both arms around me and leaned backward. I felt like I would fall. I took a deep breath as our lips met and didn't try to stop myself. In my head, a voice exulted, *I am kissing Martin Weigel!*

Lizzie

Chapter 48

Martin wanted to walk me home, but I declined, not wanting to face Mama's inevitable questions. So at the Wagon Hotel we parted ways, and he went off a little disappointed.

"You managed that quite properly," said Rosanna.

"Were you really asleep? Or were you peering at us the whole time?"

"You'll never know," she said, raising her eyebrows.

"At least tell me what you think of him."

"Why, I approve of him."

"Is that all you can say?"

"He will be more handsome when his beard comes in."

"He is already handsome!"

"My, it's easy to rile you up. Of course he is nice looking. And he seems thoughtful and cautious. Neither of you is likely to lose your head in love."

"But what if I want to!" I spun around until I was giddy.

"Then go ahead," said Rosanna, laughing and throwing up her hands. "But it's my obligation as a knowing widow to warn you."

"Pish and bother," I said, wrinkling my nose. "Oh, Rosanna, this has been the best birthday ever!" I hugged her, then skipped the rest of the way home, stopping in enough time to compose myself before

Mama could see me and guess what I had been up to. But she was away at a meeting.

Alone in my room, I folded my new silk shawl and caressed the fashionable bonnet before putting them away. If I were going to be courted by a fellow, I would need a new dress or two. Would a tartan skirt be too bold? Wearing only my shift, I tilted the mirror on the bureau and stood back to examine myself. I decided I owned a pleasing face and figure—not a beautiful one, certainly, but no longer the awkward, childish body I thought I would always have. I shivered at the memory of Martin's embrace. How would I react when I saw him again? Would Mama allow Martin to court me, and when Papa came back, would he approve?

Papa's absence cut into my joy like a small, sharp knife. I went to bed and prayed that another birthday would not pass before I saw him again. And the very next day, the same providence that brought Luke and Rosanna to Gettysburg delivered a letter from Papa! Though it was dirt-stained and battered, the sight of his unmistakable handwriting brought tears of happiness to my eyes. Mama unfolded the letter with shaking fingers while Ben and I crowded around her. I noticed the date on the letter was almost two months ago.

Near railroad depot and Pamunkey River
August 30, 1863
Dear wife and children,
I suspect the few lines I wrote weeks ago never made it into the post as I had nothing to bribe the guard with. Nor do I now but I will take my chances. I am worried about your welfare after hearing of the battle at Gettysburg, and only a letter from you would put me at ease again.

I am tolerably well at the moment as I have avoided the prison camps thus far. The others taken in the raid were marched away at once. My foot being injured, they kept me behind and more or less forgot me. The ambulance that was to take me to a Richmond hospital never came, so I spent weeks playing checkers and cards with my captors. A good bunch of men, though blind to the evil of rebellion and slavery, and I could not convert their minds.

When my foot healed somewhat they sent me and others by train to a holding camp along the James River, where we expected an exchange of prisoners that never came to pass. Conditions there were poor. I was given a square of wormy cornbread and 2 oz. of salted meat per day. With no shelter, my clothes and boots rotted on my body. My wound broke open and started to fester again due to damp and filth. A kind Southern doctor finally sent me to a Richmond hospital, where my foot was pronounced gangrenous and the necessary operation conducted at once.

The good news, at which you should rejoice, is that I am alive and with both my arms, to embrace you when the war is over. I have only lost my lower right leg. In my ward are two men with no legs, and one missing half of his face. When I am back in the good hands of the Union medical corps, I will get a wooden leg that straps on like a harness.

However, for the time being I expect to be sent to Belle Isle or Libby Prison in Richmond. I don't mean to scare you if you have heard of the misery in these *places. But I must have a letter from you! The hope of seeing your beloved faces again is what keeps me alive. Remember as I do to pray every day for an end to this war and the birth of a lasting peace & freedom.*

Your loving husband and father,

Albert

I was too stunned to speak or even to cry.

"They cut off Papa's foot, just like that?" cried Ben in disbelief.

Mama let out a sob, and I put my arm around her shoulder, wondering what I could possibly say to comfort her. But she didn't need comforting.

"Dear Jesus, he's alive! Oh, praise God," Mama cried. "I must write to him now."

"I'll get a pen and paper for you," Ben said, jumping up.

The letter from Papa had bolstered Mama's hopes, but I couldn't stop worrying. All the letter assured us was that he had been alive two months ago. Why hadn't he written since then? I skipped my literature class and went to the shop, where I shuffled pages in the account books while my feelings shifted between hope and despair.

An hour later Amos pulled up with a cartload of squealing pigs.

"Why that's great news 'bout your pa!" he called out.

"Yes, it is," I replied, watching Amos's nimble, vigorous movements as he wrestled a wandering sow through the gate.

"Why're you lookin' so low spirited, Miz Lizzie?" he asked, wiping his face on a handkerchief.

"My father will never be able to do that again—what you just did," I said, trying to keep my voice from wavering, the tears from coming.

"He don' need to, 'cause I kin do it for him."

"Oh, Amos, I can't bear the thought of him being crippled forever!"

"Your pa still has his head, don' he? His heart ain't in his foot, is it?"

At this I had to smile.

"Don' you worry. He ain't goin' to be that different at all."

"If he ever comes home . . ." My voice trailed off.

"Now Miz Lizzie, you got to have faith," insisted Amos. "That's what I lived on, an' look how the Lord rewarded me—I have Grace and baby Lincoln, a freeborn chile, growin' bigger as we speak." His face shone with pride at the thought of his son. "You, too, go an' count up your blessings."

I tried. I sat down and wrote a long letter to Papa in which I described the battle for Little Round Top, Luke's surprising visit, and the excitement of Rosanna's return. We had all come safely through the battle, I wrote. Business was good. Amos and Grace had a new baby. Martin Weigel had given me a birthday present. By the time I finished the letter, I did feel blessed, and I had hope that Papa would come home.

I recopied the letter and mailed one to Libby Prison and the other to Belle Isle. Surely one of them would find him. But Papa's letter reached us first, on the last day of October, when the air bit the skin with the venom of coming winter.

October 15, 1863 Belle Isle Prison

Dearest wife and children,

How I pray that your letters to me are crossing paths with this one.

I arrived with dozens of other prisoners packed into a roofless boxcar that swayed terribly. I could not stand up, lacking my foot, so mercifully the others let me lie down, but then I was nearly crushed. From the depot we were herded like cattle through the Richmond streets. I hopped on crutches, my stump throbbing. Many in the crowds jeered, while the Negroes simply stared at us, fellow captives, with emotions that must have been extreme and complicated.

So many prisoners had arrived that we were left on a sandbar in the James River to be baked by the sun for three days. Finally we were sorted out and roughly accommodated at Belle Isle—a mistaken name for this grim, unlovely place. I will not appall you with details of the suffering here: the fevers, miasmas, and mosquitoes. A fellow Pennsylvanian, a young lawyer, contracted septicemia from his infected bites and died. Many starve for lack of food. I am healthier than most, despite being crippled. I was easily able to barter my salt beef ration for the ink and paper to write this.

There is some cause for hope, however, as sick and wounded prisoners are sometimes released because it is impossible to care for them. They must fend for themselves and agree not to bear arms against the Confederacy again. As a one-legged man I am a good candidate, though I push in vain for my case to be reviewed.

Two years and four months have passed since I kissed you, dear wife, and beheld the lovely faces of little Benjamin and Lizzie. How much longer must I endure the separation from all I love? Until justice triumphs and God remits His anger against this warring nation.

*Pray for that event, and yet be patient, as it may take
me still longer to get home to you.
    Ever your loving,
    Albert and Papa*

"At least we know where Papa is, and that he is managing to survive," I said, as Mama finished the letter and sat in silence. "Surely he has received our letters by now and they will cheer him up."

"Maybe Papa's injury is not such a bad thing, if it means he'll be freed from that terrible prison," said Ben, sounding hopeful.

"He simply cannot spend the winter there," said Mama, and from the look that crossed her face, I knew she was afraid he would die from the cold.

That very day she wrote again to her brother, insisting that he use his influence to get Papa released, and she paid a courier fifteen dollars to get the letter to Richmond speedily.

"If I don't hear something in ten days, I will get on a train and go to the prison myself," she said.

The idea of my mother leaving made my stomach clench with fear.

"But it wouldn't be safe for you to go alone. At least let me come with you," I protested.

"No, Lizzie, you will stay here with Ben."

"What good can you do? They'll just turn you away. And think of all the diseases you might catch. You can't go," I said stubbornly.

Mama's eyebrows shot up. "I am the head of this household, Lizzie. Do not presume to give *me* orders. The matter is decided."

I barely managed to keep my temper. In the days that followed, a tense mood settled over our house. No letters or telegrams brought news from Richmond. One afternoon in early November a snow squall blew down from a heavy cloud, and for an hour or more you couldn't see fifty feet in front of you. The snow melted the next day, but my mind was changed. Now I wanted Mama to go to Richmond, the sooner the better. On Wednesday, November 11, she packed her valise.

"How will we know if you get there safely?" asked Ben, who had taken over the worrying from me. "When will you be back?"

Mama pulled him to her with one arm, kissing the top of his head.

"Don't worry. I will be with your aunt and uncle McGreevey."

"You'll miss the dedication of the Soldier's National Cemetery next week," he said. "You won't get to see President Lincoln when he comes."

"That can't be helped, I'm afraid," Mama replied. "Now carry this bag."

At the depot, Ben played with the stationmaster's cat while we waited for the train. Mama laid her hand on my arm.

"Lizzie, when I am gone, you must be careful of what people might say." She paused and I looked up at her questioningly. "About you and Martin."

I gulped and felt my face grow red, despite the chill in the air.

"But we've only kissed a few times, Mama," I said meekly.

"I trust you, Lizzie. But you and Martin should not be together without a chaperone such as Margaret."

How Mama knew about us, I was too embarrassed to ask. But I also felt the urge to confide in her. The train grated to a slow halt, giving me a moment to pick out my words.

"Mama, I've realized . . . that Martin's been a steady friend . . . through everything. And now—well, I think . . . I'm in love . . . with him." I stammered my way through this unfamiliar territory of words.

Mama smiled but her eyes teared up as she kissed me and hugged Ben, then boarded the train for Richmond, waving from the window until the train disappeared from sight.

I didn't worry about Mama while she was gone. I knew she was stronger than she had been when the war started. She would find Papa. They would be reunited in the prison and embrace in tears. I remembered how I had run out to tell Papa good-bye the morning he left for war. He had lifted me up like I weighed no more than a sack of beans. He had been vigorous and full of confidence. What did he look like now?

A few days after Mama left, a letter came from Luke. They were camped near the Rappahannock River in Virginia, where nothing significant had occurred besides a few skirmishes. He wrote that he was still in good spirits from seeing us in July.

Ben and I behaved well. We did our chores without quarreling. My brother didn't even tease me when he caught sight of Martin and me holding hands after church. On the days Martin worked at the butcher shop, we hardly said a word to each other, for Amos kept him occupied every minute. But when he arrived in the morning, he would smile at me in a way that let me know there was something between us. Then I thought about him so much I hardly got any work done. I recalled the way his lips felt on mine, the deep gray of his eyes, the clean smell of his skin.

One day after the shop was closed, he startled me by coming up behind me, putting his hands on my shoulders, and turning me around to face him.

"How do I go about courting you?" he asked abruptly.

"Well," I said, easing out of his grasp and looking around to be sure we were alone, "since Papa and Mama are both gone, you'll have to ask *my* permission."

"But what if you say no?" He tilted his head and smiled in a way that seemed to invite me to kiss him. I reached up and, tangling my fingers in his hair, drew his head down and touched my lips to his temple right where a pulse throbbed under the skin. When he kissed me back, on the lips, I felt the thrill all the way to my toes.

Then to tease him, I pretended to consider the matter.

"I *think* I'll agree to be your girl," I finally said, and we both laughed.

"I'll talk to your ma the minute she comes home. D'you think she'll allow me?"

"That depends on whether she learns we've been kissing in secret," I said. "Are you sure Amos is gone?"

"Amos?" Martin burst out. "He knows all about how I feel!"

❦

For the entire week after Mama left, a tide of people flowed into Gettysburg to attend the dedication of the new cemetery. Not since the rebels arrived had there been such a stir in the town. By Wednesday not a single room could be had in any inn or hotel. Visitors were staying in people's houses and sleeping two or more to a bed.

The president's train was due to arrive on Wednesday evening. Ben and I joined the crowd waiting at the depot. A band stood poised to begin playing at the moment the train appeared. We stood shoulder to shoulder with Annie Baumann and her mother and Mrs. Brodhead.

"It's too bad your mother isn't here, Lizzie," said Mrs. Brodhead with a sympathetic smile. Her eyes widened when I told her that Mama had gone to Richmond to find Papa. "Now I know where you come by your bravery."

"Let's move closer," said Annie, pointing to the dais where the president would step off the train. Just then the band struck up "John Brown's Body." The train had been sighted. Cheers interrupted the singing as the cars eased into the station with a loud squealing. Men lifted their hats, and women waved handkerchiefs. The next tune fairly lifted the tile roof off the depot, and I sang as loudly as anyone.

"We'll rally from the hillside, we'll gather from the plain, shouting the battle cry of freedom."

The passengers began to alight, but everyone's eyes were seeking the president. A cheer went up and I turned my gaze from the dais just as he stepped off the train farther down the platform. He was easy to pick out, for with his top hat he stood almost a head above everyone in the crowd. But though I stood on tiptoe, I couldn't see his face.

"Why, he rode in an ordinary coach with the other passengers!" said Mrs. Baumann, sounding horrified.

Judge Wills and Mr. Kendlehart scurried over to greet Mr. Lincoln.

"What is he wearing on his hat?" asked Annie.

"A black mourning band," murmured Mrs. Brodhead. "Poor man, it's been nearly two years since his little son Willie died of a fever."

Soon the president was lost to view, and we were caught up in the crowd heading toward the judge's house on the Diamond, where Mr. Lincoln would spend the night. People were hoping Mr. Lincoln might give a speech. He went inside, then appeared in a second-story window, without his hat. His hair was black and his face looked worn and craggy. My heart went out to him, thinking of the grief he had to bear for all the dead soldiers and for his own son. He waved but shook his head to the cries of "Speech! Speech!"

The crowd began to disperse, and Ben and I turned to go home. It was nearly dark. As we crossed Stratton Street, I happened to look toward the depot and saw a man hunched over in the middle of the street. A shabby coat and trousers that once might have been blue hung loosely on his thin body. He moved slowly, with the exaggerated up-and-down gait of someone using crutches that were too short for him.

"That man looks as if he is about to fall," Ben said.

"He must have been on the train," I said. "Poor soldier. I wonder if he's lost."

"Look, there's someone with him, carrying a bag," said Ben.

As the man swung forward again, I saw that one of his pant legs flapped. The man's arms trembled against the crutches.

Ben and I took a few steps toward the two figures.

"Do you need help getting to the inn?" I called.

Just then the man paused, raised his head, and shoved back his hat with a gesture of his wrist that was familiar. The light from a gas lamp fell on a gaunt face that was mostly hidden by a full beard. Yet I recognized this man. And the woman standing next to him. Goose bumps broke out and spread across my skin.

"Papa!" I shouted. "It's me, Lizzie."

In seconds I covered the distance between us and gathered him to me, easily lifting his bony body off the ground with the sudden strength in my arms.

Rosanna

Chapter 49

November 18, 1863 Gettysburg

Mr. Lincoln's visit has put Margaret in a frenzy of excitement, sewing decorative trappings for the horses that will ride in tomorrow's parade. She also made Jack and Clara new double-breasted uniforms for the occasion, as they have outgrown their old ones. Tomorrow morning she plans to leave at dawn to reserve a place near the speaker's stand, although the dedication of the cemetery will not begin until the afternoon.

I have decided to attend Mr. Lincoln's speech, for I am curious about this man who is regarded as a second Moses.

November 19, 1863

This has been a historic and unforgettable day, memorable not for its horrors, but for its hope.

The morning dawned cold and foggy, but the sun as it rose in the sky dispelled the dampness and promised unseasonable warmth. I arose early to help Margaret, who was frantic over some detail of the trappings that had to be changed at the last minute. After she left, Lizzie burst into the house, trailing her green bonnet and shawl, her eyes ablaze with joy. Aunt Mary has come home, and Uncle Albert with her!

Lizzie poured out her thanks, for it was my father who helped gain her papa's release. Not only is Uncle Albert freed from that terrible prison, but my father and Aunt Mary, after years of estrangement, have reconciled.

Lizzie also reported that her papa and mama rode in the same rail coach as Mr. Lincoln, who shook their hands before settling down to work on his speech, the one he is giving today!

As she relayed the good news, cannons boomed from Cemetery Hill, giving the signal for the parade to begin from the Diamond. We waited in the street, listening to the band approach. A crowd preceded the parade, eager to arrive at the dedication site ahead of everyone else. The cavalry and ranks of infantry passed, then the dignitaries and politicians, their horses resplendent in Margaret's cloth. Mr. Lincoln was unmistakable among them. He wore a top hat and rode a dark stallion, but the way his legs hung down made the horse seem too small for his great height.

Lizzie and I, with Jack and Clara in tow, fell in behind the procession. Once inside the cemetery gates, the crowd spread out over the grounds like a river released from its channel, while horses and carriages drew up along the perimeter. The new cemetery for soldiers, unlike the grassy Evergreen Cemetery, is raw and stony, marked by mounds of dirt and still-empty graves, for the process of identifying and reburying the dead is not yet finished. Attendants tried in vain to keep people from trampling the new graves or stumbling into empty holes.

Except for the tall pines in the old cemetery, most of the trees were bare. The beeches, however, still clung to their russet and gold leaves, which seemed to shake with expectation as the breeze stirred them.

We found Margaret beside a small boulder, defending her little territory against the encroaching crowd with nothing more than a blanket and picnic basket. Jack immediately took possession of the rock and glared at anyone who stood in front of him. The speaker's stand was a mere twenty yards away, but hundreds of people filled the space before us, pressing as close together as the ladies' wide skirts would allow.

"At last you're here. It's almost time for the dedication!" said Margaret with relief. Of course she was overjoyed at the news of Uncle Albert. Lizzie stood on the rock beside Jack and flung her arms wide.

"I want to tell the world that Papa's home!"

Amos spotted her and wove his way through the crowd with Grace and the baby. "That's the best news in months," he said, lifting Lizzie right off the rock in his huge arms. "Are they here today?"

"No, Papa is too weak, and Mama is happy just to sit beside him and hold his hand. You should see how they look at each other," said Lizzie wistfully. "They are writing a letter to Luke together—imagine how happy that will make my brother!"

I said that after the speeches I would go home with Lizzie and see if Uncle Albert required any medical treatment. Then Margaret touched my arm, for the music had stopped. The noise of the crowd subsided to a murmur, then to absolute quiet as a white-haired man stepped up to the podium.

"It's Mr. Edward Everett, the country's greatest living orator, according to Mrs. Pierpont," whispered Lizzie. "Did you bring your journal to take down the speech?"

I replied that I was not the one in school! Yet I had brought paper and pen, meaning to take notes, in case the speeches should be worth transcribing later.

Mr. Everett began his speech with the heroes of ancient Greece, slowly making his way through time to the present war. He spoke from memory, hardly glancing down at the papers before him. When he described the dramatic ebb and flow of the three-day battle, the tumultuous attacks on the hills around Gettysburg, and the ill-fated charge on the final day, I felt as if I were viewing the events with the eye of a bird hovering over the field.

My own "History of the War"—this journal—is quite a different work, small in scope, comprising only my own experiences. Indeed, how can one person paint the vast canvas of war truly, as he can witness so little of it? Yet I hope that someday my jottings will be read, to reveal how this war affected the common persons of our divided nations. For in a time of war, the humble as well as the great, the civilian as well as the soldier, make sacrifices and endure suffering.

The audience listened with keen attention to Mr. Everett's lengthy oration. They stood shoulder to shoulder, for it was too crowded to sit down. Jack had run off to play in the dirt, and Clara began to whine that she was cold. Margaret led her away so as not to distrub those straining to hear the speech. The breeze shifted, carrying Everett's words with it, and people moved around the edge of the crowd to pick them up again. Grace's baby slept peacefully in her arms, and Amos stood beside his wife, proud and protective.

Finally the two-hour oration was over. Clapping ensued, and people coughed, stretched their legs, then pressed close again, anticipating the president's speech.

"That was longer than any sermon I have ever sat through," said Lizzie. "I wonder what is left for Mr. Lincoln to say."

"He ought to explain how General Meade missed his chance to destroy Lee's army," said a disgruntled gentleman nearby. "I want to know when this war will end before I vote for Mr. Lincoln again."

The man's wife nudged him into silence, but I suspect his concern is widely shared. Despite the losses at Gettysburg and Vicksburg, Lee's valiant army rallied again. Now it seems certain that the two armies will spend another winter in a stalemate, riding out the season's cold fury in camp and guarding their capitals from each other.

Then Mr. Lincoln took the speaker's stand. He was hatless, revealing a high forehead over his craggy, dark eyebrows. Deep lines creased his face. He reached into his pocket and withdrew a pair of spectacles that he set on his nose. Returning his hand to his pocket, he pulled out a sheet of paper. Then he began to speak, not in deep, resonant tones like Mr. Everett, but in a high tenor voice. Yet his phrases were chosen with exquisite care. The entire speech lasted but a few minutes and, as it was frequently interrupted by applause, I was able to write down much of it.

He began, "Four score and seven years ago our fathers brought forth upon this continent a new nation, conceived in Liberty, and dedicated to the proposition that all men are created equal."

Applause broke out. Baby Lincoln woke up and smiled like a dusky cherub at the sight of his mother's face.

Unlike Mr. Everett, Mr. Lincoln did not speak of the past, only of the present, pausing to take in the rocky sweep of land surrounding him. Was he trying to imagine the battle raging there, the soldiers dying? He said that we could not dedicate or consecrate this ground, for the brave men who struggled here had already done so, and we must never forget them. Mr. Lincoln's next words touched me most deeply, reminding me of John:

"It is for us, the living, rather, to be dedicated here to the unfinished work that they have thus far so nobly carried on. . . . to the great task remaining before us—that from these honored dead we take increased devotion to the cause for which they here gave the last full measure of devotion. . . ." Applause stopped the president from speaking, and I wrote down his words while people around me wept openly.

"We shall be here another two hours at this rate," said the man who had criticized Lincoln earlier. His wife and several others glared at him.

Drawn by the excitement, those on the fringes of the crowd moved closer to hear the president as he issued this ringing resolution: "That the nation shall, under God, have a new birth of freedom, and that the government of the people, by the people, and for the people, shall not perish from the earth."

The president stepped back from the podium. I thought he had misplaced the remainder of his speech. But he only raised his hand and nodded to the cheering crowd. He was finished. The band played "The Battle Hymn of the Republic," and children began to run around and shout again.

"Well, that was short," said Margaret, sounding disappointed.

"The world might forget what he said here, but I will remember this day forever," said Lizzie solemnly.

"Mr. Lincoln blessed all of us, the living right along with the dead," said Amos.

I too was affected by Mr. Lincoln's humanity. I had expected denunciations of the Southern rebels, but he uttered not one word against my countrymen. Rather he expressed grief at our division and hope that the nation will not perish. He also prayed for a new birth of freedom, by which he surely meant the day when no Negro is enslaved, and all men's hearts will be reborn. Who cannot love that ideal of liberty, even if it means the defeat of the Southern cause?

I was moved to demonstrate to Margaret that she and I now stood on common ground. I said that I believed every Negro should possess the freedom that Tom Banks, Amos, Grace, and Lincoln enjoy.

"Why, Rosanna, you truly have changed!" she replied, her eyes glistening.

"Moreover," I continued, "if the nation was founded on a belief in equality, as Mr. Lincoln reminded us, the Negro ought to benefit from equality as well as freedom."

"Ah, you are still a dreamer, sister. Equality is a distant ideal, for every man wants to have a greater mind and fortune than his neighbor, and most believe themselves superior to the Negro."

"But before God and the law, Negroes ought to be the white man's equal, don't you agree?" I persisted.

"I suppose they are, in God's eyes," she admitted.

"Then, if Negroes ought to be so elevated, why not women?"

Margaret's eyes narrowed. "A woman, equal to a man? With that notion, Rosanna, you will never get another husband."

"Perhaps I do not intend to marry again. Though I am sure you will," I hastened to add. Samuel Pierpont, now that he is recovered, may be a good prospect for her. He is only a year or two younger than Margaret and much less intimidating than his mother.

Leaving Margaret staring at me in surprise, I turned to see Lizzie standing on the rock, her hands resting on Martin Weigel's shoulders. He held her waist and smiled up at her with the unmistakable look of a man badly smitten. She tipped her head down and the brim of her hat hid both their faces from view. Oh, it gladdens me to see her so happy!

After the lovers said their reluctant good-byes, Lizzie and I walked home together. She was like a twittering bird, while I was a sage owl, my mind stirred with serious thoughts.

"You're not listening to me!" said Lizzie, stopping so suddenly that a woman walking behind us almost collided with her. She put her hands on her hips.

"I was listening, dear cousin," I protested. "Then my own thoughts distracted me. I am sorry. But do you remember how Mr. Lincoln spoke of the great task remaining before us, the work that is not yet finished?"

"Of course. Who could forget such a speech?" Lizzie sat down on a stone wall beside the road and immediately became serious.

"Well, Camp Letterman is closed now, but the work of healing is still not finished. The war and the suffering go on. I'm not ready to give up my work. I want to learn more about treating infections of the blood and different types of gangrene. Lizzie, what do you think about my going to Washington to study nursing?"

She frowned and said, "I thought you would stay in Gettysburg."

I explained that as much as I loved her and Margaret, I did not belong in Gettysburg. Ever since I began following John's regiment as a nurse, I've known that I want to help others in this way. But it was Mr. Lincoln's speech today that moved me to act. I said that I would begin making inquiries. Perhaps I can study with the Sisters of Charity, live at the convent, and work for wages in one of the new general hospitals. I promised I would come back often to visit, then glanced at Lizzie, awaiting her protests and persuasion.

But when she looked up, she was smiling.

"One day, Rosanna, you will be a famous physician."

Her words took me aback. A woman doctor is such a rarity I had not even considered myself in that role. Now that the idea is planted, I feel it taking root.

"And what do you wish for?" I asked, thinking my lovestruck cousin would reply that she wished to be Martin Weigel's wife.

"I know that I don't want to be a teacher any longer. Yes, after all the fuss I made about going to Mrs. Pierpont's school . . ." She stood up and began to walk again. I hurried after her.

"Papa will be so disappointed," she whispered.

"Lizzie, the problem is that you're too smart for her poetry and music classes. You should go to college—Pennsylvania College, right here in Gettysburg."

"But that is a school for men. I would have to disguise myself, cut my hair, and wear pants. I could hardly get away with that," she said, glancing down at her figure.

I thought sadly of Kate O'Neill and her determination. Then I renewed my efforts to persuade Lizzie.

"Why shouldn't you be allowed the same education as a man? Didn't Mr. Lincoln just speak of the great task before us, the unfinished work of freedom and equality?"

Lizzie grasped the thread of my thoughts, but pulled it in a new direction. "Why, it's Amos who deserves to go to college. He has learned to read and figure as well as any man."

We were silent for a moment at the greatness of the idea that women and Negroes might someday attend colleges.

"Rosanna, the truth is, I've gotten used to being in charge of the butcher shop."

I regarded her with dismay. "You want to be a butcher?"

Lizzie laughed. "No, of course not! Papa will manage the shop again, and Martin will continue working there—if Papa approves him—until Luke comes home. No, I want to have my own store. A bookshop."

My cousin, a businesswoman! Now I was the one startled into silence.

"Even if I can't go to Pennsylvania College, I can study textbooks on economic principles, and I do have experience running a shop. I will ask Papa to supply the capital."

"And I will invest in your shop as well," I said, my enthusiasm growing.

Thus encouraged, Lizzie continued building her castle, stone by stone.

"I could use the profits from the shop to publish new books. You must let me print your history of the war. We could call it *The Memoirs of a Confederate Field Nurse*. It will sell hundreds of copies. Then I will help Grace write the story of her years in slavery. It will be so heartbreaking that Jefferson Davis will read it and issue his own Emancipation Proclamation."

I had never seen Lizzie so animated. My down-to-earth cousin was on fire with bold ideals.

"So I will learn to cure gangrene, and you will change the hearts of men through books," I said with a wistful laugh.

Lizzie took me by the shoulders. In the middle of the road we faced each other. Her bonnet had fallen from her shoulders, and her wheat gold hair escaped from its pins. I saw her girlish self like a faint shadow behind her present womanly features. She seemed lit from within, like a lamp.

"I am not joking, Rosanna. These are not dreams for a far-off future. These are plans," she said emphatically. "It is like deciding to picnic at Culp's Hill. We will not do it *someday*, but *tomorrow*."

"Whether the sun shines or the rain falls," I said, echoing her conviction.

Lizzie smiled, her green eyes bright with hope. I began to feel that everything we had spoken of was possible. The waning sun shot its beams through the bare-branched trees along Cemetery Ridge as this memorable day slipped into dusk, while Lizzie and I resumed our way along the deeply rutted pike that led at once toward Gettysburg and away from it.

Author's Note

This is a work of fiction. Any resemblance to actual, historical persons and events is . . . completely intentional!

If you're like me, when you read a novel about a historical event, you ask, "How much of this really happened?" My answer here is, "More than you might realize." It all *could have happened* exactly as written, for all the fictional characters and events occur within a framework of actual events that I did not alter, not even to make a better story.

For example, Lizzie Allbauer is drawn after the fifteen-year-old Matilda "Tillie" Pierce, the daughter of a butcher with a brother in the Pennsylvania Reserves. She spent the second day of the battle at the farmhouse of Jacob and Sarah Weikert on Taneytown Road just behind Little Round Top. In 1889, Tillie Pierce Alleman wrote a memoir of the battle (*At Gettysburg: Or What a Girl Saw and Heard of the Battle*) that first gave me the idea for this book. But I changed Tillie enough that I gave her a new name. The rest of the Allbauers are made up. Ginnie Wade was a real person (called "Jennie" by her family), as was Sarah Brodhead and Mr. Kendlehart. Other citizens of Gettysburg and soldiers in Company K are invented but based on real people. Rosanna McGreevey and her family are entirely made up, as are Amos and Grace. There was a ladies' seminary in Gettysburg run by a Mrs.

Eyster, but I have rendered her as Mrs. Pierpont. The Weikerts have become the Weigels. My rule of thumb was that any historical person who appears under his or her own name has not been fictionalized. This includes the military personnel such as generals George Meade, Robert E. Lee, and Gouverneur Warren, and, of course, President Abraham Lincoln.

There is so much written about the Civil War and especially the battle of Gettysburg, and the truth is so compelling, that there is really no reason to make anything up. For the military campaigns and battles I relied on Richard Wheeler's *Gettysburg, 1863: Campaign of Endless Echoes* and Bruce Catton's *The Civil War.* The movements of John Wilcox's regiment follow closely the account in *John Dooley, Confederate Soldier: His War Journal,* and the actions of the Pennsylvania Reserves follow Henry Minnigh's *History of Company K* and Samuel P. Bates's *History of the Pennsylvania Volunteers.* For the Gettysburg battle itself, nothing matches the compelling volume by David J. Eicher, *Gettysburg Battlefield: The Definitive Illustrated History.* Thanks to the three-dimensional drawings, it is possible to envision the flow of battle hour by hour. The many photographs that exist of Gettysburg and the battlefield also served as a great inspiration and research aid. William Frassanito's *Early Photography at Gettysburg* and *Gettysburg Then & Now* make it possible to stand almost anywhere and imagine the scene 150 years ago. E. F. Conklin's *Women at Gettysburg, 1863* has a wealth of true stories of ordinary yet heroic women. Robert E. Denney's *Civil War Medicine: Care and Comfort of the Wounded* consists of excerpts from contemporary sources detailing the drama of saving lives under horrific conditions. And I used Garry Wills, *Lincoln at Gettysburg: The Words That Remade America* for my account of the dedication of the Soldiers' National Cemetery. I did some research at the Adams County Historical Society (located in the Lutheran Seminary building that served as a hospital during the battle), where knowledgeable Civil War buffs and historians such as Tim Smith hang out, chatting about the battle in phenomenal detail. But if you really want to experience the past, visit Gettysburg during Remembrance Day weekend in November or Civil War Heritage Days in early July, when there are parades, reenactments, and thousands of visitors in period costumes. I promise you that history will come incredibly alive.

It was a visit to Gettysburg with my family six years ago that made me want to write a novel about the Civil War. I was fascinated by the photographs of civilians on one wall of the Visitor's Center at Gettysburg National Military Park. Each of their lives was marked with tragedy and moments of heroism due to the battle that unfolded at their very doorsteps. I had never before thought about the ordinary people who were caught up in the war, and I wanted to write about their fears, their sacrifices, and their everyday joys. Lizzie and Rosanna took shape as opposites, two halves of a divided country, and in them I tried to imagine the opportunities for heroism in the lives of two girls coming of age during the most shattering events of our American history.

In three days at Gettysburg, nearly eight thousand soldiers died, and another thirty-seven thousand were wounded, captured, or missing. Jennie Wade was the only civilian killed. When writing fiction about the Civil War, one can invent scenes of battlefield bravery, human tragedy, freakish accidents, and near miraculous escapes, only to discover, with enough reading, that something even more amazing or terrible actually happened. Yes, this book is a work of fiction, but everything in it could have occurred just as described to real, historical people living between June 1861 and November 1863, when the cataclysmic Civil War touched the lives of every man, woman, and child in our divided nation.

For Further Reading and Research

Bates, Samuel P. *History of Pennsylvania Volunteers, 1861–5.* Harrisburg, PA: B. Singerly, 1869–71. Available online at www.pacivilwar.com.

Bennett, Gerald R. *Days of "Uncertainty and Dread": The Ordeal Endured by the Citizens at Gettysburg.* Littlestown, PA: Gerald R. Bennett, 1994.

Billings, John D. *Hardtack and Coffee: or the Unwritten Story of Army Life.* Boston, 1887. G.M. Smith & Co.

Bloom, Robert L. "'We Never Expected a Battle': The Civilians at Gettysburg, 1863." *Pennsylvania History 55,* no. 4 (October 1988): 161–200.

Brodhead, Sarah. *The Diary of a Lady of Gettysburg, Pennsylvania, from June 15 to July 15, 1863.* Privately printed. (Copy in State Library of Ohio).

Catton, Bruce. *The Civil War.* Boston: Houghton Mifflin, 1987.

Chesnut, Mary Boykin Miller. *Mary Chesnut's Civil War.* Edited by C. Vann Woodward. New Haven: Yale University Press, 1981.

Coco, Gregory A. *A Strange and Blighted Land: Gettysburg: The Aftermath of a Battle.* Gettysburg: Thomas Publications, 1995.

Conklin, E. F., ed. *Women at Gettysburg, 1863.* Gettysburg: Thomas Publications, 1995.

Denney, Robert E. *Civil War Medicine: Care and Comfort of the Wounded.* New York: Sterling, 1994.

Eicher, David J. *Gettysburg Battlefield: The Definitive Illustrated History*. San Francisco: Chronicle Books, 2003.

Faust, Drew Gilpin. *Mothers of Invention: Women of the Slaveholding South in the American Civil War.* Chapel Hill: University of North Carolina Press, 1996.

Frassanito, William A. *Early Photography at Gettysburg*. Gettysburg: Thomas Publications, 1995.

————. *Gettysburg Then & Now: Touring the Battlefield with Old Photos, 1863–1889*. Gettysburg: Thomas Publications, 1996.

History of Cumberland and Adams Counties, Pennsylvania. Chicago: Warner, Beers, 1886.

John Dooley, Confederate Soldier: His War Journal. Edited by Joseph T. Durkin. Washington, D.C.: Georgetown University Press, 1945.

Leisch, Juanita. *An Introduction to the Civil War Civilians*. Gettysburg: Thomas Publications, 1994.

Minnigh, Henry N. *History of Company K*. Gettysburg: Thomas Publications, 1998.

Pember, Phoebe Yates. *A Southern Woman's Story*. Columbia: University of South Carolina Press, 2002.

Sheldon, George. *When the Smoke Cleared at Gettysburg: The Tragic Aftermath of the Bloodiest Battle of the Civil War.* Nashville: Cumberland House, 2003.

Small, Cindy L. *The Jennie Wade Story*. Gettysburg: Thomas Publications, 1991.

Volo, Dorothy D. *Daily Life in Civil War America*. Westport, CT: Greenwood Press, 1998.

Wheeler, Richard. *Gettysburg, 1863: Campaign of Endless Echoes*. New York: Penguin Putnam, 1999.

Wills, Garry. *Lincoln at Gettysburg: The Words that Remade America.* New York: Simon & Schuster, 1993.

Web Sites:

www.civilwarmed.org (National Museum of Civil War Medicine)

www.americancivilwar.com (timelines, battles, people)

www.nps.gov/gett (Gettysburg National Military Park)

www.civil-war.net (outstanding site for research; many photographs)

Acknowledgments

I wish to thank Julie Romeis and Melanie Cecka, gifted editors, along with the Bloomsbury staff—particularly, Sandy, Jill, Melissa, Jennifer, and Donna. And, of course, dear Carolyn French, my agent. Finally, Rob, David, and Adam, for putting up with a wife and mother who is sometimes absent from the here and now.

Shakespeare created a powerful tyrant in *Macbeth*.
Lisa Klein has given him a force to reckon with . . .
a daughter.

Read on for a sneak peek of *Lady Macbeth's Daughter*

Determined, I face Fleance in the small clearing. With a shield in one hand and a sword in the other, I feel balanced and secure. I match his every move. My knees are bent and I lean a bit forward, waiting for the opportunity to thrust. Has Fleance noticed that my sword is now sharp?

"Just so you know," I say, with a hint of teasing in my tone, "if I hurt you, I don't mean to."

Fleance laughs in a loud burst. "I think I can defend myself. I've had harder opponents."

At that moment his attention falters, and I bring my blade briskly down upon his wooden war-toy. With a crack it shivers into pieces and he is left holding the hilt. He lets out all his breath at once and stares at me, stunned.

Now it is my turn to laugh.

"By Saint Brigid!" he cries. He looks me up and down, his eyes stopping at my waist. "Could the old woman have woven some magic into that girdle?"

"If so, I must never take it off."

"Let me see that sword."

Beaming with triumph, I hand it to him and slip the heavy shield from my forearm.

"It is the same one, surely, but you had it sharpened," he observes. "Did you put a charm upon it, too?"

"I am no sorceress! But I have been building my strength. See?" I hold out my arms, letting the loose sleeves slip back, and tense them so that my sinews show, small but hard.

Fleance grasps my wrists, then slides his hands along my forearms, cupping my elbows. He presses upward, bunching the cloth of my sleeves until he is holding me by the shoulders. There he stops and regards me, his eyebrows raised, mutely asking, *May I?*

I feel the tingling start up again beneath the girdle, deeper this time. I clap my hands against Fleance's back. It is damp with sweat, and the muscles ripple beneath the skin. I pull him to me.

Where is the harm?

I press my lips as hard as I can against his. My teeth bump into his. He kisses me back and we almost fight to hold each other the tighter, until he lifts me off my feet. Soon I feel my strength begin to falter and release my arms, letting him hold me in the air, with nothing to ground me.

❧

Rhuven comes for me the very next day, like one of the priest's angels who save those who are about to lose their souls. My pulse is still racing from kissing Fleance. How could Rhuven have known what happened between us?

Of course she does not know. The reason she has come, she says, is that the pestilence infecting Scotland has reached the Wychelm Wood. My mother is very ill. In fact, she is dying.

We leave Dunbeag at once. Even on Rhuven's palfrey, we cannot travel fast enough to satisfy me. I yearn to see my mother. But my thoughts are also full of guilty desire for Fleance. When I fall asleep sitting up, I feel his hands on me and with a start realize that it is Rhuven holding me up as we ride.

We stop for the night and I have a dream about Banquo. His face is pale beneath his beard, like a ghost's. His look reproaches me as he whispers through bloodless lips, "Avenge me, daughter of evil!" The dream frightens me. It makes no sense. I ask Rhuven if Banquo is my father.

"What gives you that idea?" she asks, looking at me as if I am crazy.

"Never mind." I decide to wait and ask Mother who my father is. But she is dying. What if we are too late?

When we come to the edge of the wood, I leave Rhuven and run ahead. The spreading branches of the wychelms reach out to welcome me home, but they are leafless. The burn rushes along as always, but there are no flowers blooming on its banks, and the birds sing plaintive notes as if protesting the loss. The roundhouse looks darker and more ancient than before, as if it conceals an entrance to the Under-world. Helwain stands in the low doorway, her eyes sunken and her hands twitching. She says nothing, yet her eyes speak of the fear that her sister will die.

Inside Mother lies, too weak to rise from her bed, yet glowing with gladness to see me. If she can smile so warmly, perhaps she is not dying after all! I kneel down and take her hand, and then I see that her skin is as thin and white as the bark of a birch tree.

"Mother, I am sorry that I left you last time, without even a kiss!" The words tumble out of me. "But why did you send me away? You must have been sick even then. I should not have left you. Will you forgive me?"

"There is nothing to forgive, daughter," she says, shaking her head. "Tell me, are you happy at Dunbeag?"

Like a child I am eager to tell her everything.

"It is never dull there. I have learned to read and write. I can even fight with a sword. Don't look surprised, it is more for the sport. The lady Breda dislikes me, but the lord Banquo is most kind and fatherly to me, and Fleance—" Here I blush. "He is . . . as rough as one would expect of a brother."

Mother smiles. "They are good people and will see that you are married well." She closes her eyes.

"Married? Mother, I have no wish to marry. I only want you to be well!" The tears fill my eyes, leaving her face a blur. "Helwain, can you cure her?"

Helwain pays no attention to me. She is plying Rhuven for news of the king.

"My lady suffers terrible dreams and wakes nightly, her clothes as wet as if she had fallen in the well," says Rhuven, her face creased with distress. "She cries over and over, 'What's done is done and cannot be undone.' Your potion of poppy did nothing to calm her."

"I will make a stronger elixir with nightshade and belladonna," says Helwain. "Better yet, something that would hold a child within her loins. What of the rue that was meant to strengthen the king's seed?"

"He tasted its bitterness in his wine and demanded to know who poisoned him," says Rhuven. "I think he suspected me and my lady. I was as afraid of him as on that terrible night!"

I listen in disbelief. How can they fret over King Macbeth and his queen at a time like this?

"Then what poison shall I concoct for His Majesty?" Helwain's voice drips with malice. "The deadly nightshade, ground with the bones of night-flying bats. That is the way to end a tyrant's life. It does its deadly work inside, where the evil dwells."

"Nay, you shall do no such thing, nor shall you even think it," says Rhuven fearfully.

Finally I can bear it no longer. I stand up to Helwain, inches from her hairy chin. My hands shake and the words seethe from me. "Enough! How are the troubles of the king and queen any business of yours? My mother is dying. Why don't you heal her!"

"I have tried and it is beyond my powers," says Helwain in anguish.

"O peace. Between you two, peace," pleads my mother.

Helwain sinks down on the hearthstones and begins rattling

bones in her hands. The sound irks me as always, but at least she is no longer ranting.

I take a deep breath. If I do not ask Mother about my father now, I will never again have the opportunity. I kneel down beside her again and smoothe her thin hair. I am loath to displease her while she lies at the brink of her death. But I must learn a simple truth.

"Mother, tell me please, who was my father?"

The soft hiss of the peat fire answers me. The rattling of bones stops.

"Please. I am old enough to know whose name I bear."

From the corner of my eye, I see Rhuven stiffen. In the silence and the swirl of smoke, I hear the intake of my mother's breath. She exhales without speaking.

"It is time for her to know the truth," says Helwain.

After a long pause, my mother speaks. Her voice is barely above a whisper, and I must strain to hear.

"Macbeth, Scotland's king, is your father."

I sigh and turn to Helwain. "Does her mind often wander so?"

The old woman shakes her head.

"I am dying, Albia, I cannot lie." My mother's voice is stronger. She lays a hand on my arm.

I suppress my tears and decide to humor her. "How did you come to bear Macbeth's child? It would have been long before he became king. Tell me, it must be quite a story."

My mother shakes her head. Then she confesses, with the little breath remaining in her, that she is not my mother at all.

"You were born of Grelach, Macbeth's lady. Though I have loved you all these years as truly as any mother."

I stare at her, openmouthed. Then I turn to Rhuven. "Your *mistress*?"

Rhuven nods. Her face is twisted with sorrow.

"No. That can't be! You're both lying."

I see my mother—no, not my mother, simply *Geillis*—wince with pain.

"Then explain why I grew up here," I demand. "Did the faeries steal me from this Grelach and leave me . . . in this pitiful house?" My voice is full of scorn.

Rhuven says, "In a manner of speaking, yes—"

"Don't lie to her!" thunders Helwain. "She is no child. She must know the truth, black as it is!"

"What truth? That I am kin to that painted warrior you conned on the moor? The tyrant who seizes land and lets his subjects starve? That is madness! The king is not my father."

"Your hair is exactly the color of his," says Rhuven, reaching out to me. "And you have his temper."

I push her arm away. "How should that make me his daughter?"

"Albia, you are Scotland's daughter, and here is proof," says Helwain darkly. She holds out a gold armlet set with a large gem the color of thickened blood. I gaze upon it in fascination but recoil from touching it.

"What is this bauble?" I demand.

"It belonged to your mother," Rhuven says. "My lord gave it to her when they were wed. Now it is yours."

"That proves nothing. For all I know, you stole it last week."

Rhuven is on the verge of tears. "Do you think we would make all this up? We would never torment you so."

"Then let me take this gem to Dun Forres and see if I am welcomed as the long-lost daughter of the king and queen." I try to sound defiant as I thrust out my hand for the armlet, but my voice wavers.

"Foolish girl," says Helwain, snatching it away. "Do you want to be killed?"

Her words, like a wintry blast, pierce to my very bones. Clearly there is more to this matter than learning who gave me birth.

"Tell me everything," I say in a small, tight voice. "Tell me who I am and how I came here."

Throughout the remaining hours of that long night, Geillis, Rhuven, and Helwain unfold the long and complicated tale. From hand to hand they pass the thread of my life, until I am dizzied by the whirling, falling spindle and vexed by the tangled strands they weave. I hear how the lady Grelach bore me and tried to hide my lame foot from her husband; how Macbeth, believing me cursed, seized me from her arms and put me out as food for the wolves; how Rhuven saved me and brought me to Geillis, who raised me as the child of her own, never-filled womb.

"Do they even know I am alive?" I ask, my voice rising as if it would leave my throat altogether.

"No, and they must never find out," says Rhuven.

"You are not to seek out Macbeth and his lady," Helwain orders.

"Why not?" I ask, lifting my chin. The time when I let Helwain tell me what to do is long past.

Rhuven shakes her head at Helwain. There is something else she does not want spoken. But Helwain says that I must know, despite the risk.

So I hear the dark and terrible secret that Rhuven has shared with no one but her sisters: that Macbeth and his wife, whetting their ambition until it was sharper than a steel blade, slew King Duncan as he slept under their very roof, innocent and unsuspecting.

Thus I learn that I am the daughter of a murderer and his wife, Macbeth and Grelach—my father and mother? No, monsters who did not scruple to kill their very own flesh and blood, and hardened by that first crime, boldly took the life of a king and his harmless servants. How can I live with this terrible truth? It shakes me to the marrow of my bones. I no longer know myself. Why did I not leave the past buried?

I hurl bitter words at the sisters, charging them with malice against Macbeth for slaying Gillam and making them homeless. I accuse them of raising me in hopes of restoring me to the queen for reward. But my ranting subsides when I see the grief in Geillis's eyes, Rhuven's fear, and Helwain's pain. They have done me no wrong. They are also victims. Now I understand that it is because of Macbeth and his wife that all of Scotland suffers.

"I hate them! Not you," I cry. "And I am their fruit. I fell from that rotten tree." My voice rises to a wail. "Oh, I hate myself, too!"

"Nay, Albia, their crimes cannot stain you," says Geillis with earnest feeling in her failing voice. "You have none of their wickedness in you."

I think of my quick temper with Colum, my hatred of Helwain, the times I struck Fleance, and my sudden passion for him.

"Aye, I do have a violent nature," I whisper.

The peat fire has died down to embers. A few birds begin to twitter. Soon it will be the morning of another sunless day. Geillis's breath grows ragged.

"Come here, Albia," says Helwain.

I get up and obey her. She puts my hand through the armlet with the red stones. The chill of the metal goes through me like a knife blade.

"I don't want it, if it was hers."

"You cannot refuse it. Wear it," she orders. "Your mother is descended of a just king. Macbeth has corrupted her. But you can remedy their evil." Her eyes are shining with conviction. "Albia, you have been chosen!"

A harsh laugh escapes me. "What shall I do? Ride up to Dun Forres and kill Macbeth for you?"

"This is no matter for jesting," Helwain says sharply.

Rhuven adds her own rebuke. "Albia, never speak of what you have learned. It is dangerous—for all of us."

"I didn't ask for this," I say, shaking my head.

"Leave her be, sisters," Geillis pleads. "It is too much for her. Dearest Albia, give me your hand."

I kneel down and put my fingers in her dry palm. The red gem in the armlet gleams like an eye between us.

"Forgive me, daughter. Forgive us. All that we did, was done to save your life."

❧